THE
MERZETTI
EFFECT

NORAH WILSON

THE MERZETTI EFFECT

PUBLISHED BY:

NORAH WILSON

Note re Bonus Material

Please note that bonus material in the form of an excerpt from NIGHTFALL, another Vampire Romance, appears at the end of this book. That bonus material will make this book appear several pages longer than it actually is. Bear that in mind as you approach the end and are anxiously trying to judge how much story is left!

Chapter 1

AINSLEY CRAWFORD STEERED her 1993 Crown Vic to the empty curb, wincing at the ugly crunching sounds her power steering made as she cranked the wheel. Great. Fluid must be leaking again. She needed another repair bill like she needed a bladder infection.

What she should do is dump the old boat and get something smaller, something easier on gas and maybe with a bit of warranty left so she wouldn't have to pour money into it so regularly. Of course, if she ever wanted a new car, she was going to have to learn to keep her mouth shut.

Right. Like *that* was gonna happen. She'd pretty much sabotaged her prospects when she'd reported that handsome anesthetist who was dipping into the anesthetic agent, shortchanging patients in the process. Although the situation was dealt with promptly and appropriately, it turned out no one liked a whistleblower.

Well, at least she had a lead on a new job. A better paying one, even, and God knew she needed the money. Lucy and Devon were depending on her, maybe for their very lives.

Which was why she was here. Except *here* looked pretty creepy. She glanced around, reluctant to kill her engine or release her door locks.

Okay, not *creepy*, exactly. It was a respectable enough commercial zone; not a slum by any stretch of the imagination. And she'd lived here in St. Cloud, New Brunswick, long enough to know she was less than three or four blocks from the club district, which would be hopping even on a Wednesday night, so it wasn't like she was in the middle of nowhere. But the quiet buildings gave off a different vibe once they were abandoned for the night.

Beneath the streetlights, the empty avenue shone after the warm August rain.

Ainsley turned off the ignition and the engine stuttered and coughed to a stop. The *tic-tic-tic* of her cooling motor sounded overly loud in the ensuing silence. Then the rain started up again, drowning out other sounds. Raindrops pattered on the car's roof and smeared her view of the urban landscape, intensifying her sense of isolation.

Before the cast of her thoughts could get gloomier, she grabbed her umbrella from the passenger seat and shouldered her door open. She fumbled with the umbrella a moment to get it open, then stepped out into the night. Closing the Crown Vic's door, she peered around. Not a soul moved on the street. Though lights burned in the office building windows, she knew they were deserted.

Well, mostly deserted. Her prospective employer, Dr. Delano Bowen, waited for her in one of them.

She'd balked when he'd asked for an evening interview, and his warm-whiskey voice had cooled over the telephone line. He had a conference to attend in San Francisco, he'd informed her, and he intended to fill the position before he left, one way or another. Desperate as she was for the job, she'd agreed to the nighttime interview.

Of course, that hadn't stopped her from checking him out. If the research sponsor, a major bio-medical company, hadn't confirmed his claims, she'd have cancelled. But he had checked out. According to Bio-Sys Genomix, he was analyzing the DNA of individuals afflicted with a particular blood disorder in the hopes of unlocking a cure.

What he needed, he'd said, was a cross between a phlebotomist to draw blood, a research assistant to help with his investigations, and a secretary to deal with the paperwork.

She stood there a moment, rain spattering up on her legs as she contemplated her utter lack of experience in the foregoing areas. But dammit, eight years as an OR nurse in a Level 1 Trauma Center had to count for something.

She pulled the folded piece of paper out of her purse and checked the address again — 420 St-Laurent Street — compared it with the number on the closest building, then headed west. Shouldn't be more than a half a block.

As it turned out, it was more like a block and a half, which carried her closer to the club district than she'd expected. The rain fell harder and she picked up her pace, cursing. Her low-heeled leather pumps were going to be ruined. She dashed up the walkway to the building's front door and tried to yank it open, but it didn't give. Another tug. Locked.

Great. She glanced around for a buzzer, but instead found a note taped to the glass door from the inside.

Ms. Crawford. My apologies. Please use the entrance at the back of the building.

Freaking wonderful.

She backtracked to the sidewalk and dashed westward, stopping at the alley running between Dr. Bowen's building and the next building. The lane was narrow, barely wide enough for a single vehicle to pass. It was also liberally spotted with puddles. Her shoes would be ruined for sure if she slogged through that.

Maybe she'd be risking more than her shoes.

The thought sent a jitter of uneasiness through her. She glanced around quickly. Nothing moved on St-Laurent. She looked back down the alley. At the midway point, a single security light mounted on the brick facing of the adjacent building cast enough light to show the alley was empty. No nooks or crannies for an assailant to jump out of; no doorways, no garbage bins for them to hide behind.

So why were the hairs on the back of her neck lifting?

She chewed her lip a moment, then made her decision. She had Dr. Bowen's phone number on the paper in her purse. She'd dash to the nearest bar and use a payphone to call him. If he still wanted to do the interview, he could damned well meet her at the mouth of the alley to escort her into the building. Or better still, in whatever warm, dry pub she found from which to make the call.

She turned to continue up St-Laurent, but a blur of motion caught her eye. She swiveled toward it.

A man, black clothing and a white blur for a face. Where had he come from? Before she could so much as gasp her surprise he was on her, pushing her into the alley.

She brought the umbrella down, intending to defend herself with it, but he was too fast. He squeezed her wrist in a grip that shot paralyzing pain up to her elbow. She dropped the umbrella. And then he was driving her deeper into the alley, bearing her along as though her resistance presented no more challenge than a feather.

Crackhead. Had to be. No ordinary man had that kind of strength. Fear surged as she remembered the one she'd seen in the ER last month. Out of his mind on a dose of crystal meth that should have killed him, he'd shaken off three cops like they weighed no more than dandruff on his shoulders.

She gathered her breath to scream, but again he was too quick. He clamped a hand over her mouth and slammed her against the unyielding brick wall. Tears leapt to her eyes, blurring her vision.

Think.

Resistance was likely to get her killed.

Reasoning was out of the question.

Cooperation … He probably just wanted money. For these guys, it was all about feeding the habit, buying more gack to snort up his nose or shoot into his veins.

Her right hand dropped to her purse, which was still slung over her shoulder. She pushed it toward him. "Take it." She mumbled the words out against his palm, hoping he'd understand. "Money. Take it."

His lips curved with real amusement, which stirred a far deeper fear than had his physical attack. For the first time, she looked closely at his face. His eyes gleamed an eerie yellow-gold under the security light. They were most definitely not the eyes of a hopped-up junkie.

"It's not your money I want."

Oh, God. She was going to be raped in a rainy alley while everyone huddled indoors where it was warm and dry. Where they wouldn't hear her cries.

"No, sweetheart, I don't want that, either."

His lips parted on a smile and her gaze dropped to his bared teeth. As soon as she saw his incisors, she knew what he did want. Her rational mind rebelled against the truth, but her blood knew. Her pulse leapt into overdrive.

"No!"

The word was smothered against his hand. He angled her neck and sank his teeth deep into her throat. She felt the pierce of his grossly elongated incisors like the hot stab of IV needles. Adrenaline arced through her, lending her strength as she fought him, but she might as well have tried to knock down the brick wall at her back.

On and on she struggled, but he clung to her, oblivious of her efforts. But he didn't seem to be doing much more than just hanging on. Why wasn't he sucking or otherwise working the wound? Wasn't that what vampires did? Or did they tear throats out and lap the blood?

She shivered. God, she was so cold ...

Cold. Blood loss. Shock!

Oh, shit, she was going into *shock*.

Goddammit, he'd pierced her carotid artery. He was letting her own thundering heart pump the lifeblood out of her. A bubble of hysterical laughter rose in her chest at the irony.

Seconds later, she sagged against the building, mirth — and strength — gone. Only his weight against her held her upright.

A violent tremor shook her. *Cold.* She was going to die here in this alley.

And her shoes were ruined.

Then, miraculously, he released her. She crumpled to the wet asphalt. Dear God, she was so cold. Was she dead?

No, not yet. If she were dead, she wouldn't feel the cold rain or the hot abrasion of the asphalt on her hands and knees.

So why had he left her?

She managed to lift her head to peer through the driving rain, searching for her assailant. There, deeper in the alley. And dear God, he was locked in combat with another man! A man who must have pulled the creature off her.

She wanted to shout, to warn her would-be savior that he wasn't dealing with your average thug, but her vision wobbled. Feeling oddly detached, she put a hand to her throat and it came away red. The rain quickly washed her hand clean, but a downward glance confirmed she was still bleeding. Her tan trench coat was streaked with red.

Oh, man, she was tired. More than anything, she wanted to lie down. She wanted to just curl into herself and let the hovering blackness take her. But the man who'd tried to save her ... the Good Samaritan ... if she didn't get help, he'd die.

She pushed herself to her feet and stumbled toward the mouth of the alley, one hand pressed to her neck to try to stem her bleeding and the other pressed against the building's wall to keep herself upright. She'd lost one shoe, so she kicked the other one off. Almost there.

Then the world started to swim. She blinked and blinked, but the blurriness refused to clear. She found herself on the ground again, felt the asphalt burn her already scraped knees. Then the same abrasive surface kissed her cheek as she pitched face-first onto the street.

Too late, Ainsley. As usual. You're nobody's savior.

Delano Bowen watched the beaten vampire's retreat long enough to be certain the creature was really leaving. He expelled his breath. *Thank God.* It had been close. For a moment, he'd thought he was going to have to destroy it. Black-hearted devil hadn't wanted to give up his kill.

Well, they'd soon see who killed whom.

And speaking of dying, he'd better see to the woman before she succumbed to shock. He strode to the mouth of the alley where she lay crumpled on the wet asphalt. Kneeling, he rolled her over, bent close and deftly arrested her bleeding. He drew away from her to find that her eyes had fluttered open.

"It's okay," he said. "I've got you. You're going to be all right."

The assurance seemed good enough for her, for she slipped back into unconsciousness. He gathered her into his arms and stood.

"Come on, Ainsley Crawford. We have work to do."

Hot sex.

No, not just *hot* sex. Incredibly erotic, deliciously forbidden *stranger* sex.

Ainsley knew it was a dream. Knew it wasn't really happening. But dear God, it was good. And it felt so damned real. She could almost smell him, musky and male and incredibly arousing ...

A small sound tugged at her awareness, but she clung to sleep. She wanted to stay in the dream, wanted the stranger to keep on stroking and licking and sucking her as her hands clenched in his hair. She wanted him to keep his mouth on her intimate flesh, his hands on her body. Just a few minutes more ...

Then the sound came again. A beeping. Familiar but wrong. Out of place in the dream. What the hell was it? It sounded like a ... oh, hell, a monitor alarm!

She came awake with a start.

The first thing she saw was the bedrail on the left side. Then the IV pole with the suspended bag of deep red fluid. She glanced down to see an IV line disappearing into her arm.

Holy shit. She was in hospital. And the beeping *was* a monitor. It blinked at her from its position right beside the IV pole.

Glancing at her hand, she saw the pulse oximeter had slipped off her finger. She slid the clothespin-like device back on and the beeping stopped. A quick glance at the monitor showed her oxygen saturation was okay.

Oh, man, she was really in hospital? Being *transfused*?

She pressed her legs together beneath the blankets, and the last traces of arousal from her sex dream withered. Urinary catheter. *Ugh*. She was definitely being transfused. But why?

Omigod, the alley! Heart suddenly hammering, she struggled to sit up.

"Ah, you're awake. That's good."

She yelped, more at the unexpected hand on her shoulder urging her back against the pillows than at the masculine voice from the right side of her bed.

"Easy. You're safe now. I'm a doctor."

Her gaze locked on him and she let out a gasp.

It was *him*. The man she'd been imagining, the stranger/lover.

Okay, she was still dreaming. She must be. How else could she have conjured him to look exactly like the man in her dream?

Then another thought struck her: *maybe she was dead.*

Maybe she never escaped the alley after all. Maybe her lifeless body lay there still in a blood-darkened puddle, and this vision, this whole hospital room encounter, was just the result of her oxygen-starved brain dying.

She closed her eyes for a second and reopened them. The man beside her remained unchanged. Shoulder-length black hair, glossy under the lights, sprang back from a widow's peak. Behind the lenses of Italian designer frames, dark brown eyes glowed like banked coals under heavy, slashing eyebrows. Dark, intense, sexy.

She started to lift a hand, thinking to touch his face to test if he were flesh and bone, but — *ow, ow, ow* — was quickly reminded that her arm had been harpooned with an IV catheter.

Okay, so it looked like she hadn't dreamed him, she wasn't dead, and she really was being transfused. So she had to be in hospital. But oh, baby, if this was the ER, this guy was new to the rotation.

"Where am I?"

"You're under my care, and you're currently being treated for blood loss and shock."

Blood loss.

She shivered convulsively. The alley. A creature straight out of her nightmares had attacked her, driven his teeth deep into her neck and —

No!

Her mind shied away from the memory. Better to stick with the rational, the world she knew. Medicine.

Her gaze flicked back to the IV pole. "Whole blood?"

"Yes."

"How much have I had?"

"We're coming up on 2000 mls."

She felt her face go slack. "So much?"

"By my estimate, you'd lost almost forty percent of your blood, Miss Crawford."

Holy Hannah. Her gaze leapt back to the unit of blood suspended from the IV pole, her brain ticking at a hundred miles an hour. "Then you wouldn't have had time to crossmatch the blood..."

"It's perfectly crossmatched."

She blinked. How'd he manage that feat? With this kind of blood loss, they usually started pushing the O-neg while they waited for typing and crossmatching, switching to the precise match as soon as they had the info. In any case, if they'd pushed that much blood, her coagulation factors would almost certainly be out of whack...

She lifted her right hand — carefully this time — to her neck, only to find her puncture wounds covered by a dressing. She clapped her gaze back on the hunky doctor who sat so quietly at her bedside. The doctor who in her dreams had blazed a trail of kisses down her body ......

She blinked the image away, cleared her throat and asked, "What about the possibility of a bleed?"

He lifted a dark eyebrow. "You know your transfusion medicine."

"I should. I'm an OR nurse."

"Indeed." The corner of his mouth lifted in what might have been a smile, but he obligingly ran down the numbers — hemoglobin, platelet count and the rest. "Based on what I'm seeing, I don't think we'll have to worry, but we'll keep monitoring the situation."

Okay, so she seemed to be out of immediate peril. Time to tackle the hard stuff.

"How'd I get here?"

One beat, two, three, as though he were weighing how much to tell her.

"I brought you."

"*You* brought me?"

"Yes. I was there, in the alley. I saw the attack."

"No." The denial emerged on an exhalation. She wasn't even sure what she was denying.

"Yes. I witnessed it. I saw that creature attack you."

Her heart started banging again. A man fiercely grappling with her attacker. A black-haired man.

"You were there." A statement, not a question. She remembered now. And she remembered something else.

His was the face she'd seen when she'd surfaced from that cold hell she thought was death. Then she remembered what had wakened her from that icy place — his mouth, hot on her bare throat, like a lover's.

No. No way. It hadn't happened. It couldn't have. Just a dream, like the other one.

She wet her lips. "Where are we?" Lifting her head, she scanned the room. No nurses came and went. Nothing fit her experience with various wards at the hospital. "This isn't the Regional."

"You are in my home. But I assure you it is as well equipped as your hospital to deal with your particular emergency. Better equipped, in fact."

This was his *home*? It looked more like a trauma treatment room. And how freaky was it that he'd brought her here to treat her? *Scary*-freaky. Fear warred with anger. By the slimmest margin, the latter won.

"I can see for myself that you're well equipped. My question would be, *why*? And while we're at it, why didn't you call an ambulance to take me to the emergency room? That would be the logical response."

Those glowing eyes narrowed to dark slits. "And what would you have told them at your ER, Nurse Crawford?"

She lifted her chin. "That I'd been attacked by ..."

"A vampire?" he finished.

"Yes! You know I'm telling the truth. You were there. You saw it."

He didn't move so much as a muscle, but for all his stillness, he emitted an odd leashed energy. It poured off him in waves so potent, she could almost imagine she saw an aura of energy surrounding him.

"Indeed I did witness it. But the ER staff who would have attended you weren't there. They didn't see it."

"You could have hung around and explained."

His lips turned up at the corners in a flash of amusement that was gone so quickly she wondered if she imagined it. "Yes, I suppose I could have given them the *Readers' Digest* version of events, but I rather value my professional reputation."

"Okay, yes, they'd be skeptical in the extreme, until they'd seen *this*." She lifted a hand to her throat, where she could still feel the pain of her wounds beneath the bandage.

"Remove the dressing."

She blinked. "What?"

He opened the drawer on her bedside table and extracted a hand mirror, which he offered to her. "Remove the dressing and have a look."

Panic flared. Did she really want to view those puncture marks? She knew the attack had happened. She remembered it in horrifying detail. But to look on her wounds would make the proof of it incontrovertible. If she looked in the mirror, she couldn't then decide she'd dreamed it. She couldn't then conclude, for the sake of preserving her own sanity, that she'd had some kind of psychotic break.

"Not up to it? I see." He started to return the mirror to the drawer.

"Give it to me."

"Are you sure?"

Her answer was to peel the adhesive dressing away with one swift motion.

"So be it."

She accepted the mirror from him, angling it to get a look at the puncture marks. Once again, her pulse skyrocketed. The skin of her throat was smooth and unbroken, with nothing but some faint bruising and some redness from the adhesive removal to suggest any kind of trauma.

Impossible.

She put a hand to her throat, running her fingers over the area to confirm what her eyes had already told her. Sweet Jesus.

"You see why the medical staff at the hospital might question your story?"

"But how? I was bitten … I can still feel the burn. Where did the puncture marks go?"

Behind the lenses of his glasses, his eyes seemed to blaze even stronger than before. "These creatures cover their tracks by infusing their victims with a substance that promotes coagulation. It's similar to the MPH beads you might use in surgery to stem a bad bleed, but it also promotes ultra-rapid healing of the wound."

She laughed, a choked sound that bordered on weeping, which God knew was closer to what she felt like doing.

"You're telling me vampires walk around with Bleed-X in their pockets, ready to sprinkle it on their victims' wounds afterward?"

"They secrete the substance at will." He pried the mirror out of her hand and put it back in the drawer. "Of course, the victim of an attack like this typically expires from shock shortly after the evidence fades."

"Well, that must give the Coroner's Office fits on cause of death." She heard her own words and marveled at how reassuringly sarcastic they sounded. Was she really having this conversation with this stranger about *vampires*?

He shrugged. "Occasionally. Though many victims are street people — drug addicts, prostitutes, vagrants, runaways. No one investigates too closely when one of them turns up dead."

The truth of the latter statement was undeniable. She'd seen for herself the ease with which street deaths were accepted. She'd even protested it. Until the business with Lucy. Until she decided she couldn't afford to make waves over something she wasn't going to be able to change anyway.

She forced her numb mind to work. "I still don't understand why you brought me here. Why not call an ambulance and let someone else worry about it?"

"Because, as you must be coming to appreciate, I have a special expertise in these matters that conventional medicine lacks. Indeed, I think it's safe to say I'm alone in my field."

Well, there was something she had no trouble believing.

"Besides," he added, "had you not been coming to meet with me, you would not have suffered the attack. For that, I feel a burden of guilt."

Going to meet him? Then he must be ... "My God."

A smile ghosted over his lips. "No, not God, Ms. Crawford. Though on occasion, I have been accused of harboring a God complex." He offered his hand. "Dr. Delano Bowen."

Chapter 2

DELANO WATCHED EMOTIONS chase each other in the depths of those lovely violet eyes.

A few moments ago, he'd seen the exact instant when she remembered the events in the alley. Terror, followed quickly by doubt of her very sanity. He knew how hard it was for the human mind to confront the unacceptable. He also knew some minds splintered under the stress. But not this one. Through the window of her eyes, he'd seen her emotions roll and tumble together as she grappled to integrate that one simple, shocking, world-changing bit of information. *Vampires are real.*

But now it was surprise and confusion that warred in her eyes.

"Dr. Bowen?"

"At your service."

"But why ... how ...?"

"A belated attack of chivalry, I guess you'd call it." He leaned back in his chair, consciously relaxing his posture. But not *too* relaxed. *Don't want to look like you're selling it too hard. She's smart.* "My access code to override the alarm on the front door quit working, which is why I redirected you to the rear entrance. That alarm operates with a key, and was still functioning. But I started thinking that was no way to begin a potential employer/ employee relationship, leaving you to navigate a dark alley, so I went down to meet you. You know the rest."

He saw her breath catch, knew she was thinking what would have happened if he hadn't intervened. Once again, she mastered herself quickly.

"I'm glad your chivalrous streak chose that moment to assert itself."

If she but knew.

He smiled. "Me too."

She returned his smile, but hers looked distinctly strained. "I guess a job interview's not in the cards this evening then. Can we reschedule when you come back from San Franciso?"

Ah, yes. He'd thrown that artificial time constraint into the mix to pressure her into keeping their rendezvous. "San Francisco is no longer in my plans. I'll be staying here."

"But I thought it was pressing?"

"My priorities have changed."

A new gleam came into her eye. "Then maybe we *can* do the job interview after all."

His eyebrows shot up. She was one determined lady. "Now?"

"Why not? I'm here. You're here. You need a research assistant, and I need a job."

"At this juncture, I've got bigger problems on my hands than finding an assistant. And you, quite frankly, have bigger problems than finding a job."

She smiled again, this one more genuine if somewhat self-mocking. "Ah, but that's where you're wrong, Doctor Bowen. I need immediate employment and I intend to find it."

"But there's no way —"

"You think this'll slow me down?" She nodded toward the IV assembly. "I'm stronger than I look. I'll be back on my feet and will have landed a job by week's end. You can bet on it."

"But Ms. Crawford —"

"If this job's off the table, just say so. I'll find another."

"Ms. Crawford, you were bitten by a vampire tonight," he said. "Has it not yet crossed your mind that you might have been infected?"

From her sharply indrawn breath and the way her fingers dug into the blankets, he realized the notion had not occurred to her. And he was the worst kind of bastard for raising the specter, particularly when he knew it wasn't even a remote possibility. The vampire had been feeding, pure and simple. He would not have imbibed so deeply and weakened her so thoroughly had he planned to turn her. And in any case, he'd have had to abandon the carotid artery in favor of the jugular vein, which he had not done. The blood that spurted from Ainsley's neck was definitely the bright red of arterial blood, not the slower, bluish-tinged venous blood. Ergo, no infection could or would ensue.

"Infected?" The word emerged on a faint breath.

He forced down the self-revulsion that rose in his gorge. "Yes. As medicine will one day be obliged to accept, vampirism is an infectious disease, viral in nature, inducing an extraordinarily rapid genetic mutation in the afflicted. We'll need to monitor you carefully for the foreseeable future, take frequent blood samples to screen for the virus and so forth."

"Omigod, I could be *infected*."

"There's an equally good chance you're not," he said gently. "But we have to treat it as a possibility."

She threw back the covers and tried to swing her legs out of the bed.

He restrained her easily. "What are you doing?"

"I need to get to the hospital."

"They can't help you."

"I know a virologist. If I could just —"

"Listen to me carefully, Ms. Crawford." He waited until she subsided again on the pillow before continuing. "This is one disease state to which mainstream medicine is willfully blind. If you try to open their eyes to it, I can guarantee you that the local psychiatric ward will quickly become your new address of record."

"But —"

"And if you're actually infected ... well, God help you. Your attempts to feed, to *survive*, will be greeted with restraints and higher and higher doses of antipsychotics and sedatives, until you die a slow, excruciating death from starvation approximately 26 days after onset. And this despite all the nutrients they will force you to ingest through a digestive system that can no longer sustain you."

She covered her mouth with her hand, but a moan escaped.

He cursed himself, but didn't let up. "Do you see what I'm saying, Ms. Crawford? They can't help you. Worst-case scenario, they will literally kill you with their ignorance. Best-case scenario, you turn out not to have been infected and will eventually be released, albeit permanently stigmatized by your *mental illness*. Do you understand?"

She didn't nod or otherwise signal comprehension, but the spreading bleakness in her eyes was all the confirmation he needed.

"They can't help you," he repeated. "But *I* can."

Hope flared in her eyes, taking a savage bite out of his conscience.

"This is my domain," he continued softly, hypnotically. "It's my sole area of inquiry and has been for my whole career. I assure you, if anyone can help you, it's me."

"That's the blood disorder you're investigating!"

Ah, so she'd checked his credentials. Smart girl. "Someone's been doing their homework."

"I'd hardly make an evening appointment with you if I hadn't already checked you out. Though much good it did me." She narrowed those unusual violet eyes. "So, how much did you pay them to say you were legit?"

"I assure you, Ms. Crawford, I *am* legit." Granted, he was the majority shareholder of Bio-Sys Genomix, but it was as legitimate as the next bio-pharm company. "And just because conventional medicine isn't ready to accept the research is no reason not to do it. I would remind you that when penicillin was first introduced, it languished for over a decade before it found acceptance."

"But vampirism? They actually advanced money to investigate it as a ... what? A phenomenon? A disease state?"

"It *is* a disease state. And I would say it's a very fortunate thing for you that I persevered in this line of inquiry."

❦

Ainsley blinked rapidly. Dammit, he was right. The hospital was not an option. Not unless she was prepared to forfeit what was left of her professional reputation, or her freedom, or oh God, her very life. Suddenly, she wanted to cry, badly. But no way was she going to do that in front of this man with the disturbing eyes that seemed to see deeper than they should.

The man who a few moments ago, in her dream, had lifted his head from between her thighs to lock that intense gaze with hers.

She pushed the image away hastily. Good God, what was *wrong* with her? How could she be thinking about sex when she needed to be thinking about her very dire situation?

She took a deep, calming breath, then released it. Then took another and another. Better.

"Okay, you're right," she said. "The hospital is out. They'd lock me up in the psych ward and sedate the hell out of me. If I'm not infected, they'd eventually let me go when I stopped babbling about vampires and the mad scientists" — she shot him a pointed look — "who study them. On the other hand, if I am infected —"

"If you are infected, the only way you'd get out of that hospital is in a pine box."

No! She couldn't die. She wouldn't die. She cleared her throat to ease the ache of unshed tears. "And what will you do, Dr. Bowen, if I start to turn? Will you sedate me, too? Will you confine me? Will you let me starve to death?"

He leaned closer to the bed, fixing her with the full force and intensity of that burning gaze. "No harm will come to you so long as you are in my care. That's a promise, Ms. Crawford."

He spoke the truth. The calm certainty he projected was no bedside routine to boost the patient's morale. This was rock-solid confidence. She'd seen enough to know the difference. For the first time since she'd awakened to a radically changed world, her anxiety level dropped a notch.

"I think I believe you."

"You should. On this score, you absolutely should."

She drew a deep, calming breath and exhaled slowly. "So, I guess this means I'm committing myself into your hands."

He nodded once, leaning back in his chair again. "A wise decision."

"I'm sorry about that stuff earlier."

"Don't worry about it. You've had a lot to absorb."

The understatement wrung a choked laugh out of her. "Dr. Bowen, I left my apartment tonight for a simple job interview. Now I'm lying here in a hospital bed — in your *house*, no less — thinking about the possibility that I might turn into a ravening monster like the one that attacked me. So, yeah, I guess you could say it's been a lot to absorb."

He inclined his head. "I can only reiterate that you are in the best possible hands."

"The irony is a little hard to ignore, though, isn't it?" She lifted a hand to brush her hair back from her face and wondered belatedly how bad she looked. She wished she had that mirror back. "I mean, I was attacked by a vampire on my way to meet a man who apparently specializes in studying them?"

Something flickered in his impassive face. "Ironic, yes. Now, if you'll excuse me, I do have to go out briefly."

As disconcerting as it was to have him near, the prospect of his leaving was even more disturbing. Like it or not, she now relied on him, possibly for her life.

"You're going out?"

"Only briefly. And you won't be alone, I assure you. My friend Eli Grayson will be here. He's an RN. In fact, he should be in any minute to check on you again."

Omigod, he was going after the vampire who'd attacked her!

It wasn't a hunch, not some leap of intuition. She just looked into that intense, still face and knew it as clearly as though he'd just announced his intention. She knew it so bone deep, she didn't even stop to question where her certainty sprang from. She was too busy fighting off a new wash of fear.

What if something happened to him? She shuddered as she remembered how easily the creature had overpowered her. Back in that alley, Delano had somehow driven off the vampire, but would he win a rematch? And if he didn't, where would that leave her?

"Send your friend."

A dark eyebrow arched. "Excuse me?"

"Stay here with me and send your friend Eli What's-His-Name to do whatever needs doing so urgently."

The dark eyebrows drew together in a frown. "Impossible. I must do it myself."

"What if that thing kills you?" she demanded. "What will happen to me then, huh? Can your Eli save me? Is he also an expert on vampirism?"

She'd thought those eyes couldn't burn with more intensity, but she was wrong. She felt her skin tingle under the brush of his gaze.

"What makes you think I go to confront the vampire?"

"Please, Dr. Bowen. You couldn't be more transparent. I could practically hear your thoughts."

He drew back, more startled than offended.

"No denial? Well, thank you for that, at least."

"Just at this moment, Ms. Crawford, you do not look like a woman to be patronized."

His tone was gently mocking, the first sign she'd seen that he might not be totally lacking in humor. She thrust that thought aside. "But you're still going?"

The sensual line of his mouth hardened. "I must. But I assure you, I will return. I'm somewhat of an expert at this, as well."

Vampire slayer?

Yes. She felt the truth of it as the words resonated in her mind.

Healer and slayer both. The implications made her shiver. If her transformation were inevitable, if it could not be stopped, would he see it as his moral imperative to destroy her? Her pulse took a jagged leap.

"What exactly is the focus of your research, Dr. Bowen? Is it a cure you seek for this affliction, or a weapon to wield against the afflicted?"

His eyes hardened. "If you're quite finished accusing me of plotting genocide, I really have to be going." He pushed his chair back and stood. "I'll send Mr. Grayson in."

※

Eli Grayson turned out to look more like a linebacker than any-one's idea of a nurse. Native American, probably early thirties, though it was hard to tell. He had the kind of face she suspected hadn't changed much in the last decade. Average height, but with the kind of body that required a lot of gym time to build and maintain. He was also competent and gentler than his forbidding physique might suggest as he attended to her.

"Delano tells me you're a nurse also," he said, when he'd checked her IV assembly.

Delano. The name sounded exotic, which probably had less to do with the slight drawl with which Eli delivered it than it did with the mind-picture it conjured.

She nodded. "Mainly in the OR in recent years."

He whistled. "I did a few years in OR myself."

"Here in St. Cloud?" She lifted her arm so he could get the blood pressure cuff on her.

"Abroad." He paused a moment to complete her BP check, then took the stethoscope out of his ears. "US Army. Iraq, mostly. A little in Afghanistan." He peeled the cuff off her arm.

Wow. Well, that explained the linebacker body. But why would a man like that temp himself out? Or did he work for Delano Bowen in a more permanent, full-time, multi-faceted way?

"Trauma, huh?" she said.

"By the busload."

"I'm sorry. That's got to be hard to see. But the adrenaline's addictive, isn't it?"

He grinned. "Very."

And now for the payoff question: "So," she said casually, "how'd you get from there to here?"

He glanced up from checking her catheter bag. His easy expression didn't change, but she sensed a new edge in him. "I found a new war to fight."

She inhaled sharply. There could be no mistaking his meaning. "The vampires, you mean?"

He produced an instant digital ear thermometer, applied it to her ear canal and nodded his satisfaction. "Normal."

Ainsley refused to be distracted. "You didn't answer me. Is the new enemy the vampires?"

"They are a contagion that has to be contained."

A contagion to be contained. She swallowed to ease her fear-dried mouth. If she were infected …

Think about something else, Ainsley.

Her gaze locked on the nurse again. Given what she'd pieced together so far about Delano Bowen's activities, she figured it was a safe bet he'd picked Eli Grayson with a view to more than just his nursing skills.

"What do you do for Dr. Bowen, Mr. Grayson?"

The big man finished making an entry in a hand-held electronic gadget and dropped the PDA in the pocket of his lab coat. Then he met her gaze with a level one of his own, letting her see the soldier beneath the nurse persona. "Whatever he needs me to do."

She suppressed a shiver. He meant what he said. And he intended her to know it. Her mind reeled. A soldier who'd left the service of his country to lay his fealty at Delano Bowen's feet … Who was this Dr. Bowen to command such devotion?

"And now, if you don't mind, I'd like to draw just a wee bit of blood so we can check on a few things."

She stopped breathing, watching as he prepared to draw blood from the vein in her left arm. "You'd be able to detect it already?"

He'd moved away from the bed for a moment, returning with a tray of blood collection tubes. "Detect what?"

"Whether or not I've been infected."

He looked up from the task or organizing the tubes by their color-coded stoppers, no doubt arranging them by order of draw. Which color was for the vampirism test?

"Infected?" he echoed, surprise clearly etched on his face. "You mean, with HIV or hepatitis?"

"With the vampire virus."

"Ah, no." He cleared his throat. "No, nothing like that at this stage. Just the standard stuff you'd look for after such a massive transfusion. You know, hemostatic abnormalities, citrate toxicity, acid-base changes, that kind of thing."

Of course. Talk about getting ahead of herself. At this stage, they were just guarding against post-transfusion complications. "Sorry. Go right ahead."

Again, his touch was deft as he worked.

"That's it for now," he announced. "I'll be back at frequent intervals to check on you, but if you need anything at any time, you can page me with this." He drew a small device from his pocket and placed it on the bed table within easy reach. "Just push the button if you need me, and I'll be here in under a minute."

"Eli?"

He was halfway to the door with his cargo of blood-filled tubes, and turned. "Yes?"

"The catheter ..."

He smiled ruefully. "Can't take it out yet, I'm afraid. But very soon."

"That's not the issue. I know you'll need to monitor my output for a while. But I was just wondering ... did you ... I mean, who —"

Fortunately, he deduced her question before she had to stutter the rest of it out.

He smiled. "Yeah, it was me. Dr. Bowen called ahead, so I was here and ready for you when you arrived. He did help me get those wet clothes off you and get you into that dry gown and wrapped in some heated blankets, but I did the rest. He may be the MD, but he knows we nurses are the experts at this stuff."

She smiled back, unaccountably relieved that it hadn't been the intense doctor who'd touched her so intimately, if clinically.

"Thank you."

"No problem."

"Eli, can I ask you one more question?"

"Sure."

"I know he went out after that vampire who attacked me. He said he'd come back safely, but I know how freakishly strong that creature was. What do you think? Will he come back?"

If she hadn't been studying his expression carefully, she might have missed the brief flash of surprise in that flat, handsome face.

"You don't miss much, do you, Ms. Crawford?"

"Ainsley," she corrected. "And I try not to."

"Well, here are two more tidbits you should know about Dr. Bowen. First, if he says he'll do something, he'll find a way to do it. And second, he can handle himself very well."

On that note, he exited the room with samples in hand, leaving Ainsley alone with her thoughts.

Her thoughts immediately turned bleak.

Lucy, I messed up. I messed up so bad. I'm sorry.

Fortunately, exhaustion overtook her before she could berate herself anymore.

Chapter 3

DELANO'S PULSE POUNDED as he strode down the darkened street. Not from exertion, and certainly not from fear. His pulse pounded because he couldn't get that picture of Ainsley Crawford out of his mind.

He'd watched her writhe in her sleep, knowing her dreams were sex-drenched. Watched for long minutes as she touched her breasts and arched her body, until decency finally reasserted itself. He'd been about to wake her when the monitor alarm had gone off, saving him the trouble.

And saving her some face, no doubt.

Had he woken her himself, there'd have been no hiding his awareness of her arousal. In which case he would've had to explain her state was literally a chemical by-product of her vampire encounter. Powerful, inescapable, but fortunately temporary. Indeed, it was clearly fading as they'd spoken.

Too bad he couldn't quell his own reaction quite so easily.

He shook the thought away and focused on the task. To his annoyance, he found he'd overshot his target. Cursing under his breath, he retraced his steps and turned down the correct boulevard. Two more turns and he stood before Edward Webber's lair. Of course, he'd staked the place out three weeks ago, so finding it again tonight was no difficult feat.

Delano found the place unlocked. Carelessness or arrogance?

Arrogance, he decided. Webber was a mere 50 years old, 21 of those years natural ones. He was a veritable infant among his kind. Short on guile and long on brutality, was our Eddie.

Eddie was also on death's door. Delano found him prostrate on the Oriental rug in the living room.

Closing himself to the smell of fear and impending death, Delano carefully set up his blood centrifuge on the marble-topped table near the spot where Webber had collapsed. Then he knelt beside the vampire to examine him.

Respiratory distress was patently obvious. The nasal flaring was a dead giveaway, but it was the way Webber's chest, abdominal and neck muscles labored for each breath that spoke to the depth of his distress. Delano pressed two fingers to Webber's carotid artery and was not surprised to find the pulse far, far too rapid.

It did not look good for young Edward.

Delano opened his medical bag, retrieved the materials he needed, and quickly drew blood for his tests.

"Bowen …?"

"Ah, he wakes." Finished, Delano removed the tourniquet and lifted his gaze to meet Webber's. Eyes fevered and glassy. Another symptom for his mounting list.

"Have you … come … to finish me … off?"

Yes, Webber was not long for this world. No wind at all to get his words out. "No."

"Good. Gotta say … feel like shit. Be a sitting duck."

"Small wonder you feel bad."

Delano stood and crossed to the table, where he slipped a tube of blood into the centrifuge and turned the machine on. Then he returned to Webber's side.

A tremor shivered through Webber's frame. "What's wrong with me?"

Delano dragged a blanket from the unmade bed and draped it over the dying vampire. No, correction: dying man. "Give me a few minutes and I'll tell you for sure."

"What do you *think* is wrong with me?"

Webber had to pause after every word or two. Bowen was tempted to tell him to save his breath, but there was little point. He wasn't getting out of this room alive.

"What do I think? I think you ate something that didn't agree with you."

A harsh growl. "Fuck you, Bowen."

"Indeed."

The centrifuge stopped, and Bowen went over to retrieve the tube of blood.

"What is it?" Webber called. "What ... are you doing?"

Delano lifted his eyes from the tube of blood he'd extracted. It was all he could do to contain the exultation that rose in his chest. None of it showed in his voice as he held up the tube.

"I just fractionated your blood, so we can get a clear look at your plasma, your white blood cells and your red blood cells. See that severely red-tinged layer on the top? That's your plasma, the liquid portion of your blood."

"What about it?"

"It's supposed to be yellow."

"Jesus," Webber croaked. "What are you ... saying? Goddammit, Bowen ... what have you ... done to me?"

Delano bared his teeth in a smile. "It's not what I've done, Edward. It's what you've done."

"What do you mean?"

"You picked the wrong woman to make a meal of."

"Wrong woman?"

Webber lifted his head. He looked like he was having trouble focusing. He'd be dizzy, no doubt. Probably nauseous, too.

"Which one?"

Delano sucked his breath in through his teeth. "You fed again? After I drove you away from the woman?"

"Had to. Felt weak ..."

Dammit. This clouded the matter. "Did you kill that one, Webber? Hmmm? Did you drain her and leave her to die in some alley?"

He shook his head. "Got away. Too weak to —"

A mighty spasm wracked the vampire's body, dragging an agonized groan from deep in his chest.

Delano watched, crushing the emotions that rose in his own breast. This rogue didn't deserve pity. He'd slain hundreds — no, thousands — of humans. He'd left a trail of corpses from Halifax to Miami, from Vancouver to Mexico City, and points in between, for nearly 30 years. He was an unrepentant predator, and he richly deserved his fate.

Delano's mind slid away to another time, another place, another rogue to whom he'd given the benefit of a doubt. A creature who rewarded his act of compassion by going on to slaughter legions of defenseless men and women.

"What in God's name ... have you done?"

"*God's* name?" Delano lifted an eyebrow. "Not a bad idea to invoke it now, if you're ever going to, Edward Webber. Because you're dying."

Webber bared his fangs in a threatening hiss that normally would have made Delano leap back, but this time he made no attempt to move out of range. The vampire, or what was left of him, was too weak to threaten a kitten.

"Fuck you, Bowen." Webber's chest rose and fell rapidly, abdominals pumping ceaselessly like a fish trying to breathe on dry land. "You're crazy."

"I'm afraid you're the one who's fucked, as you so crudely put it. The first one you fed on — she was the bad choice. She carries the Merzetti blood."

"No!" Another shuddering spasm, another sustained, guttural groan. "No," he rasped, when he had breath enough to talk again. "That's a goddamn fairy tale. Told by long-tooths like you to keep the rest of us in line. Won't work."

Slow as that message had come out, Webber had to pause a moment to recover his breath, signaling with an upraised finger that he wasn't finished.

"They're prey, Bowen," he said when he could continue. "*Prey!* When you gonna get that through your head? Fucking food is all they are. And we're at the top of the food chain."

"Not anymore, Edward. Not you, anyway."

"Shit." Another shudder, this one weaker. "Merzetti Effect ... it's real?"

Delano nodded. "As real as the genetic mutation reversal that's going on inside you right now."

"Reversal? Jesus Christ. I'm really ... going back?"

"Yes."

"Sucks, but I don't … see why it means … I'm dying."

"Trust me, Edward. You're dying. Of acute hemolysis, to be specific. But thanks to your feeding again, I don't know whether this attack on your red blood cells is being mounted by the Merzetti blood or whether it's your second victim's blood that's killing you."

"Merzetti bitch … Had to be."

"Not necessarily. The mutation reversal might already have begun when you infused yourself with your second victim's blood. Maybe she just wasn't your type."

"My type?"

"Your blood type, Edward. You could be suffering from a simple but catastrophic ABO incompatibility."

"No!"

"I'm afraid so. You're having an acute transfusion reaction. The mutation reversal would leave you open to it."

"Jesus!"

"For what it's worth, the Merzetti woman's blood *was* your type, or at least what your type used to be, pre-mutation. I hoped it would reverse the mutation, but I didn't know what else it might do. Now, thanks to your muddying the waters with your second meal, I still don't know."

"You *picked* me! *Motherfucker!* You lured me … with her … as the bait."

"Guilty as charged."

Webber made a weak lunge. Delano didn't even bother to retreat.

"Kill you! Rip out your heart while it's still beating … suck it dry." The fight slowly went out of Webber as he realized the futility of his threat. "Must be something … you can do!" He clutched at Delano with clammy hands. "For God's sake … Bowen … have mercy!"

Mercy? Delano felt his face harden. He removed Webber's hand from his arm.

"First, Edward, you'd do better to ask for God's mercy. I have none to give you. And secondly, you're too far gone for my help. You were too far gone before I drew that blood. Even if I wanted to, I can't offer you the support you need here. I just don't have the tools. And you'd never make it to hospital, even supposing they knew what to do with you when you got there."

Another tremor. "Then don't leave me."

Delano arched an eyebrow. "To die alone, you mean? Like you left every one of your victims to do?"

"Please ... I'm sorry."

Black-hearted sonofabitch wasn't sorry. He'd do it all over again if he had the chance. But he was dying and he was frightened and he was human, dammit.

Bowen sat on the nearby bed. "I'll stay."

Chapter 4

AINSLEY JERKED AWAKE. The room was dark but for a pool of yellow light cast by a small reading lamp in the corner, but she felt none of the usual waking-in-a-strange-room confusion. She knew instantly where she was. And she knew *he* was there.

"Dr. Bowen?"

A soft laugh. "You have extremely keen night vision, Ms. Crawford."

She angled her head in the direction of his voice. There. A shadow, to the left of the door. "I don't know about that. Pretty average, I'd say. But I could sense you in the room."

He stepped into the light, or at least his black-clad legs did. Rather long legs, she noticed.

"I'm sorry. I didn't mean to disturb you. I just wanted to check on you."

"I'm feeling much better. Stronger."

"So Eli told me."

Another step carried him further into the circle of light. Lean hips, the gleam of a belt buckle, the first two buttons on a black shirt, hands hanging loosely at his sides.

His hands . . .

A memory flickered in her brain, shrouded and diffused like sheet lightning pulsing behind a bank of clouds. Those hands . . . she'd felt them cradling her head, lifting her torso, felt his lips pressed hotly to her throat . . .

God, what was wrong with her? Fantasizing about her rescuer again, for pity's sake. It was that damned dream. It had been so vivid.

He took a seat beside her bed, leaning forward to rest his elbows on his knees. The light spilled over his face then. A sharp thrill — half fear, half fascination — shot through her. Oh, man!

A few strands of wet hair fell forward from that widow's peak she'd admired before, suggesting he was fresh from the shower. But his jaw was still darkened by the shadow of beard stubble. Had he had that earlier tonight?

Yes. She'd felt it when he'd carried her. Or at least, she thought she remembered it. And his eyes still burned with all the intensity she remembered. She found herself wishing he'd take off the glasses.

A panther. That's what he reminded her of. Powerful, glossy, breathtakingly vital. And extremely dangerous.

She swallowed to moisten her mouth. "The vampire?"

"He won't trouble you again."

She couldn't quite suppress a shiver. "He's dead?"

A slight pause, but no flicker of expression. "He's dead."

She digested that, or rather, she tried to.

Her first reaction was profound relief. It flooded every available brain receptor like a blast of narcotics. Relief that the beast who'd come so close to taking her life had paid with his own life, damn him. Relief that the creature that might have infected her — goddamn him again! — would infect no one else.

But her relief was followed immediately by horror. Horror at her own reactions. Horror at the actions of the dark Dr. Bowen. If he were right, if vampirism was a blood-borne pathogen, then her attacker was just a man. Granted, he'd treated her as though she were little more than a walking Tetra Pak, but he was nonetheless afflicted and in need of curative treatment.

And what of her? What if she were to develop this mutation? Would Dr. Bowen dispense with her as easily as he had her assailant? Would his brow be just as unruffled afterward? God, she'd seen Botoxed newscasters with more expression in their foreheads than this man was displaying. And this after admitting to a kill. Or at least, not denying it.

A *kill*.

She wet her lips. "I was thinking, if I'm feeling this good tomorrow, I'd like to go home."

His eyebrows shot up. Expression at last.

"Impossible."

Impossible? The single word caused a fist of tension to close around her stomach. Impossible because he didn't judge her well enough, or impossible because he refused to let her go?

"What, am I a prisoner here or something?"

"Of course not."

Another jolt of relief. "Then I want to go home."

"Have you forgotten you may be infected? I'll have to monitor you. We'll need frequent blood checks. No, you must stay here."

She propped herself up higher in the bed. "Of course I haven't forgotten my exposure, Dr. Bowen. But I don't see why I can't go home. Send Mr. Grayson over as often as you like. Or send him over to stay with me. I just need to go home."

"Why?" He leaned closer as though he genuinely wanted to know the answer. "There's no one waiting for you there. No husband, no children, no pets, no dependents. Why do you need to go home?"

Pain, raw and unexpected, sliced through her. Is that how he saw her, alone, lonely?

"Thank you for highlighting so succinctly what you consider the barren nature of my life. But it just so happens that I believe there's more to life than marriage and children. Like career. Like making a difference in people's lives."

"Ah, yes, your career." He sat back in his chair, raking back the strand of hair that fell on his forehead. "I understood it was dealt a serious blow last month when you resigned from the hospital authority under a bit of a cloud. A charting episode?"

Jesus, Mary and Joseph! Her heart lurched, then thundered. How did he know that? How the *hell* did he know it? Who had he been talking to?

She paled as another thought struck her. How did he know about her domestic living arrangements? How had he known she lived alone?

That eyebrow again, lifting eloquently. "What, no comment on the charting debacle?"

Anger surged, choking coherent thought. "The circumstances of my leaving the hospital are nobody's business but mine!"

"You don't think a prospective employer should be permitted to investigate a potential employee's track record?"

"Who did you talk to?" she demanded.

"I hardly think that's relevant."

"It sure as hell is relevant. They agreed to give me a clean, if not particularly enthusiastic, reference." She found the hydraulic lever on the side of the bed and raised the head of it while she talked. "That was the deal, in exchange for my leaving. That's all they wanted, to get rid of me. The allegations were bogus and they knew it, but they didn't care."

"So you were framed?"

"Yes, I was framed, dammit!" She paused a few seconds to bring herself under control. When she continued, her voice sounded more like her own. "Okay, I know that probably sounds pretty lame, but it's true. They saw me as a whistleblower, not a team player. So when these allegations were raised, they jumped at the chance to get rid of me."

"I know."

"This all happened because I reported an anesthetist's gross criminal misconduct. But I had to! Those surgeons, or at least some of them, had to have known about his drug problem, yet no one would come forward. Sooner or later, someone would have come to harm, maybe even died, and —"

"I know. You did what you had to. I wholeheartedly approve of your decision."

That brought her up short. "You know about all this?"

"Of course. When I pay as much for information as I did in this case, it has to be comprehensive."

She blinked. "You paid for information on me?"

"You should be pleased to know the personnel department is keeping up its end of the bargain. Your reference is clean enough, for anyone making a conventional inquiry."

"But that wasn't good enough for you?"

He shrugged. "As you can see, my research is a little sensitive. I need people whose discretion I can trust absolutely."

She snorted. "You found it *reassuring* to learn that I was a whistleblower? I would have thought that little detail would be a deterrent. What, for instance, makes you think I wouldn't rat you out? Something tells me your research might not be in strict compliance with the Tri-Council's ethical standards for research involving humans."

He smiled. It started slow, then spread until it suffused his whole face. And oh, Christmas, he was gorgeous when he did that. Which was the absolute last thing she should be thinking. This man had violated her privacy!

"Okay, what's so funny?"

His smile faded much quicker than it had appeared. "You are a fearless little thing, aren't you?"

Her neck prickled. "What do you mean?"

"You've been sitting in that bed, thinking what an unprincipled rogue I am, what a disgrace to the healing arts. You've wondered about your own safety, about the wisdom of staying here under my care. Indeed, you've wondered whether I would let you leave. Even now, I can see you second-guessing whether the hospital might be a better bet, after all. And yet you dare to raise the specter of reporting me to Health Canada for regulatory breaches. You are, Ms. Crawford, quite a piece of work."

Dammit, she'd let her mouth run on again. When would she learn? Ignoring the heat that rose in her cheeks, she tilted her chin.

"If that sounded like a threat, I apologize. I hardly know enough about your research to even speculate about compliance issues. And I would certainly not reward you for saving my life by jeopardizing either your livelihood or your research. As I'm sure your investigation revealed, Dr. Bowen, I have trouble staying silent in certain situations. Which begs the question again, what made me look like a desirable employee for such a … delicate project?"

"Your financial situation."

Ainsley gasped. "You investigated my finances?"

"I believe I mentioned I expect a thorough job when I commission an investigation."

Of course! That's how he knew about her domestic situation. Did he know about Lucy and Devon?

She schooled her face into what she hoped was an expressionless mask. "So, what did that highly illegal investigation tell you, Dr. Bowen, to convince you that I was the candidate you wanted?"

"It told me that until you left your employment last month, you earned very good money. That you'd been working as many extra shifts as you could safely work without compromising your patients' safety. That you live in a modest bachelor apartment and drive a vehicle that was bequeathed to you by an elderly patient, a vehicle that is sadly past its prime. You take very little vacation, and spend virtually nothing on yourself, and you have no drug habits to support. Yet you have a significant appetite for money. Money which barely has time to hit your bank account before it gets transferred offshore."

For the second time in the last ten minutes, her heart hammered against her ribcage like a wild thing. Which made it hard to keep her face impassive. "Again, you viewed this as a good thing?"

Another smile, this one tight and controlled. "Quite definitely. You need immediate employment to keep the dollars flowing into that bank account. And despite your former employer's agreement to stay mum on that little cloud over your head, your employment opportunities are limited unless you're prepared to relocate, which takes time and money. Just as obviously, you need your employment to be lucrative, stable and predictable. All of which augured well, I thought, for a mutually beneficial relationship. Your need for cash, my need for discretion ..."

"And did your impeccable source tell you any more?"

"About the money? No. Certainly I could have pursued it further. I'd have had to switch channels, but I assure you, the information could be had. Information is the one commodity that can always be purchased."

"So ... what? You decided you'd already spent too much money on your little investigation?"

"Hardly little. And money was not the issue, you may be sure."

"Then why not pursue it to the bitter end?" Her voice broke and she had to pause. Goddamn him. "Just think — my humiliation could have been complete." She blinked rapidly to forestall the tears that burned the backs of her eyes and tickled her nose. "You could have fed my Big Secret back to me and watched me sweat even harder."

"*Humiliate* you?"

His face turned thunderous and he came to his feet.

Despite herself, she shrank back, just the merest of movements, but he detected it. And it seemed to infuriate him further.

"Ms. Crawford," he said through thinned lips, "as hard as this may be to comprehend, I couldn't give a damn about what your so-called big secret is. You could be using your money to bankroll an insurgence in Haiti or to establish a training camp for white supremacists in Arkansas for all I care. The only thing that matters to me is that it exists."

"But you had me investigated."

"I did. And if you want to accuse me of exploiting your situation, I guess you could make a pretty good argument. But I will not wear the mantle of your torturer. If you believe that, I'll have Eli drive you home tomorrow, or to the hospital, or wherever you wish to go, and you can take your chances on your own. Now, if you'll excuse me, I've been up all night. I'd like to get a little sleep before we take this conversation up again."

He turned on his heel and strode toward the door.

"Wait!"

He'd moved outside the circle of light cast by the lamp, but the room was already beginning to lighten with the approaching dawn. A new day on the way. A day she would live to see because of his intervention. He'd stopped just short of the door. Though he didn't turn, he did angle his head as though to listen.

"I'm sorry. You saved my life. I know that. And I know I must sound ungrateful. It was just such a shock, hearing you talk so ...

knowledgeably about my employment situation and my finances. I just —"

"Do you still want the job?"

She'd sensed him angle his body toward her a little more, but she could tell by the way his voice bounced off the wall that he hadn't completely turned around.

Did she want the job? Oh, man, crunch time. Could she take the leap of faith? Did she have any choice? She wet her lips. "What are your terms?"

He turned fully around to face her and named a figure that surpassed her annual income last year by a good margin, even with the crazy extra shifts she'd logged.

What on earth was he expecting for that princely sum?

"I won't have to do anything ... illegal?"

"Not even close."

His answer came without hesitation, but just like before when she'd intuited his plan to hunt down and destroy the vampire who'd attacked her, she detected the space between what he said and what he thought. What he actually thought was he'd take care of any shady stuff himself.

That knowledge should have sent her running for the hills, but she found it oddly reassuring. He clearly didn't know — or maybe he just didn't care — how transparent his thoughts were to her. Certainly it would make a refreshing change from the minefield of politics, ego and subterfuge she'd had to navigate every day at the hospital.

"You said there'd be a phlebotomy element?"

"Yes."

"These subjects I'd be drawing blood from ... would they be human or vampire?"

A sigh. "I thought we'd agreed vampires *are* human."

Whoops. "Sorry." She chewed the inside of her cheek a moment. "So they're vampires, then? Infected, mutated, however you want to describe them."

"Yes, they're vampires. But they pose no threat. They're nothing like the rogue that attacked you. These people are civilized.

They come voluntarily, and they have a vested interest in the continuation of my research."

"They want to be turned back, you mean?"

The room had lightened sufficiently for her to see him shrug. "Some hope for that outcome. Others are quite happy with their lot, and just come for the free lunch."

Free lunch? She laughed, a short, startled sound. "You supply them with *blood*?"

"Think of it like a Methadone clinic. If opiate addicts can get their regular dose of Methadone at a clinic, they stay off the streets and out of trouble. They lead productive lives instead of engaging in round-the-clock criminal activity to support their addictions. Vampires are no different. If these people can get human blood through a legal, or at least not out-and-out illegal source, then everyone wins."

She felt her forehead crease into a frown and immediately lifted her hand to smooth it. God, she had to stop doing that or her forehead would look like a roadmap. Or rather, more like a roadmap than it already did.

"Aren't they worried about what you'll use this research for?"

"Oh, I make full disclosure. I'm working on a vaccine to protect the very high-risk populations — the homeless, the drug-addicted, the mentally ill who roam our streets. The prime targets for the predators like the one who attacked you. Still, I've had to work hard to gain their trust, particularly those who don't embrace a so-called cure. They have to trust that the vaccine won't be turned against them, or used to deprive these peaceable citizens of viable sustenance."

Her mind whirled and spun. In a world where pharmaceutical policy decisions were dictated by the bottom line, how could he hope to control the fruits of his labor?

"In all conscience, can you offer them that assurance?"

"I *have* offered it, so let us hope I can deliver it." He cleared his throat. "Now, shall we discuss the hours of work? As I suggested when we talked by telephone, we're a dusk to dawn operation here. Now you understand why."

As she'd told him on the phone, day or night made no difference. She was quite accustomed to shift work. What she wanted to pursue was the sunlight thing. "It's true, then? The mythology about vampires and daylight?"

He laughed, a low, amused sound. "Yes and no."

She arched an eyebrow.

"No, vampires don't explode into columns of fire, nor are they instantly reduced to a pile of ash. But they do have a severe photosensitivity."

"Like a sun allergy?"

"Precisely. But more profound than anything you've ever seen in one of your ERs."

She called on her memory to dredge up what details she'd retained. Somehow the immune system started treating the sun-exposed skin as "foreign," triggering an allergic reaction. She'd even seen a few cases in the emergency department over the years.

"How profound are we talking?"

"Acute solar uticaria."

Hives ... "How acute?"

"Very. If it were a hand or a forearm that got exposed, and if the exposure were brief, it would probably be manageable. Anything more is deadly. Full-on anaphylactic reaction."

Her stomach clenched. What a way to go. Lips swelling, airway closing ... She shook the mind-picture away. "Why don't they just carry an EpiPen?"

His face had gone flat, expressionless. "Usually the poor bastards are caught out in the open, without shelter. A single-dose injection of epinephrine isn't going to save them in that instance, even supposing it operates the same on a vampire, given their genetic mutations. Which we don't know for sure. Understandably, no one wants to volunteer for that particular trial."

She let her breath escape. "That really sucks."

"Yes, it does."

"I'm not much of typist or a filing clerk."

He laughed. "That's okay. I'm not very good with dogs."

She laughed, too. A dizzy, giddy, flirting-with-hysteria kind of laugh. Man, she must be tired. "You know what I mean. For the job. The clerical component. I'm a great charter, but I've never had much to do with that other stuff."

"Ah, of course. I think it's safe to say you'll be better than me. You certainly couldn't be any slower."

"Okay, then."

"Okay you'll take the job?"

She ordered her twanging nerves to settle down. "Yes, I'd like the job."

"Excellent. I think we'll deal very well together."

Deal very well together? Sometimes he used the strangest turn of phrase. "When do I start?"

"I think we'd better put you on the payroll immediately," came his wry reply. "After all, you wouldn't be lying there if you hadn't come for the interview."

Immediately. Thank goodness. An infusion for her desperately dwindling bank balance. "It could be a day or two before I'm up to scratch," she cautioned.

"There's no hurry," he said. "You need to recuperate. And remember, we'll have to do frequent blood work to monitor your situation. In fact, I'd like you to stay here for the immediate future so we can keep a close eye on things. Would that be agreeable?"

A shiver went through her at the reminder of her exposure, which she'd almost managed to forget for a few minutes. And once again, he was right. It made sense to stay here while she needed close monitoring.

Whoa, Ainsley! Ten minutes ago, she'd been ready to fight her way out of here. What had changed?

Well, number one, despite his slayer routine, he seemed genuinely devoted to helping the vampire community co-exist peaceably with the broader community.

God, had she just framed the thought *vampire community*?

She forced her thoughts back to why she felt better disposed to staying here.

Well, he'd actually *asked* this time, more of an invitation than a decree. She didn't feel so much like a prisoner.

Plus her future didn't look quite as gloomy as she'd assumed. Worst case scenario, if she were infected and Delano ... er, Dr. Bowen were unable to halt the progression, it didn't mean she'd automatically turn into a ravening predator like her attacker. Clearly, there were kinder, gentler vampires.

"Ms. Crawford?"

"Ainsley," she said. "If we're going to work together, I guess you'd better call me Ainsley."

"And you can call me Delano."

"Delano." She said his name experimentally, surprised at how easily it rolled off her tongue. "Okay, Delano, if I'm going to stay here, I'm going to need some things from my apartment. Can we make a trip over there tomorrow?"

"I'll have Eli do it. Just make a list of what you'd like to have and he'll see to it."

"Thank you."

"And now, I really must snatch some sleep. Vampire hours and all that." With that, he left as quietly as he'd come.

Vampire hours.

Suddenly, the fundamental, frightening paradigm shifts she'd been forced to make in the last hours caught up with her. Finding the lever, she lowered the head of the bed so she could lie prone again, adjusted her pillow and closed her eyes. She'd think about it all tomorrow.

No, not tomorrow. *Tonight.*

Vampire hours ...

Chapter 5

CRAZY. FOUR DAYS, and he was going quietly crazy.

Currently, she was in a completely different room, and still she tortured him. She saturated his senses, aroused every lustful hunger he possessed. He hadn't counted on that when he'd hatched this plan.

That damnable scented soap she used. Oh, it was very subtle; most people probably wouldn't even notice it. But it had wormed its way into his olfactory system, right into his permanent memory. His scientist's brain had catalogued the component parts insofar as he could distinguish them: sandalwood, vanilla, soft musk and some spice or other — nutmeg? Saffron, maybe? God help him, he could tell how far or how near she was from her scent alone. For pity's sake, he could all but hear the blood in her veins. *Surge and whisper, surge and whisper ...*

Four short days and the frustration was a living thing under his skin. Last night, for the first time in decades, he'd been tempted to take to the darkest, most desperate streets of St. Cloud's underbelly in search of a rogue. As restless and raw and as he felt, it would have been hugely therapeutic to pull a rogue off a victim and dispatch him straight to hell.

Except that's what he paid professional hunters to do. He couldn't afford to indulge himself by engaging the rogues at that level. If a hunt went south, the research would die with him. Like it or not, his place was here in the lab.

Besides, he knew from experience the therapeutic effect would be short lived. Hunting was better left to those with a genuine appetite for it, like Aiden Afflack. Handsome, smiling, easy Aiden. The man could dispatch a rogue without ruffling his evening wear, then head out to seduce his newest conquest with an equally unruffled conscience. Or maybe RJ. One part laconic, one part cryptic and two parts pissed-off. The man had been on the payroll forty years, and Delano still didn't know what "RJ" stood for. Those men were natural hunters.

You could visit those dark streets in search of something else . . .

For a moment, Delano actually let himself consider the idea. Maybe with a stranger, a prostitute . . . Perfunctory, impersonal, detached. Maybe it would be safe.

No! Not safe.

He pushed the subversive voice back into his subconscious. *Not. Safe.*

He lifted his head, nostrils flaring. She approached!

Quickly, he bent to press his eyes once again to the viewer of the electron microscope. Not that there was anything especially fascinating to see yet; after all, it had only been a few days. But he needed some time to collect himself.

"Dr. Bowen?"

"A moment." He made several superfluous adjustments, completely destroying the focus. When he'd taken a grip on himself again, he lifted his head, brushed his hair back from his face and replaced his eyeglasses. Glasses he wore not to correct his vision, but because it helped him fit the mold people expected. They civilized him, masking the intensity of his eyes.

"Sorry," he said. "How went the clinic?"

She slid a hand under her hair to lift it from her collar and gave it one of those very female flips, causing a resultant wave of fragrant warmth to billow toward him.

"Great," she said. "Although it was kind of creepy, going back to your building after having been attacked outside it."

"Of course. I'm sorry. But you understand, I can't have the clinic in my house. The traffic coming and going . . ."

She grinned. "Of course. Your neighbors would have the police investigating you for suspicion of trafficking in something else entirely."

"I trust Eli's presence helped allay your concerns?"

Another flash of white teeth, which drew his attention to her lips.

"I'll say! People literally cross the street to avoid us when he puts his game face on."

Focus, Bowen. He lifted his gaze back to her eyes. "The blood samples?"

"All squared away. The paperwork, too."

Efficient. Of course, he'd known she would be. Pity he didn't have more real work for her. At this rate, he'd have to drum something up just to keep her busy enough to make a full-time position plausible.

"And what about your clients? They were all well-behaved? You didn't feel threatened or frightened?"

She smiled. "You know I didn't. I heard you checking in with Eli. I figure that's why he hovered over me the whole time."

He shrugged. "After what happened on your first visit, I wanted to make certain your first clinic was as anxiety-free as we could make it."

"Well, thank you. I appreciated it. I think I fully relaxed when I recognized the fifth donor."

"Someone you know?"

"Yeah. Well, sort of. I don't *know* know him, but I recognized him from the all-night video rental spot on Arcadia Boulevard." She shook her head as though she still couldn't get over the wonder of it. "That's when it hit me. They're everywhere, aren't they? Doing all kinds of night work. Running gas pumps, re-stocking shelves ... "

"Yes, and DJ-ing at radio stations, hosting late-night call-in shows, driving taxi cabs. And there are still more working from their homes. Telecommuting has been the biggest lifestyle improvement for these people since the all-night diner."

"Wow. They're everywhere."

"Not everywhere, but more commonplace than you might imagine."

"It was strange, though. Doing a venipuncture and thinking, this guy is probably thinking about what my blood would taste like. And then thinking, no, he's probably thinking how I'm thinking that he's thinking about what I'd taste like, and what a rube I am for thinking it."

He laughed, a short bark of hilarity that surprised him.

"Ah, you were right the first time."

"Oh, my Lord!"

"Just think of it the same way you would a regular male patient. It's as instinctive to a vampire to speculate about sampling your blood as it is for a normal man to think about what it would be like to have sex with you."

She goggled at him. "Men really think about that when I'm sticking a large-gauge needle into their veins?"

A red-blooded man would be thinking about sex with Ainsley Crawford even if she were preparing to slice into their flesh with a scalpel without benefit of anesthetic, but he thought better of sharing that thought. "I'm afraid so. Blame it on the power of the male drive to procreate."

"Procreation . . ." Her brows drew together. "Is that something vampires do?"

He sobered quickly. "No."

"They don't have sex?"

Christ, how had this discussion gotten started? "They don't produce offspring. They are physically incapable of conception, whether you're talking vampire on vampire, or vampire on non-vampire."

Her frown deepened. "That is so sad."

"No," he said. "No, actually it isn't. A vampire infant doesn't bear thinking about."

She pulled back. "Why not?"

"For a vampire, the thirst is constant. The men and women you met tonight, it takes extraordinary discipline for them to live their lives the way they do. The call to feed, to take what they want from their relatively weaker, vulnerable human brothers and sisters . . . it's unimaginably hard to resist. As is the idea of their own superiority. They are infinitely stronger, faster, more physically vital."

"Okay," she conceded. "I see what you're saying. We must look like dumb cattle. Or maybe sacrificial lambs, tied to the stake."

"To some, yes. But not to the ones you met tonight. The difference between them and the creature that attacked you is that they cling to their humanity. The hunger is no less powerful, but the discipline is there. A child vampire, however ... well, let's just say that in the world of vampires, it's completely taboo to turn a child. An adult vampire needs to feed enough to maintain himself or herself. They need to take in enough blood to sustain them and to fight off the day's aging. But a child ... their needs are phenomenally heavy, given the burden of growth, and they lack the self-control to be integrated into the shared world. They are both innocent and deadly."

"Omigod, it's true. Vampires don't age!"

God, there she went again with the Hollywood stereotypes. "They most definitely *do* age. They just do it in a profoundly slower manner than un-mutated humans."

"Like turtles, you mean? Negligible senescence?"

He managed a tight smile. "Yes, like turtles. And rockfish and sturgeon and bivalves. Once they reach physical maturity, the aging process is all but halted. And just like those species, vampires typically succumb to accident or predation long before they would meet their natural end from old age."

Her eyes shone. "This is so exciting! Just think of it, Del, if you could bottle that ..."

Del? He was Del, now? He didn't know whether to be honored or horrified. He'd been Lane once, briefly, an eternity ago, but never Del. He chose to ignore her use of the diminutive.

"Believe me, there are R&D companies trying to extract that mutation as we speak. Unfortunately, they haven't been able to separate that characteristic from the compulsion to gorge on human blood."

She goggled at him. "You mean every other bio-pharm company knows that vampires walk among us?"

He laughed, a cold, cynical sound. "Ainsley, sweetheart, you don't even want to know what they know and aren't telling. You could keep Senate committees busy for years if they knew the whole of it."

"I can imagine."

She chewed her lower lip a moment, and all he could think was *let me do that.*

"So, do they do it?"

He shook his head, but the words didn't realign to make any more sense. "Does who do what?"

"Do vampires have sex? You've clarified they don't procreate, which apparently is good because baby vamps are voracious, conscienceless blood leeches. But you didn't say what they do about sex."

He cleared his throat. "They are more than capable of sex."

"With each other?"

God, the woman's curiosity was boundless. As was her temerity. "Very rarely."

She arched an eyebrow. "Why not?"

"Mainly because it's not very satisfying. Typically, vampires have no appetite for vampire blood."

This time her eyebrows soared. "And vampire sex involves the exchange of blood?"

"Most definitely. But with human/vampire couplings, it's one way, human to vampire. Otherwise, the vamps would have converted your ranks pretty swiftly."

She scoffed. "That's presuming there are ranks of females just waiting to be bitten. 'Cuz speaking as a card-carrying member of the once-bitten, I can assure you the experience would not be high on the must-do list for most females."

"Ranks of *females*?" He shook his head. "There you go again with the generalities. For your information, some male vampires prefer male partners. And female vampires take their share of partners, too, thank you, from both the male and female ranks. Basic sexual orientation isn't altered by this mutation."

"I didn't mean to —"

He held up a hand to forestall her. "All I'm saying is that if every time a vampire had sex with a non-vampire, they opted to turn said partner, then the food supply would have been exhausted long ago. The vampire ranks would swell until there were no un-mutated humans left to feed them. Presumably, that's why vampires have evolved in such a fashion as to not be sexually attracted to other vampires."

She grinned. "Securing the food supply. Smart."

"And again, for your information, it's not an unpleasant experience for a woman. Or a man, for that matter, or so I'm told. Quite the opposite. It's quite an extraordinary experience. So extraordinary, in fact, that certain people engage in relations only with vampires."

Her jaw dropped. "Vampire groupies?"

He couldn't suppress a smile at her expression. "If you want to call them that, I suppose it's fair enough, at least in your view of the world. But I assure you, they have a very different view of themselves."

"What would you call them?"

"Me?" He pushed his hair back. "I don't know. Holy women?"

Her eyes widened, fascinating written in their violet depths. "Holy women?"

"Or men. Let's not be sexist here."

"Wow."

"Think about it: why wouldn't they be revered? They provide sustenance, comfort, pleasure, companionship, all at the same time."

"Why indeed? Shoot, I want me one of them."

That surprised a laugh out of him. "Sorry. You don't qualify. Mutant variants only."

Her face got very still. Uh-oh.

"What?" he said.

"I was just thinking about what you said ... does that mean there are circumstances when it's safe to be bitten? When there's no risk of infection ensuing?"

Stupid, Bowen. Real stupid. What now?

He decided to stick with the truth, or at least enough of it that the lie could be in the omission.

"Absolutely." He leaned back in his chair, the picture of relaxation. "The vampire controls the exchange. Obviously, in the sex situation, he — or she — wants to keep their partner not just alive and well, but uninfected. However, in your case —"

"In my case, he was doing his damndest to drain the very last drop of my blood, so he probably wasn't being too particular about whether or not he infected me."

"I'm sorry," he said. And he was. A *sorry sonofabitch*, that is. "Don't think about it. Besides, I told you no harm would come to you, and I meant it."

She held his gaze, her violet eyes shadowed, and Delano felt another lash to his conscience.

"You're right. No point worrying about it. My blood work has been fine so far, right? No abnormalities?"

He nodded. "Definitely normal, and no post-transfusion reaction."

"I still can't believe you typed and crossmatched me so quickly. If I'd gone to the ER, they'd have started me on O-neg while they were waiting for the lab."

He gestured to the equipment around him. "As you can see, there's not much I don't have at my disposal, and no competition for the resources. Not to mention lots of blood."

"And speaking of blood, isn't it time for me to roll up my sleeve again?"

He checked his watch. Two o'clock in the morning. Precious as those vials were for his research, he hadn't planned on drawing any more until at least four.

She rubbed the back of her neck. "I know it's a little early, but I wouldn't mind turning in for some rest, if we're done here. I'm feeling a little wiped."

The last thing she needed was an iron deficiency, which wasn't out of the question the way they'd been harvesting samples. By rights, he should postpone the next draw until she got up. But he had a solid four hours left in the lab tonight, if he had new samples to work with. And her hemoglobin was fine ... "Sure, we can do that. I'll just buzz Eli."

"Oh, don't do that," she protested. "He's been on call pretty much around the clock since I came here, and he only just got to bed. Let the poor guy sleep."

"Very well." He inclined his head. "We'll take the next specimen tomorrow. I'll ask Eli to wake you for it."

She laughed. "No, I didn't mean postpone it. I meant you could do it. You did run the clinic by yourself before I came, right? Or you and Eli."

Good God! *Draw her blood?*

In a flash, he saw himself tying off the tourniquet, swabbing that warm patch of skin on the inside of her elbow, probing the delicate blue veins, introducing the needle ...

Bad idea. Very bad idea. He cleared his throat.

"Eli is paid very handsomely to do what I ask of him. He certainly won't mind being roused for this. He's as anxious as I am to find ... to know that you're going to be all right."

*

There! She wasn't imagining it. Ainsley blew out an exasperated breath. For some reason, he was completely loath to touch her. She'd been here for days, under his direct care, and he'd yet to lay a finger on her. Well, apart from carrying her here that first night.

What exactly was his problem?

He sure as hell wasn't a germaphobe — hell, he'd performed countless venipunctures on vampires. Creatures who were capable of visiting a blood-borne, gene-warping, physiology-altering pathogen on their victims, at will.

So if it wasn't disease or germs he feared, it had to be her.

"Why are you afraid of me?"

He snorted. "Afraid of you? Ms. Crawford, believe me when I say there's very little in this world that frightens me."

His words rang with the authority of a man who dealt with deadly forces every day, but dark patches of color now rode his cheekbones.

Interesting.

She smiled. "I don't doubt your ability to hold your own in this … underworld. But I was thinking … maybe it's the fairer sex that scares you?"

His forehead, which had been pleated in a fierce frown, relaxed, and he laughed. He actually *laughed*, dammit.

"Ummm, how shall I put this? No. Women hold no terrors for me, Ms. Crawford. Not even women as smart, attractive and driven as you."

Her smile suddenly felt strained. Yes, she was smart. Yes, she was attractive, in a blond ambition kind of way. And damn right she was driven. But somehow when he put all those attributes together — all attributes she happily owned up to individually — the picture didn't feel terribly flattering.

Ignoring the stiffness in her face, she let her smile broaden. "Then you won't mind drawing this little bit of blood."

A slight hesitation, long enough to make her rethink pushing the issue. What was she doing anyway, aggravating her new employer like this? The man had literally saved her life, then handed her a job that solved all her problems, and here she was baiting him. She really did need to learn when to keep her mouth shut.

He shrugged, as if it were of no import. "Certainly. If that's what you want."

Huh? What was he up to now, with the sudden acquiescence? Because despite the six-of-one, half-a-dozen-of-another attitude he currently projected, she'd lay strong odds he wasn't nearly that blasé about it. She couldn't have misread him that badly. She angled her chin in a challenge.

"Great. It makes infinitely more sense than waking Eli."

He nodded agreeably. "Then by all means, I'll do it. I thought only to keep the employer/employee relationship as straightforward as possible. You may be my patient for now, but I hope you'll be in my employ much longer than you will be in my care."

That rat! With his reasonable tone and his plausible explanation, he'd turned the tables on her.

Well, she refused to feel like she was being unreasonable. It did make more sense for him to do it than to rouse poor Eli, who seemed to be on call 24-7.

Plus, she knew his rationalizations were just that — rationalizations. She'd felt his reluctance like a palpable force between them.

She lifted her eyebrows. "Oh, but we're both professionals. I hardly think either one of us is going to get confused if you draw my blood this one time."

"You're the boss," he said, his voice loose, a little mocking. Casual, casual. "Just sit tight and I'll get the kit."

He left the room to retrieve the phlebotomy supplies.

Ainsley wilted immediately. God, she was a fool to antagonize him. And he was antagonized. As smooth as he was trying to play it, he was pissed. No question about it.

She didn't have long to flay herself about it; he was back in under a minute. Plunking the kit down, he readied the materials and donned fresh sterile latex gloves.

He looked up, his eyes cool, thoughts purposely shrouded. "Left arm?"

"Seems to work best." She extended her arm, having already rolled up her sleeve.

He tied the rubber tourniquet off, then reached for an alcohol prep pad, which he tore open. Grasping her arm, he swabbed the inside of her elbow efficiently. Then, with every bit as much practiced ease as Eli displayed, he probed for the best vein, introduced the needle and quickly filled the requisite number of tubes, each with a different colored cap. Though she watched his face carefully, he didn't betray by so much as a twitch any untoward emotion.

Stranger and stranger. Had she been that far off base? Had she completely imagined his ambivalence?

"There. All done."

He applied a gauze pad to the site and withdrew the needle. Automatically, she took over, applying steady pressure to the site while he released the tourniquet.

Okay, Ainsley, you're an idiot. A vain, self-centered jerk. You pose no more of a threat to this man's composure than a gnat circling his head.

Then he stood so abruptly that his chair shot backward, careening into the wall where it left a small but definite dent in the drywall.

"You can run off to bed now. We're done here." With that, he left the room, samples in hand.

Ainsley watched him thoughtfully, wondering when it would strike him that the samples had to come back to this lab.

Chapter 6

AINSLEY WOKE TO a violent thunderstorm.

She lay there a moment, wondering if she'd imagined the ear-splitting crack of thunder that still echoed in her head. Then another boom sounded, shaking the house and rattling the windows. She jack-knifed up in bed, heart pounding. Holy Mother of God, that had to have been close!

She reached for the lamp at her bedside, turning the switch. Nothing. That's when she noticed the clock radio that usually glowed at her bedside had been extinguished. Great. No power. The electrical storm must have knocked the electricity out.

Or, oh shit, had lightning struck the house itself? It sure sounded close enough. Was the house already on fire?

She swung her legs over the edge of the bed, grabbed her clothes and began to struggle into them. She was poking her bare feet into her athletic shoes when her door burst open.

"Ainsley? Thank God you're all right."

The voice was Delano's, but she couldn't see him.

"Del? What's happening? Has the house been hit?"

"We have to leave. Now."

Another boom and a flash rocked the house and briefly revealed Delano, closer now than his voice had suggested just second ago.

"Are you sure we should go out there in that? I mean, unless the house is on fire, wouldn't we be safer in here?"

"That's mortar fire," he clipped. "The house is under attack."

Under attack? "But who ... why — ?"

"Just come." He grabbed her arm and pulled her toward the door.

"My purse!"

"Quickly."

She dashed back to grab her bag from her bedside, then Delano was tugging her forward again. Within seconds, they were racing through the halls at a dead run.

"We're going too fast. I can't see anything!"

"I can see. Just stay close."

"Where are we going?"

"There are tunnels below. But save your breath. We have to get clear before they get close enough to get a lock on our infrared signatures."

He was worried about their *infrared-freaking-signatures*? That had to mean they were dealing with attackers who had heat-seeking weapons ...

She stumbled, but he righted her before she could fall, then tugged her onward at a pace even faster than before. Which was way faster than she was capable of running. It was his speed and strength that impelled her. She forgot to worry about slamming into unseen objects and merely concentrated on keeping her feet churning beneath her fast enough to avoid stumbling again.

They ran for what seemed like forever, but was probably a matter of minutes. Delano quickly learned to announce corners before they negotiated them. "In five seconds, we've got a left turn, 90 degrees. Left again in five. Right. Steps. Left. More steps. Five, four, three, two, one ... ramp."

By the time they reached the ramp, her leaden legs could no longer respond fast enough to keep up. He'd merely slid an arm around her and lifted her clear of the ground, pelting down the ramp without losing a fraction of his speed.

Before she could marvel at his endurance, he stopped and set her back on her feet.

"We're here."

"Where is here?"

As though in response to her question, a very dim light came on. She was standing in a cavern of some sort. And in the center of the cavern, resting like a great sleeping beast on the rock floor, sat the strangest looking aircraft she'd ever seen. A helicopter, she realized. Well, maybe a helicopter. It had rotors, anyway. That's about where the resemblance ended.

"What's that?"

"That's our ticket out of here."

Out of here? Reflexively, she glanced up, straining to see the roof of the cavern. Though she could not discern it through the inky darkness, she felt its looming, containing presence, heard it in the way their voices bounced off the walls. How was a helicopter going to get them out of this cave?

A man detached himself from the shadows, a pair of helmets in hand. "Fuelled up and ready to go, boss."

Eli! A pang of guilt pierced her. She'd forgotten all about him in the headlong rush to escape the bombardment above.

"Oh, thank goodness, Eli! You made it out."

"Yes, ma'am. Now put this helmet on. We've gotta strap in, pronto."

She accepted the helmet, but before she could put it on, the floor beneath her feet started to vibrate. Her gaze flew to Delano, who pointed upward. She glanced up to see the ceiling above them sliding open, exposing cold pinpoints of starlight in the pre-dawn sky. A retractable roof!

She should have been relieved that an escape route had opened up, but all she felt was scared and confused. Who was Delano Bowen to command these resources? More importantly, who was he to attract a military-style attack on his house? "I don't understand this. I don't understand any of it."

"I'll explain later. But trust me, we have to get out of here, and we have to do it quickly."

Her answer was to jam the helmet on.

Minutes later, she finished strapping herself into the seat Delano indicated. He and Eli sat up front. Even before their seat-belts were fastened, they'd run through an ultra-rapid pre-flight check. Then Eli powered up the engines. Faster than she would have imagined possible, the beast lifted smoothly off the ground.

Ainsley squeezed her eyes shut. She would have characterized herself as a comfortable flyer, but one glance at the cavern walls closing in on them as the craft ascended convinced her that this was one takeoff she was better off not watching.

"It's okay."

At the soothing sound of Delano's voice inside her helmet, she opened her eyes.

"Eli can fly this thing in his sleep, and it's very maneuverable. Oh, and his helmet is equipped with night vision sensors. He can see like it's high noon."

Good. That was all good. "What about the heat-seeking technology you mentioned?"

"It won't be a problem now that we're inside the craft. It's equipped with the latest in low-observable technology."

Dear Jesus, stealth technology? Wasn't that restricted to military use? "This is a stealth helicopter? We're invisible?"

"Nothing is invisible, especially to the naked eye. But the craft is designed to minimize its radar signature and hide its heat signature. Once we're away, we'll be very hard to track."

"Yeah? Well, it's the getting away part that has me concerned right now. They'll be able to see us, won't they? And hear us?"

"Not to worry. I left them a little something to keep them preoccupied."

"Clear," came Eli's voice in her ear.

She glanced out the window to see the lights of the city on the horizon, a scant three miles away. They were indeed clear of the cavern.

"Time to give our visitors their present."

On cue, a spectacular explosion erupted perhaps a thousand yards away, tearing the west-facing, ivy-covered stone wall right out of Delano's house. Flames leapt high into the air. In the orange illumination provided by the fire, debris drifted gracefully to the ground.

Ainsley gasped, recognizing the corner of the house that had just been destroyed. "Your lab! Del, they blew up your lab!"

"No, they didn't. I did."

Just then, Eli nailed the accelerator, or whatever the equivalent of an accelerator was in a big-assed stealth helicopter, and they screamed off. In what seemed like a matter of seconds, they were racing along at what felt like an altitude of mere inches above the surface of the glittering river that bisected St. Cloud.

He'd blown up his own lab? "Delano Bowen, you've got some explaining to do."

"More than you know. But I'm afraid it's going to have to wait."

"No!" Her voice rose on a note of hysteria, which she clamped down on immediately. She hadn't done all those years in as an OR nurse in a major trauma center for nothing. "You're not putting this off," she said, and this time her tone was calm, authoritative. "I want to know what's going on here, and I want to know it now."

"I'd love to oblige, but I'm afraid it's impossible just at the moment. See that on the eastern horizon?" He released his safety harness, removed his flight helmet and crawled out of the cockpit.

Her heart leapt into her throat, scattering her composure. Were they being pursued? Was he going to man some hidden high-tech defense system? She craned her neck to scan the eastern horizon for hostile aircraft, but the pre-dawn sky was empty.

"I don't understand. What am I supposed to see?"

"The sun," he said dryly. "It's about to rise. Which means I need to seek shelter."

She felt her heart thudding in her chest, hard enough that she could count each and every painful contraction. Time seemed to bow and wobble, and the very air between her and the rest of the world turned liquid, heavy, oppressive.

Omigod, omigod, omigod, omigod, omigod.

She sucked in a shallow breath. Then another, deeper one. On the exhalation: "You're a vampire."

"I'm afraid so. Though I had hoped to break the news in more favorable circumstances. "

"Did you? Did you really?" It was a struggle to keep her tone of voice out of the fishwife register. "Or did you plan to keep me in the dark indefinitely?"

His brows came together. "Look, I'd really like to have this out with you, but in five minutes, I'm either going to be dead to the world or just plain dead. I strongly prefer the former. So if you'll excuse me ..."

With that, he brushed past her to flip open the top to what she'd taken for some kind of cargo storage box. Then he climbed inside its satin-lined cavity and sketched her a casual, self-mocking salute. "Until tonight."

Then he lay down and pulled the lid shut.

The lid!

To. His. Fucking. Coffin!

Montreal at night. One of his favorite spots on earth. Delano gazed out over the sea of lights spread virtually at his feet, and waited. And waited still longer. But for once, the pulse of the city failed to steal into him to quicken his own heartbeat.

Instead, he felt ... nothing.

Dammit. It was a sorry vampire whose blood was not stirred by the prospect of all that vibrant life down there on the streets.

Of course, it was a sorrier vampire still who had to be carted into his penthouse, in full daylight, delivered up like an inanimate piece of furniture.

Or a numb, cold piece of statuary.

His brows drew together in a frown. What was this odd feeling dragging at him? What was this strange mood? He looked inward and saw the answer.

Melancholy.

His gut clenched. *Sweet Jesus.* Bring on the mortar shells. Let a hundred enemies rain fire from the sky. But please, God, keep the monkey of depression off his back. Stronger men than he had stepped outside at dawn to witness their last sunrise, impelled by an unrelenting weariness too profound to resist.

The woman. Ainsley Crawford. That's what brought it on.

These past few days, she'd looked on him as though he were an ordinary, if not entirely trustworthy, man. Until that moment in the helicopter. He'd seen the shock, the shift in her eyes when he'd had to seek shelter from the sun.

What he would give to have her look at him again the way she had before ...

Delano heard the door open behind him but did not turn. That would be Eli, bearing sustenance and a status report.

Eli came to stand beside him at the window. "Ah, Montréal," he said, pronouncing it the French way. "Good to be back, isn't it?"

Delano sighed and turned his back on the nighttime tableau. "I must be getting old, Eli. The blood doesn't pump like it used to."

Eli looked singularly unconvinced, but said, "It's been a rough twenty-four hours, I'll grant you that much."

Delano raked his hair, still wet from the shower, back from his forehead. "It was our Czech friend, of course."

"Yeah, it was Janecek, all right." Eli moved away to place the unit of blood he carried in the blood warmer. "Our sources in Prague confirm he was Stateside as of last week, and he was spotted in New York two days ago. And just in case we might have had any lingering doubts, the blast you left for them took out one of his key lieutenants, a merc by the name of Liam Hanlon."

Delano whistled. "Hanlon? Are we sure about that?"

"Absolutely."

Janecek would be extremely pissed. As would Hanlon, if he were still around to reflect on his fate. Word had it Hanlon had made a deal with Janecek. When he'd served long enough and faithfully enough, he would be rewarded with his master's eternal kiss. If nothing else positive came out of last night's firefight, the world was far better off without a merc-turned-vamp rampaging around it.

"The body?"

"Our people let their people retrieve it."

"What about police?"

"Nothing to worry about there. The scene was sufficiently sanitized before their arrival. The HAZMAT team that went in was 100% ours."

Always good when the contingency plans one laid so carefully actually fell into place. "The media? How did they characterize it?"

"Natural gas explosion. No injuries, since you were out of town and your staff had the week off."

More good news. "Repairs to the lab?"

"Already underway."

He nodded his satisfaction. "Sounds like everything is under control."

Eli coughed, to disguise either a laugh or a snort. "Under control. Absolutely. Except for that little detail that the Butcher of Bohemia is apparently out for your head."

"Indeed."

Eli shot Delano a hard look. "You know, I can do my job better when I have the full picture."

"Point taken. When I have the full picture, I'll fill you in."

Eli blew out an exasperated breath. "Okay, I appreciate it's a little early for definitive conclusions, but if you had to speculate, what would you say? What's this about?"

"If it were just me he wanted, he could have ambushed me any number of times over this past week, but he chose to strike my home, my lab. So I would say I have something Radak Janecek wants. Or perhaps something he wants to see destroyed."

"The fruits of your research?"

"Definitely. Also the woman."

Eli's lifted his left eyebrow, which for him was tantamount to gaping. "The Crawford woman?"

The Merzetti woman, he thought, but instead he nodded. "Ainsley Crawford, yes."

"But why?"

Delano inhaled, released his breath slowly. It was past time to tell Eli. He was right about that; he couldn't do his job unless he knew the situation. "Because she's the key. She can bring it all down, the whole vampire kingdom. And somehow, Radak must have figured that out."

This time Eli's face showed no reaction. "Bring the Kingdom down? How?"

Delano waved his hand dismissively. "It doesn't matter how. What matters is keeping her safe. She is now my number one priority, Eli. The research must continue, but above all, her life must be preserved."

Eli held his gaze for a few beats. "Does she know?"

"No."

"When will you tell her?"

He ran a hand over the back of his neck. "With any luck I won't have to."

The soaring eyebrow again. Twice in a single night. A record.

"Delano, I don't like this —"

"In the long run, it would be better for her if she doesn't know."

That was the understatement of the century. And if she did know, she could very well withhold her consent. He'd seen the look on her face when she realized her attacker was dead. Relief so profound she couldn't hide it, but mixed with an equally strong measure of guilt and remorse. If she felt that conflicted thinking that he had killed Edward Webber to avenge the attack, imagine the turmoil she'd feel to know that, strictly speaking, it was her blood that caused his demise. Even though her role in his death had not been an active or deliberate one, even though the responsibility still lay squarely on Delano's shoulders, he knew she would suffer for it. And if he went on to use her blood to bring down other rogues, which indeed he planned to do, she could multiply that guilt a hundredfold.

Once upon a time, taking the decision out of her hands would have been beyond him. As a physician — hell, as a morally upright human being — he could not have crossed that line. But he was infinitely older now, and his once black-and-white world had long since dissolved into gradations of gray, a world where he frequently had to choose between the lesser of evils.

"What about her safety? Doesn't she have the right to know?"

"She'll remain under my protection until all threat is removed. And if I'm not satisfied she'll be safe in her ignorance, I will certainly tell her the truth. But mark my words, Eli, it would pain her greatly to know. I seek only to spare her the burden. You know the work must go on."

Eli held his gaze for a long moment, measuring the veracity of his words. "Okay," he said at last.

Delano inclined his head in acknowledgement.

"But I still don't like it."

Delano narrowed his eyes. "Nevertheless, it's my decision."

This time, Eli inclined his head in acceptance. "You should eat."

Eat. Delano's lips twisted. Despite being a medical professional, Eli clung stubbornly to language that characterized Delano's nightly infusion as some manner of meal. And Eli well knew he never ingested anything, beyond the occasional sip of whiskey he took just to feel the alcohol sear his throat, or maybe a sip of ice water to feel the cold.

For better or worse, caffeine could not jolt him. No amount of alcohol consumption could produce the warm, welcome, barely-remembered buzz of inebriation. No matter how many cigarettes he smoked, they couldn't create, and then fill, receptors in his brain to give him an instantaneous nicotine rush. The only, the sole intoxication available to him whispered in the veins of humans.

And that was an intoxication no vampire could indulge freely, lest he become ruled by it. That was how creatures like Edward Webber were born. Far better to imbibe disembodied blood from a bag. Granted, it was like eating a K-ration when a sumptuous, aromatic buffet beckoned, but it was the only path he dared walk.

Eli handed him the unit of blood. "You'd best eat. Ms. Crawford knows you're awake and is probably preparing to knock down that door this very moment. I won't be able to hold her off much longer."

Delano's fingers closed around the bag of blood. Warm. Thirty-seven degrees Celsius. Body-temperature. "She waits outside?"

"I expect so."

"Then send her in."

"But —"

"Send her in."

Eli sighed. "You don't have to do this, Delano."

Ah, but he really did. "She's a nurse, Eli. I don't think she'll develop a case of the vapors. You didn't."

"I've also killed men in hand-to-hand combat."

"Show her in, Eli."

Without another word, Eli turned to do his bidding.

Chapter 7

AINSLEY'S MOMENTUM AS she entered the study carried her right past Delano. Belatedly, she caught a glimpse of him in her peripheral vision, standing still as a statue just to the left of the door.

"Over here," he drawled. "You seem to have overshot me."

She rounded on him, a flush warming her neck. The rat. No doubt he'd positioned himself there strategically so she would blow right past him. Well, she refused to feel like she was overreacting.

"Dammit, Delano, why didn't you tell me?"

"Because I thought you'd had quite enough rude shocks to cope with."

She made no attempt to stifle a snort of disbelief. "Really? So it was my welfare you were concerned about?"

"Absolutely."

"And the fact that I might have declined the job had I known the boss was a blood-sucking vampire didn't enter into your decision-making process?"

His face hardened. "I shouldn't have to explain to you, of all people, that there's no sucking involved. And to answer your question, yes, that did enter into the equation. But frankly, I don't think it would have been a deal-breaker, had I told you. You still have that crippling need to feed your bank account, and a decidedly lackluster reference from your employer."

"But I deserved to know!"

"Know?" His face hardened still further, making him look even more remote. "You want to know, Ainsley? Then you shall know."

Suddenly, he was beside her. Just like that. One second he was standing twelve feet away, his features perfectly distinguishable. Then, the very next instant, he was there, right there, mere inches away, too close for her to adjust the focus. All she'd seen was a blur of motion.

"Jesus!" Her hand leapt automatically to the pulse hammering in her throat.

"Not even close."

He drew his lips back in a caricature of a smile, and before her eyes, the two upper cuspids telescoped into pointed fangs more fearsome and lethal looking than those of her attacker. Reflexively, she jerked back, but his hand shot out to grasp her wrist.

"Don't go all weak-kneed on me now, Ainsley. You want to know? Then watch and learn."

Then he raised what she realized was a unit of blood and sank his teeth into it. Holding her gaze, he squeezed the plastic bag, creating the pressure required to push the blood into his venous system.

She watched, half revolted, half fascinated.

It took thirty seconds. Maybe a little longer. When the bag was all but empty, he wrenched it from his mouth. Her eyes dropped to his teeth, to the elongated canines that gleamed red with blood. Then, drawn by motion, her gaze dropped to his chest. Beneath the black cashmere sweater he wore, his chest heaved as though he'd just run a marathon.

Or as though he was sexually aroused.

Her gaze jerked back to his face, and she sucked in an audible breath.

Jesus, Mary and Joseph.

Pure need had chiseled his features into brutally hard planes and angles. It blazed from his dark eyes and escaped in gusts from his still parted lips.

And deep in her belly, a dark, matching excitement unfurled.

Oh, God.

He'd said it was pleasurable for a woman. Intensely so. She'd doubted it then; nothing about her own experience had been anything but horrifying. Of course, that had been an assault, an act of violence, the equivalent of a rape. This would be different.

Her blood thrummed with the certain, inborn knowledge that Delano Bowen could bring her pleasure beyond imagination.

Her skin tingled. His breath on her flesh was a caress. Beneath the man's shirt that Eli had procured for her, she felt her nipples tighten and her stomach muscles contract. Oh, God, yes.

She let her eyelids drift down, let her head fall back, tilting it to the right to expose her neck. Trembling with the force of a raw and unfamiliar need, she waited for the searing kiss of his teeth.

His grip on her wrist tightened to the point of pain. She gasped. Her eyes flew open, but he'd already released her. Once again, he stood on the other side of his study, this time with his back to her, shoulders tight and tense.

"Delano?"

"That was nothing personal."

She blinked, watched him dispose of the spent blood bag in a bio-hazard waste disposal unit mounted on the wall. Calmly, he took a paper towel from a dispenser, wiped his mouth, then disposed of it, too.

"Excuse me?"

He turned to face her, his face once again composed and controlled, though his voice was slightly thicker than normal. "It's just the bloodlust. It's awakened when we feed."

She blanched. This happened to all vampires when they fed? "You mean all those males who came to the clinic ...?"

"I'm afraid so." An apologetic smile curved his lips. "And perhaps more than a few of the females. Which is why we offer them a private, safe environment for their infusions. It takes a few moments to regain complete control afterward."

Great. Her face burned. He'd had what amounted to a basic physiological reaction that would have happened with or without her presence, and she'd practically leapt on him. She closed her eyes again, this time in utter humiliation.

"Lighten up on yourself, Nurse Crawford. You may not have known about vampires and the delights of blood-sharing, but your primitive brain does."

She blinked. "My primitive brain?"

"The primitive arousal center of your brain, yes. It knows, Ainsley." His voice was like velvet brushing against her skin. "It's as deeply embedded in your instincts as the fear of serpents or saber-toothed tigers or lightning. Don't punish yourself for what it remembers."

No. Un-uh. She wouldn't have reacted the same way had this happened with any of the clients she'd processed in his clinic. Not even the one who bore a strong resemblance to Alan Rickman, right down to the voice, and she adored the hell out of Alan Rickman. Truly, madly, deeply adored him. But she was happy to take the out he offered.

"Well, that's a relief. I was beginning to think—" Omigod! Her words trailed off as another thought occurred to her. That's why he hadn't wanted to draw her blood that time. But she'd pushed and pushed until he relented. That's why he'd practically fled afterward. What might have happened if she had but looked into his eyes?

"Ainsley?"

She blinked. "I'm sorry, what?"

"You didn't finish your thought."

"That's because I had another one." Feeling off balance and not liking it one little bit, she went on the offensive. "Is there anything else I should know at this juncture?"

His expression did not change perceptibly, but somehow he was closing up on her. Damn him! He had no right —

"Ask me whatever you would."

Huh? "Really?"

He extended his hands, palm up. "Really."

I'm an open book, the gesture said. But gestures could lie, or speak partial truths. Time to see how much he would tell her.

"Who attacked your house?"

His left eyebrow shot up. "I thought Eli told you that much."

"He did. Now I want you to tell me."

"Very well." He pushed a strand of long hair back from his forehead. "The assault was launched by a vampire, a rogue by the name of Radak Janecek. He knows the nature of my work — the search for a vaccine to inoculate the vulnerable. Clearly he fears I am getting too close, and chose to make a preemptive strike. Fortunately, he destroyed nothing that can't be reproduced."

"So you plan to resume your research?"

"As soon as possible."

"When your house is repaired?"

"No." He shook his head. "That will take months. I'll set up a clinic here immediately."

Her jaw dropped. "Here? In Montreal?"

"Yes, here."

"But it can't be as easy as that. Surely you can't just literally drop from the sky in your helicopter and open a clinic? What about the local health authority? What about the Quebec government? What about Health Canada?"

He smiled. Not the polite, automatic social smile, not the apologetic one, not the rueful one. A real honest-to-God amused smile. It was, she thought, just the second real smile she'd seen from him. It flashed suddenly and was gone, further proof of its sincerity.

"I'm afraid this particular clinic is going to be an unsanctioned one. It would take far too long to get approval from the proper channels. But you may be certain the clientele won't betray us."

"Us?" She took a half-step backward. "You expect me to go back to work, then?"

"Ah, you have concerns about your safety."

Ainsley lifted her chin. "After the last twenty-four hours, I'd have to be a fool not to have concerns about my safety. And I assure you, Dr. Bowen, I am no fool."

"Indeed not, Ms. Crawford. Nor am I a fool. We shall have security worthy of a king. The clinic itself will be underground, and therefore there will be no official paper trail to lead my friend Janecek to it. That will buy us some time."

"Underground, like the cavern in St. Cloud? Or underground, as in illicit?"

He shot her a reproving look. "The latter, although I prefer to think of it as unsanctioned rather than illicit."

She nodded. "Is that it? You're going to rely on hiding it?"

"That's part of the picture, but hardly all of it. We will move it around, alternating locations. And before you ask, no vampire who would patronize our clinic would breathe a word to a rogue. He will not find us quickly, and when he does, we will be prepared."

"*When* he does? Not *if* he does?"

"As passionate as I am about creating this vaccine, that's how determined he is to prevent it. He won't stop until he destroys the research."

Ainsley felt a cold frisson of fear skitter along her spine. "And you."

"What about me?"

She shot him a reproving look. "You know what I mean. He can't rest until he's eliminated you, too. He knows the research won't die until you die."

"I was rather planning on not letting that happen, but yes, that sums up his intentions quite fairly, I should think."

"But all he needs to do is find out where you're staying, right? He can launch another military-type attack and take the top floor of this high-rise right out. Probably the entire building, if he wanted." In her mind, she saw a replay of the Twin Towers collapsing.

"No." Delano shook his head decisively. "He won't use the same approach again. Even if he were inclined to, by the time he finds us, he'll know we'll have sophisticated anti-aircraft capability in place."

"Anti-aircraft capability?"

Those heavy eyebrows drew together again in a fierce frown. "He won't catch us napping again."

Oh, man, was he for real? Probably. After all, he owned a freaking stealth helicopter. And she hadn't even known such a thing existed. She crossed her arms beneath her breasts. "Sitting on an oil well, are we?"

"An oil well?" His eyebrows drew together.

"It's an expression, Del. An idiom. I was alluding to your seemingly bottomless pockets."

"Ah." His frown cleared.

"So, is there no limit to your resources?"

His eyes glinted with humor again. "There's a limit to everything, Ainsley, but I'm happy to say not even I shall live long enough to exhaust my resources."

"Shut up!"

He laughed. "Ah, another idiom. I know that one."

"No, I mean *shut the hell up*! That's appalling. You're saying you have more money than you can spend in a century? Centuries? Omigod, that's obscene."

Again, he laughed. "When one has a surfeit of time and a sufficiently long look at human behavioral trends, you'd be amazed what the markets will yield. Oh, and yes, I am sitting on an oil well. Or twenty."

It was her turn to laugh. Dammit, she was supposed to be grilling him, but she couldn't help herself. "Why does that not surprise me?"

His smile faded. "Not much throws you off stride, I've noticed. You're very ... resilient."

She sobered too. "Resilient, yes. Bulletproof, no. I don't like this, Delano." She held up a hand when it looked like he might interrupt. "I don't have nine lives like you appear to have. Maybe I should go back to St. Cloud, look for more conventional work. Or maybe I could pack up my stuff and go west. Pay scale's much better in Alberta or British Columbia. Or maybe south of the border, although that would take paperwork ...

"That sounds like a very reasonable plan."

His easy acquiescence was like a blade, slicing into her with no forewarning. He was going to send her on her way just like that, with no protest?

"But not quite yet, I'm afraid," he continued. "There's still the matter of your possible infection. Beginning a new job for a new employer in a new city is not where you want to start getting all toothy around a bloody trauma case."

"Oh, right. That." She glanced away. "Surely it won't be much longer."

"A few weeks, I should think. If you're not evidencing antibody activity by then, I think we can declare you unscathed from your adventure."

"Unscathed?" She snorted. "My life has been threatened twice, once by bite and once by bomb. I was whisked away in the night and left to deal with the knowledge that my boss is playing for the skins team when I thought he was playing for the shirts, and now —" Her voice broke. Mortified, she turned away.

Damn, damn and damn again. She was going to cry. No, she was already crying. He detected the betraying salt smell of her tears.

"I'm sorry, I'm suddenly not feeling all that resilient."

He suppressed a groan. Every chivalrous instinct he owned urged him to take her in his arms, offer her the physical comfort she so clearly needed. Except there were other instincts to be considered. Like the call of her blood to his, the all-but-audible surge of it in her veins ...

Damn, maybe he should call Eli.

Her head snapped up. "Don't even suggest it!"

What the hell? "Pardon me?"

"Don't you dare offer Eli for me to use as some kind of security blanket." She dashed tears away with the back of her hand.

By all the saints, she'd done it again! Deduced his thoughts as though she'd plucked them straight from his head. Just like the other time, when he'd gone out to find Webber. He scowled. And drew a shield tight around his thoughts.

"There you go again, thinking you can read my mind. For your information, Nurse Crawford, I was not about to offer Eli's services, in that or any other respect." Hearing his own words, Delano could almost credit them. He hoped she would, too. "Believe it or not, there are one or two things I can do for myself without resorting to a proxy." *Pray God this was one of them.* He took her hand and pulled her toward him. "Now, come here. My shoulder is quite up to the job, I assure you."

He expected an argument. Wariness. At the very least, he expected to have to reassure her that such intimate contact was perfectly safe. That having fed mere moments ago, he was unlikely to be overcome with lust. But she turned into his arms with a choked sob, making it unnecessary for him to utter yet another lie.

"I'm sorry." The words were mumbled against his shirt. "I never do this. Really. I'm always the one who holds it together."

"Hush, Ainsley. I know. Don't worry about it."

His arms closed awkwardly around her, and her arms gripped back as though he were a lifeline. Her breath warmed his chest through his shirt, and he felt a fine tremor shudder through her. And oh Jesus God, it was good to feel the touch of another human, let alone the press of a woman's flesh against his own. How long had it been?

Very quickly, the steady thudding of her heart impinged on his awareness, distracting him from the simple comfort of warm contact. He felt the pumping of her heart as distinctly as his own. At this range, the muted surge and whisper of her blood became a roaring in his ears. To his heightened senses, her body felt like a blazing furnace, even through the layers of clothing they wore, and her heated scent rose to tantalize his nostrils.

He tried to keep a lid on things, reminding himself that she was distraught. She needed his comfort, not his lust. Even now her tears burned him through the fine cotton of his shirt, and sobs wracked her body.

Despite his best efforts, a sensory image of how she would taste — her lips, her skin, her blood — flooded his senses ...

Jesus, Bowen. Get hold of yourself!

He fixed on her heart sounds, imagining the corresponding functions. Better.

Right atrium contracting. Now, the right ventricle. Back surge as the blood tried to flow back into the right atrium. Both right and left atrioventricular valves closing.

Lub.

Pressure building, blood squeezing out of the right ventricle, through the pulmonary semilunar valve, and into the pulmonary artery. Pulmonary semilunar valve and the aortic semilunar valve closing.

Dub.

Lub, dub. Lub, dub. Lub, dub.

No, no, no. Not good. Tune it out. Think of something else!

He found himself stroking her hair, though he had no conscious memory of lifting his hand to her head. Lord, it was like spun silk, fine and warm and fragrant and straighter even than his own. His fingers itched to pull out the clasp that trapped it in that twist at her nape, but that would never do. Such actions were for lovers. And he would never — could never — be that.

For to taste her might be to die.

His blood cooled fractionally.

At the same moment, she pulled back, wiping her eyes. "Oh, God, I'm sorry. That was ... embarrassing."

Delano stepped back. Thank God. Space. Layers of air between them. He could breathe again.

"No, that was merely human, Ainsley. In the last week, you've had to absorb more than most people could cope with and still keep their sanity. I think a few tears are allowed."

She laughed, daubing at her eyes again. "Well, that was more than a few tears, but thank you. I guess everything just sort of caught up with me."

He nodded. "Exactly so. And if you don't feel like returning to work under the circumstances, I will understand entirely. Of course, whether you attend the clinics or not, I will see that your salary is deposited."

Her chin came up. Her violet eyes, washed almost blue from her tears, sparkled with temper.

"My need is great, as you've pointed out on numerous occasions, and your pockets are clearly very deep, but I could hardly take your money if I'm not working."

"Nonsense. You wouldn't be in this position if you hadn't answered my advertisement."

"But —"

"But nothing. Had you not answered my ad, you would not have ventured near that alley, and thus you would not have been savaged by Edward Webber. And had you not been bitten, you would not have been under my care, indeed under my roof, when Janecek attacked. In short, you would not be here, in the particular situation in which you find yourself. So, whether you choose to work or not, your salary will continue."

She inclined her head. "That's very generous of you, Dr. Bowen, but I insist on earning my pay. But before you rush to canonize me, you should know that I'll be insisting on something else."

Something else? His pulse kicked. "And what would that be?"

"Danger pay." She fixed him with a steely look. "I think twenty-five percent over the basic compensation package ought to do it."

Danger pay? That was all she wanted? He'd been half afraid she was going to try to extract something much harder for him to give. Money, however, was not a problem. Hell, he could easily afford to pay her ten times the salary she was earning, and he wouldn't begrudge a penny of it. Unfortunately, he couldn't risk handing her so much money that her financial pressures evaporated altogether. Her financial need was a major tool in keeping her close. But surely twenty-five percent he could do without jeopardizing the situation. And she was quite right — danger pay was definitely in order.

Still, he mustn't grant the concession too easily. She wasn't the type to enjoy a victory if it were too readily ceded.

"Twenty-five percent over an already generous base?" He lifted his eyebrows in what he hoped conveyed surprise. "You realize our armed forces would be lucky to get that, even as they march into imminent danger."

"Twenty-five percent," she repeated. "And as far as I'm concerned, we *are* in imminent danger. You're lucky I'm not asking for it retroactively."

"Then excuse me while I thank my lucky stars."

Her chin came up higher. "No need for sarcasm, Dr. Bowen. Oh, and I expect you'll make the same adjustment for Eli."

Delano's snort of disbelief was genuine. "You're bargaining for Eli now? What's this? A union?"

"Both of us. Twenty-five percent."

Wait until Eli heard about this! He already protested that Delano paid him far too much. "What about the security I'll be providing? Throw the cost of that in with the compensation package, and it's a pricey office overhead I'll be paying."

"True, but it's a risky enterprise you're engaged in, particularly here, where your activities will be unsanctioned, in an underground clinic."

Delano thought about prolonging the exchange just to keep her looking at him with that fire of determination in her eyes. But the time had come to cede her point.

"You make a good argument, Nurse Crawford." He pretended to consider the issue for another moment. "Okay, twenty-five percent it is, for both of you."

"Thank you."

"Now, if there's nothing else, I really must be going. I need to make contact with potential clients."

The change of subject left her blinking. "You're going trolling for vampires?"

"Precisely. We have to get the word out on the street if we expect to do business by tomorrow night."

"Of course."

He started to move toward the door when she spoke again. "Delano?"

He turned back toward her. "Yes?"

"Be careful."

He knew she wasn't alluding to the law-abiding vampires he'd be recruiting in the all night establishments down on the street. She meant Janecek.

Something lurched painfully inside of him, something rusty that hadn't moved in a long time. He turned away from the concern in her eyes before it undid him.

"I'm always careful," he said. Then he left.

Chapter 8

AINSLEY FOUND ELI on the phone.

"Can you hold on just a sec?" he said into the telephone, then covered the mouthpiece. His eyes took in her face, which was no doubt still blotchy and hideous from that crying jag. "You okay?"

She grimaced. "Small meltdown, but I'm better now."

"Long overdue, you ask me." He gestured toward her suite of rooms. "We got you some clothes, if you'd like to ditch that shirt. Not that there's anything wrong with you in that shirt, you understand."

She laughed, buoyed by his easy, uncomplicated masculine appreciation. "Thanks. I'll go check them out." It occurred to her to tell him about his new pay hike, but thought better of it, seeing as he was in the middle of something. She waved him back to his phone conversation and headed for her rooms.

Ten minutes later, she'd examined everything in the four bags piled on her bed.

Two pairs of flat-front trousers, size 10, one pair chocolate brown, the other navy, just like the ones she'd left in St. Cloud. Two Eddie Bauer wrinkle-resistant, two-pleat khaki pants. One pair of designer jeans she knew must have cost the earth because, in a fit of self-indulgence, she'd paid $80 for an identical pair at a 75% off sale. A waffle-knit top, a long-sleeved v-neck tee, a ribbed v-neck sweater. Two Oxford shirts, one long sleeved and one short. A couple of tanks. The pants were precisely the same issue as the ones she'd abandoned, and the tops were close enough.

The final bag contained underwear. 36C underwire bras that fit, along with matching thongs and boy shorts and hip-hugging briefs. Underwear that mirrored almost exactly the intimates she'd left behind, though the stuff back home had seen better days.

Definitely not Delano's work. The very versatile Eli must have phoned back to the house in St. Cloud to get the particulars of her wardrobe, then paid a shopper to reproduce it as closely as possible. No wonder he was so invaluable to Delano.

Ainsley tossed the underwear into a drawer, gathered the clothes off the bed and hung them in the closet. Then she stretched out on the bed.

Lord, she was tired. Bone-deep weary, the way she used to get after stringing together too many consecutive 12s at the hospital. Except she didn't have long shifts to blame for her exhaustion this time. Just one nasty, psyche-rattling shock after another. But at least she knew the score, now.

Or did she?

Delano didn't seem like he was hiding anything more from her. Of course, she hadn't thought he'd been hiding anything significant before, and look how wrong she'd been.

She sat up on the bed, drawing her knees up and hugging them to her chest. How was it possible that she could read him so easily one moment — God, it was freaky ... like she could hear his very thoughts — only to discover he'd effortlessly concealed something as humongous and critical as, "Oh, by the way, I'm a vampire."

Unless he projected the things he wanted her to know, or things he flat out just didn't care if she knew, but shielded the rest?

She lifted her chin off her knees. Dear God, she was starting to think about this stuff as though she really had some kind of weird telepathic connection with Delano Bowen! How bizarre was that?

"Argh!" She flopped back against the pillows again.

Her eyes, still slightly puffy from crying, wanted to close, so she let them. God, but it would be good to just crash. If only she could shut her mind down like a computer. Clear the cache. Ctl-Alt-Del. Re-friggin'-boot. That's what she needed to do. If she could just sleep, she could forget about vampires for a while. And Delano's murderous nemesis Janecek. And her possible infection with the vampirism virus. And the way Delano's hot, black gaze had burned straight back into hers, touching her soul.

Her lids sprang open. That was no way to think. Nobody touched her soul, not without her permission. And she was extremely picky.

She let her lids drift closed again. It felt so good to close her burning eyes. But aaaaaaahhhhh, she couldn't sleep. Not now. Not yet. If Delano was planning to have a clinic up and running by tomorrow night, she'd better stick to the night rhythms, and sleep by day.

Besides which, if he were hiding something more from her, she'd have to match his hours so she could keep an eye on him. Groaning, she rolled off the bed and headed for the shower.

Delano stayed out until almost 4:30.

By 2:30, he'd already recruited more candidates than he needed. After all, these were familiar stomping grounds. He knew where to find the usual suspects. But he just wasn't ready to go back that soon. So he inserted himself into the current of humanity moving from bar to bar to after-hours club.

From Ste-Catherine Street, he moved northward along St-Denis Street, through the Quartier Latin, letting the scent of sweat and sex and booze and perfume and high spirits wash over him. He rarely walked among people like this, choosing not to torture himself with what he could not have. What he could not *be*. Except tonight, the hot, bright, slightly desperate gaiety was his salvation. Sweet, sweet distraction.

Eventually the sky started to lighten in the East. Only then did he head back in the direction of the high-rise.

It was her fault, dammit. The smell of her, the sound of her pulse, the way it quickened when he moved close to her. He'd had to tell her, had to show her, what the blood lust did to his kind. But she hadn't recoiled from him, as he half hoped she would. Instead she'd offered him her slender, delectable, innocent white throat. It had taken every shred of discipline he could summon to step back.

And this even knowing it could be the death of him. Literally.

Damn Edward Webber to the furthest reaches of hell for muddying the waters. Delano still didn't know if it was Ainsley's blood itself that killed the rogue outright, or whether her blood merely started a rapid reversal of the mutation.

The legends were murky. This particular strain of the Merzetti family was said to be lethal for vampires. But interestingly, not all vampires who partook of the blood died. According to the old tomes that Delano had unearthed, some vampires who infused themselves with the fabled toxic blood were reputed to have been mysteriously restored to a "state of grace". Delano interpreted that to mean their mutation was reversed, leaving them once again human.

And knowing what medical science now knew about transfusion medicine, it was entirely possible that those who died did so because the Merzetti blood reverted them to type, so to speak. Unaware of what was happening internally, they might have gone on to feed upon another victim whose ABO type was incompatible to their resurrected blood type.

Is that what happened with Webber? Would the Merzetti blood have killed him outright, even if he hadn't taken the second victim's blood? Or had the Merzetti blood already reset his genetic code, setting off the reversal?

Somehow, he hadn't imagined the reversal could be so quick. But why not?

Certainly the original mutation had acted quickly enough. Contrary to what he'd led Ainsley to believe, it generally took just over twenty-four hours for the change to begin, once the virus was imparted. Thirty at the outside. Why shouldn't the reversal be equally expeditious?

Clearly, what he needed to do was orchestrate another attack on Ainsley. Only this time, he'd be right there, *right goddamn there*, to monitor the situation. It had been frighteningly close the last time. The shock of the blood loss might have killed her if he'd been a moment later arriving.

The thing that had lurched in his chest earlier made another jerking wrench. His hand went to his breastbone as though to still the pain.

Damnation. This couldn't possibly be good. It happened every time he thought about putting her in the path of another rogue. But it had to be done. He didn't see a way around it.

And dear Lord, all that talk about taking blood from a sexual partner. It made him hard just to think about it. Hard and angry with himself.

Oh, it was all true, the incomparable rush, the full-on body-brain-soul connection. But what he'd failed to tell Ainsley was that he hadn't shared that sacred act with a living soul in almost 80 years.

How safe would she feel in his penthouse if she knew that?

And, oh Christ, how safe was *he*?

Well, that was a question for tomorrow. Tonight was all but gone. He glanced to the eastern horizon and picked up his pace.

Two minutes later, he entered the building's lobby, only to be braced by security. The shift must have changed in the night, because the security guard was different than the one he'd passed on his way out earlier. This one was older, military haircut, and clearly unimpressed by Delano's claim to be the owner of the building. As was the German Shepherd at his side.

"All due respect, mister, I don't care if you own the entire Island of Montreal. You're not taking that elevator or the stairwell until or unless I see some identification. So let's have it."

The dog growled, its hackles rising.

Delano ignored the dog. It didn't do to make eye contact with them. He always wound up in a pissing contest, and in this case, he didn't want to leave the security guard with a permanently cowed guard dog.

"So, Douglas," Delano said, reading the name from the nametag on the guard's his uniform, "you must be a friend of

Eli Grayson's." He fished a laminated card out of his wallet and proffered it.

The guard accepted the ID from Delano, leaned closer to his computer and hit a button, then toggled the cursor. Within a few seconds, he apparently found what he was looking for and handed the card back. "Sorry about that, Dr. Bowen, but I've got a job to do."

"Don't apologize. I'd have bent Eli's ear if you didn't challenge me." The dog sat back on his haunches, the motion drawing Delano's gaze. At the eye contact, the dog pinned his ears back, narrowed his eyes and growled. Delano looked away. "Has Eli told you what to expect?"

The guard's expression remained placid. "Pretty much anything, up to and maybe exceeding what I might expect to see in a combat situation."

Well, that about summed it up. "Glad to have you on the team, Doug."

On the 27th floor, Delano emerged from the elevator to a similar scene — security guard behind a desk with monitors. But this one was sans dog, thank God, and Delano had already met him earlier tonight. After checking in briefly, he strode to a second elevator and rode to the 29th floor.

The first elevator went no higher than the 27th floor, and the second started at 27 and went straight to 29. The 28th floor, where Delano's lab resided, could only be reached via the stairwell, and only from the 29th floor. Which was one of the reasons he'd bought this building. Couldn't be careful enough.

The suite was in near darkness when Delano entered, but he had no difficulty picking out Eli's form reclining on the couch. Damn. He should have known Eli wouldn't sleep until he was safely in before sunup. He should have called. Or come home sooner.

Delano keyed in the alarm code, then turned to his friend. "I see you've got security under control."

Eli stood, stifling a yawn. "The basics. More to do tomorrow."

"Today, you mean. Go to bed, Eli."

He scratched his chest. "Don't mind if I do."

"And don't set the alarm too early."

"Did you round up lots of Nosferatu? Nosferati? Oh, hell, vamps?"

Delano laughed. "More than enough for our clinic." He glanced around. "How's Ainsley? Gone to bed, I take it?"

"I think so." Eli rolled his shoulders, and cricked his neck, first one way, then the other. "She was restless, roamed around a while, but I haven't seen her since we shared a nightcap an hour or so ago."

Delano raised an eyebrow. Eli never drank alcohol. Ever.

"Okay, she had a nightcap. I had a coffee."

"A decaf, I hope."

"Decaf?" Eli yawned, which ruined the offended look he was trying to project. "It was an espresso, thank you very much. But don't worry. It won't keep me up. 'Night, boss."

"Goodnight, Eli."

As soon as Eli moved off, Delano headed for his own windowless rooms in the center of the penthouse. Five steps from the door of his suite, he halted.

Someone was in there.

A light burned inside, casting a dim glow into the corridor, but that's not what alerted him. Eli always left a small lamp burning for him. But he could feel a presence. He stood stock-still, and listened. There it was! Someone breathing. Quiet and regular. He flared his nostrils and caught the scent of sandalwood and vanilla.

Ainsley.

His heart leapt. Oh, hell. Had she crawled into his bed to await him, her imagination fired by the look that passed between them in his study earlier tonight?

Feeling disembodied, almost as though he were watching himself from above, he pushed the door to his bedroom open. It swung inward silently on well-oiled hinges, and there she was. Not in his bed, thank God, but in his chair. Specifically, the antique French wingback chair beside his bed. And she was sleeping soundly, bathed in yellow light from the 40-watt bulb in the bedside lamp.

A fierce pang, as sweet as it was painful, pierced his chest. God, she was beautiful. She slept slumped to one side, her head resting against the chair's upholstered wing, hair swept to one side to keep it out of her face. Her cheeks bore the faintest of flushes, and her mouth had a softness about it he'd never seen while she was awake.

Unable to help himself, he drifted closer until he stood not a foot away from her. At this range, he could almost feel the moisture of her respirations, see the fine blue veins in her eyelids and the dark sweep of lashes against her pale skin. With her lids lowered like that, veiling the strength and determination that normally blazed from her eyes like fire, she looked deceptively fragile. Ephemeral.

He closed his eyes against a new onslaught of yearning. Heart, mind, body, soul — oh, Christ, it all ached. All he wanted to do was sink to his knees on the fine old Persian carpet and bury his face in her lap. He wanted to feel her hands tunnel into his hair, skim his shoulders, slide down his back ... He wanted her naked. He wanted to glide his hands up the outsides of those slender thighs, skim his mouth over the inside of her thigh, letting his own heart beat match the pulse of her femoral artery ...

Merciful Jesus.

Step back, his mind ordered, but his limbs refused to comply. He swayed, balanced on the exquisite knife-edge of temptation.

Don't do it.

Silently, grimly, he fought the gravitational pull, the inexorable force that demanded he bend his knees and pay homage —

"Delano?"

His eyes sprang open.

Her voice was husky and sleep-thickened, but she sat up abruptly enough.

Spell broken, he stepped back.

"What are you doing here?" The question came out sounding harsher than he intended.

"I'm sorry. I must have fallen asleep." She leapt up, and something hit the floor with a soft thump, something that must have been lying in her lap as she slept.

They both reached for it at the same time, narrowly avoiding knocking heads. Ainsley pulled back at the last moment, and Delano came up with the object. As soon as his hand closed on it, he knew what it was.

A new pain flooded in, pushing out the other.

Gitta.

✳

Ainsley watched as Delano's face lost all expression.

There was no other way to describe the transformation. She'd awakened to find him looming above her, his eyes closed, jaw clenched, his whole face wreathed in a torment of sexual need. God help her, her heart still banged against her ribs from the memory of it. But now his face was carefully, scrupulously blank.

"I see you've been exploring." His voice was as bland as his facial expression.

"I'm sorry," she said again. "I was restless, and I didn't want to inflict myself on Eli any longer. I was keeping him from his work." She realized she was plucking at the sleeve of her sweater and forced herself to stop. "I just ventured in here for a minute. I was curious about where ... I mean, I wanted to see —"

"My coffin?"

An almost smile touched his lips, but his eyes were ... what? Cold?

"As you can see, I make use of a bed, like everyone else. Just not much of a view."

Flushing — because yes, she had expected a coffin, or at least something like the affair he'd climbed into on the helicopter — she glanced around the dim, windowless room.

"Cosy."

He elevated an eyebrow. "Disappointed?"

She shrugged. "I don't know ... I just thought your bedroom would be different."

He made no remark, but she knew he was angry. Possibly *very* angry. Not that she blamed him; she'd invaded his privacy shamelessly. It had seemed like a smart idea earlier tonight, when her brain was teaming with paranoia about what he might yet be hiding. Now, it just felt unforgivably rude.

Her gaze dropped to the pewter-framed black-and-white photograph he held in his hands. The one she'd been studying when she decided to just rest her eyes a moment. An old photo, judging by its graininess and by the high-necked gown the woman wore. The subject herself was an older lady, probably close to sixty years old, but with warm, laughing dark eyes and an aura of youthfulness that belied the marks time had left on her face.

"Is that your mother?"

Delano stiffened. "No."

"Your grandmother?"

"She was my wife," he growled.

Oh. *Oh!*

He crossed the room to place the photograph carefully back on the dresser from whence Ainsley had taken it. "It's been a long night," he said without turning. "Maybe we should both retire."

"I'm sorry. Your wife ... of course ... Oh, hell, I'm sorry, Del. I didn't stop to think —"

"Ainsley?" He angled his head, not so far that he was looking at her but enough so she could see his profile.

She moved a tentative step closer. "Yes?"

"Go to bed. Now."

"Of course. Sorry."

She took her leave as quickly as she could without actually appearing to flee. Oh, man, what an idiot she was. A minute later, she was safely in her own rooms, where she could castigate herself in private.

Why hadn't she thought about the possibility that the woman in the photo could be his wife?

Well, duh, because she was old and he was young.

Except he wasn't young. Not really. Vampires didn't age, he'd told her, or not perceptibly. Dammit, she'd even speculated about his possible age while she'd waited for him to waken tonight, but she'd been too caught up in her own anger to dwell on it much.

How old was he? Judging by that dress his wife wore — God, why hadn't she read more historical novels? — she'd say that photo was early 20th century. Like, way early. So give him close to a hundred years.

And his wife was probably younger than him when they married, maybe significantly younger. At least, that was the way of it in the romance novels, wasn't it? So give him another ... what? Forty years? So conservative estimate, he was probably 140.

A hundred-and-freaking-forty years old!

Of course, given her poor grasp of the history of fashion, that could easily be 150, 160. Who knew? Maybe 200.

God, that was so weird. He looked like a man in his prime. No, he *was* a man in his prime.

She peeled off her clothes and reached for the man's shirt Eli had furnished earlier, tugging it on for sleepwear.

Lord, she must be tired. She should have figured this all out. It's not like she hadn't had time, having studied that woman's picture for a good twenty minutes. But somehow, she hadn't thought about Delano in connection with family, or at least not in the context of a continuing relationship. She'd presumed that after he'd been infected, he would have fled not just the light of day, but a society that reviled him.

But she was certain now that he had to have been the man behind the lens of the camera that captured that woman's picture. She harbored still less doubt that he'd put that all-knowing expression in her eyes and that Mona Lisa smile on her lips. Envy, sharp and surprising, twisted in her gut.

Oh, God, Ainsley, could you be any more of a jerk? She buttoned the shirt's buttons swiftly. Begrudge the poor man a conjugal relationship with his own wife. A long-dead relationship.

She raked her hair back. What had it been like for him, to watch his wife age while he himself stayed vigorous and youthful? And what heartache it must have been for her.

Did he think of her still? Miss her? How long could a heart ache?

She thought of the woman in the photograph, with her mysterious smile. And she thought of Delano, the way he held himself so still. The way his eyes lost their focus sometimes, as though he were looking at something across a great distance.

A long time, she decided.

A very long time.

Sighing, she drew the heavy curtains across the bedroom's window to shield against the coming daylight and crawled into bed.

Take heart, she counseled herself. Tomorrow's another ... well ... night.

Chapter 9

AINSLEY SLID THE final ruby-red tube of blood into the last available slot in her specimen container and closed the insulated case's lid. Another night, another thirty vamp venipunctures.

"All set, Ms. Crawford?"

She glanced up at the young man who'd been assigned to shadow her this past week. He looked just as fresh as he had four hours ago. She hadn't checked a mirror lately, but she was willing to bet she looked considerably more wilted than he did. Of course, she had a few years on her young bodyguard. With that boyish face, he looked more like a junior executive than the highly-seasoned professional Eli assured her he was. She reached for her sweater. "Ready, Freddy."

For about a millisecond, he looked as though he might smile, but he conquered the impulse. Man, there was just no fun to be had since Eli had flown back to St. Cloud to take care of business and Delano had locked himself in the lab on the floor below the penthouse.

Not that she felt abandoned.

She understood Eli had to get the reconstruction effort going back in St. Cloud, not to mention re-establishing a ready blood supply for the donors who'd become dependant on the clinic there. God only knew what other business Delano had charged him with.

Delano had accompanied her the first night to this new clinic, making sure she was comfortable with the clientele, so she had no complaints there. He'd also hired an amazing array of people to protect her. Fred Carstairs was just the most obvious fixture in the team.

A man, dressed like a derelict and reeking of cheap wine, took up position nightly just outside the door of the ageing, nondescript building that housed the clinic. From atop the tenement house across the street, a marksman kept watch with night vision goggles, or so she was told. She'd never caught sight of him. And when they pulled away from the clinic's shabby address, a pair of headlights always fell into position behind their perfectly ordinary-looking SUV, to guard their rear.

Except there was nothing perfectly ordinary about the vehicle they traveled in. According to Fred, the windows were fashioned from ballistic glass, the body covered with an opaque armor comprised of ballistic nylon and steel. Who knew?

No, she didn't feel abandoned. Not at all.

Okay, maybe a little bit. But she wasn't afraid.

They made the fifteen-minute trip back home — yes, after the chaos of the past weeks, she'd actually started thinking of Delano's high-rise penthouse as home — without incident. As was his habit, Fred accompanied her into the building. And as was also his habit, he insisted on accompanying her all the way up to the 29th floor. She'd tried to persuade him that she could navigate the elevator ride herself, given there were two separate levels of security before she even reached the penthouse door, but apparently he was an old-fashioned kind of guy. He refused to leave her until he'd either handed her off personally to Delano or until he'd assured himself the penthouse was empty and the security unbreached.

Tonight, Delano was still not back, so she had to wait for Fred to do his check.

"All clear, Ms. Crawford."

"Thank you, Fred," she said, meaning it. Every time she was tempted to think these elaborate precautions were overkill, she remembered the mortar attack in St. Cloud. "I know I bust your chops sometimes, but I really do appreciate everything you do for me."

"Just doing my job, ma'am."

His words were delivered in the same flat monotone he always used, but she swore he blushed. She was still smiling when she closed the door behind him and re-armed the alarm. She turned and leaned against the door. Alone at last.

Except she didn't really want to be alone. She'd had too much of that since Eli left.

Okay, strictly speaking, she hadn't been alone more than a few waking hours, but the company of bodyguards who were paid to be there just wasn't the same. Nor did the strangers who presented their arms to her, trading their blood for a liquid supper, fill the void.

She was lonely, dammit.

She sighed and headed for the kitchen, which Eli had stocked magnificently with chocolate. Specifically, a stash of Hershey's milk chocolate bars. Clearly he'd had his people size up the contents of her pantry when they'd sized up her wardrobe. The chocolate might have been a lucky guess, but the Australian Shiraz that appeared in the wine rack and the smoked Gouda in the refrigerator tipped his hand. She could get used to that kind of consideration, if it weren't a little scary vis-à-vis the invasion of privacy. For heaven's sake, the man knew her bra size and her food addictions. At least he hadn't furnished a replacement for her vibrator. That would have been too humiliating.

Of course, if he had furnished it, then at least she'd have it. The dreams she had almost nightly left her frustrated and aching. She slipped one of the chocolate bars out of its sleeve, peeled the foil back and bit into it. Mmmmmm.

Maybe she'd coerce Fred into stopping at one of the sex shops that abounded on what seemed like every street corner. She grinned, imagining Fred's reaction.

It had been hard enough persuading him to stop three nights ago so she could use a payphone. He'd refused initially, citing security concerns and pointing out there were plenty of phones back at the penthouse. He'd only relented when she told him she'd just hire a taxi and go out and find a public phone booth after he dropped her off. Fuming, he'd offered her five minutes. She'd argued for twenty. They split the difference.

The twelve minutes hadn't been nearly long enough, and it had been tricky as hell explaining to Lucy that her time was limited without alarming the other woman. Breezily, she told her friend she'd been lured away from the hospital to take a very cushy private job for a researcher doing top-secret clinical trials. A great job, but she was on the road with her boss right now and her schedule was crazy.

What's that? Was her boss cute? Yes, actually, he was very handsome, but he was also old. Very old.

Then she switched the topic to the one thing guaranteed to divert her friend's attention — Lucy's daughter Devon. Too soon, Fred had walked up to the booth and tapped his wristwatch meaningfully. She'd said a rushed goodbye and hung up, missing Lucy but lighter of heart knowing that both she and Devon were still safe.

No, Fred would definitely not be receptive to stopping at a sex shop, but it might be worth it to ask him, just to see his reaction. Poor guy. He'd probably offer to send someone to make the purchase for her, if she would describe what she wanted. Her smile broadened.

But apart from the distraction that tormenting her straight-laced bodyguard would afford, a stop at the sex toy shop wasn't going to help her. Her smile faded. They weren't that kind of dreams.

Oh, they were hot, all right, and Delano featured in every one of them. As did gleaming, massively elongated cuspids, arched throats, thudding hearts and slick, mating bodies. But the dreams were also incredibly tender and . . . well, sacred, for lack of a better word. As raggedly aroused as the dreams left her, she felt strangely averse to seeking release. Somehow, it seemed tantamount to blasphemy.

Or maybe she was just turning into a masochist, preferring to walk around all day — or rather, all night — carrying that sweet ache low in her belly and in her tender, swollen breasts.

And as for the man who put it there, he'd all but disappeared. She saw him briefly each night before she left for the clinic. He dutifully drew her blood to test for the vampirism virus and/ or antibodies to the virus. Typically, he inquired after her level of comfort with the security he was providing, then quickly excused himself to start his night's work at the lab. Occasionally, he returned shortly before or after she did, giving them a few moments together, but on those occasions he'd looked so exhausted, she hadn't the heart to delay him from seeking his bed.

Shoot, she didn't even know what would happen if he didn't get to bed. Did sleep claim him wherever he happened to be, if he didn't make it to his rooms? Or could he postpone it, like regular people did? And what happened if he did? Would he age? She distinctly remembered him saying that sleep erased the previous day's — or rather, night's — aging. And what did he look like in his sleep?

Chocolate. Now.

She glanced down to see the empty wrapper she clutched in her hand. Ack! She'd eaten the whole thing.

Dammit, that did it. She wasn't going to grow fat eating comfort food to ease her loneliness. Delano was responsible for her being here; he'd admitted as much. So he could damn well take some responsibility for her current social vacuum.

Tossing the candy bar wrapper in the garbage, she headed for the stairs, the ones inside the suite that traveled just one short floor to the 28th level.

Delano had been looking into the amber depths of a forty-year-old whiskey in an even older Waterford glass when he heard the trill that signaled someone was on their way down to the lab. An intruder? Eli was still away.

He put the glass down and picked up the 9mm he always kept handy. Cocking the pistol, he took up position beside the door.

The door opened and Ainsley stepped into the lab. Moving with maximum speed, Delano grabbed her by the wrist and whirled her out of the way. Partially shielded by the door, he trained his pistol into the stairwell.

The empty stairwell.

Thank God. He dropped the nose of the gun until it pointed at the floor.

"God, Delano! Didn't you see it was me?"

"Of course I did." He decocked the Walther, conscious of her horrified gaze following his every movement. "But if I were an intruder, I'd have held you at gunpoint and forced you out the stairwell first, as a distraction and a shield."

She looked at the closed doors shielding the stairwell. "Of course. I'm sorry. I didn't mean to alarm you." Her gaze drifted back to the gun, regarding it as though it were a snake coiled to spring.

"No harm done." Wanting to get rid of the gun but not wanting to just lay it down on the workbench again, he deposited it in the right-hand pocket of his lab coat. Of course, he then had to jam his left hand in the other pocket to counterbalance the weight of the weapon. "I was just about ready to finish here for the night. Let me shut a few things down and I'll ride up with you."

"Oh, but I'd love to have a look around. Can I?"

Dammit. Had he left anything incriminating lying around?

"Please? I won't contaminate anything. I just want a quick tour."

No, he'd secured everything. He'd only been delaying going upstairs in the hope that she'd retire before he returned. He pasted on a smile. "Then a tour you shall have, but I warn you, there's not much to see."

It turned out to be anything but quick. She was full of questions. Some things she recognized — microscopes, centrifuge, incubators, autoclave for sterilizing instruments, biological hoods to provide a sterile environment for working with specimens. But other equipment needed explanation.

"Holy cow, you're as well equipped as any hospital lab. Better, probably."

"Most definitely better, unless they're doing primary research and have need for a DNA sequencer or gene mapping software."

She glanced around the lab. "Where's that?"

He indicated a room to their left with a nod of his head. "But it's nothing special to look at. A big box and a computer."

"So is this a genetically engineered vaccine you're working on? I mean, as opposed to a traditional vaccine like polio or flu?"

The conversation was veering into dangerous territory. He'd have to choose his words carefully, and shield his thoughts even more carefully.

"Exactly. My aim is to engineer such a vaccine. Unfortunately, as I've mentioned, vampires are immune to practically all blood-borne diseases. However, there are recorded cases of vampires dying from the blood of certain victims who gave every evidence of being completely healthy. Such reports date back to the earliest days of vampire history. Thus, the focus of my work has been to search out such individuals whose blood has proven lethal. Armed with their blood, I'm confident I can eventually isolate the anti-vampire gene from the genome."

Her brows came together. "There are people walking around with an anti-vampire agent in their blood?"

"Precisely."

"And have you found such a person?"

He rubbed the back of his neck. "They grow harder and harder to find."

"Wait a minute — can't you create your own vaccine without such a person?"

He shook his head. "I'm afraid not."

"But I thought every vaccine started with the infectious agent itself." The skin between her eyebrows pleated in a frown. "Shouldn't you be working with a weakened version of the vampire virus, if you want to immunize people against infection by that same agent?"

Ah, but she was a smart one. "I've already done that. I took the vampire virion, crippled it and produced a vaccine. I even used the vampire virus as a gene delivery vector. And yes, it works flawlessly. Specifically, it changes the genotype that makes the cells susceptible to infection in the first place."

"So what's the problem?"

"The problem is, even if I render you immune to the vampire virus, it won't stop a vampire from killing you. No matter how invulnerable you may be to infection, no matter how many anti-bodies you express, your blood won't harm a hair on the head of the rogue who drains it from you."

"Doh." She rolled her eyes. "Guess it's late. I didn't think of that."

He laughed. "It was a fair question. Until I tested it, there was every reason to hope it *would* deal serious harm to the attacker, or at least put them off the victim before they'd taken life-threatening amounts of blood. If I hadn't had high hopes, I wouldn't have labored so long to create it."

"You must have been very disappointed."

Disappointed? Try devastated. His hopes had been so high. True, earlier, cruder vaccines had failed, but he'd thought altering the genotype —

Enough. It hadn't worked.

He smiled, consciously smoothing his expression. "Very much so," he agreed. "But the work must continue."

Her eyes rounded. "You have one, don't you?"

Delano blinked. "Have one what?"

"You've found someone with the anti-vampire blood!"

His heart stopped, then leapt into a hard thudding. "What makes you say that?"

She gestured to a workbench where incubators hummed. "You must think you have at least a possibility or you wouldn't be doing all this."

Ah, of course. A logical deduction on her part, not a lapse on his. For a moment there, he feared he'd let the barrier around his thoughts slip. He smiled. "Perhaps," he conceded.

She angled her head and studied him through narrowed eyes. "More than a perhaps, I think."

His smile broadened. "Perhaps."

She smiled back at him, her eyes sparkling with shared mirth. But then, in an instant, everything changed. Their smiles faded and the air between them grew thick.

And his heart suddenly felt as though it housed a hundred birds, all of them frantically beating their wings and clawing.

"Delano."

She said his name on a sweet exhalation of breath, and stepped closer. Desire rolled off her in palpable waves. And God help him, he heard the leap of her heart, the sudden urgency of the blood surging in her veins.

He leaned closer. Sweet Christ, the heat and smell of her! He smelled her arousal, could all but taste the chocolate that lingered in her mouth, the metallic, copperish flavor of her blood ...

Her blood. Her potentially *deadly* blood.

Backpedal. Godammit, Bowen, backpedal for all you're worth. "Ainsley, I don't think —"

Whatever he thought, she clearly didn't want to hear it, because she closed the small remaining distance between them, grabbed the lapels of his lab coat, stretched up and kissed him.

In a reflex he could not have stopped for the world, his arms closed around her, drawing her closer.

Ah! Such warmth, so much softness. He could weep with joy just from the sensation of her arms around him. And she tasted just as he imagined she would, like chocolate and heat and dark, dark temptation. Then she tasted him right back, swirling her tongue over his lower lip and into his mouth. The thunder of his own heartbeat almost drowning out the sound of hers, he pulled her closer still.

And she went rigid, pushing against his chest.

Damn, damn, damn. No ignoring that signal. His hands tightened on her waist at the thought of releasing her so soon, but he forced his grip to slacken, letting her pull back.

"I'm sorry. Forgive me." Did he look as stiff as he sounded? Probably. But casual seemed to be beyond him at the moment. "That shouldn't have happened."

"What? Are you kidding?" Her eyes blazed up at him in disbelief. "That's been coming for weeks. Don't even pretend otherwise. I just want you to get rid of that thing."

He might have corrected her — he'd been thinking about this for exactly twelve days — but his mind was distracted by her last comment. "What thing?"

"The gun." She glanced pointedly at his lab coat pocket. "Could we put it aside, please, just for the next few minutes? I'm sure it's perfectly safe, but I don't like them. I've seen too many gunshot wounds roll through the OR to be comfortable with firearms."

He drew the offending Walther from his pocket and placed it on the workbench. "Better?"

"Much better." She gave him a smile, knowing and sexy and intimate.

His heart kicked it up another notch, and it struck him afresh that he was courting disaster.

Disaster? Hell, he could be courting death itself. He needed to stop this madness before —

She slid back into his arms and he forgot to think because her mouth was on his again, and oh, merciful God, there was no way he was stopping. Not yet. Not before he absolutely had to. With a groan, he cupped her head, angling her face for better access and also to slow her down.

This was all there could be, all he dared allow, this mating of mouths and the agonizing sweetness of bodies brushing together. Oh, precious Jesus, he had to make it last.

He lifted his head, and when she tried to recapture his lips, he restrained her. "Slowly, Ainsley. Slowly."

＊

Better?

Yes, this was definitely better, she thought, as she surfaced from yet another long, drugging kiss. Better than any dream. Better even than her last lover, and he'd been very, very good. Of course, between her shifts at the hospital and Clay's shift at the police station, their relationship was more of a "hi, bye, thanks for the orgasm" kind of thing. Then Delano nibbled the corner of her mouth, and she forgot about Clay Davidson.

Again, he took his time exploring her mouth. Again, she tasted the inexplicable but unmistakable flavor of a fine scotch. She'd never seen him drink any beverage, let alone something alcoholic, but there was no mistaking the taste of scotch whiskey on his tongue. Yet beneath the smoky, slightly mossy taste lay pure Delano. Dizzy with the pleasure of it, she pressed closer.

His hands still cupped her head, and she desperately wanted them on her body. On her breasts. On her ass. And oh, yes, between her thighs. She wanted it with a violence that left her trembling. She wanted him buried deep inside her, with his mouth at her throat, gleaming cuspids elongated and grazing her skin, tantalizing her with the promise of a joining more intimate, more thrilling, than anything she'd ever known.

But dammit, she also wanted this slow torture. She wanted to spin it out as long as they could possibly stand. This first exquisite exploration came only once.

He pulled back again, but this time she didn't protest. This time she trusted him. And she wasn't disappointed.

Winding one hand into her hair, he tugged her head back, exposing her throat.

Okay, straight to the main event. That worked too.

Her pulse leapt, and she closed her eyes. In her mind's eye, she saw herself as he must see her, her throat exposed and vulnerable. Raw excitement shot straight to her core as she waited for him to lower his mouth to her throat, to rake his teeth over her skin . . .

"Ainsley, look at me."

Dazed, she opened her eyes to find him looking at her with an expression that seemed torn between scorching need and tortured regret.

Regret?

He released his grip on her hair, but he didn't pull away as she half expected. Instead, he lifted his hand to her mouth, drawing the pad of his thumb across her lower lip. Swollen and sensitized as her flesh was from his thorough, meticulous attention, the light caress made her shiver.

He closed his eyes, as though to better absorb even that fleeting sensation. When he opened his eyes again, they blazed with a ferocity that should have frightened her.

She opened her mouth on his thumb, and let the salt taste of his skin bloom on her tongue, mingling with the whiskey taste his mouth had imparted.

"Delano —"

"God, I love your mouth." His words were thick. "It was made for this."

Unbearably aroused, she bit the fleshy pad of his thumb.

"Ainsley!"

His body went rigid, but she wasn't sure if it was rigid good or rigid bad. But he hadn't withdrawn his thumb, so she ran her tongue over it. Soothing, soothing.

Then she bit it again.

His control snapped. Suddenly, his hands were everywhere she'd wanted them to be, hard and demanding, his mouth fierce on hers. Oh, yes, please. He pushed her up against the nearest workbench, the better to grind his lower body against her. The urgent thrust of his arousal against her belly inflamed her beyond reason, and his hands left trails of fire on her skin.

Mindless with need, she rubbed her breasts against his chest. God, was that her making those noises? He was making her crazy. She wanted him to tear her clothes off before she burned up. She wanted to hook a leg behind his and take him down to the floor. She wanted to free the impressive erection straining against his trousers, and climb onto it. God help her, she wanted to scream, "Fuck me already!"

Instead, she did the next best thing. She insinuated her left hand between them to cup the bulge of his erection. Oh, Lord, it was nice. She squeezed gently.

He growled against her mouth, and she swallowed the gratifyingly desperate sound. Then, before she could guess his intention, he lifted her and deposited her on the edge of the workbench. She felt something hard poking into her back, but then he moved between her spread thighs and she forgot about the discomfort. All of her attention focused on the hard heat of him pressed against the center of her universe. Could he feel how wet and ready she was?

"Del —"

He covered her mouth, cutting off what surely would have been the plea she'd suppressed a few seconds ago. He thrust his tongue into her mouth, penetrating it in the way she wanted his engorged —

The thought died when she heard the unmistakable sound of a pistol being cocked.

Chapter 10

"Hi, guys. Did you miss me?"

Delano's blood froze. Goddammit. He was the world's biggest idiot. Worse than an idiot. He was a fool.

He released Ainsley, careful to pull her t-shirt down from where he'd thrust it high atop her breasts before moving the shield of his body away.

"Okay, Eli," he drawled. "Point made. That was terribly careless of me."

Eli held the pistol Delano had left on the workbench, letting it dangle harmlessly in his hand. "In more ways than one."

Delano met Eli's steely gray gaze. "I repeat, point made."

"God, Eli, you scared the hell out of me." Ainsley's voice was high and thin. Her lips were red and swollen from their kisses, the delicate skin of her face and neck pink from the abrasion of his stubble-roughened face. She smoothed her hair, her clothing, as though she could smooth her composure back into place with her hands. "Maybe next time you could just call out 'I'm back' or something like that."

"Sorry." With a smooth motion, Eli uncocked the Walther again and laid it back on the workbench. "As our boss so quickly surmised, I was making a point."

Ainsley blushed, though whether from the not-so-subtle reminder that the man she'd been making out with was her boss, or just the fact that she'd been caught making out, was anyone's guess. Then her chin came up.

"This was my fault, Eli. Really. Del wanted to head up to bed. I mean, *his* bed. Oh, you know what I mean." Her flush deepened. "Our respective beds. Alone. But I detained him."

Before she could stammer out any more, Delano interrupted with a question for Eli. "How was St. Cloud?"

"Busy."

"The blood supply?"

"Back up and flowing. Though we're not taking blood. I figured you had that covered here."

Delano nodded his approval. "And the house?"

"Repairs'll be done within the month, complete with refurbished lab." He glanced at Ainsley, then back to Delano. "We really should talk."

Ainsley leapt on Eli's words, evidently grateful for the chance to bolt. "I'm sure you two have lots to discuss. I'll just make my way back upstairs." She turned to Delano. "Thank you for the tour."

He inclined his head. "No trouble."

When the door closed behind her, Eli snorted. "Thanks for the tour?"

Delano scowled. "She was bored. She just came down here looking for a little diversion."

"And you provided it, I see."

"Eli," he said warningly.

"Oh, go to hell with that tone, Delano."

"Excuse me?"

"My job, or a pretty sizeable part of it, is to protect you. But dammit, I can't do that if you're going to put yourself in front of a freakin' freight train every time I look away."

Delano stiffened. "For pity's sake, I was just kissing her. Since when did you, of all people, decide kissing an attractive woman was a crime?"

"*Kissing her?* Delano, I was here. You were about to devour the woman. And this is not some morality judgment thing. You know me better than that. This is about you not dying before we can find a tool to fight these bastards."

Delano scrubbed a hand across his face. "You're right."

"Damn right I am."

Delano looked at his thumb. It still bore the slight but unmistakable indentation of her teeth. Jesus. He wouldn't have taken her blood. Given the stakes, he had enough self-control to stop before that happened, no matter what Eli thought.

And no matter what else happened ...

But she'd bitten him. Twice. If she'd broken the skin ... Though thankfully saliva wasn't the best vehicle for transmission for most viruses. Witness the rarity of HIV transmission from oral contact, or even from biting, for that matter.

Eli just stood there, as though expecting something more. Delano raked his hair back off his face. Dammit. In his own defense, he wanted to point out that Ainsley had been the aggressor. She'd literally grabbed him by the lapels and laid a lip-lock on him. The only problem with using that defense was his natural instinct to shield a lady.

Besides, it would be a cop-out. He could have fended her off easily, had he really wanted to. He just hadn't been able to deny himself the interlude.

"It won't happen again."

Eli snorted. "Come on, man, I've seen the way you look at her. Hell, I've seen the way she looks at you. This isn't gonna go away. You have to tell her. You have to explain why it could be disastrous for the two of you to hook up."

His mouth hardened. "No."

"Delano —"

"Don't you think I've done the equation a hundred times? It still comes out the same. One way or another, her blood killed Edward Webber, even though it was not her choice. It may yet kill more predators before we have a workable vaccine to protect the vulnerable. But if we're going to curb the behavior of those rogues, Ainsley is our only hope. You and I, we're veterans of this war, Eli. We've taken lives."

Eli's hands clenched at his sides. "We've stopped ruthless killers!"

"Granted. But don't you see their faces in your dreams, Eli? Don't you see the humanity in them in those last moments before the spark of life leaves them? In the end, they are but men who lacked the strength to cling to their own humanity in the face of this mutation."

"What I see in my nightmares is that sonofabitch who slaughtered half my team in Afghanistan."

Delano lifted an eyebrow. "So you don't suffer any pangs in those hours when everyone else is asleep?"

"Shit, Delano."

"Would you have Ainsley carry the same weight? Wrestle the same demons in her sleep?"

Eli closed his eyes and sighed. "Have I mentioned how much I hate it when you pull this sensei crap?"

"A time or two."

Eli took a deep breath and expelled it. "Okay, fuck it. Forget about this vaccine thing. We can hunt them down and kill them, one at a time."

Delano rubbed a hand across his forehead. "We could. But as long as there are vulnerable populations, there will always be another predator to take the place of the ones we slay. We have to make that ... lifestyle ... untenable. Which brings us back to Ainsley's blood."

Eli looked away. "I don't like it, Del. She should have the chance to choose for herself."

Del? Ainsley must be rubbing off. "And what if she chooses to withhold her genetic gift?"

Eli swore.

Delano pressed his advantage. "Our security is top notch. You made sure of it personally. Janecek is not going to get to her. All we need to do is make sure she keeps her distance from me, and all will be well."

Eli's eyes narrowed. "Whachu mean we, white man?"

Delano smiled as though his insides weren't being eaten by corrosive acid.

"She's bored, Eli. And she's lonely. She's cut off from everything she used to know. Her whole world was literally turned upside down in the wake of Webber's attack. And now she's stuck here, in a strange city, virtually under lock and key, seeing no one but her bodyguard, her clients at the clinic, and us."

"Us. There's that plural thing again."

"You're heterosexual and unattached."

"Last time I checked."

"And you want to keep Ainsley safe, don't you? You want me to unlock the secrets of her blood —"

"Whoa." Eli threw up a hand in the universal stop signal. "I think you'd better quit right there, before I leap to the completely laughable conclusion that you're asking me to sleep with Nurse Crawford."

"Eli —"

"Jesus, you're serious! You want me to seduce her."

Delano's nails dug into his palms. "I want you to pay attention to her. I want you to entertain her, keep her preoccupied."

"And what exactly are you suggesting I do to entertain her? Huh? 'Cuz somehow I don't think you had a friendly game of Chinese checkers in mind."

"It would seem that she needs male attention." Delano managed to keep his voice calm and controlled, a major accomplishment in the circumstances. "Just give her some attention."

Delano's reasonable tone seemed to anger Eli even more. "I see. So, what did you have in mind? A little flirting? Maybe some petting on the couch? More?"

Delano sighed.

"And how should I open with her? Verbal or non-verbal? I mean, I could just come out and say, 'I think you're hot, let's go, baby.'"

"Eli —"

"You're right. That rarely works. At least not with a woman like Ainsley. It'd have to be way more subtle. Let's see ... maybe I should start by crowding her in the kitchen or when we pass in the hallways. You know, get a little too close. Just enough to make her take notice. Then maybe I could comment on her hair. She does have great hair, don't you think?"

"I really don't —"

"After that, I could graduate to brushing up against her, all accidentally-on-purpose-like. An elbow to a breast in that tiny kitchen, followed by a quick apology. Then, while we're sitting on the couch watching TV, maybe I could let my leg relax against hers."

"I'm not terribly —"

"Oh, here's a thought — a collision! Yeah, I like that. The corner where the hall comes out to the living room would be perfect. I could kind of catch her and steady her, but not before making sure she got a real good feel, if you know what I mean. In my personal experience, next to broad shoulders, a good set of abs pretty much tops every lady's wish list."

"Dammit, Eli, I don't care how you do it! Just for God's sake *do it*."

Eli's face softened. "Look, man, I'm just trying to show you why this plan of yours can't work."

"It *will* work."

"Come on. I haven't laid a finger on her, and already you can't stand it."

Delano shook his head vigorously. "You're quite mistaken. What I feel for Ainsley is responsibility. The danger she finds herself in, her social isolation, her anxiety about a non-existent infection, the removal from her ordinary world … it's all my doing. The kindest thing I could possibly do at this point is put you in her path. I just don't need to hear the details. I feel guilty enough as it is for manipulating her."

"And well you should."

"And well I should," he agreed. "That's my burden to live with. In the meantime, you'll be good for her. Hell, you'll be good for each other." As he said the words, he realized how true they were. Eli and Ainsley. They were perfectly matched. Aside from their shared nursing background, they were both handsome physical specimens, both single and unattached, both quick to laugh. A new emptiness opened up inside, lending his voice more bite. "You must do this for me, Eli."

His friend closed his eyes for an interminable moment, as though consulting some inner voice, or perhaps the voice of some long-dead Comanche ancestor. "Okay." He opened his eyes. "I'll do it."

Delano let the breath he was holding escape. "Thank you."

Eli inclined his head in acknowledgement. "You'll owe me one. Oh, and one more thing."

"Yes?"

"Don't try to sell me any more of this horseshit about how you don't care. Your guts are gonna feel like you chowed down a metric ton of ground glass, and we both know it."

Delano cursed, employing a particularly loathsome word he hadn't used in a good sixty years.

"Exactly," Eli agreed. "Now, sun's almost up. We should both hit the sack. I can bring you up to date on St. Cloud tomorrow."

*

"Rise and shine, cupcake."

Ainsley lifted her head and squinted at the imposing figure looming in her doorway. Eli? In her bedroom? Calling her *Cupcake?* Oh, thank goodness. She was still dreaming. She rolled onto her side, drew her knees up and burrowed deeper into the pillows, striving to get her dream back on track.

"Come on, sleepy head, it's way past noon."

She opened bleary eyes again, tracking Eli as he moved across her bedroom to the window. She'd tossed and turned for hours, finally falling into a light sleep punctuated by highly erotic dreams. Dreams of Delano, his hands all over her body, her hands on him …

How the devil had Eli made his way into her dream?

Then Eli swept the heavy curtains back. The dazzling light of midday flooded the room, sending a dagger of pain to her brain.

Groaning, she pulled the covers over her head. "Go away, Eli. You're wrecking my dream."

"Ouch. You're wrecking my ego."

She snorted beneath the covers. "I think it'll survive."

"No need for sarcasm."

"Okay, I'm sorry. Now, would you please go away?"

The edge of her bed depressed. "Sorry, angel."

Wait a minute, Eli in her room? She jack-knifed up to find Eli actually sitting there, on her actual bed. "Eli? What is it? Is something wrong?"

"Something's very wrong."

He said the words sternly, but the tone didn't match the dancing light in his eyes or the suggestion of an upward tilt to his lips. The latter was enough to make the knot of anxiety dissolve.

"Okay, out with it, buster. What the heck is so very wrong?"

"Delano tells me that in all the time you've been here, he hasn't taken you to see anything of Montreal. A beautiful woman sitting up here in this penthouse while the city waits down there? To my way of thinking, that's just plain wrong. And I aim to fix that, starting right now." He gave her a thump on the thigh. "So shake a leg, honey."

He stood again, and she gaped up at him. "You're going to take me out?"

"I thought we'd start with *le Vieux Montréal*."

Ainsley grinned. Touring Old Montreal in broad daylight like an ordinary visitor to the city? "Oh, *can* we?"

He feigned offence. "Did I not just invite you?"

"I mean, is it safe?"

"It is when I'm in charge."

She rolled her eyes. "What'd I tell you? The ego remains undented."

His lips quirked. "Seriously, it's not high risk. I wouldn't be suggesting it if it were. But just the same, we'll have a discreet security team maintaining a cushion around us at all times."

His gaze flickered just long enough to make her aware she was sitting in bed in her nightshirt with the bedclothes pooled on her lap.

Oh, Christmas. The clinch with Delano last night. That's probably what he saw every time he looked at her. She felt a blush rise in her neck.

"Can you be ready in half an hour?"

"Give me fifteen minutes."

Chapter 11

Two and a half hours later, Eli helped her clamber out of the *calèche* he'd hailed at Rue de la Commune, in front of the old port.

"How'd you enjoy that?"

Ainsley grinned. "You have to ask?"

He shrugged. "It's a guy thing."

She laughed. "It was great. But I'd like to come back one day to explore the Notre-Dame Basilica. Oh, and the Pointe-à-Callière."

He squinted at her. "Interesting."

"What?"

"The Basilica, sure. I mean, it's a bloody Neo-Gothic wonder. Everyone is awed by it. But I wouldn't have pegged you for the museum of archaeology and history."

She shrugged. "I like history."

And she did. Except as they toured Old Montreal, from the Bonsecours Market to the Place d'Armes, she'd found herself wondering if Delano had walked these cobbled streets in another time. Another century. She shivered.

Eli checked his watch. "We'd better head back. Both of us could stand a nap before the boss rises."

At the mention of Delano, Ainsley's face sobered. "About last night —"

He threw up a hand. "Whoa, whoa, whoa. Stop right there."

"Stop?"

"Gawd, yes." He lowered his hand. "Number one, there are several three-word phrases in the English language that are guaranteed to tighten a man's sphincter, and that, my darlin', is one of 'em. Don't wanna hear it. And secondly, it's none of my business."

"But —"

"No buts."

"But —"

"You had fun today, right?"

Ainsley blinked. "Well, yes, bu —"

"Then let's leave it lie just like that, why don't we?"

She shook her head. "You make things awfully easy for me, Eli."

"That was sort of the point." He raised an arm, flagging down a passing taxi, which stopped amid the squealing of sorely abused brakes. He opened the back door of the cab. *"Après vous, Madame."*

She grinned at his French, delivered as it was with that unique accent of his. *"Merci, monsieur."*

When she moved toward the car, he didn't move back as far as she expected. Consequently, she had to squeeze past him to get into the back seat. No doubt it was a security precaution, his standing so close, but she found herself taking notice of his sheer size and power. And not for the first time today.

Criminey, but he was nice looking. Nice smelling, too. Not to mention funny and considerate and easy to be around. And his body — oh, baby, *seriously ripped*. Under different circumstances, she'd be giving him some not-so-subtle signals, just to see if there was any answering spark there. He'd be playful in the bedroom. She'd lay money on it. And a good thing, too. That levity would mitigate all that overpowering, hulking brawn …

She blinked. Oh, God. She was having decidedly sexual thoughts about Eli. Eli! Her co-worker. A fellow nurse. What was wrong with her? She'd all but torn Delano's clothes off last night, and now she was —

"Scoot over, Angel. I have no desire to get clipped by traffic trying to get in that other door."

Face burning, she slid across the bench seat to hug the far door. Eli climbed in and instructed the driver.

He turned to her. "You look tired."

Normally, she would not welcome that kind of observation from an attractive man, but it was too good an opportunity to let slide.

"I am." She aimed an apologetic smile at him. "Mind if I snooze on the way home?"

"Go right ahead. Actually, eyes closed might not be a bad idea any time, given traffic in this city."

She gave the expected chuckle, then settled back against the seat cushions to feign rest.

Eyes closed. Yessiree. That worked just fine.

Just fine for contemplating exactly when she'd turned into the Whore of Babylon.

Delano leaned back in his chair as he listened to Eli's progress report. He heard every word his friend said, and responded appropriately, but another part of his brain was busy cataloguing scents.

Sandalwood, vanilla, leather, horse. All of these things he smelled, on top of Eli's scent signature.

Ainsley.

Eli.

Ainsley and Eli, enjoying a romantic tour of Old Montreal from the intimate confines of a horse-drawn carriage.

Good. Excellent.

He dug his nails into his palm.

"So it looks like the repairs will be effected within the month, but it may take an extra few weeks to get some of the more esoteric lab equipment. We've purchased so much of this stuff to equip all the fallback labs. I just didn't want to raise any unnecessary red flags by putting a hair-on-fire kind of rush on this."

Delano nodded his approval. "Good thinking. We've got all the capacity we need, even if we have to fall back to Calgary or Vancouver."

Eli inclined his head in acknowledgement.

"What about Janecek?"

"We've got ears to the ground everywhere, but no sign of him since the attack in St. Cloud. I've heard a rumor that he's back in

Prague, but I wouldn't trust that piece of intelligence. It reeks of disinformation."

"He won't have left the continent."

"Probably not even the country," Eli agreed. "I'll keep the pressure up until we find him. It's hard to hide for long from other vamps."

"Indeed. Okay, what about the other matter I asked you to look into?"

"The money's going to an offshore account in the Cayman Islands."

"And?"

"And those suckers are secret."

Delano raised an eyebrow. "And?"

Eli sighed. "And as usual, money talks, at least when you have as much of it to throw around as you do."

"So what did you learn?"

"The account belongs to a Lucida Machias, which is almost certainly not her real name."

"Spoken like a man who has a theory."

Eli took a photograph from the file in front of him and slid it across the table. "I think it's probably this woman. Lucy Michaels."

Delano looked down at a photo of two women, standing arm in arm and smiling at the camera. One of whom was a much younger Ainsley, probably no more than nineteen or twenty. The other woman was shorter, finer boned than Ainsley, with curly dark hair to Ainsley's straight fall of blond hair. He glanced over his shoulder, belatedly realizing he'd succumbed to an instinct to make sure Ainsley wasn't within earshot. Stupid. She was upstairs in the penthouse, sleeping, a fact he'd taken trouble to ascertain before he and Eli had come down here to the lab to talk.

"Where'd you get this?"

"Ainsley's apartment. But don't worry. It's a copy. The original is intact."

"And who is this Lucy Michaels?"

Eli passed another document across the table, this one a copy of a microfiched newspaper engagement announcement. "She used to be Lucy Heatherington. In fact, that was her name when she posed for that snapshot with Ainsley. She left for college, but wound up having a baby out of wedlock in August eight years ago. No father named on the birth certificate. Came back to St. Cloud and worked for a book-binding company. She quickly met and married the guy in this picture, Weldon Michaels, who adopted her daughter, Devon. Michaels was the deputy chief with the local police department in St. Cloud at the time, and he's now the Big Cheese there."

"Chief of Police."

"Yep."

Delano lifted an eyebrow. "And how does this lead to a secret bank account in the Caymans?"

"Fourteen months ago, Lucy and Devon Michaels did a disappearing act."

Interesting. "A missing persons kind of disappearing act?"

Eli shook his head. "There's not even a murmur of anything like that. But they up and left. I got that directly from the woman who cleans house for them. She also thought Mr. Michaels might have a bit of a problem with his temper, judging by the bruises Mrs. Michaels tried to conceal."

"An abuser."

"No doubt about it. I had a little look-see into Lucy Michael's medical records, thanks again to the power of the almighty dollar. She's suffered enough fractures and contusions to raise her doctor's suspicion, but when he confronted her, she wouldn't cop to it. Too scared, is my bet. I mean, who's she gonna turn to for help? Not the local PD, it would seem."

Delano gritted his teeth. Cowardly bastard, terrorizing a woman and child. Then another thought occurred to him.

"What about her family? If she just up and disappeared, and her husband is known to have a temper, why aren't they clamoring about her disappearance? Is she in touch with them? She must be. I mean, if he's a mean S.O.B., who's to say he didn't beat them to death and bury them in the basement?"

"No family." Eli tossed another document across the table. "She went into state care at the age of eight, when her mother, a single-parent, was shot dead at work."

"Domestic situation?"

Eli shook his head. "Good guess, but no. It was a co-worker who'd recently been fired. He went postal, killing his boss and Lucy's mother, and injuring three others."

"And she went immediately into foster care?"

"Yep. And for two of those years — approximately age 11 through 13 — she stayed with a foster family by the name of Dickinson. Albert and Gail Dickinson."

Delano frowned. Albert Dickinson? "In St. Cloud? On the north side?"

"Yep."

"The same foster home where Ainsley lived for the better part of two years."

"Bingo."

Delano raked his hair back. All too easily, he imagined the two girls bonding, clinging together ... "I guess that sheds some light on why Ainsley has sacrificed every disposable dime she's earned for the last year and a half."

"I guess so."

"Do we know where they are, this Lucy Michaels and her child?"

"Do we really need to know that?"

Damn Eli for his questions. Of course, that's what made him so valuable. Delano met the other man's probing gaze with a level stare of his own. "Yes."

Eli leaned back in his chair. "Why? So you can use the information to keep Ainsley in the fold, once she figures out she can't possibly be infected? Or that you're exploiting her for her genetic material?"

Delano felt the bite of his own nails in his palms, and forced his fists to unclench. "You seem inordinately concerned about Miss Crawford."

"Of course I'm concerned about her. But dammit, Delano, I'm just as concerned about you. I'm as passionate as you are about stopping these murderous bastards, but there's a line beyond which you go at your peril."

Delano felt the anger rise in his chest, felt the blood lust rise with it, too. He clamped down on it. *Hard.*

Eli had been there, to that line he talked about, and maybe some distance beyond. And he'd somehow made his way back. He knew whereof he spoke. That knowledge tempered his words.

"I appreciate your concern, my friend, but you can rest easy. I was actually thinking more in terms of being able to offer Ainsley an assurance that her loved ones would be safe. Because it occurs to me that if Mrs. Michaels found it necessary to go to these lengths to get free of her abuser, it's not likely he's going to shrug it off and move on with his life."

Eli rubbed his left temple. "Okay, you got me there. And no, we don't yet know where she is, but it's only a matter of time before our people find her."

"So you do have someone on it?"

"Several someones."

At Delano's uplifted eyebrow, Eli rolled his eyes.

"Let's say I anticipated your answer."

"And Chief Michaels? Is he also looking for her?"

"Oh, he's beating the bushes for her, all right. And he's got a few things going for him. Not only does he have the resources of law enforcement at his fingertips, but he comes from money, too. Lots of capital there to finance an ongoing search."

"But?"

"But his pockets aren't quite deep enough. He can keep a succession of PIs on payroll, and if he's careful, he can abuse the police resources under his control. Together, that's a pretty potent combination. But frankly, he doesn't have enough money to crack open the doors we opened. If he finds her, it will be through a serious misstep on her part, and so far, she doesn't seem inclined to careless mistakes."

"Good work."

Eli inclined his head in acknowledgement. "Would you like a report on my afternoon with Ainsley?"

Before Delano could reply emphatically in the negative, the piercing bleat of alarm rent the air.

Both men surged to their feet.

"Fire alarm," Eli opined. He whipped out his radio and conferred quickly with security staff downstairs. Seconds later, he holstered the radio. "It's the real thing. We got a small blaze on the second floor, and fire trucks on the way."

Dammit. "We'll have to evacuate."

Eli cursed. "This reeks of Janecek."

"Don't I know it. But we don't have a lot of choice. So which is it? Up or down?"

"Down." Eli's voice rang with certainty. "Even though we've got men up there, the roof would be the best spot to spring a trap. I say we take our chances on the street. Emergency Response'll be here in minutes. Probably the press, too. Harder to ambush us in that kind of public glare."

Delano nodded. That would have been his call, too, but it was good to have it confirmed by his chief tactician. "I'll round up Ainsley and keep her by my side. You marshal all hands. Except for the team on the roof, I want everyone on my Montreal payroll down on that street."

They hit the stairwell at the same time, Eli barking orders into his radio as he lunged upward, two steps at a time.

In the penthouse, Eli called a "Meet you in the lobby!", then took the second stairwell, the one that led all the way down to the ground floor.

Delano set off for Ainsley's suite. He nearly ran into her, quite literally, at the door to her bedroom, avoiding a collision only by catching her by the upper arms.

Clad in a long t-shirt, her hair mussed, she wore the dazed look of someone wrenched from a deep sleep. "What is it? Are we under attack?"

"There's a fire on the second floor. We've got to get out of here until the fire department can contain it." He pushed her back into the bedroom. Spying a bathrobe draped over a chair, he grabbed it and handed it to her. "Put this on. That's a lot of steps down to ground level."

"Of course. Can't use the elevator." She accepted the robe and shrugged into it. "Just give me one more second."

"We don't have time to fuss, Ainsley. Come on." He tugged her by the hand but she resisted.

"Wait! I need something for my feet."

He released her. To her credit, she located her runners quickly and shoved her feet into them. "Ready."

"Good job."

The reached the stairwell seconds later.

"Stay behind me," he ordered. "But not too far behind. I want you no more than a step or two away. Okay?"

She sucked in a breath. "We're under attack, aren't we?"

"I don't know. But the blaze on the second floor is real. We have to get out of here. Just stay close. I'll keep you safe."

At the nineteenth floor, Delano growled.

"What?"

"This is taking too long."

"I'm sorry," she panted. "I can't go any faster without risking a fall. I'm so dizzy from going around and around."

"Climb onto my back." Already a step below her, he crouched slightly to allow her to clamber onto him.

When she hesitated, he growled his impatience. "What, suddenly that's too intimate? May I remind you of what transpired in my lab?"

"Delano!"

"On my back. Or it's over the shoulder in a fireman's lift. You have five seconds to make up your mind."

At Four-Mississippi, he turned to grab her.

"Okay, okay! Turn around. I'll go piggy-back."

He accepted her weight with a grunt, purely out of spite. In truth, she didn't weigh enough to slow him down. "Hang on," he cautioned, "but try not to choke me."

She did, in fact, nearly choke the breath out of him with her death grip around his neck. Of course, that might have had something to do with the speed with which he spiraled down the succession of flights. Even now, all these years later, he vaguely remembered how disorienting it felt to travel so fast, back before his faculties had acclimatized.

They hit the ground floor in under a minute. Delano knelt and let Ainsley slide off his back. She reeled left, straight into the wall — a reaction that had more to do with the speed of their descent than the bit of smoke they'd encountered around the third and second floors — and he grabbed her arm. Pushing the door open with the panic bar, he pulled her out into the lobby.

"Del." Her fingers clutched at him and she leaned back against the mahogany paneled wall for support. "I'm so dizzy. I think I'm going to be sick."

"It'll pass in a minute, if you can hang in there. Just don't close your eyes."

Even as he offered the advice to Ainsley, his gaze swept the lobby. Eli was conferring with their security staff. Good. Judging by the way his orders came out in staccato puffs, he couldn't have been too far ahead of them descending the stairs. Eli glanced up and saw them. He signaled to two officers and brought them over to where Delano and Ainsley stood, just outside the stairwell.

"Delano, Ainsley, this is Bruce Shalvis and Bob Hayes," Eli said. "Do me a favor and keep 'em with you at all times. The fire department's just arriving, but don't go outside until I deploy the rest of the troops, okay?"

"You're the boss when it comes to this stuff."

"Oh, and take one of these radios." Eli handed Delano what looked like a walkie-talkie. "Channel's open. You'll hear me on it periodically. If you want to be heard, depress the button and talk."

Delano regarded the radio. "That's it?"

"That's it."

A man in his element, Eli turned away, barking orders at the remaining security guards. In pairs, they peeled away and headed outside to take up whatever position they'd been assigned. When only one guard remained, a particularly tough-looking customer, he gave the okay for Delano and Ainsley to move out.

Delano squeezed Ainsley's hand. "You okay to put one foot in front of the other?"

She pushed away from the wall, as though testing whether her vertigo had disappeared. "I'm good."

Despite her assurance, she stumbled a few times on the way across the lobby, but once outside, she seemed to regain her equilibrium. Immediately, someone from the fire department seized Delano's arm. In French, Delano identified himself as the building's owner. The fireman proceeded to give him instructions and accompanied by lots of hand gestures.

Delano clapped the other man on the back. *"Oui, oui. Merci."*

"What'd he say?"

He took Ainsley's arm and directed her across the street. The two security guards fell in behind, at a discreet distance. "He said we should be so kind as to get out of their way and stay back behind the perimeter they've set up until the fire is under control." He gestured to the east. "Down there, where everyone is gathering. That's where he told us to go."

"Didn't he also say something about a hotel?"

"You understand French?"

"Not much, but even I can puzzle out l'hôtel."

He urged her into motion again. "You heard right. He suggested we find a hotel for the night, since it will take them a while to clear the scene. Until they do that, they won't let anyone back in."

"And you agreed?"

"I told him I was the owner of the building and I preferred to hang around to see how long it's going to take."

"Don't we need to get back in there? I mean, before sunup?"

Irritation raked across nerve endings left raw by this unexpected development. Did she think he was completely helpless outside of his bedroom? Or lair, as she no doubt thought of it. "I can make do very nicely in a hotel room, as long as the black-out drapes are drawn and no one intrudes during the daylight hours to yank them open."

"But surely this place is easier to defend in the event —"

"Un moment, Monsieur Bowen!"

Delano glanced around to find a fireman approaching at a brisk pace. Maybe he had a situation report already. He signaled for the guards to fall back a few feet. The firefighter pulled abreast of them.

"You have a report for me?"

"More of a catch-up." The fireman removed his helmet and tucked it under an arm. "How've you been, Dad?"

Chapter 12

DELANO MADE A hissing sound, exactly like the noise Ainsley's attacker had made in that alley back in St. Cloud when Delano had saved her life. She recoiled, intuitively recognizing this to be a vampire-on-vampire confrontation, but Delano's grip on her hand held her fast.

"You're no relation of mine, Janecek."

Janecek!

Ainsley's already racing heart took another bounding leap. She cast a glance over her shoulder to see their bodyguards moving in. Thank God! They'd heard.

"I'd call them off if I were you, Bowen. Unless you'd like the world to see an extremely bloody shootout play out on network television."

The bodyguards froze. Ainsley whipped her head around to see that Delano had thrown his palm up in an unmistakable stop sign for Shalvis and Hayes. Then she saw the gun in Janecek's hand. Ainsley knew nothing about guns, other than what bullets did to flesh and bone, but this looked nothing like the compact pistol Delano had brandished in his lab. It looked quite capable of discharging enough automatic rounds to kill everyone. A glance back toward the high-rise confirmed that the local media had, indeed, arrived.

"Come on, Delano, I just want to have a civilized conversation."

For seconds, there was only silence. Ainsley imagined she could hear Delano's heart thudding. Or maybe it was her own.

"Hold your fire," he said at last. "For now."

"Much appreciated." Janecek bared gleaming white teeth in a smile, but he didn't lower his weapon. "Like my new duds? I gotta say, it's a little hot under this gear."

"Nice. Did you kill the fireman you stole it from?"

"Nah. I just left him unconscious. He'll be fine." His shrug was barely perceptible beneath the bulky fire-fighter's jacket. "Call it a late Father's Day gift."

Delano's hand tightened on Ainsley's so hard, it was all she could do to keep from crying out. Then it slackened again.

"I am not your father."

"Well, how do you like that?"

Janecek fixed his gaze on Ainsley, facing her fully for the first time, and she caught her breath.

Dear God, he was stunning. Wavy blond hair that touched his collar, flawless skin, strong white teeth, dark eyebrows and green, eerily feline eyes.

"But I guess you'd understand that whole foster parent thing, wouldn't you, little one? So anxious to disown us."

Ainsley's heartbeat faltered as she belatedly began to absorb the meaning of his words. Delano had fostered Janecek? His enemy?

"Del?" She glanced up at him, but his gaze was still fixed on Janecek.

"What? You didn't tell her about our relationship? I'm wounded."

"Why would I volunteer that information?" Delano spat the words out. "To think I kept your worthless hide alive, allowed you to reach maturity, and you repay me by preying on the vulnerable. It's my deepest shame. One I hope to atone for some day, God willing."

Janecek snorted. "Did you hear that, Ainsley?"

The creature knew her name! And, oh, sweet Jesus, he'd known she'd been in foster care. What else did he know? She looked into his glittering green eyes and saw the truth there. A lot. More, perhaps, than she knew herself. She sagged against Delano, clutching his arm.

The creature transferred its attention back to Delano. "And you. I should think by now you'd realize your God has forsaken you."

"Just because you willingly surrendered your own soul doesn't mean the rest of us have."

"Face it, Delano. After all these years, he's forgotten you. He's never going to come to collect your shriveled-up soul. You're stuck here, locked inside your own personal, self-loathing prison of flesh."

Delano's bicep bulged beneath her hands.

"Shut up."

Janecek grinned. "Aw, come on, Dad, call me Radak. Just once, for old time's sake."

"I should have left you in that monastery to starve to death after you killed the last of the monks."

"Now that cuts."

"Look, if you've got something to say, say it, before a real fireman comes jogging over to see why you've strayed so far from the scene."

"Straight to the point, as ever." When Delano held his silence, Janecek sighed. "I come to offer a truce. Give me what I want, and I'll leave you alone in your lab to tinker with your toys."

"A truce?" Delano snorted. "And what would your price be for that?"

Janecek's odd eyes fixed on Ainsley. "The woman."

Beside her, Delano went rigid.

Dear God! They were talking about her. But why would Janecek want her badly enough to engineer this dialogue, unless he thought it would hurt Delano?

"Forget it." Delano ground the words out.

"Think about it," Janecek urged. "I'm sure you've got plenty of her precious blood squirreled away by now for your experiments. You don't need her anymore."

Ainsley put a hand to her head, battling a new surge of vertigo. Blood for his experiments? *Her* blood? Is that why he'd been drawing it daily?

"You're a killer. I wouldn't turn a rabid dog over to you, let alone a human being. And even if I had no such scruples, I'd be a fool to accept your word that you'd keep the peace. I made that mistake once, which is the only reason you live and breathe today."

"Del, what's he talking about?"

Janecek laughed. "Don't tell me she doesn't know!"

Delano growled.

"Oh, this is priceless! He really didn't tell you?" He threw back his head and laughed again.

"Del?"

"Later, Ainsley," he said, keeping his gaze locked on Janecek. "You've had your answer. I'll give you nothing, save perhaps a hypodermic dart full of that vaccine I've got cooking."

Janecek's face went hard. "You're a fool, Delano. A fool on a misguided mission. You'd be so much happier if you'd just embrace your nature. Do you never grow weary of fighting it?"

"I never lose sight of who the enemy is. It's you and predators like you."

Janecek's mouth curved in a smile that was almost gentle. Pitying. "Is it? Is it really?"

Then he seemed to melt away. Ainsley blinked. Of course. He could move as fast as Delano. As fast as her attacker had back in that alley.

"Boss?"

Shalvis and Hayes were poised to pursue Janecek, on Delano's word.

He shook his head. "Forget it. You'd never catch up."

Gone. Thank God. Ainsley shuddered. Except now there were all these questions. Ugly questions, the answers to which she knew were going to change her. Possibly even destroy her. "Delano?"

"I'll answer all your questions. Just not now." Without glancing down at her, he lifted the radio to his mouth. "Did you get any of that, Eli?" He released the button he must have been pressing for the whole exchange.

"All of it," came Eli's voice. "And let me say, quick thinking. That heads-up allowed us to run interference with the media to keep them off you."

"Thanks."

"Now get your butts over here. Our guys have spotted some of Janecek's soldiers. We need to circle the wagons."

Delano pocketed the radio. "Come on. You heard him."

Ainsley fell into step, and this time she had no trouble keeping up, a combination of anger and fear fuelling her limbs.

Her *blood*. He was using her blood for something.

Was it because she'd been bitten but not yet turned? Did he need the blood of a victim in transition?

Transition.

God, she'd almost forgotten about the possibility of infection. Okay, maybe not forgotten. It was hard to forget when she had to roll up her sleeve twice a day, but the regular negative results had lulled her into a sense of security.

And why had Janecek tried to bargain for her? For her blood? Could he want it, too? But why? Or had he made the offer just to taunt Delano? The latter, she suspected. He had to have known Delano wouldn't deal a human life for any kind of favor. If Delano had in fact fostered Janecek, he had to understand that much about him.

She longed to grab Del's arm, make him stop, make him answer her questions now, but if Eli said they were still in danger, they couldn't afford that kind of distraction.

As they neared the knot of people, the outer ring opened to admit them — Delano, followed by Ainsley, then the two security officers.

Eli stepped forward and clapped Delano on the back. "Good thinking, transmitting that exchange."

"Squeezing that transmission button had a dual purpose, I assure you," Delano said grimly. "It kept me from going for the bastard's throat."

Eli turned to Ainsley. "You okay?"

His gaze slid over her face without ever really meeting her eyes, and the other shoe dropped.

He knew. Eli knew what Delano's real interest was in her. Oddly, she felt closer to tears than she had when she'd challenged

Delano. She'd always known Delano was keeping something from her, but somehow she'd trusted Eli to be straight with her.

She glared at him. "Do I look okay, Eli?"

He mumbled something about it being a rough night all the way around, then turned back to Delano.

"How the hell did he get in? He must have gotten past the guards in the lobby to get to the second floor to start that blaze."

"He could have hired someone to start it," Delano said.

"But he had to have been inside the building to have surprised that fireman and strip him of his turn-out gear."

"Speaking of which, do we know if he's okay? The fireman he suckered?"

"He's fine. The guys we sent over there to distract the media just reported that he was hauled out. They'll evacuate him in an ambulance any minute."

As if on cue, a siren started up and an ambulance nudged its way onto the street, before accelerating and quickly disappearing.

"But how'd he get past the guards?"

The sound of the ambulance's siren had started to fade. Delano stood looking after it. "Glamour."

"Glamour?"

"Yeah. A cheap parlor trick. All vampires use it, to some extent, to look more normal, to fit in, to fade into the background a bit. It works great for most people, who see what they expect to see. But for Janecek to have slipped past guards who are watching for him …" Delano shook his head. "He must have cultivated a talent far beyond anything he possessed when I knew him."

Eli swore. "Does this mean he can slip past our check points whenever he likes?"

Delano shook his head emphatically. "Highly doubtful. You need a certain degree of willingness on the part of the person fooled before the trick can work, and after this incident, everyone will be on high alert. Having said that, I don't think we should take any chances. From now on, I want a vampire at every post for the night shifts."

Eli coughed.

"Do you have a problem with that?"

"I hope you're not suggesting we replace our agents altogether?"

"Of course not. They'd be in addition to the current complement."

"I presume they'd be civilians, for lack of a better word. No tactical training?"

"They won't need tactical training to see through a vampire glamour. No matter how slick young Radak has gotten, he'll never slip by another vampire."

Ainsley put up her hand. "Ah, excuse me?"

Both men turned to frown at her, which she chose to interpret as leave to interject. "Umm, if Janecek couldn't fool a vampire, how come he got right up to us tonight without you sensing him, Delano? Unless, of course, your own power is waning while Janecek's is growing?"

There was a collective hiss of indrawn breath from the men who circled them.

Delano's face in the harsh streetlight looked carved from stone. "I know you're angry, Ainsley, so that was a free shot. But I assure you, my powers are as potent as the day I was made." He turned back to Eli. "Perhaps it was the clothing?"

Eli nodded vigorously. "Of course. There'd be Kevlar in the turn-out suit, and it looked like he had a hot shield around his neck, not to mention a helmet. Maybe all that shielding was sufficient to muffle his vamp vibe."

"Sounds reasonable."

"Okay, we'll add excessive shielding to the list of flags. From now on, anybody wearing more than a summer-weight business suit gets an extra-hard look. Firemen, riot police, hell, the fuckin' Marlboro Man if he's wearing an oilskin duster. I'll spread the word."

They went on to discuss where Janecek's operatives had been spotted, the situation on the roof, and so on, but Ainsley listened with only half an ear. Her brain was too busy going over the confrontation with Janecek, dredging up every word that had been said.

Delano was using her. There could be no other conclusion. And everyone seemed to know about it — Janecek, Eli, and who else? The security staff? Her personal bodyguard? Everyone but stupid, unsuspecting Ainsley?

Well, she was going to get to the bottom of it tonight. Come hell or high water, she'd have her answers before the sunrise chased Delano to his bed.

*

Delano found his gaze straying more and more frequently to Ainsley as he listened to Eli. They'd been cleared to go back into the building, but Eli had insisted a tactical team go in first to search and secure every floor, just in case Janecek wasn't the only vampire who'd gotten past their checkpoints. Delano had hoped the long wait might give Ainsley an opportunity to cool down, but she hadn't shown much sign of it.

He stole another glance at her. Nope, no cooling off happening there. If anything, she looked to have whipped herself up, imagining God knows what nefarious plots.

Too bad the truth was going to be so much worse than anything she might have conjured.

Eli's radio squawked and he answered it.

"Looks like we're cleared to go back in," he said.

Ainsley smiled, a cool, frightening thing any vampress would have been proud of. "Splendid."

Delano sighed. The hour of reckoning was upon him.

Chapter 13

BACK AT THE penthouse, Eli insisted they stick with him while he did his own thorough check, notwithstanding that the whole building had already been searched and cleared. Delano should have been grateful for the reprieve, but now he just wanted it over.

"It's clear."

"Thanks, Eli. Now if you'll excuse us?"

He grimaced. "Not quite yet, I'm afraid. I need to clear the lab, as well, since it has direct access to the penthouse."

This time Delano and Ainsley stayed put while Eli descended the stairs alone to search the 28th floor. As soon as his footsteps faded, Ainsley broke away.

"I need to make some tea."

"Fine. I'll join you in the kitchen when Eli's through."

She marched toward the kitchen with her head held high, giving no sign that she heard him. He sighed. This waiting hadn't done her nerves any more favors than it had done his, it would seem.

Eli emerged from the stairwell, immediately plugging a code into the alarm panel on the wall to prevent it from sounding. "Clean as a new penny," he declared. "And now, while there's a few hours of darkness left, I'd better go out, see if I can't recruit some vampire eyes to help staff security checkpoints tomorrow night."

"Good plan. And while you're at it, you'd better outfit them with uniforms so they can blend in better with the other guards. They'll have to drop their own glamours for optimal performance, but that will make them stand out like neon in the dark. The uniform will help camouflage them."

"You got it, boss."

At last, Eli left. Delano headed for the kitchen, where he found Ainsley seated at the small cherry wood pedestal table. His heart squeezed as he took in the line of her back as she sat bent over her cup. She'd pulled all that blond hair to one side, exposing her nape. Was there anything in the world more beautiful? More achingly vulnerable?

She sat up sharply. "Finally."

There was nothing vulnerable or soft about her tone.

"Is that tea hot?"

She blinked. "You drink tea?"

He brushed past her and helped himself to a china mug. "Once in a while I like to remind myself what a steaming beverage feels like sliding down my throat, what the tannins feel like in my mouth."

Her face softened momentarily, then the line of her jaw hardened again. "Don't try to play me. Just sit down and start talking."

"I think what I promised was that I'd answer all your questions." He filled his mug, sat down and inhaled the steam from the pale brew. Peppermint leaves, ginger root, chamomile flowers and something more. Definitely an herbal concoction designed to calm the nerves. Too bad there'd be no uptake of those soothing ingredients as the fragrant liquid made its way through his system. He glanced up at her. "I promise to answer them truthfully."

Her eyes narrowed. "Does this mean if I don't ask the right questions, you'll withhold information?"

"I'm confident you'll have a comprehensive picture of the situation when we're done."

She sat up straighter in her chair. "Okay, we'll do it your way. Why do you want my blood? He said you were using it for experiments."

"I believe your blood holds the key for the vaccine I've been trying to develop."

"Why? Because I was bitten? Because I'm in transition? Or maybe because I'm not? Did I resist infection, and that's why you want my blood?"

"No. It has nothing to do with the fact that you were bitten."

"The daily blood samples? Are you still testing them for antibodies?"

"No."

"No? Why not? Has the risk passed?" The furrow in her brow deepened. "And if you're not testing my blood for the virus, then why bother draw —"

He held up a hand to stop her. "Listen to me, Ainsley. There never was any risk of infection."

Her face paled. "What did you say?"

"There was never any risk of infection. None whatever."

Her mouth opened and closed, opened again, but nothing came out.

He dropped his gaze to his mug once again.

"Yes, I lied to you. There it is. I led you to believe you might have been exposed to the virus, when in fact, it was out of the question." His grip on the mug tightened until he realized he was in danger of crushing it. Carefully, he unclenched his hand.

"You lied?"

He heard the scrape of her chair as she pushed it back from the table, but still he didn't lift his gaze from the steaming amber liquid in the mug before him.

"Yes, I lied. You see, it's impossible to contract the virus if a vampire merely feeds from you. The pressure of your arterial blood far outstrips the pressure in his venous system. In order for Edward Webber to have infected you, he would have had to abandon your carotid artery and staunch the bleed with a self-secreted coagulant. He would then have bitten your jugular vein, exerting enough positive pressure to infuse a very small amount of his vampiric blood into yours, after which he would have closed that second wound. You'd have been left with no visible evidence of the attack, but the transition would have started within four to six hours, culminating within twenty-four to thirty hours."

"It's all been a lie?"

At her shaky tone, he looked up, meeting her wide, shocked eyes.

"Yes."

"Why?"

The simple question raked at his conscience with vicious talons. He shrugged. "Because I needed your blood."

"You needed my blood?"

He made no reply.

"Well, it looks like I made it easy for you, didn't I, getting attacked like that right outside your —"

She leapt up. Delano shot a hand out to catch her chair, saving it from crashing to the tiled floor.

"Omigod! You *engineered* that, didn't you? So I would fall into your hands, giving you a plausible reason to draw my blood twice a day for all these weeks."

"Yes."

Her chest was heaving now, as though she'd run up every one of the twenty-nine flights to this penthouse instead of having ridden the elevator.

"I can't believe this. You put me in the path of that monster? You had no right!"

"You're quite right. And I'm sorry for your pain and worry, but I had no option." Much as he wanted to let his gaze slide away, he held her furious glare. "Don't you see? I had to take a broader view."

"A broader view? Delano, this is my life. My health, my livelihood —" She broke off, but her eyes no longer seemed to see him. "The hospital ... Did you have anything to do with that? Did you engineer my dismissal? Answer me, dammit!"

"No!"

But she wasn't listening.

"Omigod, of course you did!"

Her gaze had come back into focus once more, and he felt the full weight of it. "Dammit, Ainsley, I had nothing to do with any of that business at the hospital. I swear. Didn't I promise to answer all your questions truthfully?"

"It makes so much sense now."

Delano pushed his own chair back and surged to his feet. "On my wife's grave, I had nothing to do with your dismissal."

"You got me fired, then dangled this so-called job in front of me when I was at my most desperate —"

Her gaze still looked inward, and he knew he hadn't reached her. Dammit, she had to listen to him.

"I did no such thing! You think I arranged for you to notice the anesthetist was siphoning off the product? And for you to blow the whistle on him?"

"Why not? You seem capable of orchestrating anything."

"That's ludicrous. Next you'll accuse me of somehow engineering your friend's flight from her abusive husband, thereby putting you in the financial bind that placed you at my mercy. I am not *God*, Ainsley. I am not responsible for every aspect of your predicament. I may have taken advantage of it, but I didn't create it."

She drew her next breath in on an agonized hiss and he realized his error.

"Goddamn you, Delano."

Chapter 14

AINSLEY SAW BY his expression that he realized his mistake. He hadn't meant to give that away.

"I'm sorry," he said.

"Sorry?" She heard her voice rising, but there was nothing she could do about it. "*Sorry?* You think that makes me feel better?"

"Of course not. But if you'd —"

"You said you didn't know why I needed the money. You said you didn't care. But I guess you lied about that, too, didn't you?"

"No. I didn't lie about that. Not at first. But circumstances have —"

"I can't believe this. You've invaded my life like a choking, noxious fucking ... *weed!*" She could hear her own breathing, ragged breaths as though she'd been running. "You investigated me within an inch of my life, and decided I was the perfect patsy. Then you dangled me in front of that creature — a serial goddamn killing monster! — so you could 'rescue' me, then harvest my blood under the pretense of helping me."

"Yes, I did those things, but —"

"Then you jeopardized my life again by keeping me under your roof in St. Cloud. Good Lord, I could have been killed when Janecek attacked that night! Then you dragged me here, where I've been living virtually under lock and key for these past weeks, unable to go anywhere without a bodyguard breathing down my neck." Her fists clenched and unclenched with impotent rage. "And still I was naively rolling up my sleeve for you twice a day. Do you have any idea —"

Her voice broke and she had to swallow a few times before she could continue.

"Can you for one goddamn minute imagine how terrified — I mean, how scared-to-the-bone I was, thinking I might turn into a beast like the one who attacked me?"

If she hadn't been watching closely, she might have said his flat expression remained unchanged, but she saw the flash of agony deep in his eyes. Good. He deserved to suffer. He'd hijacked her life!

"Now, your friend Janecek knows who I am. Shit, he knows *where* I am. And he seems to want me."

"We can protect you."

Ainsley plunged on, ignoring his assurance. "Could you explain that for me? What is it that suddenly makes me the prize in your deadly little father/son war?"

Delano brought his hand down on the table with a resounding thump. "Once and for all, he is not my son! I wish to God I'd left him to die, a nine-year-old monster."

"I wish you had, too! Because now he's an adult monster and he wants me. What I want to know is why?"

"Your blood."

Delano rubbed his forehead as though trying to erase a headache. She hoped, rather viciously, that it was a migraine.

"Oh, yes, my blood. We're back to that. Okay, let's have it. What's so special about my blood that every vampire wants it? For God's sake, I'm *A positive*, the same as a quarter of the population."

His face darkened. "I'm the one who wants your blood, Ainsley. Janecek just wants you dead."

Despite herself, she put a hand to her mouth. "Dead? Why?"

"Remember I told you about those rare people with the anti-vampire agent in their blood, dating back to the earliest history of vampires?"

Oh Jesus oh God oh no. "I'm one of them."

"I'm afraid it's worse than that," he said softly. "I believe you're the last of them."

"No!" She shook her head. "No way. That can't be."

"The gene was confined to the Merzetti family, a small clan with its roots in Sicily. The family was reputed to have been hunted down and eradicated by vampires centuries ago, but isolated tales persisted throughout time of the Merzetti Effect."

"The Merzetti Effect?"

"If a rogue fed on a member of the Merzetti clan, he died."

"But I'm no Merzetti. Hell, I'm not even Sicilian! Look at me." She lifted a fistful of white-blond hair and thrust it toward him. "I can't be Sicilian."

Delano smiled sadly. "All the Merzetti's of this strain were fair-haired and fair-skinned. I'm afraid it made your ancestors very easy to hunt in your homeland."

"No."

"Yes. There can be no doubt. You carry the Merzetti gene."

Ainsley's mind whirled. "But you said they were all hunted down and killed. If that's the case, how do you explain me?"

"For thirty years, I studied the Merzetti family. I pored over ancient records, studied the local lore. From every angle I examined it, it appeared that one Merzetti female — the teenaged Gabriella — was unaccounted for. I theorized that she'd escaped."

"It took you thirty years to figure that out?"

"I'm afraid we're talking about an era that predates reliable vital statistics and searchable databases. I had to put it together from family bibles, church records, graveyard markers, old diaries, scraps of gossip, folk tales, you name it. The information I uncovered eventually led me to North America, where I've spent a good deal longer than thirty years searching for Gabriella's offspring. Unfortunately, even as the search tools got better, the trail itself got colder."

It brought it all home, somehow, the reality of it all, listening to this man, who routinely made use of gene mapping technology in his high-tech lab, calmly discuss the cruder tools he'd had to work with a century ago. Ainsley wet lips gone suddenly dry. "And the trail got colder why? Because of the sheer size of geographic area to be searched?"

"That was a challenge," he allowed, "but not the biggest one. The main impediment was the propensity for the Merzetti women to bear only daughters, whom they have a habit of abandoning, immediately and anonymously, to foundling homes. And those daughters go on to have daughters of their own, which they promptly abandon to foster care. Thus the Merzetti name has long been lost to Gabriella's descendants. And as a consequence, I've had to trace every female foundling abandoned on a church step or shelter in every city, town and village, for the last hundred years."

No, no, no! Ainsley put her hands to her ears to shut out the sound of his voice. It couldn't be. It just couldn't.

In the next instant, Delano was there, pulling her hands down. "I know you don't want to hear this, Ainsley, but you must. Somehow Janecek has figured out who you are. And now that he knows, the clock is ticking."

"But how?"

"How did he figure it out? He lived with me for a time. While he showed no particular interest in my work, I expect he was cognizant of the nature of it."

"No, those women! How could they give up their babies?" A tear broke from her eyelash and streaked down her right cheek.

Delano's grip on her wrists softened. "They had no choice. It was imperative for the survival of the bloodline. The offspring had to be hidden."

She gripped his wrist now, her fingers digging fiercely into his flesh. "But how would they know? The foundlings ... if they never knew their mothers, never heard this story, how could they possibly know of the danger to their offspring? What would possess them give up their own daughters?"

"Somehow the instinct was born in them, and thank God for that miracle. Else there'd be no hope of a successful vaccine."

Oh, this was too much. Too fast. Too awful. It couldn't be true. She released her grip on him and stepped back, glancing wildly around the room.

"Ainsley? What is it? Do you need something? A drink of water?"

Yeah, she needed something. An argument to refute everything he'd said. She choked back a laugh. Lord, did she really think she was going to find one lying around the kitchen?

"Ainsley?" He moved closer. "Are you all right? Do you need to sit down?"

"No." She lifted an arm, both to fend off his concern and to prevent him from getting any closer. "I don't need anything except answers."

He didn't look persuaded, but he accepted her assurance. "Very well. Then ask a question."

She took a deep breath, exhaled, then another one. What to ask first?

"Okay, presuming all of this is true, how do you know if I actually carry the Merzetti blood? Huh? If I'm the first candidate you've caught up to on this side of the Atlantic, and if my ancestors on the other side of the pond were slain hundreds of years ago, how can you be sure?"

"DNA retrieved from the skeletal remains of one of your ancestors confirms it. You are most definitely a Merzetti, from the port town of Licata, in provincia di Agrigento."

Nausea roiled in her stomach. "Oh, my Lord, you dug someone up? You dug up one of my ancestors?"

Delano drew himself up to his full height. "Before you accuse me of grave robbery, it was all part of sanctioned research, I assure you. And yes, we obtained a legitimate exhumation order from the proper authorities."

"So that proves what?" She lifted her chin in challenge. "That I'm descended from the Lucata Merzettis?"

"Licata."

"Okay, the Licata Merzettis, then. Great. Wonderful. If the DNA says that's the case, I guess I'll have to accept it. But who's to say I have this mysterious anti-vampire agent in my blood? After all these generations, it must be well and truly diluted."

He shot her an offended look. "Of course you carry it. Do you think I'd have put you through all this if I weren't absolutely certain?"

This time, a sharp, hysterical laugh did escape. "Frankly, Delano, I don't know what to think. I no longer have any idea what degree of manipulation you're capable of."

"Okay, I deserve that, I guess."

The words came out calmly enough, but she saw the way his hands clenched into fists. Good. She hoped his leashed tension was adding to his headache.

"Damn right you do! And now you're going to tell my why you're so certain I have this agent in my blood."

He held her gaze. "Because when I located Edward Webber, he was already dying."

Oh, dear Lord. "Dying? Because of my blood?"

"The short answer is yes. Though I'm not sure of the mechanism."

She laughed, a harsh sound echoing dully in the small kitchen. "The mechanism? I should think that would be obvious. He bit me and he died. Ergo, I killed him."

"No." His eyebrows drew together in a fierce scowl. "You mustn't think of it that way. If anyone should be held to account for that, it's me. I'm the one who put you in his path. I'm the one — the only one — who knew what might result if he attacked you." The timbre of his voice dropped down a notch. "Simply put, you were victimized, Ainsley. By both of us."

"I killed a man."

"You did not!" He seized her wrist again, using his other hand to tip her head up so his gaze could bore into hers. "Have you heard nothing I said? *I* killed him. *Me.* You've known it all along. I don't know how, but that night as you lay in the hospital bed in my house, you knew I went in search of your attacker. And later, I confirmed that he'd been eliminated. Remember?"

"You think I could forget that?"

"You managed to find peace with that fact once, and you can find it again. Because I — not you — am solely responsible for his death."

"But my blood —"

"May or may not have killed him."

She blinked. "But you said —"

"Edward Webber died that night, but unfortunately, he fed again, several hours after he bit you. It's entirely possible — perhaps even probable — that your blood merely caused a reversal of the genetic mutation. If that's the case, the second feeding might be the one that killed him."

She tore her hand away from his to press both hands to a head that felt like it might explode if she had to absorb one more piece of information.

"I don't understand. How could the second victim kill him?"

"I ran blood work, Ainsley. He died of an acute hemolytic transfusion reaction. It's possible that reaction may have been caused directly from infusing your blood. On the other hand, it's entirely possible that the Merzetti agent merely reversed the vampiric mutation. If the reversal had already begun before the second feeding, he may have lost his ability to infuse blood regardless of type."

"Are you saying he might have died from a simple ABO incompatibility between himself and his second victim?"

He nodded. "Simple but catastrophic."

She blinked rapidly. "So you really don't know how this anti-vampire blood thing works?"

"No."

"Can't we test it?"

His eyebrows soared. "I'm sure you know there's a limit to what we can do in a test tube. It needs to be field-tested. Ethically, the only candidates I'm prepared to try it on are serial killers who happen to share your A-positive blood type, pre-mutation."

Geez, did he think she was nuts? "I wasn't suggesting you try it on our clinic patrons, for goodness sake. Of course it would have to be a predator."

He loosened his collar. "I'm glad we agree."

Agree? Panic made her stomach clench. "No! No agreement. I'm not agreeing to anything until I've had a chance to process everything you've told me. Am I making myself clear?"

"Of course."

Thank God. Some breathing space to think about this stuff. The tension coiled in her muscles slackened ever so slightly.

Of course, "processing" this new information was a lot easier said than done. Right now, a lifetime didn't feel long enough. On the other hand, she'd gone from thinking of vampires as mythical creatures to performing venipunctures on them, practically overnight. Amazing how quickly one could normalize the freakishly abnormal.

She wet her lips. "Okay, hypothetically speaking — because I haven't agreed to anything, you understand — I have a technical question. Why would the predator have to be my blood type?"

Immediately, she sensed his relief to be fielding a question that wasn't rife with emotional landmines. Dammit, it was maddening how she could read him like a large print book on something as inconsequential as this, yet he could conceal the fact that he'd been playing God with her life for weeks now. What was that about?

"Ainsley? "

Belatedly, she realized that he'd been speaking, and she hadn't absorbed a word. "Sorry. My brain went AWOL for a sec. Can you give that to me again, from the top?"

"Of course. The mutation renders us — all vampires — universal receivers. We are not hampered by ABO compatibility issues, antibodies, or any kind of blood-borne pathogens. But if your blood — the Merzetti blood — does indeed reverse the mutation, we need to make sure it's compatible with the attacker's original blood type. Ideally, I'd like to see what happens to such a candidate — one who is prevented from feeding again — after being infused with your blood. If your blood is compatible with their pre-mutation blood type, and we still see massive hemolytic reaction, we can assume your blood itself is the lethal agent. However, if we see only a progressive reversal of the mutation with no hemolytic crisis, we'll know it operates only to counter the mutation."

"But what about non-compatible . . ." She paused a moment to search for the right word, opting finally for Delano's descriptor.

"...candidates? Don't we need to know what happens when they receive my blood?"

"We do." He nodded. "Presuming it works the way I've theorized and produces a reversal in a compatible subject, we'd then proceed to test it on a non-compatible subject. Again, we'd have to ensure they didn't feed again after infusing your blood. Then we'd need to see if they experience the same mutation reversal. Finally, we need to observe whether or not they experience a hemolytic reaction following the reversal, brought on strictly by your blood and no one else's, and how severe that reaction might be. It's entirely possible it might be manageable. Webber's wasn't; he'd just infused too much incompatible blood."

She chewed her lip. "Then what? I mean, I know you'd use the knowledge of how the agent actually operates to create your vaccine, but what about the predators we test it on? If I knowingly lend myself to this experiment of yours and someone dies ..."

To his credit, Delano didn't try to minimize the risk. "It's a distinct possibility."

"Couldn't you ... I don't know ... extract some blood and inject it into the subject's veins with a syringe?"

His face went carefully blank. "That would work just as effectively, and with the tactical squad Eli has assembled, they could no doubt locate a predator during the daylight hours and Eli could inject him while he was immobilized by the day sleep."

That sounded easy enough. Why hadn't he suggested it before? She held his gaze, probing for his thoughts, but came up empty. No, not empty. He was shielding. Then it clicked. He couldn't do it himself, since he couldn't move about in daylight, and he couldn't bring himself to require Eli to do it for him.

"Of course!" she said. "In that scenario, if the subject were to die, that would make you — through Eli — his active judge, jury and executioner. You'd pretty much be killing him in his sleep."

"Don't worry about me. If that's the way it has to be, that's what I'll do. Same goes for Eli." He looked away.

"No! I'd feel worse. At least with Edward Webber, he attacked me with intent to kill. He got what was coming to him. Sort of."

His lips turned up in an uncommonly gentle smile, at least for him. "Come on, Ainsley. Do you think you're going to sell me on the idea that you're a fan of an-eye-for-an-eye justice? A proponent of the death penalty?"

"No, I couldn't sell anyone on that idea, because I detest the concept of capital punishment. But in this case, he effectively killed himself, in the process of trying to kill me. Not to mention the second bite victim. I guess I can live with ... Omigod!"

"What?"

"I can't believe it didn't occur to me to ask — what happened to the second victim?"

"She escaped. Webber was too weak by that point to restrain her long enough to exsanguinate her."

Thank God. "Well, there's a break. Of course, the poor woman probably now thinks she's nuts. To be attacked like that, and then presto, there's no evidence left, and no one to explain it to her ..."

"Oh, there was evidence," he said, his face grim. "Because the feeding was interrupted, there was no coagulant infusion and no sealing of the arterial puncture."

Ainsley blanched. "So, what? She staggered away, squirting arterial blood from her neck?"

"Not a pretty picture, I know. But she flagged down a motorist, who called 911 and applied pressure to the wound until the paramedics arrived."

"Did they believe her? That she'd been attacked by a vampire?"

"They believed that she was attacked, all right. By a nutcase who fancied himself a —"

"Holy shit."

"Excuse me?"

"Webber's attack on me was interrupted. I distinctly remember lots of blood, on my hands, on my coat. It was all kind of pink, diluted by the hard rain, but I remember blood. He wouldn't have had time to —"

She stopped mid-sentence, as the truth struck her. Of course. Delano. She felt a flush creep up her neck.

"You did it, didn't you? You stopped the bleeding."

"Yes."

She watched his gaze drop to her neck. Drawn there by her rising blush, or by the memory of that night? Suddenly, another memory jarred loose. The dark stranger bending over her, pressing his mouth to her throat ...

Oh, yikes! She closed her eyes. "I don't suppose you used conventional medicine to staunch the bleeding?"

A pause. "Would you like me to say I did?"

She sighed and opened her eyes. "I might if I thought I could believe it. Of course, I'd then have to inquire how the puncture marks miraculously disappeared."

"I think you know what happened."

"I think I do, too."

He'd saved her life. Of course, he was also the man who jeopardized it in the first place. The thought lent her voice a harder edge than usual.

"I hope you're not expecting a thank you?"

"Obviously not. In the circumstances, I'd settle for you not staking me in my sleep tomorrow."

She blinked. "That really works?"

"Staking?"

"Yeah."

"I should think so. Just not like on TV." Again the smile, this time slightly self-mocking. "We're fast healers, but perhaps not fast enough to heal that kind of catastrophic cardiac penetration wound. Without quick access to a cardiothoracic surgeon, I'd die just like you would."

"Dammit."

"What?"

"I'm never going to run out of questions, am I? Every time you tell me something new, I think of a dozen more questions."

He met and held her gaze. "Probably. But I'll answer them all. Frankly, fully and honestly. That's my motto from now on, at least as far as you're concerned."

She felt another little sliver of her anger slip away. Damn him, how did he do it? For heaven's sake, he'd practically kidnapped her out of her life so he could use her blood in his highly speculative, highly controversial research, without her knowledge or consent.

"Why didn't you just tell me from the start? I'm a very reasonable person."

"Agreed. In fact, you have one of the most open, resilient, nimble minds I've ever encountered. It's been a pleasure to work with you."

Hmmph, empty flattery. Except she couldn't quite stop the flush of pleasure his words caused. She lifted her chin. "So why didn't you tell me?"

"Remember your state of mind at the time." He took off his glasses and rubbed his eyes. "You were terrorized, your psyche stretched to the limit with what you'd had to absorb. Having just been so brutally savaged by one vampire, somehow I couldn't see you agreeing to hang around with another one. Nor could I see you freely offering your blood to my cause."

Her mouth firmed. "So you made up the fiction of a possible infection."

He replaced his glasses. "Yes."

"Would you do it again, if you had a chance to do it over?"

"Yes."

Just like that. Not even a pause.

Well, no one could fault him on his commitment.

"At least you're keeping up your end of the deal, the being honest thing."

"I told you I'd answer any of your questions, honestly and completely."

He finally lifted his mug, which he'd thus far ignored, and took a sip of the cooling tea. It was, she realized, the first time she'd seen him drink anything.

"Okay, here's a question." She fixed him with a fierce stare. "Why did you go prying into my past, digging up that stuff about Lucy and Devon? You said you couldn't care less what my secret was."

"That was before Janecek got wind of you, before he figured out who you were. Now that he knows, he'll be looking for a chink in your armor, something that makes you vulnerable. We — Eli and I — thought it was prudent to get to the bottom of it, purely from a defensive point of view. Clearly, you love this woman and her daughter like family, and Janecek will exploit that if he can."

Her breath stalled in her lungs. "Do you think he's found them?"

"No." He shook his head. "From all appearances, he's a few weeks behind us in terms of intelligence gathering, and we haven't managed to find them yet." His brows drew together. "You couldn't help us with that, could you?"

"You want me to lead you to them?"

"If you can. I mean, we can find them, sooner or later, but I'm thinking sooner would be better in this situation."

Her stomach flipped as she thought about Janecek getting his hands on what amounted to her only family. She picked up the pen and note pad lying in the center of the table, wrote a number down and handed it to Delano. "This phone number is all I have, but I know it's in Cuernavaca."

"Mexico?"

"Yes, about an hour and a half south of Mexico City, according to the map I looked at." She tossed the pen back down on the note pad. "So how does this work? You send a posse of security people to hang around 24–7 and make sure nothing happens to them?"

"That's precisely what we'll do."

"Does Lucy have to know?"

His eyebrows shot up. "You're proposing not to tell her?"

"Not really. Maybe. Oh, hell, I don't know." God, she was so tired and stressed. She felt like her gray matter was leaking out.

"As Eli once pointed out to me, it's easier to protect someone if they appreciate fully what the dangers are."

She rubbed her temple to sooth a ticking muscle that leapt to life there. "You're right. She deserves to know. And if I don't tell her, I'd be doing pretty much the same thing I've faulted you for. But God help me, Delano, how am I going to explain this? Where will I find the words to make this situation sound halfway believable? I mean, it's like something out of a Hollywood B-movie."

His expression softened. "She trusts you, Ainsley. She's already trusting you with her life and that of her daughter. You'll find the words."

She chewed her lower lip. "I suppose."

"But it will wait until tomorrow afternoon or evening, when you get up. You'll be more coherent after you've slept. In the meantime, I'll have Eli get a team on them as quickly as possible. They'll be safe."

"Thank you."

He took her hand in his and squeezed it. "You're doing the right thing."

It felt good, his warm, strong hand enveloping hers. Too good, dammit. She was still mad at him. She might never stop being mad at him in this lifetime. So why did he tug at her like this?

Because your emotions have been through the wringer.

Because your body is still trying to cope with the cascade of physiological responses triggered by the shitload of adrenaline that hit the fan when Radak Janecek took off his fireman's helmet and announced himself.

Because you've tasted a tiny fraction of the mind-blowing pleasure you know he can give you.

She pulled her hand away. "Does your offer to answer all my questions have the same shelf life as Cinderella's carriage, or can I take a rain check? Because I really don't think I'm up to any more of this tonight. I need to crash." To her mortification, her voice cracked. She laughed. "What am I saying? I'm already crashing."

His eyes darkened. "By all means, get some rest. There's no expiry date on my offer. I'll answer your questions whenever you like."

✸

Two hours later, Ainsley lay in bed looking at the ceiling as the sky lightened outside, etching a thin line of light above and below her floor-to-ceiling blackout drapes.

She was numb from exhaustion, but every time she started to slide down that slope to sleep, an image of Janecek — beautiful and deadly — leapt into her mind, sending another jolt of adrenaline ripping through her system. At this rate, she'd never sleep, and she'd be even more of a wreck when the time came to pick up the telephone and call Lucy. Her friend would think she'd come unhinged.

Dammit, enough was enough. Why should she cope with this fear alone? There were two men in this apartment, both of whom played a role in putting her in this predicament. One of them could damn well watch her back while she slept.

She rolled out of bed, tugged on the t-shirt and boxers she'd earlier discarded in a fit of fury when they'd become twisted in the sheets with all her tossing and turning, and marched out of her bedroom.

She glanced down the hall toward Delano's suite. The temptation to point her bare feet in that direction was almost too strong to fight off.

Stupid. He wouldn't welcome her.

Besides, what kind of guardian would a sleeping vampire make? Somehow she imagined the healing, age-erasing day sleep he'd told her about to be … well, deep and coma-like. Logically, then, Eli should be the better protector during daylight hours.

Not to mention that Delano was the one who'd manipulated her so callously. Eli, on the other hand, was just doing his job, and under protest, at that. According to Delano, Eli had voted to tell her everything. Granted, he may only have wanted to make the job of protecting her easier, but it still put him on the side of the angels as far as she was concerned.

Also, Eli was a much safer choice, emotionally and every other way she cared to contemplate it. She liked him. A lot. And she admired him. But her pulse didn't leap jaggedly at the thought of marching into his bedroom and demanding that he move over so she could get some sleep. And her virtue, such as it was, would be safe with him. Provided, of course, that she wanted it to be safe. She had no doubt he'd rise to the occasion, so to speak, if she needed him to. But despite his obvious and earthy charms, she didn't really want him.

Yes, her virtue would be safe with Eli.

With Delano, however ...

Okay, Eli it is.

Except when she reached his room and pushed the door open, he wasn't there. Judging from the undisturbed state of the bed, he hadn't yet retired. She pushed her hair back out of her eyes. No problem. She would find him and persuade him to go to bed, at least long enough for her to get to sleep.

Four minutes later, she conceded he was nowhere to be found in the penthouse, and she knew he wouldn't be in the lab. Not without Delano. Reluctantly, she concluded he was still out taking care of the details that would keep them safe.

Well, so much for that great idea.

She headed back to her own quarters, but once outside her bedroom door, she stopped. Dammit, she just couldn't go back in there to wrestle with the blankets and her own thoughts.

She glanced down the hallway and felt that yearning again.

Screw it. She'd just go look in on him. Just to satisfy her curiosity about the day sleep thing.

Chapter 15

AINSLEY HELD HER breath as she pushed Delano's bedroom door inward. It swung open soundlessly on well-oiled hinges.

Well, that answered one question. He obviously felt good enough about the penthouse's security that he didn't have a backup alarm system to alert him to intrusions into his inner sanctum.

And, damn, it was dark. Apart from the wedge of pale light stretching out on the carpet — she'd turned on a lamp in the adjoining sitting room — the bedroom was in complete blackness. Man, she'd thought her own bedroom was plenty dark. The one window in her room was heavily shaded to facilitate day sleeping, but it was nothing compared to this. Of course, this room was windowless, as she'd discovered that night she'd ventured in here to see what she could learn about her mysterious boss.

She stood in the doorway a moment, waiting for her eyes to acclimatize. Eventually, she made out the edge of bed, and there was the tall dresser, the one that held the framed photo of his long-dead wife.

Treading carefully, she moved into the room, gliding up to the bed. She paused another moment until she could make out his form. He lay on his side, on the far side of the bed, facing the wall, like any man might in his sleep. Somehow, she'd expected something different.

Well, okay, she'd half expected him to sleep on his back, with his hands folded on his breast like vampires in the movies.

She held her breath a moment, listening. There! She could hear his breathing. Deep and even. The sound was impossibly soothing, hypnotic. Oh Lord, if she could just lie there beside him and listen to his soft, regular respirations, she knew she could sleep.

She swayed on her feet, weary beyond belief.

Why shouldn't she sleep here? What could it hurt? She'd wake up before Delano did anyway. She always rose well before him.

She glanced around the room. Maybe she could drag that chair over, the one she'd fallen asleep in that night she'd come snooping. That way, she'd be close enough to hear the soothing rhythm of his breathing, yet she wouldn't be invading his space so brazenly.

Except she didn't want to sleep in a damned chair and wake up with a headache even worse than the one that pounded in her temples already.

"Delano?" No response.

She called his name again, this time a little louder. Again, he didn't stir, nor did his respirations change.

Well, that settled it. She could sleep here and he'd be none the wiser come evening. She'd rise while he slept, smooth the blankets back into place and be on her way.

Still, her heart pounded like crazy as she drew the lightweight covers back and perched gingerly on the edge of the bed, but he made no reaction to the depression of the mattress.

"Del?" murmured. Again, no response.

Carefully, she lay down on the bed, pulling the covers up to her shoulders. When he failed to stir, she let her breath escape on a sigh, rolled onto her side to face the door and drew her knees up. Finally, finally, she could sleep. She let her eyes drift shut and was gone in moments.

The dream had him again.

He loved this time, the interval between the deep, restoring sleep that claimed him each morning and the full wakefulness that came with sundown. He loved it, and he loathed it, too. For in that short space of time, he slept almost like he used to sleep. Like other men slept. That's when the dreams came. Yes, and the nightmares, too, sometimes. And as often as not, the dreams tortured him worse than the nightmares ever could.

This was one of those dreams, the kind he would pay for with a deep, persistent ache that would be with him for days. But God help him, he didn't care. He just wanted to hang onto it as long as he could.

This time, he lay on his back, with Ainsley's body curved sweetly against him, one silky-smooth leg twined with his. And her skin! The parts that touched him blazed like a furnace against his own skin, and her scent, a potent mix of sandalwood and sleepy woman, filled his nostrils. Beneath the soft sound of her breathing, he heard the strong, steady *lub-dub* of her heart and the fainter but even more thrilling surge and whisper of her blood.

His member, already engorged, grew harder still. He lifted a hand to palm her unbound breast through the thin t-shirt she wore, and felt the tip harden.

"Delano?"

"Ainsley."

Effortlessly, he rolled her beneath him.

Oh, Lord! She felt so solid, so real, so warm. And soft in all the right places.

"Del! Wait! You can't ... I mean, we can't —"

"Oh, but we can." Here in this twilight place, they most definitely could. They could do anything.

He grasped the hands pressing against his chest, pushed them over her head and pinned them to the mattress. Then he took her mouth the way he'd been dying to do since he'd ravished her in the lab. But unlike that night in his lab, she just lay there, accepting the thrust and swirl of his tongue.

He adjusted his grip on her wrists so he could keep her arms pinned with one hand. The other hand he slipped under her t-shirt, gliding over the hot silk of her skin as he pushed the material upward until his hands closed on one bare, plump breast. "Kiss me back. Please, Ainsley."

With a groan, she caught fire beneath him, arching up into his aching hardness. And her kiss! At last, she fed at his mouth as avidly as he could wish.

His hand tightened involuntarily on her breast, drawing a high moan from between her lips. He swallowed the sound, letting it thrill him to his very marrow.

More. He wanted more of those sounds. He wanted to make her sob with wanting.

Slowly, he drew his palm away from full contact with her breast, letting his fingers skate closer and closer to her areola, until they closed gently on the hardened nub of her nipple.

She whimpered, and again he swallowed the small noise.

More.

Down her side, over her hip, along a slender thigh until he found the hem of the shorts she wore. Then around to squeeze her bare, oh-so-luscious ass. Sweet merciful heaven, could anything feel better?

"My hands!" She panted against his mouth. "Let them go. I want … I need … Oh, please, Del, let me touch you."

Her words sent a bolt of excitement straight to his groin, causing him to surge against her. He released his grip on her wrists.

Her hands went to his head, shaping it, pushing his hair back. He levered himself up slightly so he could look at her breasts. Beautiful. Ripe, full, strawberry-tipped. Groaning, he bent to apply his mouth to one pink crest. Closing his lips around it, he lashed it with tongue, then suckled it.

She made a high keening sound. He would have shifted to her other breast, but she held him fast, demanding more. He obliged, licking, sucking, biting gently. Beneath him, she surged upward with unmistakable purpose. Oh, God, she was so hot, so responsive.

The blood lust rose, turning his vision dark and threatening to unsheathe his canines, but he reined it in, sending it the same message as he'd sent his throbbing cock.

Not yet. Not yet.

Sliding onto his side, he drew her with him. Her hands roamed his chest now, fingers flexing over muscle, raking through hair, palms spreading, exploring. Nails biting into flesh, thumbs scraping over a sensitive nipple, then soothing. Sweet Jesus, it felt good to be touched.

And to touch.

Remembering why he'd rolled them, he slid a hand down her rump, then around between her thighs to cup the moist heat gathered there.

She lifted her knee to give him better access. "Del!"

"Yes?"

"Touch me."

He urged her onto her back. "I will, sweetheart. Until you scream."

Delicately, his fingers found her slick heat, his thumb her swollen clitoris. When he probed her entrance with two fingers, she rose to meet him, surging against his hand. And, oh, mercy, the sobbing sounds she tried to swallow back! Another bolt of lightning shot through him. Grimly, he clenched his jaw to prevent his teeth from erupting.

Not yet.

Her hips bucked harder, and her breathing grew ragged as he drove her up, up, and still further up.

"That's it, my sweet," he praised, watching the fierce passion on her face. Her kiss-swollen lips were parted, gasping air, her eyes squeezed shut, the cords in her slender neck standing out. "Reach for it."

She came then, in panting, sobbing joy. And once again he had to fight off the twin demands of cock and tooth.

Not yet, not yet. For God's sake, not yet.

"Omigod, Del. That was … that was —"

He smiled into her eyes. "That was good, but you didn't scream."

Before she could respond to that, he'd slid right off the bed, pulled her to the edge of the mattress, and knelt between her slender thighs.

"Del!"

"Relax." He kissed her inner thigh, delighting in the way it trembled.

"*Relax?*" The word came out as half laugh, half sob. "You really expect me to relax?"

He laughed, letting his breath stimulate her most tender flesh, seeing her shudder. Lord, she was beautiful, sensitive, and so incredibly responsive. This, this was why he had to rein in the blood lust.

"Perhaps I should just say hang on."

And hang on she did. To his sheets. She buried her fists in the bedding, thrashing her head from side to side, crying out. This time, he made sure the ascent was slower and more deliberate. And this time, when she exploded in bliss, the room rang with her cries.

He kissed his way up her body, savoring all the physical evidence of her orgasm. Trembling stomach, nipples tightened to rock-hard points, heart still thudding crazily, the flush in her neck and face just beginning to subside.

Now.

Roughly, he hauled her back up fully onto the mattress and covered her with his body, nudging between her thighs. She shuddered beneath him.

"Now, Ainsley." He urged her legs wider apart, shifting until he found the moist heat of her with the tip of his cock.

"Yes!" She bucked beneath him. "Now, Del."

He pushed into her. Oh, Lord, she was tight. Her muscles still spasming from her orgasm, gripped him snugly. The glide of her, the hot, wet grip of her flesh . . . Oh, Lord, he was losing his mind. He pulled out until just the sensitive glans remained buried in her heat, then plunged in again. And again and again.

"Yes, yes, yes."

She wrapped her legs around him, rocking her hips, taking him deeper. He wanted to spin it out, make it last as long as he could, but her hands were on his back, her mouth hot on the point of his shoulder, his neck, wherever she could reach. The call of her blood rose, deafening now. He surged into her, harder, deeper, faster, until his control broke. With a guttural growl, he threw his head back and let his orgasm take him. As he pumped himself into her, his canines erupted.

Ainsley trembled as her internal muscles milked the last of his essence. Dear Lord, she'd died and gone to heaven. She opened her eyes to tell him so, only to see his face descending toward her neck, fangs bared in unmistakable intent.

A jolt went through her, part sexual excitement, part terror.

"No, Delano! Don't! You can't."

As though deaf to her cries, he used his hands to angle her head, exposing her vulnerable throat.

"Stop! Del, you don't know what it'll do." Frantically, she pushed at his chest with her hands, but he was so strong. It was like trying to stop a hydraulic press. "Stop!" she cried again. "For God's sake, it might kill you. Listen to me, Del. Where would we be then? Who'd stop Janecek? Who'd protect me?"

His eyes, black as midnight, burned into hers. "Shut up, Ainsley."

Shut up? *Shut up?*

Then he leaned down and pressed his mouth to her throat. She braced, expecting the hot, piercing pain of his cuspids, but he merely kissed her throat, grazing her skin ever so slightly with his teeth, tasting her skin, her pulse. She trembled.

"Del—"

"Dammit, Ainsley, this is my dream, and I make the rules here. So be quiet, would you?"

Dream? Oh, Christmas.

"You think this is a *dream*?" She caught him by the hair, and this time, he allowed her to hold him back.

"A very nice one. And in this dream, I'm going to find your carotid artery with my fingers, like so."

One hand splayed on her neck, and she felt her pulse hammer against his flesh.

"Then I'm going to sink my teeth into your lovely white neck until I hit that life-blood, which I'll take straight to my heart. When I'm done feeding, I'll close your wound, but even as I'm doing that, you'll feel me swell inside you. And then ... oh, then, my sweet Ainsley, I'm going to take you all over again. Only this time, you'll feel what I feel and I'll feel what you feel, and when we explode together, it will be like nothing you've ever experienced."

Involuntarily, her hips surged against his. *Christ, Ainsley. Get a grip.* The man thought he was dreaming!

She tightened her fists in his hair. "Del, this is *real*. I mean, really real. And I oughta know. You just made me come three times, and you're still inside me."

His eyes lost some of their fire. "Real?"

"As real as it gets. Real as the phone call I have to make to Lucy when I get up. Real as the anger I'm still struggling with over the way you deceived me."

He cursed and levered himself away from her with shocking alacrity. Though grateful he'd finally gotten the message, she felt the loss of contact like an ache. To cover her vulnerability, she resorted to flippancy.

"Well, I must say, I've seen smoother dismounts."

"Hell's teeth, woman!"

Hell's teeth? What kind of a cussword was that?

"I was more concerned about *your* teeth." Speaking of which, they had already retracted, but somehow he didn't look any less menacing.

"For God's sake, why didn't you *stop* me?"

She pulled the sheet over herself and sat up. "Excuse me. I distinctly remember saying we couldn't do this. You assured me we could."

"That's because I thought I was dreaming!"

"How was I supposed to know that? I thought you meant it was safe to ... you know ... fool around."

He made a strangled sound and ran his hands through his hair. It occurred to her that he made a very nice picture, naked.

"Okay, let's start here: what the devil were you doing in my bed?"

She lifted her chin. "I couldn't sleep."

"And you couldn't pop an Ambien?"

She glared at him.

"What? You have a very tidy supply, right there in your medicine chest. I took pains to stock it."

"Argh!"

"Come on, Ainsley, you're a nurse. A nurse who was known to work quite a few extra shifts. Don't tell me you've never resorted to a little chemical assistance to get the rest you needed between shifts."

"Go to hell." Ainsley ripped the sheets from the bed and lurched to her feet, wrapping the material around her. "Why don't you just admit that you sent your snoops into my apartment to find out every little thing about me. What food I eat, what clothes I wear. Christ, they even checked what underwear I favor. So I'm pretty sure they saw the meds in my cabinet. And yes, dammit, I take a sleep aid once in a while." She finally managed to tie off the sheet above her breasts in a way that felt secure, leaving her hands free to prop on her hips. "I resent your suggestion I should have just taken a goddamn pill. I wasn't suffering from your garden-variety insomnia last night, Delano. I was terrified out of my head. Every time I started to drift off, I saw Janecek coming for me, and it jerked me right out of sleep. I was worn out from battling stress hormones. All I could think about was human comfort. Companionship. Security. *Contact*. God, can you understand any of that?"

"That," he said, "is what Eli is for."

She'd been about to tell him she tried Eli first, but drew back. If that was his attitude, forget about it. It wasn't Eli's fault she was in this Godforsaken situation. Why should he be the one who had to hold her hand?

"*That's what Eli's for?*" She laughed harshly. "You make it sound like that's in his job description."

He shoved a hand through his hair again and glanced around the room. "I have to get dressed."

But Ainsley wasn't listening. She was putting two and two together and coming up with a disturbing answer.

"Omigod, that *is* in his job description, isn't it?"

He pushed past her to pick up a robe he'd left lying on the wingback chair. "Eli doesn't have a job description."

Her mind jumped back to that first night at Delano's house in St. Cloud, after the attack, when Eli nursed her. She'd asked him what else he did for Delano. His answer echoed in her head now.

Whatever he asks me to.

She rounded on Delano. "Oh, this just gets better and better, doesn't it? That's why he took me out for that romantic little carriage ride through Old Montreal."

"I wouldn't know about any carriage ride." He pulled the robe on and tied the sash with what seemed like excessive force.

"Well, doesn't that beat all? I've been squired around town by a paid escort. I think I can safely say that's an all-time low."

"Ainsley, would you please —"

"Please *what?*" She gathered the sheet tighter. "Please stop griping about little details, like how you paid someone to pay male attention to me? For pity's sake, Delano, you could have just told me you didn't want me that way."

"No. No, dammit, I couldn't." He grabbed her wrist in a painful clasp and dragged her close enough to see the turmoil in his eyes. Then he released her just as abruptly and turned away. "I couldn't."

She blinked at his silk-clad back. "Oh."

"Yes, *oh*," he said, his voice tight. "God, Ainsley, the night in the lab when Eli interrupted us ... I knew I couldn't take the chance that we'd get carried away like that again. Your blood ..." The muscles of his shoulders bunched beneath the silk of his robe. "To be so close, so intimate, and not take your blood ... I just couldn't trust myself."

"But you couldn't tell me this, because then you'd have to explain why we couldn't scratch the itch. And you knew I desperately wanted you to take my blood." She twisted the knotted sheet at her breast. "Well, okay, I also wanted wild sex."

"Yes." He ground the word out through gritted teeth.

"*Shit.*" She massaged her forehead and sighed. "This doesn't make it okay, you know."

"Believe me, I know. Nothing about this is okay."

Nothing? "I don't know about that. I kinda liked the sex part."

His back did the bunched-muscle thing again. "That can't happen again."

"Why not?"

"Why not?" He turned to face her. "Because it might kill one of us."

She paled. "Are you saying what we did just now ... there could be lethal consequences?"

He shook his head. "Highly unlikely."

"But not out of the question?"

"Nothing is out of the question, since we know so little about how this works."

Her heart stumbled. "I thought you said the only way I could be infected was if you ... I mean, if the vampire in question were to bite my jugular vein and infuse his own blood."

"Correct."

"So the fact that you ..."

He arched an eyebrow. "Ejaculated inside you?"

Ridiculously, she blushed. "That doesn't pose a risk of infection?"

"No. Nor of pregnancy."

His tone rang with a certainty that reassured. Then it clicked. "So, I'm not at risk, but you're not so sure about the other way around?"

"We know so little. I mean, we have a fair idea what happens when your blood is infused directly into the venous system, but the rest ..." He shrugged. "We have centuries of experience that says the vampirism virus is not sexually transmitted, but no such data on the Merzetti Effect."

"So my crawling into bed with you ..." She swallowed. "What we did ... what I let you do ... it might kill you?"

"Very unlikely."

"But not impossible?"

"Nothing's impossible."

Her vision narrowed alarmingly and her ears started to buzz. *Tinnitus. Vision disturbance. Anxiety.* Jesus, she had to calm down before she stroked out.

His voice cut through her panic.

"...even in the unlikely event of transmission, who's to say it would harm me? Maybe it would effect a reversal of my mutation?"

Reversal? "Omigod, you're going to have to type and cross-match your meals for the next while, aren't you?"

"Don't worry about it."

"Oh, I can't believe I let this happen."

"It's not your fault. Once you knew you carried the Merzetti blood, I should have been explicit about the risks of intimate contact."

She blinked. "I should have figured it out myself. Dammit, I'm a nurse! But any thought I did give to it was about my safety, and you'd said I couldn't be infected ... Oh, hell, I just didn't think."

To her dismay, she burst into tears.

Chapter 16

GOD HELP HIM, tears. Delano suppressed a groan.

"I need to find my clothes. I'll get dressed and get out of your way."

"Ainsley, come here."

She dashed tears from her cheeks as she continued to search among the strewn bedclothes for her nightwear. "Dammit, where are they?"

Whatever the circumstances, she'd just given him the incredible gift of her body, her passion, herself. At the memory, the blood lust clawed at his insides again, hot and urgent and vision-dimming. He forced it down.

"I said come here." He took her hand and tugged her to his side. She held her body stiffly away from him, but he exerted enough force to pull her into his arms. For a fleeting moment, she continued to resist. Then she leaned into him, her arms going around him in a fierce grip. It made his heart threaten to crack right open.

"I'm sorry for yelling at you," he said.

She sniffled against his chest. Something told him his silk robe was never going to be the same, but he couldn't care less. Unable to do anything else, he ran his hands over her back soothingly.

"I'm sorry, too," she mumbled into his chest. "I can't believe I put you at risk. I just didn't think."

"Just so you know, Ainsley, I wasn't the only one at risk."

She leaned back in his arms. "But you said I couldn't become ... I don't understand."

"I'm not talking about infection, which I assure you is out of the question."

"Then what?"

"If I'd taken your blood, I might not have stopped in time."

"What do you mean, in time?"

Her face was wet, her nose was red, and she looked perfectly lovely. He guided her over to the edge of the bed and urged her down on it, then sat down beside her.

"I've been celibate a long time."

"Me, too."

He laughed.

"What? It's true. Which you must know, from your very thorough investigation."

"Not as long as me."

She lifted a corner of the sheet she was wearing and dabbed at the wetness on her cheeks. "How long are we talking?"

"Let's just say transfusion medicine was not what it is today the last time I lay with a woman."

"Omigod. That's a long time."

"Indeed."

"Any particular reason you've tied that event to transfusion medicine?"

"You're very astute."

"What happened?"

"It had been a long time. Many years, in fact. I lost control, took far too much blood." He looked down at the carpet. "There was no saving her with the medical science available to me at the time."

"She died?"

He glanced sideways at her. She'd gone very still. *There but for the grace of God go I.* He could practically hear the thought. And she was right to think it. He returned his attention to the carpet, where he noticed a long blond hair lodged in the fibers. He resisted the urge to bend and pick it up.

"Delano?"

"She would have died, had I not turned her."

"Oh, Del. You made her into a vampire?"

"Yes. The one thing I swore I'd never do to another human being. But what choice did I have? It was that or leave her to die. I didn't even know if it would work, but it was the only way I knew to replace some of the blood she lost. And I knew the healing properties of the vampiric blood would take root quickly, if I could keep her alive long enough."

"It worked?"

"Spectacularly." He shot to his feet. "So, now you know."

Her hand darted out to grab his arm. "Hold it. You said you'd answer all my questions, fully and honestly."

"I can't imagine what more you'd want to know about that."

She arched a brow. "Can't you?"

He scowled. Dammit, it was times like this he'd trade a decade — hell, a century — to be able to throw back a shot of bourbon and feel it hit his stomach like a fireball, soothing his nerves.

"So, why did it work spectacularly?"

"It takes only a very small amount of blood to do the job. Rule of thumb, 15 ccs will do it. Any more than 25 ccs, you're asking for trouble."

"What kind of trouble?"

"The more blood you use, the more powerful the vampire you create will be. And the problem with creating a vampire more powerful than you is that often their first act is to destroy their maker."

"Was she very powerful?"

"More so than any vampire I'd ever seen, before or since."

"Did she try to destroy you?"

"No."

She held his gaze. "But you wished she would have?"

His throat ached, and it had nothing to do with the thirst that was eating him from the inside out. "Yes."

Her eyes softened. "Did you love her?"

He considered telling her it was none of her business. His promise to answer all questions surely could not be stretched to include this. But somehow, he felt compelled to tell her. Why that should be, he didn't care to contemplate

So he thought about Reina instead.

"Love her?" He sat back down beside her again on the edge of the bed. "She was intense and sensual and generous and very lovely, but no, I can't say I loved her. Not in the way you mean. But after that, we were ... connected."

"A blood bond."

"Well, a bond of sorts, yes."

"Did she love you?"

"Again, not like you mean. She might have thought so once, but she quickly learned she no longer wanted me. That's the fate of all vampires — relegated to the dark, lusting only after creatures of the light."

"And where is she now? Do you still see her?"

"She's dead."

At his flat pronouncement, her lips parted on a gasp. "But you said she was very powerful. How ... I mean, what happened?"

His gaze rested on her flushed face. No, not flushed. Abraded by his beard stubble. Whisker burned. He looked away.

"Power is no protection from depression. For some, the weight of the years becomes too much. There's so much change to deal with, yet at the same time, everything remains the same. And so much loss. The years stretch out endlessly. For some, it's beyond bearing."

"She took her own life?"

He shrugged. "She stayed up to greet the sunrise."

She shuddered and he knew she was thinking about what he'd told her. Acute solar uticaria, followed quickly by anaphylactic shock.

"I'm so sorry."

"Me too."

"Did she enjoy her life as a vampire?"

He angled a look at her.

"Well, yeah, okay, she committed suicide, so she wasn't too thrilled with it at the end. But what about before that? Did she hate it? Did she love it, but just got tired?"

Trust Ainsley to ask the hard questions. "She was ambivalent about it. She certainly didn't abhor what she was. Had she not had a deep fascination with vampires in the first place, she would not have wound up in my bed. And she certainly enjoyed her new-found power. But she didn't ask for it. She didn't actively seek the transformation." He shrugged. "It's hard to be wholehearted about it if the choice is not freely made."

"That sounds like personal experience talking."

"Funny, I thought it sounded like the end of a sad tale."

"Not quite. I have one more question in that vein before we move on."

"No pun intended, I'm sure."

She snorted. "Pure accident, I assure you."

"Then probe away."

"Oh, Gawd." She rolled her eyes. "More phlebotomy humor."

His gaze fell on her smiling mouth, still swollen from their kisses. Dear heaven, he wanted to kiss her again. And how stupid was that? He'd just laid out very plainly why they couldn't go there again. Her face sobered, and he realized he was frowning fiercely. He forced his brow to smooth, his jaw to relax.

"Your question?"

"Her name ... what was it?"

"You want to know her name? Ainsley, she's been dead now for decades."

"Yes, I want to know her name. You've been honoring her by telling me her story. Finish the job."

"Reina. Her name was Reina."

She took his hand. "Thank you for telling me."

"You're welcome. Are we done here?"

"Almost. Just one more question."

"Just one?"

"Okay, one more line of questioning."

"Then make it quick. I get cranky if I miss a meal."

She dropped his hand and jumped up. "Oh, shi ... shoot. I forgot. This'll wait."

"Just sit down and ask your question, Ainsley. I'm not in any danger of expiring. In fact, I can go several days without sustenance before it really starts to take a toll on anything but my disposition."

"You're sure?"

"Positive." And a damned good thing, too, since he wasn't going to be able to take blood for at least 48 hours. Ainsley presumed he could type and crossmatch his supper to avoid ABO incompatibility issues in the event the Merzetti Effect turned out to be sexually transmissible and triggered a reversal. Excellent reasoning. Except his mutation predated the pioneering work of Karl Landsteiner by almost a full century. Like all vampires, he was now effectively AB positive, the universal blood recipient, but God only knew what his original blood type was, pre-mutation.

"Ask your question."

"You got carried away with Reina because you'd been celibate too long, correct?"

"A long time, yes."

"But why? I mean, if it's as wondrous as you say — and I have no doubt it is — why would you cut yourself off from that? From what I've observed, you don't seem to have any particular hangups about sex."

Her voice grew slightly husky as she delivered that last comment, and he almost groaned. Man, he had to get through this and get her out of here before they wound up horizontal on the bed again. Or maybe in some other position ...

He cleared his throat. "I married the woman I loved, and wanted no other."

Her mouth softened. "You stayed true to her until the end?"

"Of course."

"Even though she aged while you stayed young and virile?"

"When I looked at her, I saw only the woman I married." He dropped his gaze to contemplate his left hand, which still bore the very slight indentation from the wedding band that now sat in the jewelry box on his dresser, with Gitta's. Like the length of his hair and the beard stubble on his face, it would persist, no matter what. He could take the scissors to his hair, shave his face clean, and plump that wedding band hollow with collagen, and look like a new man. For a single night. Because with one day's sleep, all would be restored to its original state.

"To the end, she was beautiful to me. I appreciate that might be hard to comprehend, in a culture bent on turning adults back into teenagers, but it's the truth."

She made a little noise, one of those "awwww" sounds that women made when they saw kittens or puppies. "Delano, that's just about the most wonderful thing I've ever heard."

Wonderful, indeed. He was now on par with a puppy.

He glared at her. "She stood by me when this affliction was foisted on me. The vampress who turned me counted on Margitta rejecting me in horror, but by some miracle she didn't. You think I'd repay that kind of loyalty with the most base of betrayals?"

"Of course not. She sounds wonderful. I'm sure I would have liked her."

She would, he realized. And Gitta would have liked Ainsley. The thought was oddly comforting.

"Yes, you would have liked her. Everyone did. She was very strong, and incredibly brave. Can you imagine what courage it took for her to confront what had happened to me? To accept me?"

"It sounds as though she helped you accept yourself."

"She saved me. Had she turned me away, I think I would have walked out into the next sunrise, to perish."

Ainsley took his hand. Oddly, he didn't feel the need to wrench it back.

"But she didn't turn me away. She sheltered me. She told the townsfolk I suffered debilitating migraines by light of day, allowing me to practice medicine under cover of night. Which in truth suited many of my patients."

"I can imagine."

"And she nourished me. Between the blood she freely gave me and the blood I collected from patients seeking venesections, I survived quite handily, without harming a soul."

"Bloodletting! I've read about it. Was it as widespread as historical accounts suggest?"

"Fortunately for me, yes. It was especially prevalent among the wealthy, who practiced it as a preventative measure. Of course, it looks barbaric in this day of molecular medicine, but at the time, it reflected medical thinking."

"So you remained faithful to her until she died?"

"And well beyond."

"And then?"

"Then I succumbed to the blood lust. When Reina sought me out ... well, you know the rest."

"Omigod!"

"What?"

"She was the first, after your wife died?"

"Yes."

"And since then?"

"Since then, I keep to myself."

She leapt up, clapping a hand to her chest to hold the knotted sheet in place. "Delano, you can't be serious!"

"I warned you I'd win the celibacy contest, hands down."

"But why? I mean, after that experience, I'm sure you would have exercised better control."

"Possibly, but I wasn't prepared to bet an innocent life on it."

"So, just now ..." Her gaze drifted to the bed. "That was the first time since Reina?"

"And it wouldn't have happened had I not been in the middle of the twilight sleep."

"Twilight sleep?"

"A transitional stage between the day sleep and full wakefulness."

"What's it like?"

"The twilight sleep?"

"The day sleep?"

"I don't know."

"How could you not know? You do it every day."

"It's like a mini-death. I just ... go away. The little I do know about it, I know from attaching electrodes to my own shaven head and recording EEGs."

She blinked. "Tell me about it."

"Not much to tell. In the first hours, the cerebrum might as well be switched off, so profound is its state of rest. But somehow, in that SWA state, all the patchwork gets done."

"SWA? As in slow wave brain activity?"

"Precisely. It's roughly comparable to your Stage 4 sleep, but we don't cycle up to REM sleep and back down again through all the stages, as you would do three or four times in the course of the night."

"What do you mean by patchwork happening? The erasure of the day's aging?"

"Exactly. But there's more. If I've cut myself, it will heal completely, leaving not the slightest trace. Hell, if I've cut my hair, it grows back. Shaved? Back comes the two-day stubble."

Her jaw dropped. "Really?"

"Really. And let me tell you, it's an eerie thing to watch at high speed on videotape."

"Then what?"

"Then nothing, for about five hours. That's how long we — or least I — stay in SWA. No dreaming, no awareness, no waking. But eventually we surface into something that approximates normal sleep, but it's not really normal since it's dominated so heavily by REM sleep. Whereas you might have three or four dreams a night, our dreams are packed into the last hour or two of sleep. At this point, we can be wakened. But as you can imagine, in a secure environment, I'm not accustomed to being roused before I waken naturally. Which is why I presumed you were just a part of my dream."

"I see. So I take it I must have been a frequent visitor in your other twilight dreams, and you just figured it was more of the same?"

"Guilty."

"Guilty?" She laughed. "Delano, that's the last thing you should feel. You hadn't had sex since when?"

He scowled. "That's hardly an excuse."

She refused to be distracted. "Since when?"

He looked at the carpet again. There was that blond hair. "1927."

"*1927?* Oh, fuck me!"

"I believe I did."

Chapter 17

DRESSED AGAIN IN her t-shirt and shorts, Ainsley stole back to her own rooms. Mercifully, she managed the quick trip without encountering Eli. She couldn't have dealt with that just yet.

She started the shower running, stripped her clothes off and tossed them in the hamper, then stepped under the hot spray.

Her body still tingled from their lovemaking. And when she closed her eyes to shampoo her hair, images rose to fill her mind. Delano's dark head at her breast. His head between her thighs, driving her wild with his lips and tongue and fingers. Delano hauling her back up the bed as easily as though she were a rag doll, and God, there was just something so hot about that! His strength, the way he'd taken charge ... He'd spread her legs, pushed into her without ceremony, driving her back up again to a third shuddering, helpless climax.

No doubt about it, she'd been well and truly ravished, unable to do much more than just hang on. Passivity was definitely not her usual style in the bedroom, but he'd taken complete control. Of course, he thought he'd been dreaming, and no doubt steered the dream accordingly.

What would it be like if they both went into it with eyes open, consciously choosing to make love?

"Stop it, Ainsley! It's never going to happen."

Concentrating on the very excellent reason why they couldn't indulge in sex again, she stuck her head under the spray and rinsed the shampoo from her hair. Briskly, she rubbed conditioner into the wet strands, resolving not to torture herself anymore.

But when she started to soap her body, more erotic thoughts crowded in. He'd said that if he took her blood, he would feel what she felt, and she would feel what he felt. If he were here right now, in the shower with her, and sank those fangs into her throat, would she be able to feel his intense arousal, amplified a hundred times by the infusion of her blood? And if he were to take the soap from her and run it over her breasts and between her thighs, would he feel the bolts of desire shoot straight to her core? And if she knelt and took his phallus into her mouth while the water beat down on them ...

"Argh!"

Rinsing quickly, she shut the shower off, toweled herself dry. Completing the rest of her toilette quickly, she dressed and prepared to go in search of coffee. A glance in the mirror assured her she looked normal. Well, almost normal. She reached for her cosmetic bag and applied some foundation to smooth out a few reddened blotches where his stubble had rasped her smooth skin. There. Much better.

Okay, coffee, breakfast — or what passed for breakfast at supper time — and more coffee. Then she'd call Lucy.

She started out the door, then stopped. Retracing her steps to the bathroom, she retrieved her t-shirt from the hamper. Pressing the soft cotton to her face, she inhaled. Yes, there it was. His scent. Before she could think too much about it, she folded the t-shirt, walked to her bed and slid it under her pillow.

There. Now breakfast.

The conversation with Lucy was every bit as hard as she knew it would be. After the initial pleasantries, she said, "Remember I told you that my new boss was old?"

"But hot, too, right?"

"Good looking, I think I said. And yes, he's very handsome. But getting back to the age thing, I don't believe I mentioned just how old he was."

"What? Did you seduce him into your bed and give him a heart attack or something?"

"Good Lord, no." Except she had crawled into his bed, and it might yet be the death of him. She crushed the thought. "But he is considerably older than I led you to believe."

"Okay, so how old are we talking?"

She drew a deep breath. "I don't know for sure, but based on what I've learned this past month, I'm thinking he's probably about 200."

Lucy laughed. "Okay, okay, I get the picture. He's too old to be fooling around with. Now can we get to the point of this discussion?"

"No, Luce, you don't understand. He really is 200 years old."

A pause. "Ainsley, that's impossible."

She closed her eyes and just said it. "He's a vampire."

"Oh, God, I knew it. When you quit the hospital and took this job, I knew something was up, but I had no idea ..."

"Lucy—"

"This is all my fault ... the pressure of supporting me and Devon. I knew you were working too hard."

"Lucy, I'm not crazy. I mean, I know this sounds crazy, and I don't blame you for thinking I've cracked up — or maybe that I'm hopped-up on crack — but I swear it's true."

"A *vampire*? A 200-year-old one? I'm supposed to just accept that?"

Ainsley gripped the receiver harder. "Hey, I was just as skeptical as you, until I found myself on the business end of a pair of fangs in an alley back in St. Cloud."

"You were attacked by a vampire? Omigod, are you all right?"

"I'm fine. That was almost a month ago."

"This vampire boss of yours ... is he the one who attacked you?"

"Oh, no! He saved me." She opted to skip the bit about his facilitating the attack. "He drove off my attacker, then provided the medical attention I needed. Otherwise, I'd have died from the blood loss."

"Ainsley, you almost *died*? And you never told me?"

She hadn't intended to tell her friend about any of this, until she'd learned about this whole Merzetti blood thing. Or rather, until Janecek learned about it, putting her friends in danger. "I'm sorry."

"I should hope so. Omigod, you almost died!"

"But I didn't, and I'm fine now. A hundred percent."

"Honestly?"

"Honestly."

"Okay. Now, explain to me what it is you do for this . . . um . . . vampire boss of yours."

"He really is a legitimate clinical researcher. His aim is to develop a vaccine to drive these predators off the streets."

"But you said he was a vampire himself . . ."

"The overwhelming majority of them are peaceable citizens, no more of a threat to the public than you or I. The rogues are a minority."

"God, Ainsley, you're talking as though they're all around us."

"They are. Remember I told you I was drawing blood samples for Delano's research? All the subjects who roll up their sleeves in our clinic are vampires. They let me take a vial of blood, and in exchange, I hand them a unit of whole blood as their reward."

"You're taking vampire blood samples?"

"Yup."

Another pause. Ainsley could practically hear her friend's thoughts.

"This isn't payback, is it? Retaliation for that April Fools joke I played on you when we were eleven?"

Ainsley grinned. "No. Although now that you mention it, I still owe you one."

"Ainsley, I think this has been the weirdest conversation we've ever had. And we've had some strange ones over the years."

"Yes, we have. But I didn't call just to share the weirdness. There's more."

"More?"

"Apparently Delano finding me was no coincidence. He's been looking for me, or someone like me, for a good part of his life."

"No way! You're together? As in engaged? Or maybe eloped already. Oh, honey, that's —"

Ack! "No! Nothing like that." Ainsley felt her face flushing. "He was looking for me, all right, but not for my gorgeous body, my keen mind or my razor-sharp wit."

"Then what did he want?"

"My blood."

"Well, you did say he was a vampire, right?"

She rolled her eyes at Lucy's hopeful tone. "Gawd, you are such a romantic."

"Which I consider a personal triumph, all things considered."

"Don't I know it." Ainsley gripped the phone tighter. "But trust me, Luce, his interest is overwhelmingly clinical. Apparently, my blood contains some anti-vampire agent that he hopes to capitalize on in developing this vaccine."

Another of those pauses. "I guess that explains a lot."

"How so?"

"When you told me you were quitting the hospital to go work for him, I wondered how he could be competitive on the salary package. I can't see your average research assistant-slash-phlebot-omist earning anywhere near as much as an experienced trauma room nurse."

Ainsley bit her lip. She hadn't told Lucy about her constructive dismissal. No point subjecting her friend to that kind of worry. "That's another thing. The man is rolling in money, Luce. He tells me they all are, the old ones who've been around a long time."

"Of course. Investments."

"Luce? There's still more I have to tell you."

"More? Do I need to pour myself a drink?"

"I'd recommend it, except I know you don't touch the stuff."

"Just hit me with it. It can't possibly give me more of a jolt than what you've told me so far."

"I gave Delano your phone number, so his people could trace you."

"You *what*?"

"I had to, Luce. You're in danger, and it's all my fault."

"You gave away my *location*? No, you gave away my location to a *vampire*."

Ainsley shut her eyes against the horrified disbelief in her friend's voice. "I had no choice. Luce, there's this other vampire, Janecek. He's a bad guy, one of those rogues I mentioned before, like the one who attacked me. The kind who believes we lesser mortals are merely prey. Somehow, he knows about me, knows about the properties in my blood. He wants to thwart Delano's research, and the surest way to do that is to eliminate me."

"Oh, Ainsley, honey, what have you gotten yourself into?"

Her throat ached. "Don't worry about me. I've got more security hovering around me than most heads of state. But I'm afraid you and Devon could be in danger, too. If this Janecek guy finds out about you, I'm afraid he might try to use you to get to me."

"Us? But how? I mean, if Weldon can't find me with all the law enforcement resources he can command, how can this other guy find me?"

"Believe me, if Weldy had pockets half as deep as these guys, he'd have found you long ago. In fact, Delano's security team had already uncovered your name through the Cayman Islands account. I just sped the process up by giving him your phone number."

"What? I thought that Cayman account was supposed to be top-secret!"

"It is."

"Someone sold my information?"

"That's about the size of it. And if Delano could find you, it stands to reason Janecek might be able to find you, too. So I thought it was best to put some security in place for you and Devon, as a preventative measure."

"I think I'm going to be sick."

Ainsley pressed a thumb and forefinger to her closed eyes. "I'm so sorry, Luce. You know I wouldn't endanger you or Devon for the world."

"Can't you tell this guy to find somebody else with this funky blood thing? It doesn't have to be you, does it?"

"That's the other bad news. Apparently, this property is con-fined to one family, the family from which I'm descended. An old Sicilian family. Unfortunately, Delano thinks I'm the last one. They died out there over a century ago, but somewhere along the line, my great-great-great — God I don't know how many greats to employ — grandmother found her way across the Atlantic and started a North American strain."

"And they're all gone but —"

"Yes, all gone. So you can see why doing a flit really isn't a possibility. They'd come after me, the good guys and the bad guys. And I have to say, after having been turned into a walking Tetra Pak by one of these predators, I think I want to stick it out. If I'm Delano's best shot at stopping these guys, I have to do it."

"Oh, Ainsley."

"Yeah, I know. Where do I *find* this trouble? Honestly, I don't even try."

"Okay, put this Delano guy on the line. I want to talk to him."

Ainsley blinked. "You want to talk to him?"

"Definitely. I love you more than anyone on this planet, with the exception of Devon, and I'm inclined to believe you because, well, you've been the sanest person in my life for almost two decades. But how do I know you're not suffering from some strange psychosis brought on by a stroke or some weird chemi-cal imbalance?"

"Point taken. Hang on, I'll call Delano. And that's Dr. Bowen to you. He can be a little stuffy at first."

She paged Delano, who was down in the lab. He came quickly enough, but when she told him the situation, he took the receiver from her as though it were the business end of a coiled cobra. Smiling, she stepped back to listen to his end of the conversation.

"Hello, Ms. Michaels. Yes, of course, Machias. Yes, this is Dr. Delano Bowen. Yes, it's true. That's also true. My birth date? That would be October 12, 1802. Where? The wolds of Lincornshire. Ah, a history major?"

He glanced at Ainsley, who smiled and shrugged.

"Of course I know what someone born in Linconshire was called. A Yellow Belly." A pause. "Yes, well I've lived on this continent almost as long as I lived in Europe. Eventually, you leave your accent behind."

To Ainsley's amazement, he'd switched to a British accent.

"Not that it ever truly leaves you. I am indeed a vampire. That's correct. In my 34th year. Your arithmetic is impeccable. Yes, I am a real doctor of medicine." He shot another look at Ainsley. "You may check with the Royal College of Physicians and Surgeons if you wish, although they'll no doubt report I'm considerably older than my appearance might suggest. Hematology. That is the gist of my work, yes. Precisely. A unique property in her blood." He turned away from her at this point. "She's well protected, and wants to make sure you are, as well. Of course. With my life. You have my solemn vow."

He turned back to Ainsley, handed her the phone and walked away.

With my life?

Blinking furiously, Ainsley pressed the receiver to her ear. "What'd I tell you?" she said. "Over 200. Can I call 'em, or what?"

"Ainsley, this is insane."

"I know."

A sigh came over the wires. "Okay, you can tell your Dr. Bowen that we'll accept his protection. If they need to get closer to do it effectively, they can make contact. I'll figure out something to tell Devon."

Relief made her giddy. "Thank you, Luce. And I'm so sorry I dragged you into this."

"Ainsley, honey, it's not your fault. If your blood really is the key, then I guess it was inevitable."

A moment later, emotional goodbyes said, Ainsley hung up the telephone. Thank God that was over. One more hurdle overcome.

So why did she feel like crying?

✳

Delano watched her replace the receiver, then sink down on the couch, her arms wrapping around herself in self-comfort.

And heaven help him, there was that pain again, the one that pierced him to his very marrow and started all that emotion bleeding out of him.

Dammit, he loved her.

He'd been denying it for weeks now, but he could deny it no longer.

Not the giddy drug of infatuation. Not the mind-blinding drive of unadulterated lust. Not the bone-deep need to possess.

It was all of those things wrapped up together, but so much more. It was simple, really. She had somehow become all that mattered.

Before he knew what he intended to do, he found himself standing before her.

"Del! I thought you went back down to the lab."

"Come here." He sat down beside her and urged her into his arms.

"Del?"

She tried to pull back, but he urged her head down to his chest.

"Hush, Ainsley. I just want to hold you a minute. Can we do that?"

Her answer was to slide her arms around him, and oh, Lord, this ache was going to kill him. "About earlier … I'm so sorry."

"It's my fault." The words were muffled against his chest. "If I hadn't crawled into your bed …"

"Then we wouldn't have made love. True. But that's not what I'm sorry about."

This time when she tried to pull back, he let her. "Then what are you sorry about?"

God, even this close to tears, her eyes were beautiful. Like amethysts. "I'm sorry I didn't appreciate it was for real. If I'd known it was real and not part of the dream state …"

"Again, my fault."

"No one's fault. You couldn't have known. But don't distract me. What I'm trying to say is that if I'd known it would be our only time, I would have done things differently."

She laughed, and he felt the vibration against his chest. "I don't know about that. Certainly, you won't get any complaints from me. It was ... amazing."

"It was sex."

"I noticed."

"It would have been different, if I'd known."

She leaned back. "Different how?"

He shrugged. "Just different. I'd have taken my time, savored it. And I'd have been less ruthlessly ..."

"Carnal?" Her lips curved in a smile. "Please don't apologize for that. If I left you thinking that I found it anything less than thrilling, then obviously I have to work on my signals."

He brushed a strand of silken hair back behind her ear, and watched as her eyes sobered. "I would have made love to you," he said.

Her swift inhalation drew his attention back to her parted lips. The need in his veins swelled again, but he clamped down on it immediately, praying that it didn't show on his face. "I'd have shown you tenderness, and I would have used all the skill and patience I possess to draw the same kind of tenderness from you. I'd have fed like a bee on the nectar of your sweet cries."

She swayed toward him. "Delano, I—"

"Hush." He pulled her against his chest again, pressing her head to his heart. "I just wanted you to know."

The sound of a key turning in the lock had them springing apart like guilty children.

Delano stood. "That will be Eli."

"Oh, good." She came to her feet. "I don't believe I've thanked him properly for that carriage ride."

Poor Eli. "Take it easy on the guy, would you? Remember, we need him."

"Yeah, yeah. And he was just following orders. I got that."

"In here, Eli," he called, knowing Eli would head straight for the lab.

Eli changed his course and came into the living room. "Delano? Is something wrong?" Eli's gaze strayed to Ainsley's face, then back to meet Delano's eyes again. "I thought you'd be downstairs, hard at work."

"We've just been talking to Ainsley's friend Lucy Michaels. It took some convincing, but she's agreed to accept our security. She's even offered to meet with your people, if that will make it easier."

"Excellent. I've got some local talent on her right now, but I'd like to send two of our own guys, a mixed team, to oversee things."

"Do it."

"A mixed team?" said Ainsley.

Eli answered. "A regular for daytime service and a vamp for nighttime."

"What about the clinic?"

"I put the word out."

Ainsley eyes flew to Delano's. "What's going on with the clinic?"

"We're suspending it for now. No sense making ourselves an easy target."

"Janecek knows where it is?"

"I expect that's how he found us."

She blinked. "You think he followed us here from the clinic?"

"No. Eli says you weren't tailed, and I have absolute faith in his judgment. But the mere fact of the clinic's activity would have confirmed our presence here in the city. After that, Janecek was bound to find this place sooner or later. Which is why you're moving out tonight."

"Moving out? But I thought it was safe here. I mean, you said the security —"

"With the addition of the vampire eyes for the nightshift, I would say our security is just about as good as we can make it," he agreed. "Damn near unbreachable. But Janecek knows beyond a shadow of a doubt that you're here. Why stay when I can lay on just as much security someplace else, while regaining the advantage of a secret location?"

"We're making the move tonight?"

"Yes, tonight. I charged Eli with the task of finding you a safe house, and since he's back, I am assuming he was successful."

"I was," Eli confirmed.

Her eyes narrowed. "Wait a minute ... I don't like this language. *I'm* moving out? You found a safe house for *me*? Aren't you coming, too? I mean, if it's not safe for me, it's not safe for you."

He shrugged. "My lab is here. I can hardly move all this equipment without Janecek noticing."

"But you have other labs, don't you? I'm sure you mentioned others in the west. Since the clinic has to be shut down anyway, why don't we just fall back to one of them?"

"The lab in Vancouver has been trashed."

"Trashed?"

"The equipment was destroyed. There's nothing left that's of any use to me. And the one in Calgary remains intact, but we're not sure if it's still undetected. We've put it under surveillance to see if his operatives show up there."

"No."

He frowned. "What do you mean, no?"

"I won't go without you."

His gut twisted. "But you must. If anything happens to you, then this is all for naught. You're the key, Ainsley."

"And you're the only one who can use that key, Delano. As I think you once told me, you're literally alone in your field. Who could take up your research? Or even if they could, who would?"

"You're suggesting there are safer things to investigate."

Her eyes blazed. "Yeah, like Ebola. Come on, Delano, this guy isn't going to quit until he sees you dead."

"Or until we see him dead," interjected Eli. "We're not without our own resources in this war. But in the meantime, Delano's right, Ainsley. We have to stash you someplace safe."

Ainsley rounded on Eli fiercely, and Delano braced, knowing what was coming.

"And Delano is always right, is that what you're saying?"

Eli being Eli, he didn't take a step backward at her tone, but he did shoot Delano a quick look before turning back to face her.

"I'm not sure about that, but he *is* always the boss."

"Was he *right* when he asked you to pay attention to me? To flirt with me? Was he *right* when he asked you to do that, Eli?"

He turned to Delano accusingly. "You *told* her?"

"I did no such thing. She figured it out."

"Wonderful." Eli lifted a hand to rub his temple. "I don't want to know the circumstances under which that happened, do I?"

"Good call."

"Then I take it she knows why we felt that course of action was necessary?"

"Correct again."

"Hey! Don't stand there talking about me as though I'm not here." If anything, she sounded more furious than before.

They both muttered an apology at the same time, but she looked anything but impressed. Hands on hips, she turned on Eli again.

"So, how far would you have gone to oblige the boss, hmm? What if I'd decided to take you up on those bedroom eyes, that aw-shucks-ma'am, Matthew-McConaughey grin and all those muscles on your muscles? Huh? What then? Would you have obliged? Would you have let me drag you into my bedroom? Would you have sacrificed your body to the greater good of Delano's master plan?"

"Whoa right there, babe. First of all, it wouldn't have come to that. You might have salved your pride and amused yourself by flirting with me, but we both know it wouldn't have gone further than that. And secondly, even if it did, how in God's name can you imagine I'd qualify that as a sacrifice?"

"But —"

"Silence!" Delano roared.

Ainsley and Eli broke off, turning surprised eyes on him.

"It was a very poor idea, okay? *My* poor idea, so if you want to take your anger out on someone, Ainsley, take it out on me.

Later. Right now, I don't want to hear any more about it. Not one damned word. Are we clear?"

"Perfectly," said Ainsley.

Except she was far from clear, because right now he looked like he could kill. Literally. Over the weeks, she'd grown used to his darkly ominous looks. So much so that she'd all but forgotten just how dangerous he could be. No one looking at his face at this moment could mistake either his power or his capacity for violence.

Dear God, could he be jealous? A thrill forked through her at the thought, followed quickly by dismay at her own reaction. Jealous men were dangerous men.

"Eli? Are we clear?" Delano's voice was as flat and hard as the planes of his face.

"Clear."

"Excellent. Now, this safe house you spoke of ..."

"I'm not going anywhere without you."

Delano pinned her with blazing eyes, and her mouth went dry. It was almost enough to make her reconsider her stance. Almost.

"I'm part of this now, whether you like it or not. Hell, whether *I* like it or not. And I'm not going anywhere. The sooner you get that through your head, the sooner we can start making a plan —"

"Eli, would you leave us for a moment?"

Eli shot Ainsley a look.

"Now, Eli. This is not a democracy."

Delano's tone made her gut tighten, but she smiled for Eli. "It's okay."

Eli searched her face briefly, as though to gauge whether her reassurance was genuine. "Of course. I have some calls to make anyway, to get the Mexico team off."

The door barely closed behind him before Delano pounced.

"You can't stay here, Ainsley. When Eli comes back, he's going to take you to the new location."

She squared her chin. "I don't think so."

"For pity's sake, I'm only trying to preserve your safety." His face darkened. "Why do you persist in resisting my efforts?"

"I've already told you. I'm just one piece of the solution. I accept that my blood is key to your vaccine, but if anything happened to you ... Without you, without your knowledge, my blood is ... well, just blood."

"Devil take it, Ainsley, I can't leave my lab. I'm so close." He thrust a hand savagely through his hair. "I can't leave."

"And I *won't* leave."

"But I don't know if I can keep you safe!"

Anguish, she realized with a start. Not anger. Not fury at her defiance.

"Del, do you really think I'll be safe if he destroys you while I'm tucked away in a safe house? Don't you think he'll eventually hunt me down and kill me, too? Think about it — you and Eli obviously believe he can find Lucy, even after all the care we took to cover her tracks. If he can do that, then I haven't a hope in hell of eluding him on my own."

"You won't be alone," he countered. "I'll send Eli with you. With his help, you can stay two steps ahead of Janecek."

"You need Eli here."

He swung away from her, cursing. "Why are you being so bloody stubborn about this?"

She chewed her lip. "You really want to know the truth?"

"Yes." He strode back to stand before her, not stopping until he was well within her personal space, his gaze locked with hers. "Yes, by God, I want the truth."

A moment ago, she might have stepped back from all that leashed violence, but not now. She felt the heat pouring off his body, and it was all she could do not to touch him.

"I don't think I *can* leave."

Chapter 18

"OF COURSE YOU can leave."

She wet her lips. "Not unless you knock me out with mega-doses of sedative. When you mentioned the idea earlier, I thought I would vomit. I mean, I was literally, physically nauseous."

"What?"

"I know, it sounds stupid. I can't believe it myself, but I just have to think about leaving, and suddenly there's this big wall of … I don't know … panic in my mind that won't let me even consider it. Truly, I'm not phobic. You know that, right?" She bit the inside of her lip. "Of course you do. You investigated me. But I swear to you, I just can't stand to think about it."

"You needn't be afraid, Ainsley. I'm sure Eli has a plan for your safe transport. No doubt he'll send out a decoy or two first. And all our cars are armored. There's no way —"

Argh! "You're not getting it! I'm not afraid of leaving *here*. I'm afraid of leaving *you*. If you'd come with me, I'd leave this place right now. "

He took a step back. "No."

She laughed. "Told you it would sound idiotic. I'm still pissed with you, for one thing, over that Eli-as-escort thing, not to mention —"

"Give me your hand."

"What?" She'd heard him, but his words didn't instantly compute, perhaps because he'd closed the distance between them again and was now towering over her.

"Your hand, dammit." Without waiting for her compliance, he seized her hand and pushed the sleeve of her shirt roughly up her arm until it bunched above her elbow.

"Del, what are you doing?"

He rotated her arm to expose the delicate white skin at the crook of her elbow. With a hiss of indrawn breath, he released her and stepped back. "Impossible."

She held her arm up to inspect it herself, seeing nothing but three raised reddish dots, aligned in a perfect equilateral triangle. They could be heat rash bumps, but for the fact there were so few of them, and the symmetry was unlikely.

"What?" She looked up to see Delano regarding her with an unreadable expression. She tried reaching out to catch his thoughts as she was sometimes able to do, but his mind was closed. Anxiety beat in her breast like the wings of a frantic bird. "What is it? What's wrong?"

"That mark on your arm ..."

"Omigod, I'm infected."

"No, nothing like that."

"You're sure?"

"I'm sure."

"Then what it is? What does it mean?"

He lifted a hand to rub the back of his neck. "You appear to be blood-bonded. To me. But it can't be."

"Blood-bonded?"

"Enthralled, if you prefer to use a Hollywood term. A condition characterized by a profound infatuation, coupled with an intractable reluctance to be parted from the object of your infatuation."

Oh no oh no oh no. "You *enthralled* me? It wasn't enough that you dragged me into this mess, you had to go and do a number on my head, too?"

His dark brows beetled in a fierce frown. "I did no such thing."

"But you said —"

"I also said it was impossible," he interjected. "There must be some other explanation. For one thing, blood-bonding can happen only between vampires. If, in fact, the phenomenon really exists. I'm not entirely convinced it does."

Infatuation between vampires? "I thought you said vampires didn't desire other vampires?"

"Vampire couplings are rare," he confirmed, "but they do occasionally happen. The exception that proves the rule, I suppose. And rarer still is the vampire union that gives rise to a blood-bond. In fact, I have seen only one such instance in all my years. Or I should say, possible instance. I wasn't in a position to subject it to scientific scrutiny. But as I said, it just doesn't happen between vampires and unmutated humans, no matter how much blood is taken."

"Thank God." The bird thrashing in her chest subsided to a mere fluttering. If it was strictly a vamp-on-vamp thing, there had to be another explanation. "I thought the whole enthralling thing was a feeding strategy. You know, so vamps could compel donors to bare their throats."

He snorted. "Another product of Hollywood. Which is not to say vampires don't have an impressive arsenal of tools to gain a potential donor's compliance. But like the glamour we use to obscure our — how shall I say? — *vitality*, seduction requires a certain willingness on the part of the subject to be seduced. Any human with a strong will and a dash of charisma can learn the skill, if they're taught how to focus their ..."

"Yeah, yeah, I get it. But why am I feeling like this if it's so freaking impossible?" She thrust her arm at him. "And why do I have these damned dots?"

"I don't know."

"Then speculate."

He sighed. "It could be psychosomatic."

She shook her head emphatically. "Un-uh."

"Don't be so quick to dismiss the idea. I'm not suggesting you're neurotic by any stretch of the imagination. But think about it, Ainsley. You've been under a degree of stress no one should have to endure, not to mention —"

"Not to mention the series of psychic shocks I've been subjected to. Yada, yada, yada. I won't argue that. And for the record, I'm as neurotic as the next woman. But answer me this — how can I possibly manifest weird symptoms I've never even heard of? Huh?"

Something flickered in his eyes, so quick she couldn't read the expression.

"Perhaps you plucked the details from my mind."

"No."

"No?" He lifted an eyebrow. "It hasn't escaped my notice over these past weeks that you have a certain talent for divining what's in my thoughts."

She rolled her eyes. "That's because all men think about that, all the time."

To her satisfaction, he blushed.

"I was referring to other situations."

"I know." It was her turn to sigh. "Unfortunately, it's a pitifully weak and sporadic talent. I can only catch fragments, and only when you let me. In fact, it's probably your doing, not mine. I'm probably just catching what you're projecting." As soon as she said it, she realized that was by far the likeliest scenario. Hadn't he said any strong mind could be trained to project suggestions? The idea was oddly deflating. "Which begs the question: have you recently thought about the vamp-on-vamp blood-bond and its triangle-producing side effects?"

"Not that I am aware of."

"Then I guess we can eliminate any possible psychic plundering on my part."

"Not necessarily."

His brows drew together again in that frown that made him look so fiercely intent. And sexy, dammit. It was all she could do not to put a hand to his forehead to smooth that crease away. A sweet ache filled her heart at the idea of soothing away his cares.

She blinked the image away. "What do you mean?"

"I can't guard my dreams. Nor can I necessarily remember them."

Oh, shit. "And I crawled into your bed and possibly into your head, even though I was sleeping myself?"

"It seems the most likely explanation available to us."

He was right. Dammit, why hadn't the possibility occurred to her? "Ah, I see we subscribe to Charles Peirce's theory of abduction."

If he detected her sarcasm, he must have recognized it for the defensive mechanism it was.

He smiled. "I would not be much of a scientist if I did not reason to the best explanation, would I?"

"So this isn't real? It's just something I plucked from your head while we were sleeping?"

His lips firmed into a straight line. "It has to be. We exchanged no blood, and you are not a vampire."

Dear God, she wanted to disappear into a crack in the floor. She'd stripped the symptoms of blood-bonding from his mind, then recreated them. How pathetic was that? Was she that far gone on him?

Yes. God help her, *yes.*

She'd been deeply attracted to him from first sight — okay, second sight, since he was just a blur in the alley on first sight. And her reliance on him had naturally grown after having been stranded in his alien world. And it was more than just reliance that had grown in the last weeks. Somehow, he'd slid right in under her radar, old world values and all.

But, dammit, he clearly did not return the sentiment. She'd joked about not needing to read his mind because all men shared the same thoughts, but hadn't she read those very thoughts in his mind? Pure, simple, sexual lust, coupled with a blood lust.

She drew a deep breath, expelled it. Inhaled again. God, give me strength.

"Okay, then I change my mind. I'll go to this safe house Eli found for me. And I want to go as soon as possible."

Delano stood abruptly, sending his chair rocketing across the room. He should be starting the delicate task of inserting the Merzetti Effect gene — or what he was 85 percent sure was the ME gene — into the plasmids, where they would multiply happily. But dammit all to hell, he couldn't do it. His hands shook, his palms were damp, and his mind refused to focus.

It was the thirst, of course. How could he be expected to concentrate when the need to feed swelled relentlessly every hour? It had been years — decades, probably — since he'd gone more than a day without at least a modest infusion. He just wasn't used to this kind of deprivation.

Yeah, right, that was it. It had absolutely nothing to do with the fact that upstairs, Ainsley was preparing to take her leave.

Leaving him, dammit!

No, leaving *here*, not leaving *him*.

With Eli.

Per my orders. So Eli could keep her safe.

Eli with the aw-shucks-Matthew-McConaughey smile, whatever the hell that was.

His right hand tightened around the positive displacement pipette he held until the instrument snapped. He opened his fist to see the microsyringe tip had embedded itself in his palm. Cursing, he strode to a nearby sink. Dropping the ruined pipette on the counter, he removed the micro tip from his flesh, hit the taps and shoved his hand under the flowing water.

Idiot.

He peeled off the latex glove and let the water flow over his bare hand. Good thing he'd conceded he was too distracted tonight to do the transfer as he'd planned, or he'd have a serious needlestick incident to worry about. Belatedly, he noticed the slight pink tinge to the water circling the drain, and cursed again. That's all he needed, to lose even a few drops of blood while he was forced to fast.

Shutting off the tap with his elbow, he grabbed a clean towel and wrapped it around his hand.

Please!

Delano's head jerked up, nostrils flaring.

Ainsley!

His gaze swept the room, even as he realized she couldn't possibly have gotten into the lab without his knowing. No, she was upstairs still, in the foyer. Poised to leave, not wanting to go ...

He leapt across the room and hit the intercom. "Eli, wait! Don't leave yet. I'm coming up."

Without waiting for an acknowledgement, he raced for the stairwell. Seconds later, he burst into the penthouse, his fingers automatically keying in the sequence to prevent the alarm from sounding.

"Delano?" called Eli from the foyer.

Christ, they were almost out the door.

Rage, hot and unreasoning, flooded his brain, his chest, his muscles. Moving at a speed he knew they would perceive as only a blur, he crossed the intervening space and snatched Ainsley's bag from Eli's shoulder.

Eli reacted instinctively, shoving Ainsley behind him and drawing his pistol in one smooth motion.

Delano found himself looking down the barrel of a SIG .40 caliber automatic, but he turned away from it to search Ainsley's face. Her eyes, a blaze of violet-blue emotion, locked on his.

Yes!

The lone word sounded in his mind, as strong and as heartfelt as her earlier plea.

"Dammit, Delano, you almost gave me a heart attack."

Delano was vaguely aware of Eli reholstering his pistol. "She's not going anywhere."

"You're kidding, right?" Eli looked from Delano to Ainsley and back to Delano again. "Delano, we agreed the safe house was the best course of action."

Delano's anger took another bump. Hands fisted, he fought to keep his breathing regular, to expel the rage eating at his self-control. This was *Eli*, for God's sake. His friend. A friend who was merely trying to carry out the orders he'd been given.

Breathe deep, let it out. Again. Air in, murderous impulse out. When he'd mastered himself, he announced, "She stays with me."

"Oh, for the love of Pete!" Eli exclaimed. "Can no one around here stick to a simple plan? *Your* plan, I might remind you. This is the only way we can be certain she'll be safe." Eli grasped Ainsley's elbow, maneuvering her toward the door again.

At the sight of Eli's hand on Ainsley, Delano's tenuous grip on control snapped. With a snarl, he lunged for Eli, pinning the other man against the wall with one hand around his throat.

"Del!" Ainsley cried.

Eli's hands came up to grip Delano's hand, trying to pry open his grip. "Get ... the hell ... off me!"

"Nobody touches her." Delano tightened his grip remorselessly. "Nobody takes her from me."

Eli's face was red now, his eyes starting to distend. He beat at Delano's arm and head with savage blows, but Delano was beyond feeling it. What he did feel was the bone-deep, total-body need to feed, together with a powerful need to punish. The combination was dizzying. Growling, he dropped his jaw and let his canines erupt.

"Stop it! My God, you're killing him! Delano, let him go!"

Through a haze of blood-lust, he felt Ainsley tugging at his arm and heard her agonized pleas. And he heard something else in her voice. *Unadulterated horror.*

Suddenly, he saw what he was doing. He held Eli suspended a good four inches off the ground, and his friend's struggles were weakening by the second. And oh, shit, Eli'd been beating him with the butt of his gun. A gun he could have used very effectively in his own defense.

Jesus, God, what had he done?

"Shit." He eased Eli down until his feet met the floor again, taking the gun from his now lax grip. "I'm sorry. Eli, I'm so sorry."

Eli started to fall forward. Delano would have caught him, but Ainsley stepped between them, catching Eli and easing him to the tiled floor.

"God, you've crushed his airway!"

Delano bent to help her stretch a coughing Eli on the floor. Thankfully, he was regaining his color quickly. "His airway's fine," he said gruffly. Which it probably was, give or take some potential cartilage fracture.

Ainsley fingers flew down the shirt she was wearing. Without a thought for modesty, she peeled it off, rolled it into a tube and slid it under Eli's neck, her attention focused completely on her patient. "Eli? Can you hear me? Are you all right?"

Eli responded with a cough, followed by a string of pungent curses that bore testimony to his soldiering days.

"Well, that's reassuring," she said. "No stridor, no muffled voice."

Delano frowned, thinking about other potential injuries. "The vascular structures are more vulnerable than the airway with this type of manual strangulation."

"Yeah?" Eli coughed again. "Coulda fooled my airway a minute ago. Now help me up."

Delano helped Ainsley ease Eli up to a sitting position, braced against the wall.

"I am so sorry, my friend." Delano handed Eli's pistol back to him. "I don't know what to say, except that you should have used that weapon the way it was intended. You'd have been completely justified."

"Damn right I should have." Eli wiped the gun on his pants before slipping it back into its shoulder holster. "On the other hand, looks like I did a pretty good job with the butt end." He gestured to the left side of Delano's head. "You oughta get a look at yourself."

Delano lifted a hand to probe his scalp. It came away covered in blood from several lacerations. Shit. More blood loss. Well, he had no one to blame but himself.

He grimaced. "Fortunately, I'll be handsome as ever come tomorrow night, whereas you will no doubt have some colorful bruises."

"That sucks. I won't even be able to say, 'You should see the other guy.' "

Delano laughed and Eli joined in.

Ainsley made an exasperated sound. "It's not funny, Eli Grayson." She turned to glare at Delano. "Nor will it be funny if he develops delayed airway troubles later tonight."

Delano sobered. "She's right. We need to get you to hospital for some soft tissue scans."

Eli waved him off. "I'm fine."

"You're *asymptomatic*," Ainsley corrected. "That could change in the next hours."

"And if it does, trust me, I'll call 911 myself. But until and unless my status changes, I have no intention of visiting the ER."

Ainsley turned to Delano. "Delano?"

He shrugged. "He's a nurse. It's his call."

"Thanks, buddy." Eli extended a hand, which Delano grasped to haul him up to his feet. "Now, if it's not too much to ask, would you mind explaining what the hell happened here? I thought we were agreed it was best for everyone if Ainsley went to the safe house."

Delano sighed heavily. "We did."

"Then what happened? What changed?"

Delano rolled back his sleeve and thrust his arm toward them. "This."

Ainsley's heart slammed in her chest, but it wasn't fear that made her pulse hammer. It was exultation, so fierce that it stopped the breath in her lungs; a dark, savage delight flooding her neurochemical system. For there, on the inside of his elbow, were three raised dots in the form of a perfect equilateral triangle.

Yes, came Delano's voice. *You are mine and I am yours.*

Her eyes widened as she realized his lips had not moved.

"A little uticaria?" Beside her, Eli snorted, although the effect was somewhat spoiled when his snort turned into a cough. "That's supposed to flip some switch in my head to make this whole soap opera comprehensible?"

"Show him your arm, Ainsley."

Ainsley, who still had not recovered her shirt, extended her own left arm.

Eli caught her arm and examined the dots. "Well, I'll be damned. Matching his-'n-hers hives." He released her arm. "I presume this is something more than a curiosity for the medical journals?"

She glanced at Delano, who bent to scoop her shirt off the floor. He shook it out and handed it to her, catching her eye as she took the garment from him.

Let me field this.

There it was again! Not precisely a voice sounding inside her head. More like her own thoughts, only not hers. *His.* In *her* head.

Delano turned back to Eli. "We are blood-bonded."

"Blood-bonded? Holy hell, Del, do you mean to say you —"

"No." Delano held up a hand to stop Eli. "I'll grant you that after that appalling display just now, you have every reason to think me mad, but I assure you I am not. I took no blood."

"Then how the devil did you get blood-bonded?"

"It's a mystery to me. I wasn't even sure I believed in blood-bonding, to begin with. I thought it merely another of the myths that have grown up around my kind, like warding off vampires with garlic, holy water or crucifixes, or vampires casting no reflection in a mirror."

"But you believe it now?"

He inclined his head. "I am obliged to re-evaluate my position."

"But still, I don't get how you wind up with a blood-bond without the blood-taking part. Unless —" Eli's gaze strayed to Ainsley.

Blushing fiercely, Ainsley busied herself putting her shirt back on.

"Indeed," Delano said.

"I see."

She felt her blush rise all the way to her hairline, which was patently stupid. They were all adults here.

"But even so," Delano continued, "it should have been quite impossible. Ostensibly, a blood-bond is possible only between vampires."

"I don't know." Eli's eyes narrowed. "When you think about it, maybe the two of you aren't really all that different. Maybe it's a two-sides-of-the-same-coin sorta thing."

Ainsley's gaze collided with Delano's and her fingers stilled on the buttons of her shirt. "Or two sides of the same mutation."

"Exactly." Eli massaged his neck. "Now, can someone tell me what this means?"

Ainsley returned her attention to fastening the last two buttons, but her mind strained toward Delano, waiting for his answer.

"It is purported to be a rare union between vampires, a union involving a bonding of the two on a physical, mental and spiritual planes."

"Hence the triangle?"

"Supposedly."

"The triumvirate." Eli grimaced. "Sounds a lot like marriage to me."

"Except I would challenge you to show me a marriage where one partner can't let the other walk out the door," Delano rasped.

Ainsley glanced at Delano again to see that his expression matched the tone of his voice — grim. Her heart squeezed painfully in her chest. He resented being bonded to her. He didn't want this link. *Oh, Ainsley, what have you done?*

You didn't trap me, little one. I'm just angry with myself that I lack the strength to put you away from me, even for your own protection.

I need no protection but yours. I want nothing but to guard your back as you guard mine.

"Can it be undone?"

Delano blinked at Eli. "Sorry?"

"Can the blood-bond be undone?" Eli repeated.

Ainsley caught the slight lift of an eyebrow, which for Del bespoke profound surprise.

"I really don't know. In all my years, I've encountered only one couple who were purported to be blood-bonded, and I lost track of them long ago."

Ainsley wet her lips. "What does legend say on the subject?"

Something flashed deep in his eyes, but he quickly lowered his lids. She reached out to his mind to try to catch the thought, but he'd veiled it as thoroughly as he'd veiled his eyes. When he lifted his lids again a second later, his expression was matter-of-fact, his thoughts unreadable.

"According to the legends, it's forever. The blood-bonded stay together as long as they live, which as you will appreciate can be a very long time. And when one of the partners dies, the other is said to follow."

"Like old married folk, you mean?" Eli coughed again, a reminder of the recent trauma to his throat. "You see it all the time. One goes and the other declines rapidly over the next months or years."

"This is more like the next day. Specifically, the next morning."

"Omigod!" Ainsley clapped a hand over her mouth.

Eli looked from one to the other of them. "Omigod what?"

"The sun," she said from behind her fingers.

"It's only legend," Delano said softly.

Stifling a cry, she spun and raced from the room.

Chapter 19

"WHAT WAS THAT about?"

Delano shot Eli an exasperated look. "For a man of above-average intelligence, you can certainly ask some asinine questions."

"Oh, shit. Of course. She has the life expectancy of a fruit fly, compared to yours, which makes her a bad bet for this blood-bond thingy."

"Eloquently put."

"Okay, how 'bout this for eloquent: if legend proves true, then we can hypothesize that your own life expectancy will be severely truncated."

"Much better."

"Thank you. Now what the hell are we gonna do about this?"

"We're not going to *do* anything about it. Ainsley will obviously stay here. I will continue to work on a vaccine. You will continue to keep us safe."

Eli snapped his fingers as though remembering something important. "Wait here. I'll be right back."

Before he could protest, Eli was gone, returning a moment later with a small paper bag bearing a local drug store's logo. "Here."

Delano took the proffered bag and peered into it, though he hardly needed to. The odor of latex was clearly discernable to his sensitive olfactory system. "Condoms?"

"Hey, you said it yourself — my responsibility is to keep both of you safe. I'm just trying to do my job. Now, if we're through here, I have a team to transport to Cuernavaca."

"That's a very thoughtful gesture, Eli, but I won't be needing them." He held the bag out for Eli to take back, but the other man ignored it.

"You know, for a man of above-average intelligence, you sure can say some asinine things."

✳

Ainsley sat up in bed before the knock sounded on her door, swiping at her cheeks. "Go away, Del. I'm tired."

The door opened. He stepped across the threshold, closing the door behind him. "I'm sorry, I can't oblige. We need to talk."

Why? She lifted her chin. *Why not just do this?*

"Because it takes a lot more energy to project a thought than it does to just say it, especially when you're just learning." He crossed the carpeted floor to stand by her bed. "Although I must say, you demonstrate an extraordinary raw talent for it, both projecting and receiving."

"That's me. A veritable walking transistor."

He sighed. "We could talk about why that analogy is woefully inadequate, or we could talk about us."

She laughed. "Oh, that's rich. *You* wanting to talk about *us*. Or about anything personal, for that matter."

"I'd say touché, but then you'd accuse me of being stuck in a seventies romance novel or something."

"Which seventies?"

"Good one."

She lifted both hands and raked them through her hair. "I'm sorry. I'm being a bitch."

"Which still leaves you miles ahead of me." His eyes grew bleak. "I behaved like an animal out there. Like the very creatures I've been working so hard to curb."

She shook her head emphatically. "Never that. But you did scare me."

"Not nearly as much as I scared myself."

He turned to examine the top of her night table, and she wondered what he'd make of the loose change, well-thumbed paperback and Hershey's chocolate sitting there, within easy reach.

"Eli is the closest thing to a brother I've ever had."

Ainsley made no reply.

He picked up the paperback and turned it over to examine its back, but she had the distinct impression he wasn't really seeing it.

"He's tough as boot leather, as talented at taking life as he is at saving it." Delano replaced the book on her night table and turned to face her again. "He's been my closest friend in over a century, and I love him dearly. But I almost killed him tonight. If you hadn't been there, if you hadn't intervened ..."

"Delano, if I hadn't been there, it wouldn't have happened in the first place."

He lifted an eyebrow. "True."

"Oh, Del, what are we going to do? Is this real? Or could it be as you suggested, a psychosomatic thing?"

"Push over."

It took her a moment to process that he wanted to sit on the edge of the bed. She scrambled back, making a space for him.

He sat, angling his body toward her where she sat propped against the headboard with her knees drawn up to her chin. "To answer your question, no."

She dragged her gaze from his thighs, encased as always in those civilized worsted wool trousers that utterly failed to disguise the powerful musculature beneath, and wondered what her question had been. "No?"

"I'm not suggestible."

Ah, the psychosomatic thing. "Well, aren't we feeling superior."

He sent her an admonishing look.

"Sorry." She grimaced. "There's that bitchy thing again."

"I'm not saying my mind — *the vampire mind* — is stronger than yours, or better, it's just ... differently organized. The interaction of mind, brain, body and social context, while still present, is not precisely the same. In a stressful situation, for instance, we do not produce cortisol to the same extent as would an unmutated —"

"You can skip the vamp biology lesson for now," she interjected. "I believe you."

"Good."

She worried the cuticle of her thumb with her teeth for a moment. "So this can't be in our heads?"

"It seems doubtful." He dropped his gaze to her mouth.

Whoops. She dropped her hand to her lap again, feeling as self-conscious as a kid. "Then I guess we'd better figure out how to undo it, huh?"

A pause.

"Did I say I wanted to undo it?"

Her pulse leapt, as much from the husky note in his voice as from the content of his words. "But it's tantamount to a death sentence for you!"

His lips curved in a wry smile. "Maybe I wasn't clear. If the legend is true, the same applies for you. If I should die, you may very well be driven to seek your own end. Though obviously not by sunlight."

"But compared to you, I'm so ... fragile." She twisted her hands together in her lap. "I'm subject to illness, disease, decrepitude, death. These things don't even have to enter your vocabulary."

He took her hand in his, the same one she'd gnawed on a moment ago. "You think your mortality frightens me?"

"I'll grow old! Wrinkles and gravity and post-menopausal weight gain—"

"Ah, yes. The aging process. Ainsley, have you forgotten that I've been there before? I cherished every minute of every day I had with Margitta, and she was never anything but beautiful to me. Never. I can assure you that the prospect of your aging holds no terrors for me."

"But it does for me!" she wailed.

He turned her hand over and stroked the incredibly sensitive flesh of her palm, the pad of his finger moving in a slow, seductive circular motion. "Then I shall have to do as I did for Gitta, proving every day how lovely she was in my eyes."

Ainsley's breath caught, partly at the sensations he was arousing from the brush of his fingers against her palm, but mostly at the idea of his making love to her like that, as though she were the most beautiful woman in the world. It took an effort of will to force her mind back to what she wanted to say.

"In your wife's case, I have no doubt that you succeeded. One look at that photo you keep in your bedroom and anyone would know she felt beautiful."

He'd adjusted his grip on her hand and his caress moved to the inside of her wrist. Her pulse, already hammering frantically, kicked up a gear. God, he must be able to feel it. Hell, he could probably hear it.

Concentrate, Ainsley.

"But if that relationship was so wonderful, why have you been alone so long?"

His fingers stilled. "I believe I related the experience with Reina, did I not?"

She pulled her hand away from his clasp. "I'm not buying it."

His eyebrows soared. "You doubt my veracity?"

"Of course not. I don't doubt your story for a moment. But clearly it was the result of an unfortunate set of circumstances. A long period of celibacy after your wife's death, followed by a purely carnal encounter with a vampire groupie."

"Ainsley ..."

"Okay, okay." She held up a defensive hand. "Negative characterization withdrawn. But the fact remains that you didn't love Reina and she didn't love you. You obviously had no such control problems with your wife."

"Perhaps it had something to do with the fact I was enjoying regular conjugal relations with my wife?" he suggested dryly.

"What about us? You were able to stop with me," she pointed out. "And your period of celibacy was much longer this time, correct?"

A muscle in his jaw leapt. "Correct."

Her triumph at scoring the point sputtered, as the obvious occurred to her. "Unless —"

"Unless what?"

Oh, Lord, how pitiful was she? Ainsley lifted one shoulder in a stiff shrug. "Nothing."

He laughed softly, knowingly.

No fair! Her chin came up. "Dammit, Delano, I thought we were going to stay out of each other's heads."

He lifted a hand to cup her cheek. "I can state unequivocally that I did not find Reina remotely *hotter* than you, to use your own vernacular."

She gritted her teeth. "Well, here's some more vernacular for you. *Screw you, Delano.* I don't care what you find hot. Or who you find hot."

"No?"

His gaze swept her face, dropped to the curve of her breasts, to her hands clasped so primly on her knees. His gaze traveled back up to meet hers. Without warning, his mind brushed hers in a sensual caress a hundred times more seductive than the one his fingers had bestowed on her palm.

Oh, help! He was right there. His mind was right there, barriers completely down. She shuddered.

"Don't be frightened," he coaxed. "Come in and see for yourself how much I want you."

Tentatively, she ventured further, instantly encountering a vast need, powerful and unquenchable. Moaning, she let it wrap around her, felt her womb clench and her nipples go tight with it. Heart pounding, she pushed deeper, then deeper still. And dear God, there was no end of it! A sixth ocean, unfathomable, endless.

A hundred images washed through her mind, pictures of the two of them, limbs tangling, bodies joining in every way imaginable, and some she had never imagined.

"Delano!"

He laughed. "Need I point out that not all those erotic pictures were mine?"

"Well, it's not hard to isolate the ones that weren't mine!"

He picked up her hand again, brushing her knuckles with his thumb. "And did they offend you?"

She let her breath out on a groan. "You know they didn't."

He smiled.

How do we do this, Del? How can I be in your mind and you in mine?

The blood-bond. While non-vampires can develop this talent to some extent, it takes a lifetime of dedication and discipline. You don't just develop it overnight, as you appear to have done.

Ainsley turned her hand within his grasp so she could caress his palm, and was rewarded with a fresh blaze of desire straight from his mind to hers. She closed her eyes against the intensity of it, and when she opened them again, he was watching her face with a thrilling, dark hunger.

She swallowed. "Earlier, in your bed, after we ... Well, you told me that if you were to take my blood and we were to make love again, I would feel what you felt and you would feel what I felt."

His soft chuckle fanned her face. "It would seem we arrived there by another route."

"This is the oneness of mind you share with non-vampires?"

Only fleetingly. Only while we are physically joined in the sex act. He tipped her chin up with a forefinger under her chin. *This ... this, my love, is unique.*

He bent and caught her lips with his.

With no thought except getting closer, she clasped a hand behind his head and returned his kiss, even as she climbed onto him. Straddling his lap, she slid her free hand under his lab coat to touch him through the Oxford cloth shirt he wore.

And oh, mercy, this desire ... so sweet, she could die of it. It filled her, flooded every nerve ending, burst forth from her pores, spilled from her mind. Urgent, aching, and incredibly sweet.

"Yes, my love." His lips left hers and his hand urged her chin up. Without hesitation, she bared her throat for the hot exploration of his mouth.

Oh, Jesus, I want your teeth right there. I want to feel the burning pierce of them.

His own excitement leapt fiercely, but she felt him force it down with ruthless control. *We can't.*

"I know." She clutched his shoulders, trembling violently, trying to master her own clamoring desires. "I know."

"But we can do everything else." With dizzying speed, he rolled her onto the bed, coming down to cover her torso with his own, pinning her there with his weight and strength.

Pulse thundering, she pulled back a few millimeters to make sure she was reading him right. "You're kidding? What about all those good reasons we talked about?"

He pulled away slightly, fumbled in the pocket of his lab coat and produced a box, which he held up for her examination.

"Condoms?"

"Courtesy of Eli."

"But *condoms*? If it's that simple, why didn't we think of it before?"

"We weren't blood-bonded before."

She heard the echo behind the words: *We had a choice before.* Her happiness dimmed a few watts. A man of reason and science, did he begrudge the hijacking of his higher brain by this mystical bond?

He took her hand and drew it down to press against his erection, which currently tented the fine wool of his trousers. "Does this feel like I begrudge our bond?"

She laughed, and his mouth caught hers.

Okay, she thought. *Okay*.

Chapter 20

Delano caught the laugh as it left her mouth, taking the joy straight into him. He was drunk on her. Her fragrant hair, the rising musk of her arousal, the soft silk of her skin, and yes, the slide of his thoughts against hers. It was the most erotic thing he'd ever known.

He lifted his head. "Listen to me, Ainsley. You mustn't let me take your blood."

She smiled up at him. "We talked about this. I trust you, Del."

He let the reins of control slip the merest bit, just enough so she could feel the breadth and scope of the blood hunger.

"Oh. *Oh!*"

She tried to struggle up, but he held her there until she subsided on the mattress again.

"Why didn't you tell me you were fasting? My God, Delano, I'm such an idiot. I can't believe it didn't occur to me that you wouldn't know your own blood type."

He pushed the blood-lust back down. "It didn't seem important to mention until now."

"Not important? What are you going to do for sustenance?"

"I can go without blood for a couple of days with minimal impact."

"Really?"

"Really. It certainly didn't cause that scene out there with Eli. At worst, I get a little ... how do you say? Bitchy. The other was caused by ... well, you know."

"I know."

She traced his mouth with a delicate finger, and it was all he could do to keep from drawing it into his mouth. Patience.

"So how long do you need to fast?"

"Forty-eight hours should do it. If there are no changes in my blood chemistry by then, we can safely assume there will be no reversal and I'll go back to my regular infusions. And if there are changes, I won't need to worry about typing and cross-matching, because I'll be looking for a rare steak and a pint of dark ale."

Her lips curved in a smile, but her eyes stayed sober. "You sure you're okay for this?"

Let's hope he was, because he wasn't about to stop now. And that thought he kept carefully shrouded. He bit her finger gently, delighting in the shiver that went through her. "With a little help from you, it won't be a problem."

"As in don't go begging for the teeth again?"

"Exactly."

He felt her hands pushing against his chest. *Roll over.*

He obliged, but pulled her with him, not ready to lose contact. She stretched for something just beyond her reach, flattening her breasts against his shoulder in the process, then came back with the prize — the box of condoms. She pulled one out and waggled it, smiling wolfishly.

"I'm guessing you've never had occasion to don one of these, huh?"

"You'd guess right."

"Then let me do the honors."

He started to sit up so he could remove his clothes, but she pushed him back again.

"No. I want your clothes on."

Clothes on?

He couldn't have stopped the probe he sent into her mind if his life depended on it, and she was right there, ready for him. His heart literally skipped a couple of beats, then fell into a heavy thudding. She meant to take him as he had taken her, thoroughly and relentlessly, and all she required of him was a promise of passivity.

"That's *all*?" He groaned. "Lord, woman, this will kill me."

The smile she gave him was all sin, and his heart rate took another jump.

"Okay, do your worst."

Laughing, she leaned forward and kissed him briefly. When he would have deepened the kiss, she pulled away. "My worst is very, very good."

She slid off the bed, her fingers already working on the buttons of her shirt. The garment floated to the floor, and she turned her attention to the khaki pants, making short work of them. In fifteen seconds flat, she stood there beside the bed in her bra and panties.

"Can I talk?"

She grinned. "You're *required* to talk. Or at least think loudly. The only thing you can't do is take control."

Lord, this *would* kill him. "You are so lovely."

"Wanna see more?"

Yes.

She popped the front clasp of her bra, freeing her breasts. The bra slid down her arms to join the other clothing at her feet.

She angled her head. "What's that? Did you say something?"

"The rest," he croaked.

Holding his gaze, she slid her fingers into the waistband of her lace panties and pushed them down over her hips. With a little encouragement, they settled around her ankles and she stepped out of them.

Perfect.

She stepped closer to the bed and he started to sit up, intent on touching her. She pressed him back down with a hand to his chest. "I want you like this, flat on your back with your feet on the floor."

His sex jerked beneath the fabric of his trousers, drawing her attention.

"Poor baby," she cooed. "Would you like me to let you out of there?"

This is going to be hard.

"Ah, but incredibly rewarding." She stepped closer and he widened the stance of his legs to allow her to get as close as possible. Then her fingers were at his belt, working it loose, and unfastening the button at his waist. Her hair, which she'd flipped to one side, trailed against his left side. With the skill of a nurse, she eased his zipper down.

"Boxers! I knew it."

Despite his intense arousal, he laughed. "There have been many scientific and technological advances over the years that I've taken full advantage of, but spandex briefs is not one I've — *ah!*"

She'd eased his boxers down, and his sex sprang free. Her eyes fixed on him, pupils dilating, nostrils flaring. And oh, God! He hardly needed to read her mind to know she was frankly savoring the scent of his arousal, feeling it do its work to intensify her own arousal state. He could practically hear the blood rush to her genitals, congesting the tissues, slicking her vagina ...

He groaned. "Ainsley, honey, have mercy on me."

"What?"

"If you're going to think thoughts like that, I might not last long enough for you to ravish me."

She flushed. "You *heard* that? I didn't mean to project it."

"Forget what I said. Don't edit. I want to feel everything you feel."

"Good, because obviously I have some work to do to master that editing thing." She picked up a condom from the spilled box and tore the wrapper off. "Showtime." She positioned herself to apply the condom, but hesitated.

He caught her concern and laughed. "Don't worry. I know it'll be different, but that's a good thing. It'll be the perfect reminder why that luscious carotid artery of yours shall remain unmolested."

Needing no further assurance, she applied the condom with a practiced touch.

"Does it bother you?"

He didn't pretend to misunderstand. "Not for a minute. Everything that you've done was all part of a path that led to this moment. How could I wish it otherwise?"

"Good answer."

With that, she bent and took his phallus in her mouth. And by all that was holy, she was better at shielding her thoughts than she'd thought, because he hadn't seen that coming! Then she swirled her tongue around his latex-sheathed glans, and coherent thought fled. There was only sensory input. Her hot mouth doing unspeakably wonderful things, her warm breath and hair tickling his skin, the thrilling surge of blood in her —

No, don't think about the blood. No blood. No blood.

Instead, he focused on the erotic picture she made at his groin, completely naked while he was completely clothed. And that just about put him over the edge. Fortunately, she pulled back before he had to beg, though he wasn't sure whether he'd have begged for her to stop or keep going.

"Not a chance, Bowen. Not this time, anyway. I planned to ravish you, remember?"

"I remember. That's the kind of detail a finely-honed scientific mind like mine tends to keep a firm grip on."

"Yeah?" She climbed fully onto the bed, straddling him with her thighs. "Well, here's another instruction for that steel trap of a mind of yours. No touching. I'm sure you can remember it."

No touching? His fingers itched to catch those breasts, to guide a tight, rosy nipple into his mouth. "You can't mean it."

"Oh, but I do. You'll take control if I give you half a chance, so no touching."

He groaned. "This is going to kill me."

"Not unless the condom breaks."

A bark of laughter escaped him. "That's one black sense of humor you have, my love."

"Meshes nicely with yours, I've noticed."

"Okay, no touching," he conceded. "Although in that event, restraints might have been a good idea."

Her eyes blazed. *Next time. You can even use them on me.*

He couldn't help it; his mind immediately conjured a picture of her spread-eagled face down on the bed, bound with soft ties and blindfolded so she couldn't see him. He'd shield his thoughts so she wouldn't know what sensory assault was coming next —

"See? Give you an inch, and you've got me tied up. No touching."

"Yes, Mistress."

A wicked smile curved her lips at his mock submission. "That's better." She moved up his body, bending low to loosen the top two buttons of his shirt. Then she kissed the vee of skin she'd exposed. He shivered involuntarily as she made her way up his neck, over his chin. When she found his mouth, her tongue invaded aggressively. He caught it and sucked gently, rewarded by the surge of excitement in her mind. She lifted her head.

"What?" he reasoned. "You offered it to me."

"Okay, your mouth only," she allowed.

Then give my mouth what we both want.

Patience, my sweet.

She tortured him some more, raking her hands through his hair, nuzzling his ear, and all the while rubbing her arousal-swollen breasts against his shirt-covered chest. And then, finally, finally, she arched over him, presenting him with one pink-crested breast. He sucked it greedily into his mouth, savoring not just the taste and texture of her, but the abundance of blood just beneath the skin, the blessed vasocongestion of sexual arousal. God, if he could just use his hands, he'd lift and shape those luscious mounds.

Of course, if he could use his hands, he'd seize her hips and urge her down onto his straining cock. Now.

She moaned and surged against him, reacting to his thoughts, and it occurred to him that he had other tools at his disposal besides his mouth.

Pushing aside the last veil of privacy, he opened his mind completely to hers. Explicit, wild, unedited, savagely carnal. He opened the gates and let it all pour out, and suddenly he had no need of his hands to urge her onward.

She reared back, guided his impossibly engorged cock to her entrance, then sank on him, impaling herself to the hilt with one screaming thrust. He gripped the bedclothes and felt the material shred beneath his fingers like tissue paper. And then — dear merciful God in heaven — then she was riding him. Wildly, recklessly, mindlessly, and he couldn't tell her pleasure from his. The ascent was swift. Her orgasm took her with a force that carried him right along behind. When she collapsed on his chest, she trembled like an aspen.

And so, God help him, did he.

"Omigod, that was so ... much." She lay there, feeling as though she'd literally melted over his hard body like hot wax. A part of her wondered if she would ever be able to pull herself completely back together, or whether they were permanently merged.

His hands caressed her butt. "Too much?"

"Never!"

A muffled laugh. Then, in a more serious tone, "Ainsley, I have to get up."

"Oh. The condom. Of course."

"That, too."

She pushed herself upward, intending to search his eyes, but her gaze never reached that far. It caught and held on his teeth. His very long, pointy teeth.

"Nothing to worry about. Just a little post-coital reaction."

He rolled her to the side, easing out of her. She felt the loss like a physical ache, but she was too preoccupied with this new development to dwell on it.

"I'm so sorry, Delano. You must be miserable. It's all my fault."

He laughed. "Yeah, miserable. To think I was just twenty years away from the century marker in the abstinence competition, and you had to come along and ruin my record."

She smacked his shoulder. "You know what I mean."

"I know what you mean. And this is a momentary thing. It will subside quickly, I promise you."

"But —"

"No buts. Compared to what we just did, it barely signifies. Now, don't move," he ordered. "I'll be right back."

He rolled off the bed and headed for the bathroom. He was quick, but by the time he returned, she was already self-conscious enough to have gotten up and found her robe.

"Suddenly shy, are we?"

"No." She lifted her chin. "We're cold."

His low laughter sent a frisson skating over her skin.

"You know better than to do that with me," he said.

Right. He could read her mind. "Okay, I'm feeling a little ... strange."

His face sobered. "And I'm feeling like throwing you over my shoulder and hauling you off to my rooms so that after we finish making love, you'll be there with me when dawn drives me into the day sleep." His Adam's apple bobbed as he swallowed. "How's that for strange?"

It sounded wonderful. Incredible. Too good to be true. She wet her lips. "What? You're not going back down to the lab?"

He shrugged. "There are only a few hours left of the night anyway. And my concentration is not the best for what needs to be done."

She smiled. "Well, I guess you can take one night off. When's the last time you played hooky?"

He blinked. "I can't remember."

Oh, Delano. "Then I'd say this is long overdue. And you do have a lot of lost time to make up for in the sex department ..."

Without a growl, he did exactly as he'd threatened, scooping her up into a fireman's lift and bearing her off toward his suite of rooms.

"Del! What if Eli sees?"

His laugh vibrated through her body, and she savored it. How many times had he laughed tonight? This was the man who gave serious a whole new dimension.

"Have you forgotten who donated the condoms?" His stride slowed. "Whoops, speaking of condoms, we left them in your room. I'll drop you off and go back for them."

"No we didn't."

They'd reached his room and he deposited her back on her feet. She pulled a handful of wrapped condoms from the pocket of her robe. "See?"

"All nine of them?" He laughed, closing the bedroom door behind them. "My recuperative powers are formidable, but that might be a challenge even for me."

Man, he was deadly when he smiled like that. Not that he wasn't smolderingly gorgeous when he brooded, but this laughing Delano made her heart overflow.

She smiled past the ache of happiness in her chest. "Right now, I think I could be happy just looking at you."

"Happy to oblige."

His clothes came off with his usual efficiency, as though he were oblivious of his own masculine beauty. She'd seen his body before, but the quarters had clearly been too close to permit full appreciation of the total package. Now, she stepped back and actively appreciated.

Broad shoulders tapered to lean hips, which flowed into powerful thighs. Even his feet were finely formed. For a man who never saw the sun, his skin was surprisingly dark. Still, the black hairs dusting his impressive pectorals and arrowing down to his groin stood out starkly. And oh, glory, the muscles!

I please you?

Her throat tightened. *If you pleased me any more, I don't think I could stand it.*

"Your turn," he said softly.

She shrugged the robe off, and stood for his appraisal. His dark gaze slid over her body like a physical caress, pausing here, lingering there, and his approval was patently evident.

Blinking back tears, she smiled. *I please you?*

You please me in every way imaginable.

He opened her arms and she went into them. He crushed her against his chest, pressing her face into his neck, kissing her hair, running his hands roughly over her back. Moving backwards, she tugged him along until the backs of her legs collided with the bed. They went down onto the mattress in a tangle of limbs, and just the feel of him — his warm, solid, glorious weight and hair-roughened skin — was almost enough to make her come. Mouths caught and held, hands searched and found, minds touched.

She broke their kiss, clutching his shoulders. "Del, we need a condom."

He levered himself off her and returned seconds later with the contents of her robe pocket. Taking one packet and dropping the others on the night table, he turned his attention to the condom.

She took it from him with fingers that trembled. "I know you could use the practice, but next time, okay? Right now, we need this on you."

Seconds later, his weight was back, pressing her into the firm mattress. She shifted, parting her legs, and he pushed into her. And oh God she wanted it to last and last, but she just couldn't hang on. A dozen thrusts and she exploded in a short, sharp orgasm. He stilled to let her wring every last drop of pleasure from it, then started moving again, his thrusts slower and more deliberate.

"Delano?"

"Hold onto me, Ainsley. I want to feel your arms around me. Don't let go."

She twined her arms around his neck, and knew that he'd lied for her. He hadn't played hooky because he wasn't up to whatever delicate task awaited him in the lab. He was here right now because he feared they might never have another chance to love each other like this.

Tears slid down her cheeks, and she gripped him harder, closing her legs around him, enveloping him.

Their loving went on forever. Slowly, he built that sweet tension in her again and again, until one climax rolled into the next one and the next one. When she could literally stand no more, he let his own release claim him, shuddering and trembling in the tight clasp of her arms.

Delano disposed of the condom and stepped into the shower, letting the hot spray hit his chest.

He hadn't wanted to leave the embrace of her body. He'd been busy cursing the condom and the consequent need to get up when it struck him that the other need to get up was mysteriously absent. His canines had not erupted following his orgasm. Before she could notice or comment on that development, or non-development, he'd rolled away, mumbling something about cleaning up.

He turned to let the water sluice his back and flinched. Ah, Ainsley had marked him with her fingernails. He grinned, finding himself wishing the small hurt could stay with him beyond the next hours. Unfortunately, it would be erased in the day sleep, leaving no lingering evidence of their shared passion.

The shower door opened, letting in a draft of cool air. "Is it safe for me to come in?"

He took her hand and pulled her inside the enclosure. He gave her a second to close the door behind her, then tugged her into his arms for a kiss. She melted against him, into him. Lord, he loved her.

He pulled away. "Let me wash you."

She acquiesced, letting him soap her body and shampoo her hair. When he'd finished finger-combing the crème rinse into her hair and rinsing it smooth, she picked up the soap and returned the favor. He had to bend to let her shampoo his hair. Gently, she worked around the lacerations Eli had inflicted, and the tenderness in her fingertips was almost enough to make him weep.

Afterward, he helped her blow her hair dry, and she reciprocated. Then they turned out the lights and climbed into his bed. Both of them could feel the approaching dawn.

He pulled her close and felt her sadness. "What's wrong, little one?"

She blinked rapidly. *I know you could push your way in to find out what's troubling me. Thank you for not doing that.*

He smiled. "There's such a thing as etiquette, even among the psychically linked."

"Yikes! I hope you'll tell me if I overstep the bounds."

"Not to worry. You'll know when an unwelcome psychic foray has been repulsed, I promise you. Now tell me why you're sad."

She drew a deep breath, let it out, then drew another. "I'm afraid I'll wake up tomorrow morning — or rather, tomorrow evening — and this will have been a dream. I'll be in my bed, alone. Or worse, I'll be here and you'll be angry at me again."

"Sweetheart." He kissed her as sweetly as he could. "It's not just real. It's forever."

"Promise?"

"Promise. Now I need a promise from you."

"Name it."

"Don't let me get carried away in the dream sleep."

"We can't fool around when we wake up?"

He grinned. God bless her. "We can definitely fool around, but just make sure I'm properly awake, for safety's sake. Lord knows what I might do — or not do — if I think I'm dreaming again."

"Of course."

He kissed her one last time, and found that incredible well of tender emotion right there beneath the surface, as deep and endless as before. He brushed a strand of hair behind her ear and looked deep into her eyes, memorizing their exact shade of violet. "Sleep now, love. I can feel your exhaustion from exercising those psychic muscles."

"Mmmm."

She moved away, just far enough to break contact, but close enough that he could still feel her body heat, hear the beat of her heart, the whoosh of her blood, the soft in-and-out of her respirations. Obviously she'd sensed his need to be untouched in the day sleep. He sent her a psychic thank you, followed by a powerful sleep suggestion. Within the minute, she was slumbering. It took considerably longer for sleep to claim him.

Chapter 21

DELANO DREAMED OF the Sahara. Even as he struggled up one dune and stumbled and slid down the next, he kept thinking, "But I've never been to Africa". But somehow he knew it was the Sahara. On and on he slogged, the desert stretching endlessly in front of him, with nothing on the shimmering horizon to promise relief. He was dreaming. He knew he was dreaming, but *Christ on the cross*, it felt so real. The merciless sun searing his skin, the heat sapping his strength and fuelling a terrible bone-deep thirst ...

Wait a minute — sun searing his skin? Definitely a dream. He'd never make it fifty feet in the Saharan sun before collapsing from anaphylactic shock, let alone trekking for miles in the burning sand.

But the thirst! It was so real, so urgent and all-consuming.

"Delano?"

Confused, he turned full circle, scanning the barren landscape. "Eli?"

"Delano, wake up!"

He cocked his head at the female voice. Ainsley was here, too? This was too strange. Why couldn't he see them? Had he gone blind from the sun?

"Delano." This time, Eli's voice held a note of command. "You have to wake up. We have a problem."

Someone laid a hand on him, jerking him out of the dream state. He jackknifed up, causing both Eli and Ainsley to spring back.

"What is it?" His heart banged against his ribs. "Are we under attack?"

"No, but I have some grim news from the team we sent to Mexico."

"What's happened?"

"They're gone."

Delano swallowed. Christ, his mouth felt like the desert of his dreams. Clearly, it had been a very long time since he'd last fasted. He didn't remember the physical symptoms being so ... well, *physical*. Even his pulse felt skittery. Skittery and feeble at the same time. *Concentrate, Bowen.* What had Eli said? They're gone. Who were *they*?

Holy Christ!

"Mrs. Michaels and her daughter?"

"Yes, and the local operatives were slain. All four of them."

Janecek!

Delano shot a glance at Ainsley, who looked like someone had unplugged her power supply. She sat there with the bedspread wrapped around her naked body, her eyes vacant, her mouth gone slack. Shock. It wouldn't last.

He took her left hand in his and chafed it with his own hands. She showed no awareness of his attempt to comfort, but he didn't release her hand. The contact comforted *him*, dammit.

He turned back to Eli, doing his best to pretend that he was facing his lieutenant across a table, rather than sitting here bucknaked in bed with a sheet covering his privates.

"Okay, let's hear what you know. Start from the beginning, and don't leave anything out."

Eli grimaced. "It's a short story, I'm afraid. Our day/night team went wheels up shortly after 1:00 this morning, and reached shelter for our vamp before dawn. Digger Harris took the day shift, but couldn't make contact with the locals we hired. After he failed to reach a single member of the team at the coordinates we provided, he made a personal reconnaissance of the subject's house."

Delano swallowed again, no easy task given he seemed to have no saliva available. "Which is when he found the whole team slaughtered and the Michaels woman and child missing."

"That's it," said Eli, rubbing the back of his neck, "in a fuckin' nutshell."

"We're sure it was Janecek?" Delano knew the answer but had to ask the question.

"I think it's a safe assumption, particularly given that they were all exsanguinated."

"Where are they?" Beside him, Ainsley stirred at last, extracting her hand from his. "What has that creature done with Lucy and Devon?"

Ainsley's eyes no longer looked vacant, but Delano wasn't entirely certain their new expression was much of an improvement. Her beautiful violet eyes had gone volcanic with a hot fury with which Delano was only too well acquainted. He didn't have to probe her mind to appreciate what she was feeling. Her lust for vengeance spilled from every pore, permeating the room.

Easy, baby. "He won't have harmed them."

She glowered at him. *Yet, you mean.*

He wished he could refute her assessment of Janecek's intent, but she'd know he was lying. But what Janecek intended wasn't necessarily what would come to pass. Not while he still lived and breathed.

"He'll use them to negotiate. And to do that, he'll have to bring them to us. When he does, we'll simply have to figure out how to wrest them away."

She stared at him, unblinking. "You know what he's going to try to negotiate. Us for them. Plus destruction of your labs and the work you've done."

"I know."

"Whoa right there." Eli held up a hand. "Don't tell me you're seriously thinking about agreeing to his demands?" He looked from one to the other. "Goddammit, he'll kill you both! And when he's done, he'll kill the Michaels woman and her kid just to put an exclamation point on his victory."

Delano tried to work up enough spit to swallow again. "At the risk of sounding repetitive, I know."

"And then there would be nothing standing between Janecek and his prey." Eli didn't raise his voice. Rather, he got quieter and more deadly as he went. "Our friend Radak and all the other monsters like him will be free to cull the herd with impunity then, wouldn't they? Alleyways and crack houses and battlefields and hospital wards and anywhere else where sudden deaths can be readily explained. That is, until the day arrives when their numbers are so plentiful that they no longer give a shit whether or not their kills go unnoticed."

Delano dragged a hand through his hair. "Christ, Eli, I know that, too. Obviously, we can't concede to his demands."

"*I* can."

Delano and Eli swiveled to gawk at Ainsley.

"The vaccine is all but finished, right? You don't really need me any more. And if there's any doubt, you can take as much blood as you like. I just need enough to stay on my feet to make the exchange."

"No!"

Both men spoke at once.

Ainsley held up a hand. "Hear me out. This makes sense. We oblige him to settle for me. He lets Lucy and Devon go. Of course, he's not really planning to let them go. He'll be planning to kill all of us, but as soon as I get close, I detonate a bomb and take him out."

Delano found his voice first. "A bomb?"

"Yes. You can wire it onto me."

"A suicide bomb?"

"No, a smart bomb that will hurt him but not me."

Delano leapt up, yanking the sheet with him. "No way. No fucking way."

Stunned silence greeted his use of the blunt Anglo-Saxon epithet, and he took advantage of it.

"Have you forgotten the blood-bond, Ainsley? You die, I follow. It's as simple as that. Then there will be no one left to perfect the vaccine, no matter how much blood you leave behind." He wrapped the sheet around himself, holding it bunched at his hip with one hand. "Christ, we might as well concede to his demands if that's your plan."

"He's right, Ainsley."

Ainsley wheeled on Eli, her lip curled in a veritable snarl. "I know he's right, dammit!" Her fierce expression crumpled, leaving raw, stomach-churning fear etched in every line of her face. "Oh, God, what are we going to do? I can't let anything happen to them. This is all my fault."

Guilt scored Delano's conscience, raking its claws deep into his psyche. The two people who gave her life meaning, the people for whom she'd sacrificed everything ... And now, because of him, their lives now hung in the balance. If he hadn't hunted her down, Lucy and Devon Michaels would still be safe. Ainsley would be safe.

"I'm the one who dragged you into this, remember? It's my fault."

Eli snorted, crossing his arms across his powerful chest. "I can't believe what I'm hearing. Janecek is the villain of this piece, make no mistake about it." He glared at Ainsley. "None of this is your fault, Ainsley. Absolutely none of it. You just happened to be born with a funky gene. Are we clear on that?"

Before Ainsley could respond, Eli wheeled toward Delano.

"And you — you coulda been more transparent with Ainsley from the start, no question. You know my position on that, so I'll leave it alone. But everyone in this room knows that it wouldn't have made a tinker's damn of a difference to the outcome. Once her eyes were opened to the predators, Ainsley could no more have turned her back on this project than I could. So if you please, a little less self-flagellating and a little more strategizing as to how we're going to bring this motherfucker down."

Amazed, Delano arched a brow. "Are you finished?"

"Gawd, I hope so. I just shot my word quota for the next four days."

Delano clapped his free hand on Eli's back. "As always, you give wise counsel. Why don't we, er," he looked down at the sheet he clutched over his nakedness, "compose ourselves and meet over the dining room table?"

Eli nodded. "I'll put coffee on."

As soon as they were alone, Delano went to Ainsley and gathered her into his arms. She shuddered, and he held her closer, absorbing her fear and dread and guilt and misery. "I'm so sorry, little one."

She let herself lean on him a moment, then pulled back. "I've got to go get dressed," she said, her voice thick with unshed tears.

"Of course." He released her immediately, although it was the last thing he wanted to do. He wanted to hold her. He wanted to tell her what this past day had meant to him. He wanted to hear what it meant to her. He wanted the equivalent of morning-after assurances, in the evening. But this was not the time. He gave her arm a last squeeze. "I'll see you shortly."

When she'd left, he headed straight for the bathroom. Standing at the basin, he turned the water on. He gave it a few seconds to run cold, then cupped his hands beneath the faucet to capture the crystal-clear liquid, bent and drank deep. Then he repeated the process a half-dozen times, until the sweet, clean water had knocked the edge of his thirst. Shutting off the tap, he reached for a hand towel and swiped it across his face. Catching his own gaze in the mirror, he cursed. "Great timing, Bowen."

He was about to go up against an enemy who was among the most powerful vampires alive.

Cursing, Delano started the shower, adjusted the water temperature and stepped under the hot spray, letting it bathe the scratches on his back with tongues of fire. Scratches that had failed to heal during his day sleep, because, God help him, he was no longer a vampire, or fast achieving that state. A fact he was going to have to keep from Ainsley and Eli, who were going to need every ounce of courage they could muster for the confrontation to come.

Ainsley managed to stay in her chair out of sheer willpower. They'd been going over different scenarios and what-ifs and contingencies for hours now, and she was ready to scream.

No, she wanted to hit something, to lash out. She wanted to tear this room apart. She wanted to hurl her coffee mug against the wall, overturn the table, smash the stupid speakerphone that refused to ring.

She glanced at Delano, and felt some of the desperate edge come off. Poor Del. He didn't look to be in much better shape than she was. Not that he looked bad; she'd come to believe he was incapable of that. But he looked ... what? More vulnerable, maybe. Suddenly, she wanted to circle the table and put her arms around him right where he sat, holding him as tightly as he'd asked her to do last night.

He looked up and caught her eye.

Tell me again that it's going to be all right.

Instead of replying to her silent plea, he reached across the table and covered her hand with his, giving it a reassuring squeeze.

Of course. He wanted her to conserve her psychic energy. He'd been right about that. Her mental exhaustion in the wee small hours before dawn had been profound. When Delano sent her a sleep suggestion, it had been lights out. She couldn't remember the last time she slept so soundly, even with the help of a sleep aid.

The speakerphone rang, jolting everyone visibly.

Delano stabbed a button. "Bowen."

"So curt." Janecek's voice filled the dining room, but there was a great deal of background noise, a rhythmic *whup-whupping*. "And after I've come all this way to see you."

Eli muted the phone. "Chopper," he said, then depressed the mute button again.

"I'm touched," Delano drawled.

"It doesn't look like it from up here," shouted Janecek over the beating of the helicopter's blades. "It looks like you've got a SWAT team up here ready to take us out on your command."

Ainsley's stomach churned. He was here, in a helicopter, hovering close enough to see the guard posted on the roof!

On cue, Eli's radio erupted with a report from the roof of an incoming aircraft, potentially hostile. He stabbed the mute button on the phone, then depressed the transmit button on his radio.

"Roger that, B-Team. Hold your fire. Repeat, hold your fire. There are hostages on board that helo. Over."

When Eli's radio had crackled a "Roger that", Delano took the mute off again.

"You expected us to roll out the red carpet, perhaps?"

"What I expect," he said, "is a little respect for my cargo."

Unable to stand it a moment longer, Ainsley jumped up. "Goddamn you, you monster, they better be all right!"

"Ah, Ms. Crawford. Good of you to confirm your presence. Because without you, this delightful duo would be of no use to me, save perhaps as an appetizer. They're neither one of them very big."

Ainsley gasped, but Delano pushed into her mind with a faint but firm command not to rise to the bait. Digging her nails into her palms, she forced herself to sink back into her chair. His eyes thanked her, and he turned his attention back to the phone.

"Come on, Radak. Skip the theatrics and get straight to the point."

"Okay, Delano. Here's my point."

Screams erupted, and the rotor blades became suddenly louder.

Eli's radio burst to life again with the voice of a team member Ainsley had met a handful of times. "Jesus, he's dangling someone out of the chopper! And not over the roof, either. Over the street. Jesus, fuck! It's a kid. Just a kid."

Ainsley leapt to her feet again, wanting to crawl through the telephone to get at the bastard. "You hurt that child and I'll kill you!"

"Tell Delano to withdraw his forces from the roof, Ms. Crawford, and nothing will happen to the child. Then you and me and Daddy Dearest can sit down and talk trade."

Eli stabbed the mute button. "We can call 'em down, but have them arrayed just inside the doors to the roof. If it starts to go sideways up there, they can be back out on the roof in seconds."

Delano released the mute. "We'll meet your demand. Just haul that kid back in."

The noise of the rotors dipped again, making the sobs of mother and child all the more audible. *Oh, Devon, Lucy, I'm so sorry.*

"Okay, she's safely inside again," came Janecek's voice. "Your turn."

Eli gave the order for his men to retreat, this time not bothering with the mute button. However, he did mute the phone to relay the order for them to hang just inside the stairwell, close to the roof's door.

"Better?" Delano asked.

"Infinitely. But before I land, I want you to tell Mr. Grayson that this handsome craft is equipped with an M6oD machine gun. He'll be familiar with it. It's standard NATO fare, I understand, and it'll be pointed at that door. My pilot tells me it's rated for 550 shots per minute, as I'm sure Mr. Grayson can confirm, although I haven't had an opportunity to personally benchmark it against those specs."

Delano glanced at Eli, who nodded grimly.

"Okay, land that bird and we'll talk again." Delano leaned forward and hit the off button on the conference phone.

Ainsley's stomach dropped sickeningly. "You hung up on him? Omigod, what have you done?"

"I've simply reminded him that we also have something he wants, and that he doesn't hold all the cards."

Ainsley was vaguely aware of Eli in the background, instructing the B-Team to move further down the stairwell and out of danger from the helo's guns.

"But he *does* hold the cards." She thumped her hand on the table. "He's got Lucy and Devon. You just heard what he did to Devon!"

Before Delano could defend his action, Eli jumped in to do it for him. "Delano's right," he said, radio still gripped at the ready. "We have to try to hang on to whatever edge we can get, even if it's psychological. And don't forget, we have our little jack-in-the-box surprise up there."

He referred, of course, to the commando they'd earlier stashed in Delano's helicopter. They'd also planted a guy in the interstitial space between the first and second floors, above the security room with its banks of monitors, which would be the logical place for Janecek to take up headquarters if he gained access to the building from below. Yet another man lay in hiding in the building they'd made use of as a clinic, in case Janecek chose that location for a rendezvous. But they'd felt all along that the roof was more Janecek's style, and he'd obliged. Still, what if Janecek sensed their man's presence?

She felt her nails biting into her palms again, and unclenched her fists. "That's presuming he goes undetected. You know the first thing he's going to do is a deep scan of the roof for any kind of hidden presence. Can you be completely certain the stealth technology of the helicopter will shield him?"

"We've been over this before, Ainsley," replied Delano. "Remember the way Janecek walked right up to me wearing that fireman's turn-out suit? If Kevlar shielded a powerful vampire so completely from my senses, then I have every confidence that the helicopter's technology will easily shield a mere man. And he's tucked completely out of sight, if Janecek is suspicious enough to order a visual."

Ainsley grimaced. He was out of sight, all right, lying in the coffin-like bed Delano had retired to during their daylight flight from St. Cloud. He'd be a sitting duck — no, make that a dead duck — if they were wrong about the shielding capacity of the helicopter's highly reflective shell. "But what about —"

Delano responded to her concern before she could voice it. "Janecek won't catch a whiff of our guy's thoughts. That's why we gave him the headphones. That's why he's been instructed to focus exclusively on the continuous incantation being relayed to him. Until and unless we interrupt that flow with other orders, he won't be having the kind of brain wave activity that Janecek can pick up on."

She gnawed her lower lip. "You should have let me do it. I'd feel better if I was up there. At least then I could —"

"Feel like you were doing something?" Eli sighed. "I know how you feel."

Eli's voice was harsh, as though he, too, wanted to be the one on the roof. Suddenly, she remembered the way he'd looked the first time she'd asked him about why he'd left the army to work for Delano. He'd said he'd found another war to fight. She'd never pursued the matter with him, but it was evidently very personal. He badly wanted to be the one to bring the monster down. What had Janecek — or someone like him — done to Eli?

"But all due respect," Eli continued, "the man up there is a former Navy SEAL. He'll get the job done if the opportunity is there. Besides, you and Delano have to be down here, to negotiate with Janecek. He'd know something was up if you weren't both here for his call."

The phone rang again.

Delano let it ring twice before picking it up. "Bowen."

"Hang up on me again, and you'll get one of these ladies back faster than you bargained for, but you won't like the condition you find her in."

Ainsley's anguished gaze flew to Delano's. *See? You angered him!*

That's good, he countered silently. *If we don't get him off balance, he won't make a mistake. And if he makes no mistakes, we're screwed.*

"So sorry," he said aloud, "I didn't realize you needed me to hold your hand for the landing."

"Ah, but you did your share of hand-holding in your time, didn't you, Delano? Not to mention a little hand *shackling*."

Delano sighed, and Ainsley noticed a tic start under his left eye.

"You were a child, Radak. An abomination, to be sure, but a child nevertheless. I tried to protect you from your own appetites. Unchecked by an immature value system, you would have wreaked horrific destruction, and then you would have died. For while you knew how to feed, you lacked the necessary survival skills."

"Ah, my father, my savior."

Delano rubbed a hand across his forehead, and Ainsley realized he was wiping away perspiration. What? She'd never seen him do that before. So much for the superior vampiric biology he'd tried to explain to her. She'd wager his system was dumping plenty of stress hormones right now.

"Once more, I am not your father. But I did try to protect you. I thought if I could supervise your adolescence, you'd eventually develop the maturity to handle yourself responsibly. I was wrong."

"You were a fool, Delano. Now enough of this. You and Nurse Crawford will come up to the roof. Delano, you will come forward first. When you reach my pilot, who will be standing by the aircraft, I will release the child. When Nurse Crawford is assured of the child's safety, then she will come forward. When we've secured her, I'll let the woman go."

Delano laughed grimly. "You're a brave man, Radak, to propose taking me first."

"Ah, but if I don't take you first, I can't be assured of taking you at all. I know you, Delano. You're the big-picture guy. You're invested in the greater good. Ms. Crawford, on the other hand, is invested in the safety of her loved ones. Besides which, we're more than prepared to handle the likes of you."

"Give us a moment." Delano stabbed the mute button and turned to Eli. "What are you thinking?"

"The report from our security cams says we've got three people to worry about — the pilot, another unidentified man, probably a co-pilot, and Janecek. Janecek is in the back, keeping the kid close, which keeps the mother docile. The co-pilot is manning the big gun."

"Lovely," Delano muttered.

"I say we comply with his demand, but activate our jack-in-the-box. He's the best sniper I've got. When the chopper door opens to let the kid out, we let our man take a shot. Meanwhile, you take the pilot out."

"And I'll dart out and grab Devon," Ainsley volunteered.

"No way," both men said in unison.

She lifted her chin. "Someone has to scoop her up. We can't leave her there while gunfire is possibly being exchanged."

"Ainsley, honey, you can't come outside that door. If we're both out there on the roof at the same time, all they have to do is open up on us with that machine gun. Then they won't have to let anyone go."

"But—"

"No buts. If you'll remember, I move a little faster than you. I can take the pilot out, scoop up the kid and get back inside before you could even reach her."

Well, that was hard to argue. He was capable of moving faster than her eyes could track him. But the plan had one flaw—a *gigantic* one.

"Okay, you're much faster than me, so that makes sense. But do you really think Janecek is just going to stand in the doorway and give you that free shot? Even if he's satisfied there's no one up there to worry about, he's not going to expose himself. He's got far too much respect for you as an opponent to do that. He'll get the co-pilot to do it."

"That's exactly what we're counting on," Delano said. "The co-pilot is the one we need to take out of commission. If our man on the roof can disable him, and if I handle the pilot, that'll leave Janecek stranded. I'm pretty sure he can't pilot that thing himself. It's not his style to do anything for himself that an underling can do for him."

Ainsley paled. "Okay, so he'll be stranded, but he'll also be extremely pissed. And he'll still have a hostage and some serious fire power."

"Once he appreciates he's stranded, his hand will be forced. Guns or no guns, he'll have to negotiate with us for his own survival."

"What do you mean?"

"When dawn comes, he'll be at our mercy."

"Couldn't he just call for another helicopter to lift him to safety?"

"He could, but he's got to know we're equipped with anti-air-craft guns we could turn on any incoming helo. He would not have dared land here without hostages."

"Hey guys," Eli interrupted, "Security cams indicate the pilot is doing a visual sweep of the rooftop, looking for booby traps. He gave our helo a careful look, but didn't raise an alarm."

"No less than what we expected," said Delano. "Give them a few more minutes for Janecek to scan —"

"Time's up." Janecek's voice came through the speakerphone. "Decide now. You have precisely four minutes to get up to the roof, or one of these pretty gals becomes dinner."

Delano hit the mute button to connect with Janecek again. "We're on our way."

"Excellent." Janecek severed the connection, leaving a dial tone resonating through the room.

Delano turned the phone off. "Okay, raise our jack-in-the-box. We're going up."

Chapter 22

DELANO SILENTLY CURSED the perspiration that slicked his skin beneath the armored vest Eli insisted he wear under his shirt. Was this the normal human state, or was the reversal in progress wreaking extra havoc on his body? It had been so long, he couldn't remember. Probably a little bit of both.

Eli stood with his hand on the door's panic bar, impatient to be off, but they had two minutes yet, and Delano had things to say to Ainsley. "Go on up," he said. "I need a minute."

Eli frowned. "Make it a literal minute."

The door had barely closed behind him when Ainsley spoke. "I should be going up there with you."

"No, my love. You know we can't run the risk of both of us falling into his hands. He wouldn't spare the hostages."

"I'm scared, Delano."

"I know, love." He put a hand to her face and felt a tremor go through her. "But it's our best chance."

She nodded, biting her lip to still its trembling.

I love you, he said silently. *If something should happen to go wrong up here, I just wanted to make absolutely certain you to know that.*

Her brow furrowed. "Delano?"

Oh, Lord, she couldn't hear him. The reversal was progressing quickly. "Sorry, I just wanted to do this before I go." He fit his hand behind her head and drew her to him for a short, sweet kiss. Just as quickly, he released her and stepped back. "I'm afraid our minute is up."

"I know. Go."

He'd reached the door when her voice stopped him.

"Delano!"

He turned to find her heart in her eyes.

"Be careful."

Heart thudding painfully against his ribs, he gave her his best reassuring smile. "I will. Now remember, don't go out there, no matter what happens. Okay?"

She nodded, her eyes solemn, and he turned away before his throat could grow any tighter. Knowing he'd used more than a minute, he leapt up the stairs. On the first landing, Eli and the members of B-Team stood waiting.

Eli clapped him on the back. "You ready for this, boss?"

"Ready as I'll ever be. Are we good to go?"

"Our man has a bead on the helicopter door as we speak."

"Time to rock and roll then."

Delano ran lightly up the last flight of stairs alone. When he reached the door, he took a deep, steadying breath. Exhaling, he raised his hands up over his head, pushed the panic bar with his hip and carefully stepped out on the roof.

The pilot stood midway between the idling helicopter and the door, holding a lethal-looking rifle. A rifle that was trained unerringly on Delano's chest as evidenced by a red laser dot. Feeling alarmingly weak in the legs — damn the timing of this mutation reversal — Delano strode toward the flak-jacketed pilot.

Then all hell broke loose.

Gunfire erupted, but from the wrong helicopter! Janecek must have detected their sniper. *Dammit, dammit, dammit!* Before Delano's horrified eyes, a hundred bullet holes bloomed on the body of the helo, and shattered glass erupted onto the helipad. For a few white-hot seconds, he considered trying to rescue the sniper, but logic told him neither of them would survive it.

Bastards!

His blood boiling with fury, Delano streaked toward the pilot, who'd let the nose of his rifle dip when the helo-to-helo gunfire broke out. And oh, thank you Jesus, he must have had some vampiric power left, because his speed was there. The startled pilot's curse was cut off as Delano struck his windpipe with the side of his right hand. The other man dropped his rifle and clutched his throat. Delano grabbed him. Using the pilot as a shield, he raced back to the door in a blur of speed. Yanking the door open, he hurled himself and his burden down the first flight of stairs, and not a second too soon. A hail of bullets struck the door, entering the vestibule and ricocheting dangerously. Dragging the dead weight of the now unconscious pilot, he plunged down the next flight, nearly plowing into Eli, who was on his way up.

"Get down! Ricochets!"

Eli crouched but didn't retreat. Rather, he slid a shoulder under the pilot's free arm to help Delano evacuate him. When they reached the next landing, the shooting, thank God, had stopped. Two soldiers reached for the pilot. Ribs screaming from the impact with the concrete floor, Delano was only too happy to pass off the burden.

"Get him inside. He needs attention."

Eli turned worried eyes on Delano. "What about you? Are you hit?"

"No." But dammit, he almost wished he was. How was he going to explain this goatfuck to Ainsley? Janecek would be livid, and the hostages ... Dammit. He cleared his throat. "Did you get a sit rep?"

"Yeah. And Ainsley will have heard it, too. I left her a radio."

I'm sorry, Ainsley. "Have you got a medical kit at the ready down there?"

"Always."

"Then let's get a move on. I think I might have hit our prisoner a little harder than was strictly necessary."

When they reached the penthouse, they found the unconscious pilot stretched out on the carpet, with Ainsley kneeling at his side.

Her eyes flew to Delano's. "Bartlett? Did he ... I mean, is he ...?"

Delano shook his head grimly. "That was a hell of a barrage. Even if he survived it, there's no way to get to him."

"And Lucy and Devon?"

His throat ached. "I don't know."

Her eyes filled with tears.

I'm so sorry, Ainsley.

He knelt opposite her, forcing his attention to the patient. "Did he take any bullets?"

She cleared her throat. "Not that I could see. I gather from the radio report that you struck him?"

"Neck area." Delano palpated the patient's throat, and swore at the crackling sensation beneath his bare fingers. Damn. The man was a goner without a tracheostomy. He sat back on his heels. "Subcutaneous emphysema."

Eli joined them, medical kit in hand. "Good thing I've got a trach kit in here. You want to do the honors, or shall I?"

"You'd better do it." He moved back to make room for Eli. "You don't want to know what equipment I employed the last time I did an emergency tracheostomy. But I'll assist." He moved around to the pilot's right, intending to relieve Ainsley, but she waved him off.

"I've got it covered."

Delano blinked. Tears still shone in her eyes, but her demeanor was completely composed. Her trauma room training, he realized. It was probably all that was holding her together. Deciding the best way to help her was to keep her busy, he backed off.

Ainsley, her hands already gloved, dug a Betadine swabstick out of the kit and swabbed the patient's throat below the Adam's apple. Eli tugged on surgical gloves and quickly laid out his supplies on a sterile pad. Feeling redundant, Delano watched as Eli and Ainsley worked quickly and calmly to expose two cartilage rings, incise them and install the tracheostomy tube.

A moment later, Eli leaned back on his heels. "Airway restored." Peeling off the surgical gloves, he nodded to the two men who'd carried the pilot downstairs. "He'll be coming around any minute now. Put him in my room and shackle him to the bed. Search him. Oh, and take his clothes and give him this to wear." He tossed one of the men a hospital-issue Johnny shirt. "That oughta keep him humble."

"He won't be able to talk," Delano added. "Tell him the tracheostomy is reversible, and that we'll be in to discuss it when our situation is resolved."

As the men moved in to pick up the patient, Eli turned to Delano. "You sure you're all right, boss? You hit the deck pretty hard."

"I'm fine." He waved off Eli's question, even though the dive onto the concrete had almost certainly cracked a rib or two, not to mention the scrapes and bruises. "I wish I could say the same for our sniper. I thought about trying to get him out of there, but they riddled the Comanche in a matter of seconds."

Eli cleared his throat and blinked, but his voice when he spoke was perfectly controlled. "You did the right thing, Del. Even if Bartlett wasn't killed outright, the both of you would have been cut to ribbons if you'd tried to get him out. And by grabbing up the pilot, you drew their fire. Not to mention that we bagged ourselves a pilot."

Delano knew he could not have done anything differently, but Eli's approval helped. He touched his ribcage surreptitiously. Yep, cracked ribs. "Thanks. Except we needed to bag two pilots to turn the tables. Janecek is going to be pissed as hell."

As soon as the words were out, he wished he could call them back. Mrs. Michaels and her daughter were still at the mercy of Janecek. Ainsley didn't need any reminders how angry their captor was going to be.

Except when he looked around, he realized she was no longer within earshot. She'd stepped clear when the men moved in to transfer the patient to Eli's bedroom, he remembered, but he hadn't seen her since. Where had she gone? His pulse jerked. Not the roof! Surely not the roof.

He whipped his head around, searching for her.

Oh, thank God! She sat at the dining room table, in front of the cursed speakerphone. A phone that was destined to ring any moment now.

His heart contracted at the picture she made. Now that the pilot's medical emergency had passed, she held herself stiffly on the chair, her face tight, limbs trembling with tension held in check.

"Excuse me," he murmured to Eli, then went to stand behind Ainsley. If she felt his hovering presence, she gave no indication. Rather, her focus was fixed intently on the phone as though she could make it ring with the sheer force of her will.

Oh, Ainsley. He wanted to place his hands on her shoulders, to pull her head back against the warmth of his chest. He wanted his touch to infuse her with courage and strength, and he wanted to draw the same from her to boost his own beleaguered faith that they were going to come out of this all right. But he dared not touch her. She looked as though she might shatter into a thousand pieces at the first contact.

He seated himself beside her and sent her a calming, centering vibe. She glanced up at him, but her face disclosed no evidence that she'd caught his thoughts. Lord, he was losing his powers, piece by piece, inch by inch. Any more of this and their blood-bond might —

Heart pounding, he casually pushed his sleeve back to examine the mark on the inside of his elbow. His stomach dropped. The triangle of dots was still there, but just barely, a faint trace of what it used to be.

Before he could reflect on that, the phone rang.

Ainsley's gaze sprang up to meet his, naked fear visible in those violet depths. He squeezed her hand, then pushed the button to answer the phone. "Bowen."

Eli slid into a seat across the table.

"I'm very disappointed in you, Delano."

Janecek's words were delivered calmly enough, but Delano heard the volcanic rage beneath the surface. He could also hear sobbing in the background. Acid erupted in his stomach, a veritable volcano of hot pain, and he grimaced.

"You used to have more respect for human life," Janecek said.

"I assure you, my respect for human life is as strong as ever." He tensed his abdominals against the next wave of pain. "If that were not so, we wouldn't be here in this position, would we, Radak?"

Janecek snorted. "I've got a dead sniper out here who might argue about that. The way I see it, if you gave a flying fuck about his life, you wouldn't have planted him in the middle of this. Did you seriously think I'd overlook him? Christ, he couldn't have announced his presence any louder, the way he was salivating as he waited for our chopper door to swing open."

"So naturally you had to kill him."

"Like he wasn't planning to kill us!"

Delano rubbed his forehead, which had begun to pound. "For your information, he was after your co-pilot, not you. And he would not have shot to kill. I reserve that for unrepentant predators. Your man just happened to be in the employ of an unrepentant predator."

"Is that what you've done with my pilot? Disabled him?"

"Indeed we have. Quite effectively."

Ainsley surged to her feet. "Shut up! Both of you!" Hands propped on the table on either side of the speakerphone, she continued: "Why are they crying? Dammit, what have you done to them?"

"Ah, yes, they are making a bit of a racket, aren't they?" Janecek's voice was easy, relaxed, charming. "Can't say I blame them, though. I just explained how long it's been since you had a child underfoot, Delano, and how I thought I'd remedy that right here and now."

Acid surged in his stomach again, as the import of Janecek's words sank in. "Don't do it!" He leapt to his feet, gripping the table's edge so hard that his nail beds screamed. "I'm begging you, Radak. If you have a shred of humanity left, you won't do this."

"Fuck you, Delano. This is what you get for screwing with me."

Screams erupted over the speaker, drawing an echoing cry from Ainsley.

That bastard. Evil, black, soul-dead spawn of Satan!

Another piercing shriek, this time unmistakably the child's. Delano shoved his chair back, intent on stopping the obscenity Janecek planned to perpetrate.

"No!" Ainsley clutched at him.

Eli had the good sense to hit the mute button just then.

"Let go!" He pried her hand off his wrist. "Goddammit, Ainsley, he plans to turn that child. I can't let him do it. I can't. You just don't know —"

"No, *you* don't know." She clung to his arm fiercer than ever. "Devon is *my* daughter, Delano. *Mine.* You know what that means."

Ainsley felt like her face was on fire. Her lips, her cheeks, her ears — everything burned. And in the background, the screaming...

Delano stared at her, his impossibly dark eyes gone blank. "What did you say?"

"Devon is my daughter." She held his gaze, willing him to grasp the truth. "If your research is correct, if what you've told me is the truth, then Janecek can't possibly turn her. But if he does this, maybe *she* can turn *him*." Her eyes begged him to understand. "It's our only chance."

He reeled backward. "Devon is *your* daughter? Not Lucy's?"

"Yes."

Devon shrieked again, a high-pitched, terror-stricken animal sound. Lucy screamed.

Ainsley clapped her hands over her ears. *I'm sorry, I'm sorry, I'm sorry!*

"Yes, she's my daughter, but I gave her away. It was just like you said about the other Merzetti women. I was driven to get pregnant, despite my normally good judgment, and then I felt equally driven to have the baby and give it away. Except Lucy wanted her. Lucy was a product of the foster system, like me, and she campaigned to claim my baby as her own from my first missed period. And God help me, I let her."

"Sweet Christ on the cross."

"I know, I know. I should have told you about this, but as you've pointed out, it's encoded in my genes to protect her by denying her."

Delano sat down again, heavily, obviously conceding the truth of her argument. An argument that would force him to stand by impotently while a child was hideously traumatized.

The screaming had stopped, replaced by Lucy's sobbing. Ainsley shuddered, feeling her friend's grief. She clasped her hands around her midriff, rocking back and forth in an effort to contain her own agony.

Then the sound of the idling copter surged, then faded, followed by another soul-ripping wail from Lucy.

"There you go, Delano. Come and get her. Maybe you'll have better luck with a daughter."

Delano leapt up, but Eli restrained him with a hand on his shoulder. "I'll extract her. If you go out there, he's apt to shoot you."

"No he won't." Delano's mouth was a grim slash. "He'll want me to suffer longer than that. He'll want me to think about the role I played in creating yet another abomination."

"Then he won't interfere with my evacuating her."

"Thank you for the offer, but —"

"He's right, Del." Ainsley closed her hand around his wrist for the second time in as many minutes. "If you go out there now, his anger is likely to get the better of him. Or he might just decide that time is of the essence, and he can't afford to make you suffer as long as he'd like. After all, the night is wearing on. He won't want to be caught here come sunup. And he knows once you're out of the way, I'll trade myself to try to save Lucy."

"You're outvoted." Eli tugged on his flak jacket and headed for the roof.

Delano snatched a radio from the table and depressed the button. "This is Dr. Bowen. Grayson is headed to the roof to retrieve the child. Can you give me a sit rep from the cameras? I want a play-by-play when he hits the roof."

"Roger that, Dr. Bowen. Stand by."

Ainsley reached for his free hand and squeezed it. He squeezed back hard enough to hurt her hand, but she refused to flinch.

Devon will be okay. You'll see. Ainsley mustered all the calm assurance she could and directed it toward Delano, wanting to return the favor he'd done for her so many times in the past. When he didn't respond, she squeezed his hand again. *Really, Del. She'll be okay, and so will Eli.*

Again, he didn't respond, and it sank in. He wasn't hearing her. Omigod, what did that mean?

And holy shit, she hadn't heard more than a handful of words from him in the last hours. She'd been far too stressed to have noticed the omission. Or if she'd registered it on any level —

"Grayson is on the roof, sir."

Delano squeezed her fingers again.

"He's picking up the child. She appears to be conscious. Yes, she's definitely conscious. She's hanging on to him pretty hard. No activity from the helo. He's on his way back. Closer, closer ... he's inside!"

"Tsk, tsk, Delano. You disappoint me." Janecek's voice came over the speaker again. Lucy's sobs had stopped, but the low, raw keening coming over the phone made the hair stand up on Ainsley's arms.

"I expected you to come storming out to try to stop me. Not only did you not try to intervene, you sent a mere man to pick up my leavings. Are you learning some sense at last?"

Delano's hands fisted. "That was my inclination, naturally, but I was persuaded that you might use the occasion to shred me with your guns."

"I'm wounded."

"You are beyond wounded, Radak." Delano said. "Now give us twenty minute's peace while we see to the child."

"Granted," he said pleasantly. "I would hate to seem ungracious."

Swearing, Delano stabbed the off button, and the room went silent. Somehow, not being able to hear Lucy's heart-rending keening was worse. Then the door opened and Eli shouldered his way into the room bearing the child.

Ainsley flew to him, taking Devon into her own arms. The little girl wrapped herself around Ainsley, clinging with the desperation of a mind stretched to the breaking point by terror.

"Oh, baby, I'm so sorry. I'm so sorry."

"I want Mama!"

"We're working on that, baby. We're working on it. But right now, you've got your Aunt Ainsley." She glanced at Delano, who gestured to the hall leading to the bedrooms. Good idea. They could shut the door so she wouldn't have to hear her mother's grief. Ainsley carried her through, bypassing Eli's bedroom where the pilot was stashed, and continuing to her own room. But when she tried to lay the child on the bed, she clung tighter, practically cutting off Ainsley's oxygen supply.

"It's okay, baby. We just want to look you over and make sure you're all right. You know I'm a nurse, right?"

She felt the girl's nod against her neck.

"And this man is a doctor. Dr. Bowen and I just want to check you over, okay honey?"

"Noooooo!"

Ainsley looked at Delano hopelessly. Short of forcibly prying Devon away, they weren't going to get her off. She clung with the tenacity of a limpet.

"Just sit down on the bed with her."

Ainsley sat, and Delano perched on the edge of the bed beside her, on the left so he could see Devon's face. Devon immediately shifted to bury her face into the other side of Ainsley's neck.

"That's okay, little one, you don't have to look at me." Delano's voice was pitched low and soothing, warm and smooth as velvet. "Just listen."

He then proceeded to weave a spell with his voice. Under its soothing, hypnotic influence, Devon loosened her death grip on Ainsley's neck. On and on he talked. Within five minutes, Ainsley felt the change in the child she held. Incredibly, Devon was asleep!

She turned questioning eyes on Delano.

"Lie her down. She'll sleep now."

"What about blood loss? Do we need to worry about replacing volume?"

Delano shook his head. "Given that he planned to turn her, he would not have taken enough blood to weaken her substantially, and he infused her with some of his own blood to compensate for the loss. Check for yourself. Her capillary refill looks very good."

"Let me lie her down."

Ainsley stood with her burden and Delano swept the blankets back. Ainsley lay Devon down, and the little girl immediately rolled onto her side and drew her little legs up into a fetal position. Ainsley took her free hand and squeezed the nail bed of her thumb. Her color bounced back satisfactorily. "You're right."

"Healing sleep is what she needs more than anything right now, but we should be ready with plenty of fluids when she wakes."

As Ainsley tucked the blankets around her fiercely sleeping daughter, she blinked back tears. Poor little mite.

She turned to Delano. "Thank you."

"You're welcome. But there's one last thing." He knelt beside the bed and put a large, gentle hand on Devon's temple.

"Can you hear me, little one?"

Devon slipped her thumb into her mouth, but she nodded her head on the pillow.

"Good girl. Now listen carefully. You were very brave out there, braver than any child in the history of the world, and your mother," he glanced at Ainsley, "is very proud of you. We're all very proud of you. But now you can forget about it. When you wake, you will have no memory of the bad man or anything he did. Now sleep, little one."

Devon burrowed deeper into her pillow, and Delano stood.

Through her tears, Ainsley smiled. "If I hadn't already fallen for you, that would have done it." She moved into his arms, sliding her hands around his back.

Chapter 23

"OH, MY LOVE." Delano swallowed, but he couldn't dislodge the ache of emotion in his throat. He pulled her closer, pressing her tear-wet face into his shirt. His cracked ribs protested the pressure, but he welcomed the pain. He was alive. He was *human*. And he was so full of love for this woman that he feared he would die of the pain of it, of the time they might not have together. If they didn't survive this . . .

Another tremor shook his whole body. God, he'd never felt weaker. The compulsion he'd worked on the terrified child had probably cost him the last of his resources, but he was fiercely glad he'd been able to do it.

Ainsley's child.

The wonder of it had him blinking back tears again. The poor wee thing might just have saved the day. Hell, she might have saved humanity.

But only if they acted fast.

Delano grasped Ainsley's arms and put her away, clearing his throat. "I'm sorry, my love, but we've used up half our reprieve. We have to get back to the table and formulate a plan."

"I know." She wiped the tears away with her palms and led the way back to the dining room.

Eli was just terminating a radio conversation when they entered the room. "How's the kid?" he asked.

"She's sleeping."

Ainsley sent Delano a look overflowing with a mother's gratitude. It was enough to make him want to weep again. He deserved no glory for that small piece of healing, not when he'd left a child to do a man's job.

She turned back to Eli. "I think she's going to forget the whole thing."

Eli nodded. "Makes sense. Believe me, it wouldn't be the first case of trauma-induced amnesia I've seen in a pediatric patient in my travels."

"I've seen it, too," Ainsley said, "but Del didn't leave anything to chance. He gave her a little help in the form of a hypnotic suggestion."

"Enough." The word emerged harsher than he intended. More softly, he continued: "We need a plan to bring this monster down, and we need it fast. We have ..." he checked his watch, "approximately nine-and-a-half minutes."

Eli scowled. "I've been beating my head against the proverbial wall trying to figure a way, but his hostage trumps everything we've got. Not to mention the big guns. If there's a way to storm that copter and extract Mrs. Michaels safely, I'm not seeing it."

Delano's eyes narrowed, as a picture came to him of another monster lying on his deathbed after infusing the Merzetti blood. Of course!

"Maybe we don't have to storm the helicopter."

Eli's face hardened. "Don't even suggest it, Delano. Neither of you are going to walk out there and turn yourselves over. You know you won't live to get off the roof of this building, and he'll kill the hostage anyway."

"I'm not suggesting that. At least not yet. First, let's see if we can get him to do our work for us."

"I'm not following."

"I think I'm beginning to." Ainsley stepped closer, searching his eyes.

"Whoa, what am I missing? What are we talking about here?"

"Remember Edward Webber, the vampire who attacked me back in St. Cloud," Ainsley said. At Eli's nod, she continued: "He died as a result of ingesting my blood."

Eli's eyebrows shot up and he glanced at Delano. "I thought he might have had a little help from you, Del."

"Afraid not. He died pretty much by his own hand. Shortly after attacking Ainsley, he started to feel weak. In an effort to bolster his strength, he fed again. When I found him, he was already dying from acute hemolysis. The mutation reversal must have already started when he fed the second time, leaving him open to ABO incompatibility."

Eli whistled. "So it *does* work!"

Ainsley gripped his arm. "But you don't know for certain that it was the second feeding that killed him, right? Maybe it was just the exposure to my blood that killed him!"

In her excitement, her nails bit into his flesh. Despite the seriousness of the situation, the irony of it curved his lips. Mere weeks ago, he'd agonized about her reaction should she discover that her blood had killed Webber. Now, she looked positively gleeful at the prospect that her blood could inflict deadly harm. Context was everything.

"God, if that's the case, our problems with Janecek could be solved, since he fed from Devon, and Devon carries the Merzetti blood. If we just wait —"

"No." Delano held up a hand to stop her. "It will take more than just exposure to the Merzetti Effect to bring Janecek down. Exposure merely initiates the reversal. For harm to come to the subject, they have to take blood again, potentially setting off a transfusion reaction. If they abstain from feeding while the reversal transpires, or if they feed on a victim who happens to be a compatible match, they'll suffer no ill effect."

Ainsley, however, was not prepared to abandon her theory that the Merzetti Effect alone might be sufficient.

"You can't possibly know that!" she said. "I know you're very close, but your research isn't there yet."

"Nevertheless, I am quite positive. The Merzetti Effect merely reverses the mutation; it doesn't kill."

"How?"

He unbuttoned his shirt and shrugged it down to expose his back, then turned to display it for her. "This is how I know."

Her sharply indrawn breath indicated she understood what the thin pink weals meant.

"Omigod! They didn't disappear with the day sleep."

"No. Nor did the lacerations on my scalp disappear. Nor will the cracked ribs I sustained diving onto that landing earlier."

Eli swore, evidently also comprehending the situation.

Ainsley was staring at him with a mixture of disbelief and some other emotion — horror?

"You're ... omigod, you're —"

"No longer a vampire." He shrugged back into the shirt and started to do up the buttons again. "Apparently, the Merzetti Effect is sexually transmissible after all."

Ainsley struggled to bring her panic under control. *No, no, no, no, no.* She couldn't do this anymore. She just could not.

The minute she thought she had some things figured out, the world shifted on her. What else could change? What new, inconceivable, fucking thing could happen to finally push her bruised psyche past the breaking point? Could the chairs walk? Would the walls talk? Was this whole life-on-earth thing a controlled experiment conducted by alien scientists from light years away?

"Ainsley, we need to talk, but there's no time." He took her hand, which hung limply at her side. "Right now, we need to come up with a plan."

She put a hand to her forehead, trying to push back the panic. "I don't know. I don't know. Dammit, I can't think!"

He cupped her face in his hands. "Ainsley, look at me."

She complied, immediately falling straight into those dark, nearly black, eyes.

I know it's a lot to take in, baby, but I love you. I love you and I'm going to take care of you. Nothing will change that. Nothing.

Ainsley felt the extreme effort it cost him to slip into her mind. She let her thoughts touch his, drew comfort from his calm assurance. Then he was gone, sliding back out of her mind like an ebbing wave retreating from the shoreline.

"Okay." She drew in a deep, shuddering breath, then let it out. "I'm okay." And as she said it, she found it was true.

"Good." He squeezed her hand. "But if it's all right with you, we're going to tell Janecek that you're not okay."

"Huh?"

"We're going to tell him you're having a bona fide, Grade A meltdown. We need to stall him, so that's what I'll tell him. I'll say I refuse to deliver you up in this shape, and he'll have to give us some time to put you back together. I'll tell him it has to be your choice, and you have to go out under your own steam."

"You think he'll buy that?"

"I *know* he'll buy it." His smile had a cynical edge. "He thinks all non-vampires are weak-minded sheep. He also knows I wouldn't let you trade yourself if you lacked the capacity to make the decision. Oh, he'll buy it, all right."

Ainsley frowned. "And while he's twiddling his thumbs, we're going to be doing precisely what?"

"If his experience is anything like Webber's, he should be starting to feel a little woozy. He'll attribute it to hunger. We're going to offer him a snack."

The speakerphone rang, the trill sounding angrier and more insistent than before, although Ainsley knew that couldn't be so.

"Ainsley, you're not here, okay? You can listen, but you can't speak. You can't sneeze. You can't make any sound to suggest you're not closeted in your room having a mental breakdown. Can you do that?"

She nodded that she understood.

Delano stabbed the button to answer the call. "Janecek, you will burn in hell for what you did here tonight."

Janecek's laughter filled the room. "No doubt you're right," he said, when he'd contained his mirth, "but not before you, Father. Which reminds me, how are you enjoying my new sister?"

"Fuck you, Janecek."

"Ooooh, I think I got to him. What do you think, Lucy, honey?"

A whimper sounded in the background, and Delano sent Ainsley a warning look not to react audibly. Ainsley covered her mouth.

Delano returned his attention to Janecek. "What you've got, *son*," — he invested the word with a wealth of disdain — "is a problem."

"What do you mean?" Janecek's voice was suddenly sharp.

"Nurse Crawford is now a basket case, thanks to that atrocity you committed on that child. There's no way I'm letting her go out there in her present condition. She's in no fit state to make the decision to sacrifice herself for the hostage."

A pause. "She'll make the decision, all right. I'll just entertain myself with Lucy here until she can't stand the sound of her friend's screams."

"That might work," Delano agreed calmly. "If I'd let her out of the bedroom so she could hear them."

"Bring her to the phone right now, Bowen, or I'll make this bitch pay."

Delano laid a restraining hand on Ainsley's arm.

"That would be regrettable, but as you've observed, I'm just too damned invested in the greater good to be trusted."

A stream of vituperative erupted from the speakerphone.

"Oh, relax, Radak. Ms. Crawford would make sure my life was not worth living if I let anything happen to her friend. But understand this, I will not send her out there in her current condition."

"And her current condition is what?"

"She's virtually catatonic, thank you. You'll have to give me at least an hour, maybe more. I'll use my powers to put her mind back together, but the decision to trade herself for her friend has to be hers. I won't push a zombie out onto that roof."

More cursing.

"Are we agreed?" Delano pressed.

"You have one hour."

"Good. Now, is there anything we can do to accommodate you while you wait? It must have been a while since you fed. I can send out a couple of units."

Janecek snorted. "Yeah, right. Like I would drink blood from a fucking bag. Blood that you've probably siphoned out of that Merzetti whore."

"Then what would be to your liking? You can't dine on your one remaining pilot, for safety's sake, and if you want me to put Ms. Crawford back together, you'll not touch a drop of her friend's blood."

A pause that seemed to stretch forever.

"Okay, here's the deal. Send me a man from your security staff, and get him up here in one minute so you don't have time to mess with his blood. I want him handcuffed, with his hands behind his back. I want him to come out on the roof, turn a full 360 so I can check him for weapons. Then I want him to approach and kneel outside the helicopter."

"I have your word you won't harm him?"

A jeering laugh. "You would trust my word?"

"It seems I don't have much choice. I want to make a good-faith gesture, in return for your concession, and for not molesting Mrs. Michaels."

"Very well. I will leave him quite able to leave the roof under his own steam."

"A moment," Delano said. "I need to speak with my security chief." Del stabbed the mute button. "We've got him! Now we just need to persuade one of the men to submit."

"I'll do it," Eli said.

Ainsley's objection merged with Delano's. "No!"

"Yes! It's perfect, Delano. After all these years, I can be instrumental in bringing down the predator who murdered more than half my company." Eli's normally impassive face was wreathed in passion. "Don't take this away from me, Del. Let me do it."

"Eli, my friend, I appreciate the gesture, but I can't let you do it. I need you here. More importantly, if anything should happen to me, Ainsley needs you."

"The success or failure of this gamble hinges on whether or not we can set off an acute hemolysis, correct?"

"That's right," Delano conceded guardedly.

Eli grinned broadly. "Then I'm your man. I'm AB-freakin'-positive."

Ainsley's jaw dropped. "You're kidding? AB positive? That's the rarest of all blood types."

"Not quite as rare as AB negative, but damned close," Eli said. "Just over three in a hundred people have it. Fortunately for me, it makes me a universal recipient in that I can receive blood of any ABO type and Rh."

"AB positive," Delano murmured. "Which means that unless our friend Janecek is a member of the exclusive AB club, the results will be catastrophic."

Eli laughed triumphantly. "Not just AB. He has to be *AB positive*."

"Perfect!"

"So I've got the job?"

Delano glanced at Ainsley, who nodded. "It's yours." Then he depressed the mute button to bring Janecek back on line.

"Radak, I've found a volunteer for you. It's my security chief. As you know, he's not exactly the trusting kind, and he wouldn't hear of jeopardizing anyone else. Insisted on doing it himself."

"Ah, the formidable Mr. Grayson." Ainsley could hear the lust in his voice. "This will be sweet, indeed!"

"What it will be is clean and perfunctory," Delano gritted, "and you will release Mr. Grayson unharmed and unmolested if you wish me to restore Ms. Crawford's functionality. Is that understood?"

"That's so like you, Bowen, to suck all the fun out of anything." A pause. When Janecek spoke again, his voice was all business. "Okay, when I say go, he's got one minute to get up here. His hands will be cuffed behind his back, cuffs double-locked and snug, and looped through his belt. When he steps onto the roof, he'll rotate a full 360 degrees so we can inspect him and ensure that you've complied with these instructions. On my signal, he will then approach the aircraft. He will kneel facing the copter, and will cross his legs at the ankles. Is that clear."

"Understood," said Eli.

"Go!"

Delano muted the phone while Eli produced his own cuffs.

"I'll get one of my guys on the landing to cuff me. It'll be quicker, and they'll do it right." With that he headed for the exit on the double.

Ainsley wanted to call him back, to tell him to be safe, or to hug him or something, but dammit, there was no time to be lost.

Oh, God, what if Janecek drained him dry?

Or what if Eli decided he couldn't wait for his blood to do its work — or didn't trust it to do it's work — and tried to take the vampire out in some other kamikaze fashion?

Her stomach lurched, and she started hyper-salivating.

Delano had already picked up the radio. While he gave a rapid-fire update to the team in the security office downstairs, Ainsley pushed back her chair and put her head between her knees.

She would not faint. Nor would she vomit. She would not.

"Ainsley, honey, are you okay?"

"I'm okay." She sat up again, wiping perspiration from her brow. Swallowing excess saliva, she wiped her mouth, too. "Just a little nauseated there, but I'm all right now."

"You don't have to stay here for this. Why don't you go sit with Devon?"

"Is she likely to waken?"

He shook his head. "Not for hours."

"Then I'm staying."

"He's on the roof," came the voice of the security command office twenty-eight floors below. "He's turning, turning …"

Delano came to stand behind her chair, placing his hands on her shoulders. She lifted her left hand to cover his right and squeezed.

"Okay he's heading toward the helo. He's stopped. He's kneeling now, legs crossed at the ankle as instructed. The helo's door is opening … and the subject is out. He seems to be scanning the roof. Now he's circling Grayson, inspecting the handcuff job." A pause. "I think … wait … he seems to be saying something to

Grayson. Now the subject has Grayson by the hair, tipping his head back. He's bending ... oh, Jesus. Oh, Christ."

"It's okay," Delano cut in sharply. "I don't need a play-by-play of this part. Just tell me when he's finished."

After what seemed like eternity but which probably was no more than a minute, the voice came back.

"Oh, thank God, he's done. Grayson is still kneeling there."

"Is he bleeding?"

"Umm ... no. Not that I can see, anyway, but I don't have the best angle."

Thank God! Ainsley knew from her own experience that if Janecek had failed to seal the wound, they'd see plenty of spurting blood, no matter what the camera's angle.

"Janecek is retreating to the helo. Grayson is getting up now. Whoa!"

"What's wrong?"

"It's okay. He's okay. He just stumbled a little, but he's on his feet now, approaching the door. Opening the door. He's in!"

Ainsley rushed to the exit and tore open the door. "Eli?" She heard the tread of several men's booted feet on the steps, and in a matter of seconds, Eli appeared on the landing, a burly man gripping each of his now uncuffed arms.

"Oh, God, bring him in!"

She almost bumped into Delano as she stepped back to clear the doorway. He caught her to save the collision, but instead of releasing her, he pulled her back against him.

"I'm okay," Eli said.

"I doubt that," said Delano, releasing Ainsley to examine Eli. Ainsley saw him squeeze one of Eli's fingernails. She saw, also, how slow the capillary refill was. "The sit rep I just got said you stumbled when you got to your feet. Sure you're not feeling a little woozy?"

He laughed, a giddy, delighted sound, as one of his men released the cuffs. "I'm feeling *extremely* woozy, thank you very much. Stupid sonofabitch took lots!"

Ainsley didn't know whether to laugh or cry, so she put her nurse face on. "Carry him to the last bedroom at the end of corridor and make him comfortable on the bed. Get that armor off him. As soon as I find the supplies, I'll be in to start him on whole blood."

"I'll get it," Delano volunteered. "Everything's downstairs in the lab. But first, a word for our friend."

He crossed to the table and stabbed the mute button. "Goddammit, Radak, do you think you took enough? You gave me your word you wouldn't harm him."

"What?" Janecek's voice came over the speaker, sounding sated and pleased with himself. "I told you I would leave him ambulatory. Did he not get back inside under his own steam?"

"No thanks to you."

"Yes, well, do tell him thanks. He was every bit as luscious as I knew he would be."

"Of course. I'll just mention that as I'm transfusing him, shall I? I'm sure he'll be thrilled. Speaking of which, I now have to address getting a transfusion started before I can sit down with Ms. Crawford. I'm going to need better than an hour now. Probably ninety minutes or more."

"Then you'd better learn how to multi-task. You have exactly one hour to put Miss Humpty-Dumpty together again, starting right now."

Janecek hung up, leaving a dial tone buzzing over the speaker. Delano closed the line, plunging the room into silence.

Ainsley bit her lip. "Will an hour be long enough for the transfusion reaction to set in?"

"Let's hope so. It certainly didn't take long for Edward Webber, and I doubt Webber imbibed nearly so deeply of his second victim as Janecek did just now."

"He drank deeply from Eli, but not from Devon. And she's so small … Are you sure this will work?"

A muscle in his jaw leapt. "It has to."

Ainsley walked over to him on trembling legs and slid her arms around his waist. He closed him own arms around her and squeezed her once, fiercely enough to crush the breath from her body, then pulled away.

"I know," she said, touching his face. "The transfusion. Go fetch what we need and I'll get him prepped."

Delano grimaced at the burning in his thigh muscles as he took the last flight of steps in three bounds and shouldered the door to the penthouse open. It was going to take some time getting used to his new — or rather, his old — physiology. He put down the heavy oxygen tank he was carrying, punched in the security code to keep the alarm from squawking, and strode to his bedroom.

Ainsley greeted him at the door, taking the carry tote from his hand and leaving him with the portable oxygen. "I'll get venous access established while you get that oxygen on him."

Delano thanked his stars for Ainsley's trauma training. Seconds counted in these situations. "How's the patient?"

Eli opened his eyes. Though his pallor was evident against the dark pillow, he still managed to look reassuringly robust. "The patient can talk for himself."

"That's encouraging." Delano started the oxygen, adjusted the flow, then lifted the mask to Eli's face. "But now the patient is going to have to shut up and take this oxygen."

Eli grinned. "Don't mind if I do."

After fitting the mask to Eli's face, Delano looked down to see that Ainsley had already managed to get the large-gauge cannula into his left arm. Eli hadn't even flinched. He was a better man than most.

"Good work," Delano told Ainsley. "Now, let's trade places so you can get this other arm, while I fix up an IV suspension system."

"You make a great team," came Eli's muffled voice from beneath the mask.

"We do, don't we? Now save your breath." Delano removed his belt, climbed onto the bed and proceeded to cinch the belt around the arm of one of the blades on the ceiling fan, leaving the end dangling.

Ainsley regarded the length of leather.

"Interesting, but I don't see how we're going to suspend the bags from that."

Delano produced one of a couple of S hooks that he'd found in the lab. "We simply stick one end through a belt hole and voila."

"Brilliant! Here you go."

She handed up both bags. Carefully, he secured them on the hook and stepped off the bed.

Delano checked his patient to see that Eli was regarding the ceiling fan IV assembly with a little less admiration than Ainsley had displayed.

"Ainsley?" Eli said.

She lifted the edge of the oxygen mask so she could hear his words better. "What is it? Are you feeling okay?"

"Never better," he replied, "but if you don't mind, could you take some of that tape and secure the switch to that ceiling fan?"

Delano had a mental flash of the fan being switched on, the blades turning, ripping out the IV. He couldn't help it; he laughed. A second later, Ainsley joined him. Even Eli was laughing under the oxygen mask.

Ainsley wiped tears from her eyes. "Thank you for the laugh. I really needed it. But you know, that's not a bad idea." She picked up the roll of tape and went to take care of the wall switch.

Delano leaned in to check the lines. Perfect. Ainsley was a consummate professional, even under these rough circumstances.

"Is there anything more I can do for you before I go back out there to monitor the phone?" he asked Eli. "I'll be back, of course, for blood samples so we can keep an eye on things."

Eli rolled his eyes, which Delano took to be a suggestion to lift the mask.

"Yeah, there's something you can do. You can bring the damned phone."

"You want to use the phone?"

"Not *a* phone. *The* phone.

"The speakerphone?"

"You must have a phone jack in here, don't you?"

"Of course, but you've given enough to the job for today, Eli. Let us handle it from here."

"What us?" he demanded. "Ainsley'll be stuck in here nursing me, or running back and forth with her attention divided. Just bring the damn phone in here. Oh, and a radio so we can stay in touch with the security cam view of what's happening on the roof."

"He has a good point, Delano. I don't want to leave him, but I need to know what's going on up there."

Delano fixed Eli with a glare. "You're not going to take this patient thing lying down, are you?" Of course, his exasperation sprang only partly from Eli's reluctance to play the patient. He'd been half hoping to shield Ainsley from the next act in this little drama. Looked like that was a non-starter.

"Did you really expect me to?"

Delano sighed. "I guess not." He retrieved the radio, which was sitting with the pile of supplies he'd brought up from the lab, and tossed it on the bed where Ainsley could reach it. "You better have this, in case it squawks before I get back with the speakerphone."

When he came back two minutes later with the speakerphone and a spare radio, Eli had the oxygen back on and Ainsley was hanging a catheter bag by clipping it to the handle of the night table with an alligator clip she'd found. Before he could compliment her ingenuity, the radio squawked.

Ainsley dove for the radio on the bed, but Delano produced the spare he'd pocketed. "Bowen here. What's the status on the roof?"

"Looks like activity in the helo, but I can't tell what's going on. It's hard to tell without sound, but it almost looks like he's trashing the inside of the helo."

"The phone!" Ainsley grabbed it from him. "Where's the jack? We need to get it plugged in. If he's frustrated, he'll call."

No sooner did she say that when the phone began to ring from the other room. "There!" Delano pointed to a phone jack to the left of his bed, situated right beside an electrical outlet. "Give me the power supply. It has to be plugged in, as well."

Between the two of them, they got it plugged in and it began to ring. Delano hit the button to answer it.

"Bowen."

"Your time is up," Janecek shouted. "Both of you. On the roof. Now."

"I told you it would take the better part of an hour. We haven't used half that much time yet. I've barely begun —"

"Changed my mind." A pause, filled by labored breathing, as though his earlier roar had done him in. "I've decided ... I'm in rather ... a hurry."

A jolt of excitement jittered through him at Janecek's breathlessness. "Radak? You don't sound so good. Is something wrong up there?"

"Nothing wrong. Just need the woman. And you."

"I'm sorry, that's not going to happen until I finish working with Nurse Crawford. She's only now starting to respond. It'll take —"

A crash and a curse. "Waste of time ... fixing her. Send her now."

"Radak, are you having trouble breathing? Is your heart racing?"

"What? What did you say?"

"Are you feeling a little weak, maybe? Or experiencing chest pain?"

An anguished howl. "How?" he demanded. "How did you do it? How did you poison me?"

"I didn't."

"Fuck you, Bowen. You did so! But how?"

"I'm afraid you partook of the Merzetti blood, Radak."

"No. Impossible. Grayson can't have ... the Merzetti blood. You would never let him spend ... so much time ... on the front lines. Too risky."

"Not Grayson. I told you, *I* didn't do this to you. You did it to yourself."

"*Noooooooooo!*"

"Yes. The girl. You didn't turn her, Radak. She's sleeping like a princess in her mother's bed. Her biological mother's bed."

"Bitch!" he snarled. "It was that little whore! You! You knew about this."

A female scream. Then the cell phone Janecek had been using crashed to the floor.

"Lucy!" Ainsley screamed. Then she turned on Delano. "Omigod, what have you done? He'll kill her now! He knows he has nothing to lose!"

"She'll be able to fend him off. He's weak as a kitten." *He hoped.* Jesus, it wasn't supposed to go this way. His plan was to make Janecek's plight plain, then dangle the prospect of medical assistance to motivate him to surrender quickly. And dammit, it was a good plan, but the vampire had let his rage get the better of him.

"Pilot!" Delano shouted. "Pilot, pick up! Pick up this phone, dammit, if you want to live. Do you hear me? Pick up the phone. Do it now!"

"Hello?"

Delano's knees went weak with relief, but he steeled his voice. "Listen carefully. Your boss is dying. I'm a doctor, and there's no doubt about the outcome. He will die, and he'll die soon. But I don't want any harm to come to that nice young woman before he dies, and neither do you. Now tell me, is she all right?"

"She's holding her own."

"Good. Because if anything bad happens to the lady, I'll no longer feel constrained not to use my anti-aircraft guns when you try to lift that bird off my roof. Do you take my meaning?"

"Guns?"

"Yes, big ones. Did you happen to notice that skylight when you landed? It's not really a skylight. And even if you should lift off safely, I've got your partner. He can't talk right now, since I've robbed him of the power of speech, but I expect he can write if I put pen and paper in his hands. And I'm pretty confident I can persuade your name out of him if I promise to reverse the tracheostomy I gave him. If this does not turn out well, I will hunt you down and feed your own liver to you. Are we understood?"

"Okay, okay! I'll help you."

"Your boss is still conscious?"

"Yes. Jesus. H. Christ, he's looking at me! He knows I'm talking to you."

"Don't worry about it. I promise you, he can't hurt you. By all means, shoot him if you feel you need to, or in defense of Mrs. Michaels, but I really don't think you'll need to. Even as we speak, his body is killing off red blood cells in a wholesale slaughter that he can't possibly survive. Is he having trouble catching his breath?"

"Yes."

"That fits. His heart will be racing, too, and his blood pressure will have plummeted. In short order, he'll go into shock and die."

"Jesus," came the pilot's reply.

"Now, I'm going to send some men out onto the roof. What I want you to do is find a way to get Ms. Michaels out of the helo. You, too. I'll give you total amnesty. You'll be free to walk away, or fly away, as you please, when this is over. But I want that woman, and I want her unharmed. Are we understood?"

The pilot swore.

"Seems like a better deal than dying for your boss, especially considering he's going to predecease you and won't be around to appreciate your sacrifice."

"Okay, dammit, I'll do it. Oh, *fuck it*! I have to go."

The line went dead.

"The radio," Ainsley cried. "Find out what's happening up there!"

"One second." Delano raised the radio to his mouth again and depressed the transmitter button. "B Team, do you read?"

"Loud and clear, Dr. Bowen."

"Janecek is critically ill. We spiked his meal, so to speak, and he's failing fast."

A cheer rose from the men, reverberating in the concrete stairwell. "Well done, sir!"

"We've also talked to the pilot, who has agreed to get himself and Ms. Michaels out of the helicopter at the first opportunity. I want your team on the roof to grab them up and hustle them inside when they make the break."

"Roger that. We're headed for the roof. Over."

Ainsley caught his arm. "What's happening inside the helicopter?"

He slid his arm around her shoulders and depressed the radio's button again. "A Team, what have you got on the roof cam?"

"Nothing much right now. For a moment, it looked like the two men might come to blows, but one of them collapsed. Just kinda folded up, you know? No idea why."

Ainsley dug her fingers into his forearm and he squeezed her shoulder again. "Which one?" he asked. "Janecek or the pilot?"

"Couldn't tell. But it's been quiet in there since."

"Presuming it was Janecek who went down, we can look for the pilot to make a break. Are we ready up there?"

"Absolutely. B Team's in position."

"Excellent. Apprise me of any changes. Over."

Ainsley's anxious gaze caught his. "If that was Janecek who went down, what are they waiting for?"

He handed her the radio he'd been using and picked up the spare. "I don't know, but I'm going to find out."

Chapter 24

"No!" AINSLEY'S HEART leapt. Though she knew better, she felt like it had lodged itself somewhere around the base of her throat. "There's no need for you to go up there."

"There is," he asserted quietly. "As you so correctly pointed out, I put Mrs. Michaels at increased risk by telling Janecek what I told him. I thought if I could impress on him the seriousness of his condition, I could persuade him to come out and seek medical attention."

She'd been about to apologize for jumping on him earlier, but that last bit distracted her. "You would save him? After all he's done, you would spare his life?"

"I doubt he could be saved in the most sophisticated of hospitals, even if he could survive the transfer, which is highly improbable. And even if he could survive a transfer, how would they begin to treat him? He's caught half way between vampire and non-vampire. An intervention would be as likely to kill him as save him. But that's neither here nor there. I merely hoped to expedite an end to the hostage situation by offering the prospect of medical salvation."

Of course. Regret scored her with merciless talons. She should have known he had a plan. And it would have worked if Janecek had listened instead of throwing the phone down. "I'm sorry about what I said, Delano. It was a good plan. But the way it worked out is just as good, isn't it? You've got the pilot on our side."

"Providing the pilot isn't the one who went down."

She cast around for another excuse to keep him here, to keep him safe. "What about the blood-bond? By risking your life to go up there, you'd be risking mine, too."

By way of answer he grasped her left wrist, pushed her sleeve up and turned her arm up for inspection.

Gone.

Her battered heart plummeted. The marks were gone as if... as if...

Oh, God, as if the blood-bond had dissolved.

"What..." She put a hand to chest as though she could somehow ease the crushing weight of loss. "It can't be. I mean, how?"

"It's only possible between vampires, remember? Or in our case, between vampire and anti-vampire. You're still anti-vampire, but I'm no longer vampire," he said gently. "My marks started to wane as soon as my powers started to leave me."

"So..."

"Your destiny is no longer immediately linked to mine. You have nothing to fear."

She swallowed. She wasn't afraid for herself, damn him. "Okay, what about the vaccine? If anything happens to you —"

"The vaccine is all but complete. If you go to my lab, you'll find I've written down the names and contact information for two researchers, one American and one Australian. They're good men — non-vampires, of course — but more open-minded than most. They might be skeptical to begin with, but they'll be too intrigued to refuse. If anything happens to me, you must contact them."

"But I don't want anything to happen to you!"

"And nothing will." He pulled her close for a quick, hard kiss. "But I have to go. Besides Lucy and the pilot, there's our man in the Comanche. If he's not dead, he'll be in desperate need of medical attention."

"But —"

"Take care of Eli," he said. "And use the radio. Tell them I'm coming out."

Ainsley suppressed the anguished wail that rose in her throat as he disappeared out the door in the direction of the roof exit. She would not call out. She would not. She and Delano were no longer blood-bonded. What would have seemed perfectly acceptable five minutes ago now seemed like the epitome of histrionics.

"Well, that was quite a show."

Heart hammering, Ainsley spun toward her forgotten audience. "I can't believe he's going out there!"

"He has to. By the way, you might want to announce his arrival, just so he doesn't spook his own team."

Oh, God! That'd be all she needed. She depressed the button on the radio. "This is Ainsley Crawford here. Delano ... I mean, Dr. Bowen is on his way to the roof. Repeat, Dr. Bowen is going out on the roof. Did you get that?"

"This is B Team. Copy that. He's already made the roof."

"A Team here. We copy. I have Dr. Bowen on screen."

She put her lips to the radio again. "A Team, can we have a running commentary?"

"Whoa! I think it's all over."

All over? What the hell did that mean? "A Team, report! What happened?"

"The helo door just opened and the hostage climbed out, followed by the pilot. B Team's all over them. Yes! They're inside."

"Janecek?"

"Nowhere to be seen."

"And Dr. Bowen?"

"I lost him."

"You lost him."

"No, there he is! Just had to tweak my camera angle. He's just entered the other helicopter, the one our guy Bartlett was hiding in."

Ainsley lifted the radio again, squeezing the transmitter button so hard her fingers hurt. "We need to send B Team back out there to help him!"

"They're already back."

"Ainsley?"

Delano's voice on the radio. Thank God! "Are you all right, Del?"

"I'm fine, but I've got another incoming. Bartlett has several gunshot wounds, and he's lost a lot of blood, but he's alive. We have to stabilize him for transfer."

"Thank God," said Eli. "Tough bastard."

She blinked. "Transfer where? Won't it raise some hard-to-answer questions if we waltz in with a multiple gunshot victim?"

"I have my contacts. Just be ready to push IV fluids. I'll be right down to help you."

Ainsley glanced at Eli.

"Go," he ordered. "I'm fine."

She raced through the penthouse, skidding to a stop as the door to the stairwell opened. One of the guards, Hayes, was the first through, followed by a haggard-looking Lucy.

"Oh, Luce!"

Lucy went into her arms for a fierce hug. "Omigod, what a nightmare, Ainsley."

Ainsley pulled away. "I know, and it's all my fault."

"Where's Devon?"

"Delano sort of hypnotized her and sent her off to sleep. He says she won't remember anything of this when she wakes up."

Lucy burst into tears. "Thank God."

"I'll take you to her right now. Then I have to attend to a wounded man."

"Just point me in the right direction. You're needed here."

Ainsley obliged. "Second suite of rooms down that hall." She gave her friend another quick, tearful hug. "I'll come see you after this crisis has passed."

Ainsley was vaguely aware of Janecek's pilot entering the penthouse, but he was quickly shuttled down the hall to share quarters with his shackled co-pilot while he awaited Delano's pleasure.

The next twelve minutes were eaten up stabilizing the critical patient, who was carried down from the roof by Delano and one of the security guards. Again, she and Delano worked together easily, as though they'd been doing this forever. When they'd done all they could do, Ainsley leaned back on her heels. "Now what?"

"Now we airlift him to a private clinic about twenty minutes away, where he'll get world-class treatment with no questions asked. I've already called ahead and they'll have a trauma team waiting."

"Isn't that highly illegal? Not to mention a blatant contravention of the Canada Health Act?"

"You left out exorbitantly expensive."

"Hey, wait a minute. Your helicopter is Swiss cheese. How are you going to airlift him?"

"Janecek's pilot is going to give our boys a ride, as a gesture of atonement for his bad judgment in choice of employers. Isn't that right, Mr. Hitchman?"

Ainsley glanced up to see Janecek's pilot once more standing in the room, with one of Delano's men in close proximity.

"That's right, sir. Whatever you need."

Ainsley returned her gaze to Delano. "But what about Janecek?"

"I'm going to remove him from the craft right now, and these men are going to load Mr. Bartlett. I'll accompany them, of course, in case he crashes en route." He glanced at Ainsley. "Can you cope here by yourself, taking care of Eli and the others?"

"Of course."

"Good." Delano tucked an extra blanket around the unconscious Bartlett, stepped back and nodded for two men to take the gurney.

Ainsley opened the door for the stretcher-bearers, and Delano went ahead to get the rooftop door. Not waiting for an invitation, she followed the procession up to the roof.

Delano turned to motion to the three men to hang back while he approached the helo himself, and caught a glimpse of Ainsley's fair head. Dammit, she'd followed them up. Her concern for his safety warmed his heart, even as he wished she'd stayed below. He glanced at the helicopter, seeing no one on their feet. It should be safe enough, he supposed, as long as she stayed back with everyone else.

He approached the helicopter soundlessly. Well, soundless except for the rumbling of his stomach. And damned if he wasn't downright dizzy from hunger. Good, old-fashioned alimentary hunger. Not that he'd given the fierce pangs much attention. His ribs ached too much for him to be aware of much else in the pain department. The rib fracture certainly hadn't been helped by his exertions in getting Bartlett out of the Comanche, and then bending over him to tend his wounds.

The door to Janecek's helo hung ajar, just as the pilot had left it after his hasty exit with Mrs. Michaels. Nevertheless, Delano employed extreme caution as he approached it. A caution that proved unnecessary, he discovered, after risking a quick glimpse inside.

Janecek lay on his back, completely preoccupied with his struggle for the oxygen his body needed. Like Webber before him, Janecek's chest, abdominal and neck muscles labored rhythmically for each breath in a way that put Delano in mind of a fish out of water, gills working uselessly.

He climbed aboard the helicopter. "Radak?"

The dying vampire looked up, struggling to focus. "Ah, come to ... gloat as I ... gasp my last?"

"I've come to evacuate you inside so you can die in comfort."

A choked laugh. Radak lifted his head and looked past Delano, out the open door to the men holding the gurney. "Don't believe this. You need ... my aircraft."

"That, too."

"Will this ... take much longer?"

Delano looked down at the incredibly handsome young man before him, and suddenly he saw Janecek as he'd found him that first day. He'd killed every one of the monks who'd taken him in, leaving the monastery littered with their bodies in varying stages of decay, but when he'd looked up at Delano, he'd done so with the same innocence of any child. A hungry, lonely child.

He looked up at Delano now with much the same confusion, as though Delano could make sense of his situation for him.

Oh, Radak, you were just not strong enough.

He cleared his throat. "I can't say for sure how long it will be. Soon."

Radak's hand clutched at Delano's pant leg. "You must help me."

"I cannot." Delano firmed his jaw. "Even if I wanted to, you are past the help of even the most sophisticated hospital, let alone what I could do for you here."

"Know that." Radak coughed. "Just want ... to make it ... fast."

Delano felt a chill move over his skin, though the night was warm and still. "You want me to finish you?"

"If you ever ... loved me, you'll do this."

Delano stepped back, out of his reach. "You ask too much!"

Radak smiled. "Always did. At least ... leave me ... a gun."

"Dammit, I can't do that."

"Begging you ... don't leave me ... like this."

Son of a bitch.

Blinking rapidly, Delano leapt out of the helicopter and strode to where the other waited. "The medical bag." He gestured to the bag that rested on the gurney at Bartlett's feet. "Quickly."

One of the men handed it to him.

"You," he said to Janecek's pilot, "Get on there and get this bird warmed up."

The pilot circled the craft, opened the other door and climbed in. Delano boarded the helo again and knelt by Janecek, plunking the bag down.

"You'll help me?"

Wordlessly, Delano tugged the bag open, found what he wanted — a multiple-dose vial of hydromorphone and a syringe — and put the bag aside. The chopper's engines turned over and caught, and their whine began to build.

Grimly, he drew up a massively lethal dose of the potent opioid, and looked down at the unsaveable man — the unsaveable *child* he'd tried so hard to save.

Janecek smiled. "Don't worry. If somebody has to ... send me to hell ... glad it's you."

"Goodbye, Radak," he said, but his words were all but drowned out as the chopper's rotors began beating the air. Within seconds of the intravenous injection, Janecek went into full respiratory arrest. After a moment, Delano placed two fingers on Janecek's carotid artery. No pulse. It was done.

Gently, he closed the dead man's sightless eyes. "May God have mercy on your soul, Radak."

He stood abruptly, turned and climbed out of the chopper, crouching low to avoid the whirling rotors, not to mention sparing his abused ribs. A crouching Ainsley darted in, grabbed him by the arm and pulled him away from the helicopter.

"What happened?" she shouted in his ear.

"He's gone."

"Thank God." Her hands roamed his arms, as though to assure herself of his soundness. "How about you? Are you okay?"

He knew she was alluding to his handiwork with the hypodermic. "Fine."

She didn't look persuaded, but she let it drop, given the urgency of their patient's situation. She glanced at the helicopter. "We need to get Bartlett loaded. What are we going do with the body?"

"Strap him into a seat for the ride."

"What?"

"He's not our problem. After the pilot has done this medevac stint for us, I'll release him. The cadaver on board is his boss and his problem." Without waiting for her reaction, Delano called Hayes over and instructed him. As they went about moving Janecek and loading Bartlett, he turned back to Ainsley. "You sure you'll be all right?"

"Perfectly sure. Devon should sleep for hours yet, and Lucy can watch over her. As for Eli —"

"Eli needs his arterial blood gases run and a half dozen other tests. As soon as Bartlett is safely delivered into the hands of the trauma team, I'll leave Hayes there and catch a lift back. If you can have the blood drawn and ready, I'll run the tests as soon as I get back." He glanced at the helo to see that everyone was now loaded. "I've got to go. They're waiting on me."

"I know." Ainsley reached up on tiptoe and pressed her mouth to his for a quick, hard kiss, taking care not to touch his injured ribs. Then she turned and dashed to the door, disappearing inside without a backward glance.

Chapter 25

BY THE TIME Delano made it back to the penthouse roof, dawn was less than twenty minutes off. Odd not to feel any urgency to seek shelter in the face of the coming day. Odder still not to feel his limbs filling with lethargy as the immutable demand of the day-sleep asserted itself. He was free to stand here and watch the sun rise over Montreal's urban skyline, risking nothing more than the pain that witnessing such beauty again would surely cause him.

Except while he was free of his vampiric nature, he wasn't free of duty. There was far too much to be done to linger here to watch a sunrise.

Lifting the radio, he called downstairs for the other pilot — the one whose throat he'd injured — to be brought to the roof for transport to the clinic he'd just left.

Ten minutes later, after his wounded partner had been loaded on board, Hitchman said, "Thanks for doing this, man. We both know my former boss would not have been so gracious if Robertson there was your man."

That, Delano thought, was the understatement of the century. "Just get your friend taken care of."

Hitchman gave him a salute — a genuine, crisp military-style salute — then climbed aboard the idling chopper. As the craft powered up and lifted off, Delano joined his waiting men by the door. They escorted him inside and down the stairs, one on either side as though they thought he might need assistance. Which wasn't far from the truth. He was exhausted and hungry and parched, not to mention his chest felt like it had been trampled by a very large horse.

Ainsley greeted him at the door, and Shalvis and Ross melted away discreetly.

"How is Geoff? Did you get a feel for his prognosis before you left him?"

Geoff? Oh, she must mean Bartlett. He smiled. The guy had worked for Delano for the last four years, and he'd never once used the guy's first name. Leave it to Ainsley.

He wanted to reach out, pull her into his arms and hold her against him. He wanted to feel the in and out of her breath stir against his skin, feel the beat of her heart against his chest. It was so strange not to be able to hear the surge of her blood in her—

"Delano?"

He blinked.

"Geoff Bartlett? How is he?"

"Right. Sorry. His prognosis is not bad, all things considered, but he's going to have the rehab from hell."

"Thank God! I've been worried sick."

She flipped her hair off her nape and he braced for the heated scent of her to invade his senses. Then blinked when all he got was the faintest whiff of her shampoo. This was going to take some getting used to.

He cleared his throat. "How about our patients? How's everyone doing?"

"Devon hasn't stirred. As you promised, she's sleeping like a newborn babe. No nightmares, no anguish, not even the hint of a frown on her forehead."

Thank God he'd had enough power left — *barely* — to give her that gift. "Good. And Mrs. Michaels?"

"Believe it or not, she's sleeping, too. Well, with the aid of a little sedative, and with one arm wrapped around Devon."

"And Eli?"

"Hard at work, managing everything from his sickbed via the radio."

Delano grinned. "That sounds like Eli, all right. Speaking of whom, I've got some tests to do to make sure he doesn't run into trouble."

Before he could turn away, Ainsley grabbed his arm. "Everything's downstairs in your lab and ready for you, but the tests will wait a few more minutes. I've made you something to … that is … I mean, I thought you might be hungry."

His stomach growled by way of reply. "I guess you have your answer," he conceded wryly. "The question is, what do you start with after 168-odd years?"

"I've been giving that some thought. Follow me." She turned and headed for the kitchen.

As instructed, he followed, touched that she had anticipated the potential difficulties.

"You've been drinking water?" She threw the question over her shoulder.

"Lots of it, with no trouble."

"Okay, I figured you can't go wrong if you start bland, and avoid anything fatty, spicy, fibrous or acidic. But then I thought, maybe it should be clear liquids." She gestured to the table, where she'd assembled about a dozen possibilities. "As you can see, I couldn't quite make up my mind."

Delano regarded the assortment of foods. Soda crackers, what looked like plain noodles, applesauce, bananas, and some other unidentifiable mushy thing, not to mention a number of small glasses filled with various clear liquids.

"What do you think?

"I think I'd like an enormous baked potato slathered in creamery butter, along with about half a cow. And to wash it down, about three pints of stout. But I take your point. Small, bland portions washed down with a little apple juice or water is probably a better reintroduction to the joys of eating."

"Okay, have a seat. I'm going to brew some tea. Tea is good." She plugged in an electric kettle. "Would you like me to make some white bread toast?" A frown pleated her brow. "Or not. The butter probably isn't the best idea."

"Relax. There's plenty here." He sat down at the table and pulled the dish of noodles closer.

"The noodles? Good choice. But let me warm them." She snatched the bowl right out from under him and whisked it off to the microwave.

He shrugged and pulled the bowl of sliced bananas closer. Spearing a slice with his fork, he popped it into his mouth and chewed it slowly, savoring the burst of impossibly intense taste on newly awakened taste buds.

"Wow," he said, when he'd swallowed it, "This is … indescribably amazing."

"Better than you remembered?"

"I never had a banana before."

"Of course." She returned with the reheated noodles. "They wouldn't have been introduced to Europe yet. I'm an idiot."

"Ainsley, you are far from an idiot. But apart from that applesauce, it's probably safe to say I've never eaten any of these things." He ate the rest of the banana slices quickly, but with no less relish than the first bite.

She plunked a glass of water down beside him. After he'd taken a bite of the steaming noodles, she asked, "So, what's the verdict?"

He chewed slowly and swallowed, considering. How to answer? He took another bite, chewed, swallowed. "Well, if bland was the object, I think you can say they were a success."

She laughed. "They're totally naked. You'll have to give them a fair chance when you're able to handle something more adventurous."

Delano put his fork down, suddenly sober. Their positions had been reversed, he realized. When she'd been so rudely thrust into his world where vampires — the good, the bad and the ugly — dominated, she'd been forced to depend on him in a milieu that was completely foreign to her.

Now the tables were turned. Now, he was the babe in the woods, learning his way.

He pushed his chair back. "Thank you, Ainsley. I feel much better. But the blood work … I really shouldn't put it off any longer."

She stood, and he knew her stiff, awkward posture mirrored his own. And when her eyes met his, he saw uncertainty there.

No doubt about it, she wanted to talk about their relationship. Females hadn't changed that much in two centuries. But dammit, he wasn't ready for that talk yet. Not feeling like this. So ... off balance.

He looked away. "I'll be back after I've run those tests."

Ainsley felt the little flame of hope in her heart sputter as she watched Delano beat a hasty retreat to his lab. He knew she needed assurance, but he was dodging her. Oh, his excuse was legitimate enough; they definitely needed the results of those tests to assess Eli's condition and plan his further treatment. But if that convenient task hadn't existed, he'd have invented another one. She didn't need a psychic link with a man to recognize when he went into avoidance mode.

And if he couldn't give her the reassurance she needed, there could only be one reason. His feelings had changed. He regretted what he'd said when he believed them to be eternally and irrevocably blood-bonded. Now that they were no longer inextricably linked, he didn't know how to break the news to her that he felt differently now.

At the thought, devastating pain ripped the air from her lungs. She sank into the chair Delano had just vacated, a wave of loss threatening to swamp her and drag her under. *Oh, Ainsley, what now? What now?*

Now, you get your ass up and get on with it.

She was a big girl, and not without some experience in this area, usually, to her shame, as the avoid*er*. And that experience had taught her that the avoid*ee* gained nothing by protesting or begging. She promised herself that if she left here with nothing else, she would leave with her pride intact.

With that vow, she pushed the sick, empty feeling down, squared her shoulders and went to check on Eli.

She found him surrounded by four of his men. At her appearance, he dismissed them.

"Don't let me break up your huddle," she said. "I just wanted to check your vitals. It'll only take two or three minutes, tops."

"No problem," Eli said, as Shalvis, Hayes and the other two, whose names she did not know, filed out of the room. "We were winding up anyway. Any word on Bartlett?"

Ainsley gave him the good news. She also told him Delano was down in the lab right now running the blood work to see what he might need in the way of coagulotherapy. She asked him a few questions about how he felt, took a quick core temperature reading with the ear thermometer, made some notes on her chart, then checked his urinary output since the last check.

"So, Nurse Crawford, how am I looking?"

She glanced up from her chart and gave him with her best squelching stare. "Eli Grayson, if I wasn't a hundred percent sure you know there's nothing to be gained from flirting with me, I might think you were. Flirting with me, that is." She picked up his wrist, found his pulse and fixed her gaze on her watch.

He laughed. "Ainsley, honey, I am a thousand percent sure it's gonna get me squat, but when has a man ever let that stop him? Besides, I'm a little giddy that this whole thing is over, and that it turned out so well. You're safe, the hostages are safe, I'm safe, my men are safe. That rapacious bastard Janecek is dead, and our small firefight at twenty-nine stories seems to have gone undetected by the authorities. And Delano is —"

"Delano is changed." She dropped his wrist.

Eli watched as she wrapped the blood pressure cuff around his bicep. "Is that a problem for you?"

"Of course not."

She put the earpieces in her ears, slid the head of the stethoscope under the cuff, and started inflating the cuff's bladder. He waited quietly while she opened the valve slightly and listened as the pressure was released. A moment later she removed the stethoscope and whipped the cuff off his arm. "Very good."

"Getting back to this Delano thing ..."

"We're not blood-bonded anymore." She forced the words past the lump in her throat, surprised to hear how normal they came out. "That's over."

"You're not ... Of course! He's no longer a vampire. Oh, Ainsley —"

"No big deal." She bundled the stethoscope and cuff and shoved them into the medical bag. "He's a regular guy now, like any other, and the whole world is open to him. He can have any woman he wants, and he should. He deserves to make up for all that lost time."

"Whoa, wait a minute. I think Delano has already made his choice."

"No, the *blood-bond* made the choice for him. And the blood-bond would never have come into play if I hadn't crawled into his bed. He never would have crossed that line if he hadn't thought he was dreaming. I took his choice away from him, even though I didn't mean to. Now he's got it back."

"But I don't think he wants —"

"It's okay. It's better this way. He should have a chance to adjust and take stock and decide what he wants to do."

"And who he wants to do it with?"

"Exactly." She had to swallow a couple of times before she could go on in a reasonably normal voice. "I just don't want him to feel any sense of obligation toward me for anything he might have said under the influence of the blood-bond, when I was literally his only choice."

"I see."

As he said the words, Eli's gaze slid to the doorway.

Oh, please God, no.

But when she swiveled to look, there was Delano standing in the doorway. From the expression on his face, it was impossible to tell whether or not he'd heard her exchange with Eli. Nevertheless, she knew he had. *Way to go, Ainsley.*

He cleared his throat and moved into the room. "I have your test results back," he told Eli. "You have some very minor coagulopathies going on that we need to monitor. Nothing that screams danger, but enough to be a concern. Which means you're going to have to stay put in that bed for a day or two and give us blood at frequent intervals."

"A day or two?" Eli looked completely horrified, a reaction that was no doubt overdone in an effort to deflect attention from what he and Ainsley had been talking about. "Oh, man, you've gotta move me back to my own room if I'm going to be stuck in bed that long. No way can I survive a stretch like that without television."

"I guess we could do that."

Ainsley leapt up. "Good plan. I'll go make your room ready."

Before either man could object, she fled the room, castigating herself as she went.

Stupid, stupid woman.

Delano's forehead creased as he watched Ainsley rush off.

"You heard all of that, I presume?"

He turned back to Eli. "Enough."

"Well, buddy, it looks like you've got a free pass to date your way through the 514 area code, to see if there's another chick out there who suits you better."

"Thanks, but I think I'll pass."

"I knew you would, but then again, I'm not the one you need to convince."

Delano massaged his forehead. "God, here I was worrying that having reverted to normal, I wouldn't be able to ..."

"Float her boat?"

"Eloquent as ever. But yes, basically. I'm *still* worried about it. But come to find out she thinks *I* might have changed my mind about *her* because I'm just a regular man again? I will never understand women."

"Well, I have every confidence you'll convince her. But a tip, if I'm not overstepping?"

Delano could use all the help he could get. "By all means."

"Ainsley isn't looking for a superman, Del. She won't care if you can't run as fast as you used to, or jump as high, or bounce back from a bout of sex like an eighteen-year-old. She fell in love with you for the same reasons I left the army to follow you."

Delano lifted an eyebrow, pretending to misunderstand. "To kill rogue vampires?"

Eli snorted. "Yeah, that was definitely an attraction for me, I'll admit, but it's not the one I'm talking about. Ainsley sees in you the same things I saw. Your dedication to protecting the vulnerable, your commitment to the greater good, your capacity for self-sacrifice in the name of your ideals. None of those things have changed just because the vampirism mutation has been reversed. Do you see me or my men lining up to leave your employ?"

"I don't know. Do I?"

"Not unless you're plannin' on firing me. The world is an infinitely better place without Janecek in it, no mistake about it. But this war is a damn sight far from over. We're not going anywhere."

Delano blinked rapidly. "Thank you. That means a lot to me, Eli."

"You're welcome," Eli said gruffly. "And here's the thing, Delano: if you give Ainsley half a chance, she's not gonna go anywhere, either."

Delano struggled with emotion. When he'd conquered its grip on his throat, he laid a hand on Eli's shoulder. "Thank you, soldier." Then he turned and left the room.

Ainsley managed to dodge Delano for the rest of the day. She spent several hours with Lucy and Devon. Thankfully, as Delano had promised, Devon awoke with no memory of how her impromptu helicopter ride had ended.

By noon, Ainsley succumbed to the need for a nap. When she arose three hours later, still slightly groggy, she discovered that Delano had also retired for his own nap. This business of moving from night to day was brutal, but she had more experience at it than most. Certainly more than Delano.

Now, evening was upon her. And although she managed to evade Delano in the flesh, she was less successful at evading thoughts of him. Her face still burned with embarrassment when she let herself recall how she'd spilled her deepest fears to Eli. What must Delano think of her? She should have had that conversation with him, and no one else. But now, she just wanted to bury her head in the sand and pretend it hadn't happened. Maybe he'd go along with that. He certainly had kept his poker face on when —

A knock sounded at her door. "Ms. Crawford?"

Recognizing Shalvis's voice, she flew to the door. "What is it? Lucy? Devon?"

"No, they're all right, ma'am."

"Eli, then? Is he okay?"

"He's fine, ma'am. Back in his own quarters, too. The reason I'm here, the boss wants you to join him in the lab."

"In the lab?"

"Yes. That was his request. As soon as you're able."

God, her hair was a mess and she needed a shower. It was bad enough that Shalvis saw her like this. She inclined her head. "Thank you, Mr. Shalvis. Tell him I'll be down in ten minutes."

"Thank you, ma'am. I'll do that."

Ainsley closed the door and raced for the shower. Ten minutes later, she combed her long, damp hair back from her face and regarded her image in the mirror. The sheer foundation she'd applied helped hide the hectic flush in her cheeks, but nothing could disguise the sheen of hope and excitement in her eyes.

Giving up, she smoothed the material of her sweater — the plunging v-neckline of which was more daring than anything else she owned — before running her hands over her hips in the slim-fitting khaki pants she'd chosen.

Too obvious?

Not nearly as obvious as the dress she'd almost chosen. But maybe the sweater was too much . . .

She glanced at her watch and sighed. She'd have to do as she was. She was out of time.

To say that she expected to find Delano alone was an understatement. To find him there with another man jolted her, but it was nothing compared to the jolt she got when she looked closer at the other man.

Vampire! Dear God, he was absolutely beautiful! And he made no attempt to cloak what he was. In the artificial light of the lab, he shone with an incandescent vitality.

"Ainsley, permit me to introduce Aiden Afflack, an associate of mine."

Keenly aware of the gorgeous stranger's personal power, she moved closer to Delano, but extended her hand. "How do you do, Mr. Afflack?"

He grasped her hand briefly before releasing it, but the sensation of power shot up her arm, spiking her heartbeat again.

"Very well, thank you. And you?"

She murmured what she hoped was an appropriate response, but her eyes had already gone to Delano.

Reading the questions there correctly, Delano spoke. "Aiden is a good friend of mine, Ainsley. Our association goes back longer than either of us like to credit."

This drew a chuckle from Aiden, a soft, easy expression of amusement that sent a tingle up her spine.

"He's right, I'm afraid," he drawled.

Lord, he had charisma! That laugh of his slid right in under a woman's defenses and said, *Like me. A lot.* She could easily see how this charmer could win over women with a dazzling smile and a flowery compliment. She could also see he was a heartbreaker. He was everything, in fact, that Delano was not. Delano had always downplayed his vitality, and easy, casual seduction was not in his repertoire.

Ainsley smiled politely and waited for an explanation.

"Aiden has agreed to do a job for me, provided you concur with our approach."

Her stomach lurched. "What kind of job?"

"My investigation of Lucy Michaels' situation discloses some unpleasant things about her husband," Delano said. "He's the chief of police in St. Cloud, correct?"

"Correct."

"And he abused Lucy to the point where she felt she had to flee, to protect herself and her daughter. Correct?"

Ainsley's fists tightened at the thought of Weldon Michaels and all the misery he was responsible for. "Also correct."

"Did you know that Weldon Michaels is bosom buddies with the director of your department in the hospital where you worked in St. Cloud?"

Chief Michaels and Dr. Demmings were pals? "Really?"

"And did you know Dr. Demmings was in the process of divorcing his wife? I understand that can be an expensive proposition. The good doctor was a prime candidate for a cash bribe, and Chief Michaels offered him a handsome one to get you fired."

Ainsley felt her blood pressure mounting. "*Weldon Michaels* did this to me? That little weasel got me fired?"

"Beyond the shadow of a doubt. You see, he must have figured out that you were subsidizing Lucy and Devon's living expenses. He probably figured if he could pauperize you, Lucy would surface sooner rather than later."

"Ohhh! I'll have his balls!

Delano laughed. "Frankly, I think we have a better idea."

"I can't imagine what that could be."

"I propose to have Aiden pay him a visit."

Ainsley's gaze flew to the stranger, who had a hard glint about his eyes now. "You wouldn't ... I mean ..." She looked at Delano again, her eyes searching his. "You're not proposing to ..."

"Kill him?" The softly-voiced question came from Aiden Afflack. "No. I won't even hurt him, unless you consider possible injury to his pride. Or unless you *want* me to."

His smile thinned ever so slightly, but Ainsley sucked in her breath at the leashed menace in it.

"I'm just proposing to spend a leisurely evening with Chief Michaels, acquainting him with the full scope and diversity of the creatures with which he shares the night. We're thinking that once he appreciates that his wife keeps company with not one, but many of us, he'll lose interest in persecuting her further. In fact, she should be able to move back home in about," he paused to consult his watch, "forty-eight hours. And of course, we'd make sure that he appreciates that this *Pax Vampira* applies to you, as well. I will make sure that he'll do whatever is necessary to ensure that you can return to your job, if you so desire."

Ainsley's head spun. *What to ask first?* "What's to stop him from reporting your ... visit?"

Aiden shrugged. "The same thing that dissuaded you from seeking treatment at a hospital when you were attacked. No one would believe him. His job would be forfeit if he makes a report of a vampire who partook of his blood, but left no evidence. A vampire who moved like lightening, but who looked like a normal man. A vampire who can leap a full story with a 200 lb. man in his arms. A vampire that knows all his dirty domestic secrets."

"Delano?" She glanced up at him.

He nodded. "It can be done just as Aiden has described. You need only give your consent. And you have our word that Chief Michaels will come to no lasting harm, while learning a new respect for coloring within the lines. Aiden will impress on him, also, that we can uncover all his many and grave abuses of power in pursuit of his wife. He'll be left with no doubt that if he so much as sneezes in the direction of Lucy, Devon or you, he'll not only be deposed as chief, but would likely face prosecution." He fixed her with an intent gaze. "This can work, Ainsley. You can go back home. You and Lucy and Devon."

But what about you? she wanted to wail. *What will I do back in St. Cloud without you?*

She shook off the thought. She had to think of Lucy and Devon. These years on the run had taken a visible toll on Lucy, and Ainsley was sure Devon, ever uncomplaining, must suffer horribly each time they were uprooted ...

And now they could go home, if she gave the word. They could stop running, stop looking over their shoulders. Thanks to this beautiful, terrifying vampire, Aiden Afflack. And thanks to Delano.

"Ainsley?" Delano prompted.

"Okay." She blinked. "Okay, do it."

"Excellent."

Aiden's smile was a fearsome thing to behold. Ainsley moved closer to Delano, who took her hand.

"Thank you," Delano said. "Aiden will leave tonight. I've got an aircraft chartered. He'll get there in plenty of time to scope out Michaels' place this evening. Then tomorrow night, our friend Weldon is in for a long night of re-education."

"Thank you," she said. "Thank you both. It will mean the world to Lucy and Devon to be able to go home at last."

"Our pleasure." Delano smiled into her eyes, but she could see he was holding something back still. "Now for the other matter."

Ainsley's heart thudded harder. So they were going to talk about it after all. Then she noticed the handsome vampire had made no move to leave. "Umm, don't you think we should have some privacy for this?"

"Actually, no," Delano replied. "Aiden may wind up playing a fairly integral part in what happens next."

Her eyes flew to the smiling Aiden and back to the unsmiling Delano. "I don't understand."

"I overheard your conversation with Eli."

It took all she had not to bury her face in her hands. "I'm so sorry about that," she said, holding his gaze. "I shouldn't have discussed our ... situation ... with Eli or anyone else."

"I wasn't being critical," he insisted. "You must feel free to discuss anything that troubles you with your friends. But the fact remains that you seem to think that now that the mutation has reversed itself, I might not feel the same about you. Indeed, I got the impression you felt I ought to play the field, so I might be certain."

Ainsley flicked a glance at Aiden. When she saw how avidly he was following the discussion, she could have died of mortification.

"That's *private*, Delano. I don't see why we need to discuss our affairs in front of your guest."

"I'm sorry, my love, but I'm going to need Aiden for this next part."

Her heart, already pounding, kicked up into overdrive. "What are you talking about?"

"When we were blood-bonded, you had your misgivings about our relationship, but they centered around causing me a premature death. At the heart of it, you were confident in my love for you, my complete and total devotion. I felt it when I held you, so you needn't deny it."

"How could I?" She swallowed to try to moisten her suddenly dry mouth.

"But since my reversal, all I can feel is your doubt, your anxiety, the worry that you trapped me into this relationship when you —"

"I *did* trap you." Her face burned with embarrassment at having this discussion in front of a stranger, but she couldn't let that stop her from saying what must be said. "But I swear to you, Del, I didn't mean to."

"You are blameless, Ainsley. It would not have happened had I not still been keeping secrets from you. And if you call that a trap, every man should be so lucky as to fall into one so sweet."

Despite her best efforts to control her breathing, a sob escaped her. "But you have *choices*, now. Choices you didn't have before."

"I do. And one of those choices is to embrace the blood-bond again, soberly, thoughtfully, and of my own volition. That's why I brought Aiden here tonight, to turn me back. It will take a matter of about thirty hours, but my vampiric powers should be restored. We can have it back, Ainsley, if that's what you want."

She started to cry in earnest, lifting the hem of her sweater to stem the tide. Delano handed her a handkerchief, which she applied to her cheeks, then used to blow her nose.

"Just give the word, my love, and Aiden will do it."

"Are you saying you love me still?" She swiped at fresh tears. "That you're ready to shackle yourself to me, forsaking all others, even though ... even though ..." *Even though it will literally kill you when I die.* She couldn't bring herself to say the words.

He grasped her face in his big hands. "Yes, that's what I'm saying. I love you, Ainsley Crawford, and I am yours as long as you want me. That didn't change just because of the reversal. Nor did my commitment to the vaccine and my life's work of turning back the rogue tide."

Her hands went to his chest, possessed of a mind of their own. "Do you *want* to go back?"

The ambivalence in his eyes raked her raw sensibilities.

"Ainsley ..."

"The truth. *Please*, Delano."

He sighed. "One of my aims all along was to reverse my own mutation, which I saw from the beginning as a vile curse, visited upon me against my will by a vampress who thought that was the path to owning me. All these years, I've sought to return to what I was. That's been my aim for so long, I knew nothing else."

"And now?"

"Now, I no longer want it. Not at this price. Not without you."

The tears brimmed again, distorting his precious face. She made no attempt to stem them this time.

"And what if you can have your mortal life back, and me too? Would you choose to have Aiden turn you then? Either way, I will stay with you. And either way, your life expectancy will be constrained." She brushed back a lock of his hair, which had fallen forward. "I swear, if I could be turned, I would ask Aiden to do it for us both, right now, so that we have eternity together. But we can't. Not with my blood."

He pulled her face closer and kissed her eyelids, one at a time. "Then I choose to age with you. You may not see the evidence of the blood-bond, and you may not be able to slip into my mind with the ease you did before, but sweetheart, it's still there. It *has* to be. Because I feel like I'd die without you."

The breath she'd been holding rushed out of her. "Oh, me too!"

Suddenly his arms were around her. She circled her own arms around him lightly, mindful of his injured ribs. His mouth closed on hers, kissing her like there was no tomorrow.

When next they looked up, Aiden had left the lab.

"Ainsley?"

She smiled at how thick his voice sounded. "Yes?"

"How 'bout we find Aiden again and get him to turn me so my ribs get better in the next five hours. Then I'll be ready to make love to you the way I want. All we have to do is lose the condoms, and I'll eventually turn back again . . ."

She laughed against his neck. "Trust me, Dr. Bowen. Making love won't be a problem," she murmured into his ear, before biting the lobe delicately. "I'm a nurse, remember? You're in good hands."

"Oh, I know it, Nurse Crawford." He laughed, but when he pulled back, his eyes sobered. "You want this, don't you? Truly?"

She smiled up at him, her heart brimming. "Truly, I do. I want to be yours and I want you to be mine. I want to wake up in the same bed with you every morning. I want to have the right to touch you like this. I want to wake up in the night and be able to reach for you."

His hands tightened on her waist. "We can move back to St. Cloud as soon as my house repairs are finished."

She turned her attention to his throat again, this time at the juncture where neck met shoulder. "I'd like that."

"And would you like children?"

Her roving mouth stopped and she leaned back in his arms. "Children?"

"That would be one of the consequences of my reversal. I'll be fertile again. Well, theoretically."

"Oh, my God."

"Or not," he said quickly. "We can change that whole fertility thing if you want. I know there's a surgery. Just so we're clear, I want you for *you*, not for any little Bowens you might produce."

Her heart thudded in her throat. Did he know what he was saying? "Del, our children . . . they'd have the Merzetti blood.

They'd be in danger from the moment they were born." Her throat tightened. "I don't know if I could stand that."

"Ah, but that's where you're wrong, my sweet. They'll be in no danger, or at least no more than the average child. Because by then, we'll be into mass production of the vaccine. Their blood won't matter." He smiled down at her. "They'll just be adorable girls, hopefully with their mother's beautiful hair and violet eyes."

"Girls." She chewed her lip. "We'd have to tell them about the Merzetti Effect. They'll need to understand. If we don't, they'll do as I did. They'll get pregnant and reject their daughters."

He smoothed a hand over her hair. "We'll tell them, my love. And we'll tell them about the fearless exploits of their mother and their half-sister Devon and their Aunt Lucy."

She blinked rapidly. "This could really work, couldn't it? I could have a baby. I could keep my baby. Our baby."

"You absolutely could."

Then, because it seemed far too long since he'd done it last, he kissed her mouth. When he lifted his head, there were no more tears glinting in her eyes. But they glinted with something else.

"We could make a little Bowen right now, couldn't we?" Her hand went to the placket of his trousers. "Theoretically."

He groaned, hardening beneath her touch. "Theoretically, yes."

"Then let's put your theory to the test."

A moment later, he lay on their hastily-shed clothing with her straddling his body, the heat of her core pressing against his erection.

He gritted his teeth, trying to hang on to reason. "Are you sure, love? I'll be just a regular guy. A human. No special powers."

"Oddly enough, *human* is kind of what I always had in mind for the father of my children."

He laughed, wishing the state of his ribs would allow him to curl up and pull her down, but as though sensing his need, she bent to him, capturing his laugh with her mouth.

"I love you," he said when she let him breathe again.

"I love you, too," she said, and proceeded to show him how much.

Thank you for investing that most precious of
commodities – your time – in my book!

If you enjoyed THE MERZETTI EFFECT, I would be
thrilled if you could help me buzz it. You can do this by:

Recommending it. Help other readers find this book by recommending it to friends, readers' groups and discussion boards.

Reviewing it. Please share with other readers what you
liked about this book by reviewing it wherever you purchased it, or at readers' sites such as Goodreads.

Again, thank you!

Look for NIGHTFALL, another Vampire Romance,
an excerpt from which appears below.

Coming September 4, 2012 from Montlake Romance:

EVERY BREATH SHE TAKES
Sensual Romantic Suspense
w/Paranormal Element

Also available by this author:
GUARDING SUZANNAH, Book 1 in
the Serve and Protect Series
SAVING GRACE, Book 2 in the Serve and Protect Series
PROTECTING PAIGE, Book 3 in the Serve and Protect Series
NEEDING NITA, A Novella in the Serve and Protect Series
(sensual romantic suspense)

As N.L. Wilson (writing partnership of
Norah Wilson and Heather Doherty)
The Dix Dodd Mysteries
THE CASE OF THE FLASHING FASHION QUEEN
FAMILY JEWELS
DEATH BY CUDDLE CLUB (Coming Fall 2012)
(funny mysteries in the vein of Janet
Evanovich's Stephanie Plum series)

As Wilson Doherty (writing partnership of
Norah Wilson and Heather Doherty)
THE SUMMONING: Book 1 in the Gatekeepers Series
ASHLYN'S RADIO
COMES THE NIGHT, Book 1 in the
Casters Series (coming Fall 2012)
ENTER THE NIGHT, Book 2 in the
Casters Series (coming Fall 2013)
(YA paranormal)

About the Author

Norah Wilson lives in Fredericton, New Brunswick, with her husband, two adult children and her beloved Rotti-Lab mix Chloe. Norah has had three of her romantic suspense stories final in the Romance Writers of America's Golden Heart® contest until she sold her first story in 2004. She was also the winner of Dorchester Publishing's New Voice in Romance contest in 2003.

Norah loves to hear from readers!

Connect with her online at:
Twitter: http://twitter.com/norah_wilson
Facebook: http://www.facebook.com/#!/profile.php?id=1053773212
Goodreads: http://www.goodreads.com/author/show/1361508.Norah_Wilson
Email: norahwilsonwrites@gmail.com

An Excerpt from NIGHTFALL
A Vampire Romance

AIDEN AFFLACK HUMMED to himself as he lifted the brass door-knocker to summon St. Cloud Police Chief Weldon Michaels to the front door of his Carrington Place residence. Rapping twice, he stepped back.

What *was* that tune running through his head? It had been with him since he'd risen this evening.

Audioslave? Nope.

Queens of the Stone Age? Un-uh.

Collective Soul? Yeah, yeah, that was it. Definitely. He cricked his neck one way, then the other and felt the satisfying crack. *Ooh, I'm feeling better now.*

The curtain in the bay window twitched, but Aiden feigned obliviousness. From inside, he clearly heard Michaels jam a clip into an automatic weapon. Aiden rolled his eyes. Nobody trusted anyone anymore.

"Who are you and what do you want?"

The voice came through the door. A very cautious man indeed.

"I'm a friend of your wife's," Aiden called. "Well, more a friend of a friend, actually, but I have a personal message for you, from her."

"Nice try. Now move on, before I call the cops."

Aiden thought about knocking the door in. It was solid oak with a good deadbolt on it, but it could have been made from cardboard and paperclips for all the challenge it would present. On the other hand, there was no reason to get messy.

He cleared his throat, did his best to summon a puzzled tone. "Well, hell, I thought you *were* the cops. Do I have the wrong address? I'm looking for Chief Weldon Michaels. Got a message for him from his wife Lucy. Pretty woman, 'bout an inch over five feet, brown hair and eyes? Oh, and a real cute little daughter. What's her name? Devon? Any of this sounding familiar?"

Silence for a few heartbeats. "What kind of message?"

"She wants to come home, but before she can see her way clear to doing that, we need to have ourselves a talk."

Another pause, then the sound of the deadbolt retracting. The door cracked open, and Weldon Michaels peered out past a security chain.

God save me from fools. Growling, Aiden pushed the door open. The hardware anchoring the security chain tore free from the wall. Before Michaels could cry out, Aiden stepped inside and closed the door behind him. In the next heartbeat, he seized Michaels' right wrist and squeezed until the other man screamed and dropped the pistol he held. It hit the hardwood floor with a clatter but didn't discharge.

"A gun?" Aiden released the other man's hand. "Now I ask you, what kind of a greeting is that?"

Michaels — clearly a slow learner — reached for a second weapon jammed into the waistband at the small of his back. Before he could get to it, Aiden had Michaels face down on the floor with his right hand way closer to his right shoulder blade than God ever intended it to go.

"Jesus, my arm. You're breaking it!"

"Not even close. You develop a feel for these things," he said conversationally. "It's sort of like braking on ice. You gotta find the threshold."

"No, my shoulder! It's gonna pop! I swear to God!"

Aiden reefed Michaels arm a half inch higher, eliciting a scream, followed by a stream of curses.

"See? Still plenty of play. It's a feel thing. Now are you gonna behave yourself if I let you up?"

"Christ, yes! I'll do whatever you say."

"Atta boy." Aiden helped the other man to his feet. "Now, let's go plug the code into the alarm, shall we? And don't fuck with me. If the alarm company or the cops call in a minute to ask if everything's okay, things will be very much not okay for you. Understood?"

"Understood."

Aiden "helped" Michaels to the alarm panel, where he keyed in a five-digit number. The winking red light went out.

"Good man. Now we're going to need your handcuffs. I know they can't be far away, since you laid hands on that pistol fast enough. So be a darling and let's go fetch them."

Michaels swore again.

"I know, I know. It's gotta sting, getting cuffed with your own bracelets, but look at it this way: they'll be a helluva lot more comfortable than the alternative if you force me to improvise."

Michaels sagged. "In that drawer."

A minute later, Chief Weldon Michaels sat cuffed in one of his own kitchen chairs, a sturdy-looking oak proposition. Michaels somehow managed to look both scared and pissed at the same time.

Aiden took a seat at the table, placing both guns — one retrieved from beneath the telephone table in the entryway and the other from the small of Michaels' back — on the gleaming wood surface. "Okay, Weldon — may I call you Weldon? — we need to talk."

Michaels glared back. "You're wasting your time. I don't keep anything of value of here, at least nothing portable enough to carry off. And damn you, you've already scored both my guns. I suggest you just let yourself out and get while the getting's good."

"You think I was bullshitting earlier, don't you? You think I was feeding you a line about your wife to get inside?" He leaned back in his chair and kicked his feet up to rest on the table. "That's rich."

Fear flashed in the other man's eyes, which he quickly attempted to hide with bravado. "Look, mister, if you have a message for me, let's get on with it."

"Afflack."

"What's that?"

"If you're gonna call me mister, you might as well make it Mr. Afflack. Or Aiden, if you prefer."

Another flash of fear. Aiden could almost hear the wheels turning in Michaels' head. *He's shown me his face, given me his name. There can only be one reason for that ...*

"Not to worry, Weldy. I think I'll call you Weldy."

Michaels tensed. Testing the cuffs and the strength of the chair's spindles, no doubt.

Aiden sighed. "For Chrissakes, I'm not planning to kill you. I'm just going to spend the night here chatting, much like we are right now."

Michaels blinked. "Spend the night?"

"Forgive me. It's probably horribly uncomfortable with those cuffs on. Let me just deal with these nasty guns. Then I'll take the bracelets off so we can talk, all civilized-like."

Aiden picked up the SIG 9mm with his left hand, grasped the barrel with his right. Closing his eyes, he slid his hand up and down the barrel a few times to attune his mind to the metal. Then he bent it effortlessly.

"Jesus Christ!"

Aiden placed the ruined pistol back on the table, picked up the .22 and repeated the process on the gun's short barrel.

"What the ... how'd you do that?"

Aiden shrugged. "A parlor trick. You should see what I can do with a dinner fork." He stood and extracted the handcuff key from the pocket of his worn jeans. "Now, about those cuffs ..."

Michaels shrank back.

Aiden lifted his eyebrows. "What? You'd prefer to keep them on after all?"

The other man collected himself, embarrassment staining his cheeks. "Of course not. Please remove them."

Aiden obliged.

As soon as his hands were free, Michaels immediately started massaging his sore right shoulder.

"Ah, yes. Your shoulder. Sorry about that." Aiden gave him his best *aw shucks* smile. "But I couldn't have you putting bullet holes in me, could I?"

Michaels said nothing, but the stiffness in his face spoke volumes. *Good. Get brave, you miserable little wife-beating worm. Get angry. Give me a reason to hurt you again.*

Michaels cleared his throat. "So, this message from my wife?"

"She wants to come back to St. Cloud. In fact, she'd like to move back into this very house, seeing as she put so much sweat equity into it." Aiden glanced around at the tastefully appointed kitchen. "I must say she did a great job."

"Of course she can come home. That's all I've wanted since she left."

"Ah, but there's a catch, Weldy. You can't stay."

Michaels made a choking sound, but quickly found his voice. "She thinks I'm just going to clear out of town?"

"That would be ideal, but no, I don't think she expects that. It will be sufficient if you leave this house and never darken the door again."

Michaels started to bluster that he owned the goddamned place and no one could put him out of it, yadda, yadda, yadda.

"Save it," he commanded. "You see, I know what you did to her, Weldy."

A pause. "I don't know what she told you, but —"

"You systematically isolated her from her friends and pressured her into quitting work. Then, when you got her where you wanted her, you escalated the abuse. You *terrorized* her, Weldy. You threatened the life of her child if she tried to leave you. Is any of this sounding familiar? No? Well how about this: you used your position and power to convince her that escape was impossible."

Michaels leapt up, his face wreathed in fury. "You don't know the first fucking thing about my family."

Aiden swung his feet to the floor, but remained in his chair. "Oh, I know quite a bit, Chief Michaels. For instance, I know you've been abusing the police resources at your fingertips to search for her, ensuring she had to stay on the run, unable to stay anywhere for any length of time. I know she's terrified for her life and that of her daughter."

"If she'd just —"

"Shut up, Weldy, and listen. I'm the messenger, and the message is that it's over. She's coming back, and you, my friend, are going to become the most obliging, most accommodating, most *respectful* ex-husband on the face of the planet. Oh, and you'll relinquish any rights to the child."

"Fuck you." Powered by rage, Michaels gripped the table's edge and overturned it, then bolted for the door.

Grinning, Aiden swept the table away as if it were constructed of matchsticks and gave chase, overtaking his quarry in a blur of speed. By the time Michaels reached the door, Aiden lounged against it, the picture of indolence.

"Going somewhere?"

"Jesus!"

Michaels' face suddenly looked like it was stretched too tightly across the underlying bones. Shock did that to some people. With others, their faces went slack, as though —

"Who are you?" Michaels rasped. "Dear God, *what* are you?"

Aiden allowed his smile to spread, noting the precise moment when Michaels caught the first glimpse of his grossly elongated cuspids. This time, Michaels' face slackened.

"I'm glad you asked."

Sam Shea burrowed deeper into her denim jacket and shifted her legs yet again. The August night was soft, and three hours ago she would have called it warm. Now, however, dew was beginning to form on the blades of grass around her. Only the patch beneath her butt and outstretched legs remained dry as she sat propped against the base of a gargoyle statue.

Yes, a frickin' cement *gargoyle*. Unfortunately, she didn't have a lot of choices about where to pitch her tripod. It was the only spot in the vicinity where she could get far enough away from the ubiquitous streetlights to see even the brightest stars in the sky. Rural shoots were so much easier.

Of course, it was anybody's guess what she was here to capture. It might have nothing to do with celestial bodies. On the other hand, what else could it be?

Well, okay, ninety minutes ago, she'd have laid bets that she was here for an electrical storm. The flashes of lightning had started to the south, illuminating the suburban landscape in an eerie purplish light. Counting the seconds between flash and boom, she tracked the storm from nearly ten miles off. She'd pack up and head for the car when it reached six miles, the safety zone. No photo was worth getting killed for, especially when she could get a decent shot from the relative safety of her rented Acura. But the storm had veered off at the last moment, making a retreat to the car unnecessary.

So if it wasn't a fantabulous light show, what the heck had drawn her here?

For the first time in a very long time, she wondered if her vision had let her down. Right place maybe, but the wrong time? Or maybe there was another Carrington Place in St. Cloud, and she'd camped at the wrong one. But what were the chances of that in a city of just over 100,000 people? Of course, maybe there was another Carrington Place in an entirely different St. Cloud.

Except she knew she wasn't wrong. She was never wrong. She'd thought so once, six years ago. After five hours of nothing more dramatic than the occasional distant meteor streaking across the night sky, she'd given up her post in disgust and gone back to the dubious comfort of her motel bed. The next morning, she'd found the local coffee shop abuzz about the dishwasher-sized meteorite that had crashed to earth in a pasture eight miles out of town. The same pasture where she'd abandoned her vigil at 4:00 a.m. If she hadn't bailed out, it would have made a hell of a photo.

No, she wasn't wrong. Despite the boredom of the past few hours, the raw energy that had drawn her here still persisted. *Something* was going to happen here, dammit.

For the umpteenth time tonight, she flicked on her hand-held infrared spotlight, lifted her infrared binoculars to her eyes and did a ground-level scan. Two houses down, a skunk made its leisurely way across the front lawn, oblivious of the surveillance. Nothing else stirred. With a sigh, she lowered her binoculars and flicked the light off.

No light show in the sky. Nothing interesting on the ground.

She leaned back again, wriggled her butt into a more comfortable position and glanced up at the leering griffin's massive head. "Don't let me nod off, okay? I'd hate to miss the fireworks. Or whatever we're going to have."

Predictably, the griffin made no reply.

"Okay, be like that," she muttered. "See if I —"

The sound of a door closing — specifically, the door of the two-story house directly across the street — cut short her one-sided conversation with the gargoyle. Automatically, she reached for the floodlight and the binoculars.

There! A man — rendered slightly greenish, thanks to the infrared technology — gliding out the flagstone driveway.

Quickly, she traded the binoculars for the tripod-mounted digital camera, flipping it to NightShot mode. A quick look through the viewfinder confirmed the target was out of range for the camera's infrared illuminator. Dammit. She squeezed the trigger switch on the spotlight again, locked it in the on position, planted its legs in the soft earth and trained it on the adjacent driveway. This time when she found her subject through the viewfinder, her mouth went dry.

Dear God! If she could give the fiercest storm a corporeal human body, this is what it would look like. Beauty and violence, all rolled up in one gorgeous, terrible package.

Zoom, focus.

God, what a face!

Hard zoom, focus, click.

Without conscious thought, habit took over. The camera clicked and whirred beneath her hands as she snapped picture after picture.

She watched him draw out a cigarette and apply a flame to it. Fascinated, she watched him inhale deeply, remove the cigarette from between sensual lips, then exhale. Then he lifted his lids and looked directly into her camera lens.

Sam pulled back, shrinking closer to the gargoyle's cold cement base. *He can't see me. Not from this distance. He's standing in the light and I'm buried in shadow. And he sure as hell can't see my spotlight.*

Carefully, she leaned forward again to peer through the view-finder. And there he was, still staring straight into the camera. And then — holy mother of God — he smiled at her. A knowing, toe-curling, sex-drenched smile.

She jerked back again, but this time, she failed to suppress a gasp. Not that it mattered, because he was gone. Vanished. She searched the sidewalks for his retreating form, but he'd melted away as completely as the smoke from his cigarette had dissipated in the night air.

She exhaled the lungful of air she'd been holding. Whew! That was ... interesting.

But even more interesting was the dawning conviction that nothing more was going to happen here. As she sat there bringing her heartbeat under control, she realized that the muted anticipation that kept her rooted to this spot for half the night had dissipated. Interesting, indeed.

Well, no point hanging around now. She got to her knees and packed her gear. Before stowing the camera, she flipped back through the pictures she'd captured to make sure she hadn't imagined the last minutes. She hadn't. There he was. Even frozen in greenish miniature, he emitted an improbable dynamism. She frowned. Could he be the force that had called her here? A shiver lifted the hairs on her arm. It didn't seem very likely. Of course, the alternative to that scenario was that her vision had been just plain wrong, which was even less palatable than the thought that a man might have drawn her here.

Sighing, she shut off the camera and tucked it carefully in the carry tote. With a last glance around the empty streets, she headed for her car. Ten minutes in a hot shower and a few hours sleep on the pillow-top mattress at her hotel would fix her up. She'd figure this thing out in the morning.

An hour later, she turned on a lamp and crawled out of bed. The dream would just keep coming back if she didn't write it down. She found a pen and hotel stationery and scribbled the words, *St. Cloud, riverbank under the bridge, tomorrow night. Call the airline and postpone your flight!*

There. Maybe now she could sleep.

Three hours later, after a poached egg and a cup of room-service coffee, Sam uploaded the images from her camera's flash card onto her photo viewer, a task she would normally have done last night. Backup was critical in this business. But since she hadn't captured anything saleable, she hadn't bothered. Now, she breathed a sigh of relief when she saw confirmation that the upload was successful.

She paged quickly through the first few photos, which she'd taken merely to fine-tune her settings. The house across the street with its foot lighting, the row of streetlights marching west, the retaining wall behind her. Then she reached the first shot of the man.

Ugh. Monochromatic green. NightShot was useful for surreptitiously framing your shot, but you then had to switch modes to get a normal-looking color shot. Of course, that required using a visible flash, which in turn required her to be considerably closer to the subject. It was great for photographing small critters in darkness, but not so great for capturing people. It just wasn't socially acceptable to creep up on a stranger and blast their night vision away with a blinding flash.

Especially this stranger.

She bent closer to the display to inspect her work. She'd zoomed in on the guy, but it was a full-body shot rather than tight to the face. He looked taller than she remembered, but the wide shoulders and narrow hips were the same, as was the longish, wavy hair. He wore what appeared to be a leather jacket over a dark shirt and dark pants.

She pulled back, feeling oddly disappointed.

He had the kind of body that would make any woman look twice, no question about it. But she just wasn't feeling that same gut punch she'd felt last night. Guess she could chalk last night's reaction up to jet-lagged giddiness and the late hour.

She toggled up the next photo, and oh, baby, there it was, that thrill low in the belly.

A high forehead pleated in a frown, and a straight nose. Several strands of curly blond hair spilled forward to graze high cheek-bones, partially obscuring his eyes. At least, she thought his hair was blond. It was too pale to be otherwise. The light also illuminated lean cheeks, a strong chin and an unsmiling mouth. Beautiful. Stern. Forbidding.

She advanced the next photo, and sucked in her breath on a hiss.

His face was tilted toward her to better reveal a sinfully gorgeous male mouth, but that wasn't what set her heart to pounding. It was his attitude of sharpened senses. She could swear he was scenting the night breeze through those flared nostrils, his head cocked to catch the slightest sound, eyes searching the darkness. She leapt out of her chair, overcome by the sensation that she was about to be discovered.

God, woman, get a grip. She snorted at her own panicked reaction. He couldn't see her. Not now, and not last night, either. At most, he may have suspected he was being watched and played to a possible audience, but standing under the streetlight like that, looking into the deep shadows … No, there was no way he could have seen her.

She seated herself in front of the viewer again and toggled up the next photo. Despite being prepared this time, her heart still jolted in her chest.

He was looking straight at her!

And oh yeah, he'd known he had an audience. An *appreciative* audience. Unlikely as it seemed, he must have sensed her.

Awareness was written there in his face, in the lift of an eyebrow and that sensual, full-lipped smile.

Sam expelled her breath. "Well, aren't you all that?"

The unknown man smiled back from the photo, his NightShot-glowing eyes maddeningly unreadable.

Magnetic.

The word slid into her mind, making her lips tighten. Last night, she'd allowed herself to contemplate the idea that this man might be the force that drew her here. The idea was no more palatable in daylight than it was in the dark of night. To think she might have delayed her return to Sioux City after the Montreal gallery opening, extending her Canadian trip to come to St. Cloud, New Brunswick, to take a photo of a mere *man*?

No. No way. It didn't bear thinking about. She'd been mistaken about the time and location, that's all. There was a first time for everything, right? Besides, last night's vision had rectified the mistake. She now had a very clear idea where she needed to be and when.

She toggled the cursor, but there were no more images. Sam moved backwards to the final picture, the one where she was sure he knew she watched him, and shivered.

Maybe she'd do a little research, for curiosity's sake, starting with finding out who lived at that Carrington Place address she'd camped outside of last night. Maybe something would surface to explain why she'd been called there.

Four hours later, she had a fix on the owners, a couple by the name of Weldon and Lucy Michaels. A Local Google search revealed that Weldon was the chief of police here in St. Cloud, but turned up nothing on Lucy. Well, that let out anything nefarious going on inside that house, him being the chief of police and all.

She pushed thoughts of Michaels and his late night visitor to the back of her mind and turned her attention to preparing for tonight's stakeout. After studying maps at the library, she drove unerringly to the downtown, parked in a parking garage, and set out on foot with her camera bag slung over her shoulder. A four-minute walk connected her with the riverfront walking trail, and another ten minutes put her practically in the shadow of the bridge. The grass was tall here, with a couple of distinct trails leading down the embankment toward the river. This was it. This was the place. She fished her digital out her bag and took a couple of shots.

The sound of crunching gravel alerted Sam to the presence of another pedestrian. She glanced up to see a young man approaching from the west. As he neared, she noted industrial facial piercings and a faux-hawk.

She lifted a hand. "Excuse me, could I —"

"Sorry," he said, side-stepping her. "I don't pose for tourists."

As if. Before she could correct his assumption, he'd walked on. She jogged to catch up.

"Hey, if I wanted to take your picture, I wouldn't want to do it here. I'd want to do it in a studio, or at least with the proper lighting equipment to do you justice. But that's not why I stopped you. I just have a question."

He slowed. Apparently flattery worked. "Whatcha wanna know?"

"Those paths back there, the ones leading down to the river. What's that all about?"

He shifted the bag he was carrying from one tattooed shoulder to the other. "Homeless."

Sam felt the truth resonate inside. Yes, that fit with the feeling the dream had left her with. "Is anyone down there now?"

Judging by the look he gave her, she expected him to say, *What am I? Kreskin?*, but what actually emerged was, "Dunno. Maybe. Or maybe they'd be out hustling for handouts this time of day."

Sam chewed the inside of her lip. "The police don't object to them living down there?"

"The cops?" He snorted. "Don't imagine they give a rat's ass where they sleep at night, long as they're outta sight. All they really care about is keepin' the panhandlin' under control." He glanced up the trail, obviously wanting to be on his way.

"Thanks for your help."

"No problem." He hiked his bag up and walked off.

She lifted her camera and took a few shots before crossing the neatly mown green to the taller grasses. She picked the closest path, which also happened to be the most well-worn, and descended the embankment, pausing occasionally to take more pictures. Passing through a thin belt of trees, she emerged to find a hard-packed footpath paralleling the river's edge.

The smell assailed her immediately. There was the usual pungent river smell that made you think of mud and fish and silt and organic rot, but underlying it was the unmistakable odor of human urine. Ugh. She snapped another picture.

She turned west and walked toward the bridge. Before she got twenty yards, she spotted the first makeshift shelters. Made from a mishmash of plywood, corrugated cardboard and blue plastic tarpaulins, the flimsy structures huddled just inside a thin belt of trees she'd just come through. No wonder none of this was visible from the walking path. For that matter, it probably wasn't terribly visible from above either, save perhaps for a few flashes of blue through the canopy of leaves.

Briefly, she thought about following the path all the way to the bridge and out the other side of the copse of tree. The riverbank appeared to be deserted, but she couldn't bring herself to go further. Deserted or not, there was something invasive and ugly about wandering past these squalid refuges like a sightseer, camera in hand. Plus, frankly she was scared. These people couldn't or wouldn't be integrated into normal society, often due to chronic mental illness. It was the same in cities all over North America. Bursting at the seams, psychiatric hospitals everywhere disgorged their long-term residents into their streets to make do the best they could.

She retraced her steps and continued west along the trail until she found another path in the tall grass. As she expected, it led down to the river, then back toward the treed area that concealed the tent community. Again, she ventured only far enough down the path to spy where flashes of blue tarp began to reappear. Though less plentiful on this side, she counted six structures, some of them no more than lean-tos.

She turned and looked west. Less than a mile away, tall condominium buildings and a handful of old brick office buildings rose up against the skyline. Sighing, she retraced her steps up the incline, through the tall grasses to the manicured green bisected by the graveled walking trail. Just like that, she was back in the shiny clean St. Cloud of the tourist brochures.

She turned back eastward and followed the trail for a hundred yards or so before veering off toward the concealing ribbon of brush and trees that shielded the shelters. A handy thing, that little green belt. It kept the homeless out of sight and out of mind for the tax-paying, job-holding, upstanding citizens of St. Cloud. That same invisibility kept the ire of the police off the backs of the vagrants.

She followed the tree line with difficulty. The grass here was knee deep, and without benefit of a beaten path, it conspired to trip her with every step. But just the other side of the bridge, she found what she was looking for — the perfect vantage point for surveilling the area later tonight.

Tucked just inside the tree line, it afforded enough cover for her, and offered the best view she was likely to get of the encampment below. Also ideal was the positioning of the streetlights on the four-lane bridge above and the towering light standard that illuminated the walking trail behind her. With any luck, there should be sufficient light to monitor goings on without having to constantly sweep the area with her infrared equipment. Likewise, it was close enough that she could step out of the tree line quickly if the commotion tonight turned out to be a light show in the sky.

Satisfied, she trekked the short distance back to her car. Just one more task and she could go back to her hotel and catch a few hours sleep. Stashing her equipment in the trunk of the rental, she walked half a block to Queen Street and found a payphone. She located the general number for the St. Cloud Police Department, plugged a quarter into the phone and dialed it.

When the receptionist answered, Sam instructed the woman to put her through to Chief Michaels, employing the tone she'd learned in her first year in business-for-self. The trick to obtaining cooperation was not to demand it, but rather to simply take that cooperation for granted. Faced with such easy, inherent authority, most people gave her exactly what she expected. The St. Cloud PD receptionist was no exception.

The phone rang twice in Michaels' office before it was answered. "Chief Michaels," a voice clipped. "Who am I talking to?"

"Good afternoon, Chief. I'm a reporter for —"

"Whoa. You can stop right there, lady. We have a communications officer who handles press inquiries. Call the switchboard again and they'll route you —"

"You had a visitor last night. Is that right, Chief Michaels?"

A pause. "I'm going to transfer you to my personal line. Please hang on."

She heard him make the transfer. Before his personal phone could manage a full ring burst, he'd picked it up.

"Dammit, what more do you people want from me?"

You people?

"I'm sorry," he said, rushing to fill the silence. "I'm just a little tense. The moving company is there right now, packing up my belongings. I'll be out by nightfall, just like I said."

Sam blinked, listening to his ragged breathing. What the devil was he talking about? Channeling that voice of authority again, she went fishing: "Very good. And the rest?"

"I won't hurt her again, I swear it. I won't even make contact. She can move back tomorrow. I'll give her a divorce, full custody of Devon, the house ... whatever she wants."

Holy crap! What had she stumbled into?

"Hello? Hello?" The chief's voice rose on a note of panic. "Are you still there?"

"Relax, Chief. I'm still listening."

"You have to believe me! I'll never lay a hand on Lucy again. On either of them. God, I won't even breathe in their direction. You'll see. You can watch me as closely as you like."

He'd been abusing his family? *Bastard.* "You can bet we'll be watching," she said in her silkiest voice. "Need I tell you what we think of recidivists?"

"No, ma'am. I'm sorry. Jesus … my ulcer. I have to go. I'm sorry."

The line went dead. Slowly, Sam hung up the receiver. Well, well, wasn't that interesting? Chief Michaels' late-night visitor had been a friend of Mrs. Michaels. And a very persuasive one, by all appearances. What could he possibly have said or done to reduce the chief of police to the jabbering wreck she'd just talked to?

She thought about the photos back in her hotel room and the peculiar energy that had emanated from Michaels' caller, and decided he was probably quite capable of decimating stronger men.

No matter. It was none of her concern. Michaels was still alive and well, and presumably newly embarked on the straight and narrow.

But who was the mystery caller? The estranged wife's new boyfriend? Hired muscle? Some vigilante out to avenge victims of violence? Random whack-job?

Well, she wasn't going to solve that mystery here, standing in a phone booth.

Correction — she wasn't going to solve that mystery at all.

Stepping out of the phone booth, she headed for her rental and the promise of a nap back at her hotel room. She had to be fresh, had to focus on tonight. Whatever the reason she'd been called to St. Cloud, it would all become clear tonight.